Tony Park was born in 1964 and grew up in Sydney, Australia. He has worked as a jou consultant and a press secretary. He also ser... ... ... tralian Army Reserve, including a tour of duty in Afghanistan in 2002. He is the author of 17 other thriller novels, all set in Africa. Tony and his wife, Nicola, divide their time equally between a home in Australia and a house on the edge of the Kruger National Park in South Africa.

Also by Tony Park

Far Horizon
Zambezi
African Sky
Safari
Silent Predator
Ivory
The Delta
African Dawn
Dark Heart
The Prey
The Hunter
An Empty Coast
Red Earth
The Cull
Captive
Scent of Fear
Ghosts of the Past

Part of the Pride, *with Kevin Richardson*
War Dogs, *with Shane Bryant*
The Grey Man, *with John Curtis*

Last Survivor

Tony Park

First published by AJP in 2020
This edition published in 2020 by AJP

Copyright © Tony Park 2020
www.tonypark.net
The moral right of the author has been asserted.

Last Survivor

EPUB: 9781922389053
POD: 9781922389060

Cover design by Leandra Wicks
Cover photo by Annelien Oberholzer

Publishing services provided by Critical Mass
www.critmassconsulting.com

For Nicola

Prologue

London, England

He was doomed. The last of his species to have lived in the wild, his extinction was guaranteed. The question was not *if* his kind would disappear from the face of the earth, but *when*.

With no females left alive in their natural habitat or in captivity there was no chance of natural reproduction.

The luckier of his ancestors had been stolen from Africa and shipped to foreign lands. In years gone by this had been done by supposedly well-meaning colonialists, who had displayed their captured specimens for generations of enchanted aficionados to gawk at.

Today it was illegal to take them from the wild, but that didn't stop the wealthy from breaking the law. Impoverished poachers were paid by middlemen to risk imprisonment, perhaps even death at the hand of an armed ranger, to satisfy the desire of proud rich people to flaunt their wealth and status by showing off something rare.

But he was now beyond rare; he was critically endangered, extinct in the wild.

His less fortunate forebears had been butchered for use in traditional medicine, hacked to pieces, ground into potions whose efficacy was spurious, at best. But worse, he was a victim of his rarity; he had been taken to serve the basest of emotions.

Pride.

Greed.

Vanity.

Envy.

These were the sins that had spelled a death sentence for a species that predated the dinosaurs and had once been seen across much of the earth's surface. Of course, scientists were looking for ways to artificially continue his existence, but it would never be the same.

He had come from a forested hill in Zululand, and while it had sometimes been misty and cool it had never been as cold as it was here, in England. His enclosure protected him from the worst of the elements and that was just as well, for if he had been left to face the harsh northern winter in the outdoors he would surely have died long ago.

So he sat, all alone, under a cold grey sky. Fertile – he had shown his captors he could produce, like some slave from bygone times being exposed and inspected by those who would use him as breeding stock – but he was nonetheless condemned.

The crime of it, Joanne Flack thought as she stared lovingly at him, was that so few people in the world even knew about him, let alone cared.

Joanne looked around, making sure no one was watching, and then reached out and ever so gently stroked one of the plant's spiky green leaves.

'Hello, Woody, my old friend. I might have some good news for you.'

Chapter 1

Pretoria, South Africa

Jacqueline Smit banged her gavel on the table. 'I call this meeting of the Pretoria Cycad and Firearms Appreciation Society to order. Are there any apologies?'

Thunder rumbled outside like a distant artillery barrage, but the lightning strike that followed was close, as loud as a direct hit. Thandi Ngwenya dropped her knitting and Jacqueline frowned.

A hadada ibis gave its drawn-out, eponymous call as it took off in fright from the water feature just outside the back-room office of the garden centre where they were meeting, sitting around an eight-seat boardroom table.

'Sorry, my Queen,' Thandi said to Jacqueline as she reached to retrieve the tiny jersey she was knitting for her third grandchild. Thandi's back ached when she bent over and SS, Stephen Stoke, who proclaimed himself 100 per cent Boer despite the shame of the Christian and surnames his English-speaking father had bestowed on him, dropped to one knee, creakily, and retrieved it for her. SS was quick to criticise the African National Congress government of South Africa and Thandi had sensed he had been distinctly uncomfortable with her, initially, as the first black person to join their society, but over time they had become friends and both, she thought, had learned to leave some of their prejudices where they belonged: in the past. 'Thank you, SS.'

SS smiled. 'Pleasure, Thandi.'

'Queen' Jacqueline Smit, as she was known to the other members, gave Thandi a curt nod and banged her gavel again, as loud and as fast as a double tap from a Glock. Her beehive hairdo, piled appropriately like a crown on her head, shook slightly.

Charles Borg, a white-haired old South African of Viking stock, sat to attention in his chair and folded his arms. 'Apart from the *obvious* apology?'

The ticking of the wall clock became audible. Laurel looked to Baye, who rolled her eyes.

'Has Joanne not officially resigned yet, or been given the chop?' Sandy Burrell asked.

Charles leaned over and put one hand on the back of Sandy's wheelchair. 'Not yet. She took off to London while you were in hospital. How did it go, by the way?'

'Well my spinal cord isn't going to fix itself, of course, but the treatment was good. Basically, I'm still fucked.'

Jacqueline cleared her throat. 'Language.'

'All right, all right,' Charles said. 'We have one apology, Mrs Joanne Flack.'

'Thank you,' Jacqueline said. 'You've all read the minutes of the last meeting, I take it, so there is no need for me to go through them?'

SS leaned back in his chair, the buttons of his farmer's two-tone khaki and blue work shirt threatening to open fire as the material stretched tight across his spreading belly. '*Ag*, enough of this what-what-what. I move the minutes be accepted.'

A quick show of hands confirmed it.

Thandi looked around the room at her friends, because despite their occasional differences and outbursts, and instances of latent racism, they were her friends. Sandy frowned; SS harrumphed; Laurel Covey inspected her latest manicure for non-existent signs of imperfection; and Baye Pigors, at sixty-seven still as lithe as a leopard in Lorna Jane activewear, regarded Jacqueline through narrowed golden eyes. Baye's hair, long, dark and lustrous, was pulled back from her olive-skinned face in a plait. She taught Pilates for the more-mature to while away her spare hours and to keep herself in shape; her regime was working, Thandi mused with not a little envy.

Charles sat up. 'Very well, I'll speak to the elephant in the room...'

'Who are you calling an elephant?' Laurel asked, finally tiring of looking for her reflection in her fingernails.

Jacqueline frowned and Thandi sighed. Laurel was the prettiest woman in the room, and had been mistaken more than once, she was keen on reminding them, for being twenty years younger than her sixty-five years. Thandi touched her gently on the arm. 'It's a figure of speech, dear, it means the big thing everyone is scared of, and knows is there, but does not want to address.'

Charles, handsome and debonair as ever in his sports coat and cravat, cleared his throat. 'I move that Joanne Flack be hereby... what's the word, excommunicated, terminated?'

Jacqueline clenched her teeth and drew her lips back from them. 'Expelled?'

Typical ex-teacher, Thandi thought as she started her knitting again. She wasn't being rude – the others knew she was able to listen to everything they said while she knitted, and it calmed her when she felt anxious. Like now. These people were messing with words. In her day, in the training camp in Mozambique, they'd known what to do with traitors.

'What do you think, Thandi?' SS asked. 'Expelled?'

She looked up from her knitting. 'I was thinking that at one time in my life, if someone betrayed the cause they would be killed. The ANC would burn them – with a necklace, you know, a tyre filled with petrol – but we Zimbabweans would simply shoot them.'

SS raised his eyebrows. 'Sheesh, man, you think we should shoot Joanne? This is not the old days.'

They were all looking at her now, as if she was the odd one out. They were no different from her. Her eyes lingered on each of her friends for a second. Charles Borg had been a South African Defence Force helicopter pilot under the old apartheid regime and had served in Namibia and Angola and, for a time, in Thandi's native Zimbabwe, flying for the Rhodesians. Ironically, Thandi's second husband – the first love of her life – had been a white man who had also flown choppers in Rhodesia. Charles had, it turned out, flown with her husband George for a short while in the same squadron. Thandi and George had been forced to keep their love a secret during the Bush War and had been estranged for many years, finally reuniting not long before dear George died of a heart attack.

SS was a former Recce-Commando, a member of South Africa's elite special forces; Jacqueline, her Majesty the Queen, had famously shot and killed a man who'd tried to hijack her car; Joanne had grown up on a farm in Zimbabwe, then Rhodesia, and had shot two Zimbabwe African National Liberation Army terrorists, Thandi's people, during an attack on her family's property. Laurel, once the wife of a Zululand cane farmer, had shot dead a thief during a farm robbery; and Baye Pigors, a banker's widow from Johannesburg's expensive Houghton Estate, had moved to Tel Aviv in 1972 after leaving school to study and found herself serving in the Israeli Army during the Yom Kippur War in 1973 before moving back to South Africa. They had all once been soldiers or involved in gunfights, living for a time on a diet of adrenaline and fear, but today they looked forward to their cycad society meetings and pensioners' discount Tuesdays at Builders Warehouse.

Even dear Sandy, the youngest of them at fifty-five, had put a bullet in a home invader's leg when he'd tried to threaten her into giving over the PIN for her Visa card—he had dropped his guard, thinking her disability, the result of a motor vehicle accident, made her helpless, and she had pulled the CZ-83 from the side pocket of her wheelchair and dropped him. She had sat there, keeping him covered, until the police tactical unit arrived at her home in Centurion.

Charles scoffed. 'Well, Thandi? It's not the liberation war now so we won't let you burn or shoot anyone to death as a punishment for betrayal.'

'No,' she tutted in reply. 'I wouldn't dream of it, and nor do I think Joanne should be expelled, or excommunicated, or sanctioned. At least not until we've heard from her.'

'Tell me exactly what I've missed over the last couple of weeks,' Sandy said. 'I want to hear it from the chair, not via the rumour mill.'

Queen Jacqueline looked down over the top of her horn-rimmed eyeglasses. 'Joanne, as treasurer, had not only the bank account log-in details, but also the keys to the storeroom.'

'Yes,' Sandy said. 'And...'

'And as you would have heard from the others already, the police brought us a fine specimen of *Encephalartos woodii*, a female plant no less, and–'

Sandy broke in: 'Yes, I could hardly believe it when Joanne told us she'd discovered a female *woodii*, but to then find out it was stolen, not once but twice, is incredible. That plant must be worth...'

'A fortune, yes,' Jacqueline continued. 'The police gave it to us for safekeeping after they caught two men with it at a random roadblock.'

Sandy shook her head. 'This is just too astonishing for words. How did the cops even know it was a female *woodii*? I think we can agree it's unlikely they'd have realised it's the only one of its kind in the world, so rare no living human had ever even seen one until Joanne and you lot clapped eyes on it.'

Jacqueline held up a hand. '*If* you will allow me to continue...'

Even Sandy, who was never afraid to speak out, had to bow to Jacqueline's typical forcefulness. She gave a submissive nod.

'The criminals,' the Queen continued, 'had it in the boot of their car. The fact that they rather foolishly tried to run from the police told the cops that the plant was worth something. The detective at the station–'

'My son-in-law,' Laurel interrupted, sitting straighter in her chair and beaming proudly.

'Yes, Laurel's son-in-law, James, asked Laurel and me to identify it. Needless to say we were shocked when we realised what it was. James later asked, begged, Laurel to bring it to us for safekeeping when she told him what it was–he was worried that once word got out about its true worth it would disappear from his evidence locker. Isn't that right, Laurel?'

Laurel nodded. 'Yes, shame, the police don't even trust one another. Poor James did actually beg me to look after the *woodii*. And this was obviously the same female *woodii* that Joanne had discovered in the garden of Prince Whatshisname?'

'I doubt there are two female *woodii*s,' Charles said patiently to Laurel, 'so, yes, this plant was first stolen from the cycad garden on Prince Faisal al Sabah's private game reserve, near Hoedspruit, and then stolen again from our storeroom after the police entrusted it to us.'

'But how can we be sure Joanne took it?' Sandy asked.

Jacqueline pursed her lips. 'Well, we can't, but you have to admit, the evidence is fairly damning. Joanne, as you know, worked for the prince part-time as his consultant horti-culturalist, and knew of the theft from the reserve. After the plant was rediscovered and left with us, Joanne flew out to London to visit her daughter, and when I next checked the lock-up, two days after her departure, the *woodii* was gone and our bank account had been emptied. Since then none of us have heard from her, despite leaving repeated voicemail and email messages.'

Sandy nodded, frowning. 'Yes, I tried as well. Nothing. And how come none of this has made the newspapers?'

'These oil-rich Arabs,' Baye said, unable to hide her disdain, 'they have enough money to buy anyone, anything, even the silence of the police and the media.'

'The *theory*,' Thandi said to Sandy, 'is that Joanne took the cycad and the money with her to the UK. She told me before she left that her son-in-law had lost his job and the family are in debt up to their eyeballs. They had already paid for her ticket to come visit before the young man was sacked.'

SS nodded. 'I'm afraid to say Joanne asked me for a loan a few weeks ago. Shame, the poor thing is in trouble. I gathered that the money her daughter used to send her from the UK had dried up.'

Charles leaned forward, hands on the desktop. 'Laurel, did you ask James to open a docket to investigate the theft from our premises?'

Laurel looked to Jacqueline, clearly bewildered. 'Should I have?'

Jacqueline frowned. 'This matter is most concerning. One of the things I wanted to discuss here today is what steps we should take next—if it is indeed appropriate to call in the authorities.'

'"*Appropriate to call in the authorities*"?' SS slapped the table. 'Our bank balance, thirty-something thousand *ronts*—'

Thandi lowered her knitting and smiled to herself at Stephen's old-fashioned pronunciation of the word 'rand' – the man lived in another era, one he would have termed 'the good old days'. 'Thirty-two thousand, six hundred and fifty-five rand and twenty cents.'

'Whatever,' SS said, 'has been *stolen*, along with a cycad we were supposed to care for until the offenders were dealt with by the courts ... I'd say it was time to call in the *bladdy* police, yes, Jacqueline, especially as this *bladdy* cycad is worth a king's ransom.'

Jacqueline glared at him. 'Language.'

'Now, now, Stephen,' Charles said. 'Like Thandi says, I think we need to give Joanne a chance to explain before we go getting the police involved.'

'But she's taken the money and the cycad, Charles, you buffoon,' Sandy said.

Charles rolled his eyes. Sandy's abrasiveness was well known, but she seemed to filter her words even less when talking to Charles. Thandi wondered why Charles put up with her barbs. They bickered like an old married couple sometimes.

Baye leaned back in her chair, one long, lycra-clad leg crossed over the other. 'That Arab prince Joanne worked for would have cut off her hands by now if he'd caught her stealing his cycad. Clearly she didn't steal the female *woodii* from her employer in the first place, unless of course she paid the guys who the police arrested to transport it for her and then had to steal it a second time – from us.' She tilted her head, lifting her nose as if she had just detected a whiff of something unpleasant. 'It wouldn't be the first time Joanne dudded someone who trusted her.'

'I say call the police,' Sandy said.

Thandi placed the little jersey back in her knitting basket. That very act made some of the others look her way.

'Comrades ...' SS looked heavenwards, as he always did when Thandi addressed them by that name. She liked using the word solely for his reaction. 'Comrades, now is not the time for burning necklaces, excommunication or amputation. We must find out what has happened to Joanne. I think she will return to Africa. Joanne told me more than once that she could not bear living in England, or Australia, or anywhere outside of this continent. She is a child of our blood-red soil, and, besides, thirty-two thousand, six hundred and fifty-five rand will not last long in England, particularly the way Joanne drinks.'

SS snorted. Queen Jacqueline frowned. Laurel had resumed her inspection of her perfect nails.

'You don't think Joanne stole the cycad?' Sandy asked.

Thandi shrugged. 'I'm saying something doesn't add up. Joanne was investigated for smuggling back in the nineties, you remember?'

SS nodded. 'I do. She was acquitted, though her husband, rest his soul, was clearly guilty, shot dead by an undercover American G-man.'

'Exactly,' Thandi said. 'Even if Joanne *was* involved she was able to expertly cover her tracks. Stealing a cycad from under our noses, from our storeroom, is not the style of an accomplished poacher. It's too obvious. If she had wanted to steal the female *woodii* she could have taken it from the Kuwaiti's garden before anyone, including the prince, even knew what it was. Remember, it was she who alerted us to her discovery of the rarest plant in the whole world.'

Laurel had taken to her nail with a file, but now she looked up, at Thandi. 'So, like, what must we do, Thands?'

Dear Laurel, Thandi thought. If it wasn't for her extensive knowledge of cycads she would think the woman a halfwit. 'We must investigate, Laurel.'

'What are we now,' SS scoffed, 'the number one old ladies' private investigation agency, headed by our own Mama Ngwenya?'

Thandi ignored the flippancy. 'But we must find Joanne and, if we cannot find her, we must ascertain what she was doing before she left South Africa, who she met with, what she was planning.'

'What about the son of the king of Arabia or whatever, Prince Sisal?' Laurel asked.

'His name is *Faisal*,' Charles said patiently, and turned to Sandy. 'Joanne told us all about her work for him while you were in hospital. Faisal's a Kuwaiti prince, a minor member of the Al Sabah family, busy building his own private game lodge near Hoedspruit. Joanne had some work advising on the landscaping. The prince is one of us, apparently.'

'You're suffering from old man's disease, Charles, you silly old fool,' Sandy said. 'You forget I was here when Joanne told us about her work for the prince and how he'd already had an *Encephalartos hirsutus* stolen from his garden. So this female *woodii* is the second valuable cycad he's lost. And what do you mean, he's one of us?'

'He's a gun nut and a cycad fancier,' Charles said quietly, somewhat chastised.

Jacqueline weighed in: 'Come to think of it, we should invite him to join the society as we need his subscription. He's a hunter – the game lodge is primarily there to stock his private trophy room, apparently.'

Sandy frowned. 'Joanne wouldn't have been involved with a hunter, would she?'

Jacqueline shrugged in reply. 'Joanne was an old-school Zimbabwean. She told me once she took her daughter on an impala hunt when the girl turned fifteen. The girl never shot again and Joanne said she no longer had the stomach for it, either, but money is money these days, and the Kuwaiti paid her in US dollars.'

Laurel addressed Sandy. 'Not only is he fabulously wealthy in his own right, but Joanne told us how he has all this ivory and rhino horn stocked away that people are always scheming to get their hands on.'

'I'm in a wheelchair, Laurel, I am not mentally deficient. I also remember Joanne telling us about the prince's other treasures.'

'Yes, well, I think this Sisal's a suspicious character, myself,' Laurel said.

'Faisal, Laurel.' Thandi had gone back to her knitting, in order to process the new information swirling around. She thought out loud: 'A suspicious member of a royal family with cash, diplomatic immunity, and a love of cycads.'

Charles raised his eyebrows. 'Are you thinking what I'm thinking, Thandi?'

'Road trip?' SS interrupted. 'Joanne told us that the prince had issued a standing invitation for us to visit his royal hunting estate if we were ever in Hoedspruit – and we very soon will be.'

11

Thandi looked to Jacqueline. 'Madam Chair, we have the Kombi organised for this year's cycad conference at Nelspruit, and a visit to the Kruger Park next week. Hoedspruit is very near.'

Jacqueline pursed her lips and slid her glasses up her nose. 'Do we have a motion and a seconder?'

All of their hands went up.

Chapter 2

London, England

By force of habit Joanne Flack looked around her.

In the bush in Mana Pools National Park in the country of her birth, Zimbabwe, she kept an eye out for elephants which, unless they were snapping off branches, were so quiet that one could walk into them before they made their presence felt. In Johannesburg, her home for the last third of her life, she watched the roadside hawkers for signs of anything other than acute sales acumen. Joanne was always amazed how the man selling the sunglasses at William Nicol could see the tiniest movement of her head or eyes that might indicate she was interested in a new pair of knock-off D&Gs.

Not that she had any money.

Now, in London, she watched the people. It wasn't that she was scared, just out of her natural environment. In Africa there was danger, for sure, and it could be random and horrible, but one could take measures, Joanne reasoned. Avoid the bad areas, keep the nine-millimetre Glock clean, try not to drive at night, keep the windows wound up, but not all the way as it was harder for a thief to smash a partially open window than a fully closed one. In Hwange National Park she didn't walk around the camp at night because she knew the hyena would be out and the snakes more active, and if she ever came across a lion on foot she knew to stand still.

There were Africans on the streets of London, which at first gave her some measure of comfort, but when she heard their voices they were speaking French, or Nigerian, or some other tongue she couldn't understand. Her people were the Ndebele, first and foremost. These people in their overcoats and beanies might be from the same continent as her, but that was as much as they had in common. She didn't understand them, didn't understand England.

There were six policemen in her field of view as she exited Kings Cross station, dispersed in three pairs, armed and wearing yellow high-visibility jackets. Cops with guns were part of her life in South Africa, but these ones in England were different from the smiling, ambling officers she was familiar with, the ones whose waistlines reflected their skill at fleecing speeding tourists with 'on-the-spot' traffic fines. She went down the escalators into the tube station.

The first time Joanne had been to London, with Peter, back in the early nineties when things had still been good for them and their country, none of the bobbies had been armed. The world had changed since then. The policemen above ground, with the sides of their heads shaved, looked like soldiers, and she wondered if some of them had been. They reminded her of her childhood, when the threat of attack had been very real and everyone seemed to carry a gun, even her own mother.

Joanne's fondest memories of her mother were of the two of them in the garden, tending to her mother's plants. She remembered going to her first Cycad Society annual general meeting in Mount Pleasant in 1979. *Members will please check firearms at the door*, the program had said. Her mother carried an Israeli-made Uzi submachine gun – 'handbag-size, darling, the ultimate fashion accessory'. Joanne smiled to herself.

How odd to have good memories of a war, she thought. A week after that meeting Joanne had shot and killed two men. While there was a terrorist threat in the United Kingdom most of these people passing her by, she realised, would never see a body oozing blood from a bullet wound or know the almost paralysing terror of an armed man coming through the night towards one's home with an AK-47. These people did not know what it was to feel the kick of the rifle in the shoulder, to smell the cordite and to know that in that instant a life had been taken and another saved. They did not have the nightmares nor feel the pats on the back in the morning from well-intentioned adults for a job well done, for taking two lives; they did not know that wine and beer could dull the pain as one got older, and bring on the tears in the same night. These people knew nothing of death and little of life. People in Africa knew these things and it shaped them, this shared experience of war and trauma, even as it chipped away at them, little by little.

She took a deep breath and hopped on the Northern Line to Embankment, then changed to the District Line and took a westbound train towards Richmond. The morning commuters had given way to tourists, mums with babies, and a noisy group of schoolchildren on an excursion. As usual everyone, apart from the kids, kept to themselves. That suited Joanne.

Kew Gardens was one stop from the end of the line, about where she felt in her life right now, she mused. She knew the route from her previous trips to the UK and wondered if this would be her last mini pilgrimage to the Botanic Gardens. The train was above ground here, and the drab outer suburbs had given way to leafier streets and old red-brick houses. Joanne exited the station and walked the five hundred metres to the Victoria Gate.

She was a member of the Gardens, a gift from Peta that no doubt could not be renewed this year, and showed her card at the entry booth. She couldn't afford to stay long–her flight left that night–but even though it had only been days since her previous visit she knew she couldn't leave England without seeing Woody again, possibly for the last time. She needed to leave this country. Extending her return ticket was not just a matter of neither she nor Peta having the money to pay the change-of-booking fee; if the events she had put in place played out as she thought they would, then it might not be safe for her daughter and her family if Joanne continued to stay with them.

When whomever stole the cycad from the society's lock-up realised what they had then there would be hell to pay. She needed to get back to Africa where she knew where and how to hide, but if she failed and her actions resulted in a loss of life, then she was determined it would not be her child or grandchild. And if that lost life was her own, she would leave this world having seen Woody once more and in the knowledge she had done her best to ensure he would not be the last of his kind.

Once through the gate she turned left. The bitumen pathway shone with dew in between the camouflage pattern of autumn leaves, but the grey sky did nothing to lift her spirits. She zipped up her imitation leather jacket and quickened her pace to ward off the cold.

The Temperate House loomed ahead, the largest surviving Victorian-era greenhouse. It sheltered plants from Africa and Asia which otherwise wouldn't have survived in the cold, dank English air. Inside, the heady, earthy smell of life calmed her a little.

Joanne went left, heading straight to the Africa section. There were cycads as soon as she entered this wing, but she bypassed them and walked purposefully to the far end, where Woody waited for her.

Joanne looked around, making sure none of the garden staff were watching, then reached out and ever so gently touched him. 'Goodbye, Woody, my old friend.'

At more than two metres in height Woody, as Joanne called him, was tall for a cycad, which was important, because anything that made him stand out from the other plants – certainly the rest of the cycads – was good, as it might make people stop and read the interpretive panel, where they would learn about the great tragedy of his story. His real name was *Encephalartos woodii* and the species part of his name was actually pronounced 'woody-eye'. He was named after John Medley Wood, an English botanist who found the plant in the Ngoye Forest in Zululand in 1895.

A little girl, perhaps nine or ten and wearing the uniform of the group Joanne had seen on the train, came wandering through the Temperate House on her own. Joanne looked past her and saw that the other children were climbing the stairs to the upper viewing level.

The girl stopped in front of Woody. 'Is this plant very rare?'

'Yes, he is.'

The girl looked up at her and brushed a strand of golden blonde hair out of her eyes. 'You call it a he. It's a plant, not a person.'

Joanne nodded and smiled. 'You're very clever, and you're right, but this plant is, in fact, a male.'

'Like a boy.'

'Yes.'

'Are there girl plants, then?'

Joanne had to be careful with her answer, in case anyone overheard them. 'Female, yes, or at least there were, once upon a time, but not for more than a hundred years. When this plant was found he was the last of his kind, and no more have ever been seen in the wild.'

'So is he the only one in the world, then?'

'Not quite,' Joanne said. 'There are a hundred and ten other cycads like this one, all related to him, and all male. They were grown from suckers, little versions of himself that he produced.'

'Like clones?'

Joanne smiled, her mood momentarily lightened. 'Yes, exactly.'

'If there are no girl plants, does that mean this plant won't ever make babies? I know you need a mummy and a daddy. I've got a little brother on the way, and my mummy said she and daddy made him, like they made me.'

Joanne drew a breath, fighting the urge to gather everyone in the Temperate House to her and blurt out the truth. 'I'm afraid that's right. This plant will never make a real baby. They're called pups, in fact.'

'Pups, like puppies?'

'Yes.'

'That's cute, but it's also very sad.'

'It is.' Joanne swallowed. 'Very.'

'Liza?' a teacher called from the end of the hall. 'Come here, please. Stay with the group.'

Liza looked up at Joanne. 'Bye, then. Don't be sad. Maybe one day your funny spiky plant will get a wife and make proper babies.'

Joanne took a tissue out of her bag and dabbed her eye. She used her phone to take a picture of Woody, made sure no one was looking, then touched one of his leaves again. She checked her watch, turned, and walked through the Temperate House and back out into the cold.

Yes, she thought to herself, one day Woody would make babies, if both she and the plant lived long enough to make that happen. If *Encephalartos woodii* was to survive and thrive into the future, then he needed to reproduce naturally. Clones took ages to grow and they lacked the genetic diversity a species needed to ensure longevity and survival. The enormity of what she had done weighed heavily on her as she retraced her steps.

From the Kew Gardens station she took the District Line to Victoria then a 170 bus through Chelsea. She had in her mind to visit the Physic Garden, a historic collection of medicinal plants, but first she needed something to eat.

She used the map app on her iPhone to find the way past the rows of beautiful Georgian townhouses. On her phone was a string of missed calls and unanswered SMS and WhatsApp messages from her friends in the society back in South Africa. She missed them, now, but she hardened her heart and tried to concentrate on her surroundings.

London fascinated her, especially the way areas of depressed poverty existed side by side with those of unimaginable wealth. The buildings were the same, but the interiors were where the money was. That and the cars on the road. On this street the Range Rovers and convertible Minis, even a Ferrari, were mirrors held up to the souls of the people who lived here.

Joanne looked up from her phone. Her son-in-law, Phillip, had warned her that on the streets where he and Peta lived in Tufnell Park she should not walk about with her phone in her hand, otherwise a mugger on a moped might grab it. Joanne figured she was safer here, in Chelsea, but kept a watchful eye out nonetheless.

As she walked, Joanne felt her eyes fill with tears. 'Stop it.'

Her admonitions to herself didn't work and she wiped her eyes as she stabbed the button at the traffic lights to summon a 'walk' sign. She had turned her back on the people closest to her in South Africa and she could not speak to the other person who had been calling her and messaging her: Faisal. Joanne was burning bridges and losing friends, but she firmly believed that her means justified the end she was hoping for. Though it was the hardest decision she'd ever made, she was confident she'd done the right thing by deceiving those who trusted her in order to reverse something the botanical world thought was inevitable.

'Are you all right, ma'am?'

Joanne half turned and looked up into the handsome face of a policeman. She blinked.

'Can I help?' he said. He looked Indian, but sounded Cockney.

'You haven't got a cigarette, have you?'

He smiled, not unsympathetically. 'Afraid not, ma'am.'

'Are you lost, ma'am?' asked his rosy-cheeked female partner.

'No.' The word ma'am made her sound old, which, as she was pushing sixty, was not entirely unwarranted. She cursed herself again, this time for wanting to smoke; she'd given up years earlier, but moments of stress brought back the old craving.

'You sure you're all right, love?' the male officer asked.

At least that made her feel younger than ma'am, she thought. Love. Hadn't had that for a long time, either.

Joanne sighed. 'My son-in-law was made redundant from his job, leaving my daughter and my grandchild with no viable means of support. My husband was shot dead, our farm in Zimbabwe was taken from us, and the pittance I used to receive from my child to keep me afloat has now dried up. I have no professional qualifications other than a keen amateur's interest in plants and garden design, no savings, no pension and no prospects.'

The two officers looked at each other, and Joanne couldn't miss their raised eyebrows.

'I'm fine,' she sighed. 'Mustn't grumble.'

They smiled and nodded and walked on, ahead of her. If anything the weather had turned colder and she felt her mood slump again. Joanne followed the officers to the King's Road and started to think about where she'd have lunch. The footpath was flanked by upmarket eateries and shops selling clothes, watches, accessories and all manner of other goods as well as food Joanne couldn't afford.

The two officers were still visible in front of her. The helmet of the man, who was much taller than his partner, bobbed commandingly, reassuringly, above the crowd.

Off to her right, in the direction of the Sloane Square tube station, she couldn't help but notice a man with a long black beard wearing a camouflage jacket. He was coming towards them, barrelling through the crowd with enough aggression to cause a woman to abuse him. The police officers didn't see him – the male constable was leaning over as he seemed to try and hear something his partner was saying.

As it happened, the man with the beard seemed to be heading straight for Joanne. She wondered if he had some sort of mental illness. She had been quite surprised and confronted to see the number of people living rough and begging on the streets of London since she had arrived.

The man with the beard was reaching into his jacket. Joanne realised that if he stayed on his path, at that pace, he would intercept her, if not run straight into her. The other people on the street were avoiding looking at him, watching the footpath ahead or talking to each other.

Joanne saw a glint of shiny stainless steel. The man with the beard drew a knife that was scarily long and he held it low, and with purpose. The police officers had their backs to her and were half a block ahead. The man came to her. Time slowed; a jolt of shock and fear could have frozen her on the spot, but instead it reignited a long since dormant survival instinct. If she couldn't flee – and she could not – she needed to fight.

'Come with me,' he said in a low voice. He showed her the knife. 'Say nothing, or I will kill you.'

'Hey!' Joanne yelled. 'Police!'

The male officer started to look around and Joanne realised with horror that she had done the wrong thing.

'He's got a knife!'

Her warning call came too late. The bearded man turned his attention from her and charged at the tall policeman from behind.

'*Allah-u-Akbar!*' The man raised his hand as he yelled the words and struck downwards with the knife, aiming for the junction between the officer's neck and shoulder, above the stab-proof vest he wore. Blood erupted and spurted over the constable next to him. She reached for her pistol but the attacker was quicker, slashing at her neck.

People screamed and ran. Joanne raced towards the bobbies and when she reached them the male officer toppled backwards onto her, pinning her to the ground. The man with the knife stepped agilely to the side.

Joanne looked up into the bearded man's eyes but he barely spared her a glance now. A man in a suit was trying to grab his arm and the attacker swung and punched him in the face. Joanne could see now that he had a knife in each hand, and he used his left to plunge a blade into the other man's belly.

Blood was flowing from the male officer's neck wound over her face and her hands as Joanne tried to wipe her eyes and fought to slide out from under the man writhing on top of her. She put an arm around him and her fingers brushed the pistol in his holster. Joanne grabbed it with a slippery grip, pulled the pistol free and stared at it.

Glock 17, no safety catch – double action trigger.

Joanne rolled the police officer off her and hauled herself up onto one knee. Having dispatched the man in the suit, the bearded man was coming for her again.

Joanne raised the pistol in a two-handed grip and fired, twice in rapid succession.

She heard the bangs and the clinking of the spent rounds hitting the pavement. The world moved in slow motion. Her moments of terror at being accosted and grabbed had been stilled, subsumed, by the speed at which everything had happened, by the familiar, reassuring grip of the pistol, by the buck and the noise and the smell of the bullets leaving the barrel.

She stood, and now the bearded man lay at her feet, gasping his last gurgling breaths of life as he looked up into her eyes. People were screaming, running, but to her they moved and spoke in muffled slow motion. She had killed, again, her brain registered.

The pistol hung loose by her side now, impossibly heavy, dragging her hand down. She wanted to crumple to the ground, spent after the rush of adrenaline. Had this just happened?

The yells of the passers-by, the wail of a siren increased in volume and pitch, bringing her back into the moment as she looked around. People were coming to her. It had not been a dream; it had been real.

She looked down at the man again. He was dead. 'Come with me,' he had said to her.

'Where?' she asked the corpse out loud.

New Jersey, United States

'Forty-five my ass.' Rod Cavanagh slammed the remote control down so hard on the kitchen bench that his twenty-year-old son, Jake, looked up from his phone.

Rain beat against the window of his modest house. The tree outside was bare, the leaves scattered by the blustery fall winds. The bleakness of the day matched his mood this morning.

The television news anchor droned on, over pictures of a crime scene roped off with blue-and-white police tape and filled with forensic investigators in one-piece white suits. '*Joanne Flack, Zimbabwean born, but now resident in South Africa, was visiting her daughter in London and sightseeing in the capital when she saw the alleged lone-wolf terrorist, Jamal Hussein, draw two knives and attack a pair of police officers in front of her. Flack took one of the injured officers' pistol and fired two shots, killing Hussein. Scotland Yard said today that Hussein, born in Mali, West Africa, had travelled to England on a South African passport. The National Rifle Association has praised...*'

'Oh, for Pete's sake...'

'Chill, Dad,' Jake said.

'Don't tell me what to do. I'm the father here, I call the shots, and that woman is *not* forty-five years old. Whatever happened to good old-fashioned fact-checking?'

'Whoa, dude. What exactly are you talking about?'

Rod picked up a piece of toast and pointed at the television screen which showed, for perhaps the hundredth time that morning, the jerky phone camera vision of a blonde woman shooting down a terrorist. For the sake of the squeamish the video ended before the impact of the bullets could be seen. 'Her.'

Jake looked up. 'The woman who killed the terrorist? She looks younger, if anything. She's badass.'

'She's at least the wrong side of fifty-five now,' Rod said.

'Wait. You know her, Dad?' Jake actually put his phone down.

'I'm glad to see I've at least got you off Facebook for two minutes.'

'Um, hello. Tinder, Dad.'

'TMI,' Rod said. 'Yes, I know her.'

'How? Can you get me her phone number? She's kinda hot, in a cougar way.'

'She's old enough to be your mom,' Rod said.

They were both quiet for the next few seconds. Rod felt the stab wound in the heart again, as, no doubt, did Jake.

'Sorry, buddy,' Rod said.

Jake smiled. 'It's OK, Dad. So, how do you know her?'

Rod shook his head. 'She's Zimbabwean, lives in South Africa. I investigated her, twenty-two years ago in –'

'The great plant sting. You may have mentioned that like, oh, maybe a thousand times.'

Rod frowned. Jake was a good kid and they were as much buddies as father and son – at least he liked to think so – and while Jake was only joshing, Rod knew he was guilty of telling the story of his biggest undercover operation too many times. After all, it wasn't every day that you busted an international ring of endangered cycad smugglers. At the time it had been news, even made the *New York Times* magazine, but in this age of the war on terror no journalist or chief financial officer cared too much about Fish and Wildlife Service investigations or the international trade in endangered plants.

Rod had been lauded by the department in public as a hero, but after the prosecutions were over his career as an investigator had been quietly but irrevocably terminated. It turned out that the end did not always justify the means and Rod had been guilty of some serious errors of judgement during the operation.

'Yeah.' Rod stared at the television, watching the re-runs of the portrait shot of Joanne Flack and the slow-motion vision of her taking down an honest-to-goodness bad guy. 'She's barely changed.'

'What was that, Dad?' Jake asked.

Rod looked up from the flat-screen on the kitchen wall. 'Oh, nothing, son.'

'Dad, are you OK?'

Rod sipped his coffee. 'Sure, why?'

'You looked a little lost, just then. Like you were flashing back or something. Was it about Mom?'

It had been two years since they'd lost Betty to breast cancer and it still hurt. Rod felt his cheeks flush. 'Yes, I guess, buddy. Go on, get off to work, now. Wall Street might crash without its latest young hotshot intern.'

Jake chuckled. 'OK. And Dad?'

He looked at his son and wiped his mouth with a paper napkin. 'Yes?'

'I'm proud of you, really. And the plant world sleeps safe knowing tough guys like you once put their lives on the line for them.'

Rod screwed up the napkin and threw it at his son. 'Get out of here. Go sell off some junk bonds to little old ladies and I hope you choke on your Dom Pérignon.'

Jake got up and put his satchel around his neck. 'Love you, Dad.'

'Ditto.'

Rod drained the last of his coffee. When Jake had left he switched channels to watch the story on Joanne Flack all over again.

Just so he could look at her.

Chapter 3

Mali, West Africa

The woman in the burqa, clutching a tattered hessian sack to her chest with her left arm, passed all but unnoticed down a dusty street flanked by an open drain whose smell ripened in the afternoon heat.

A bored jihadi in a black turban picked his nose as he leaned on the receiver of his Russian-made 12.7-millimetre DShK heavy machine gun on the back of a battered Toyota HiLux technical. The gun's nickname was Dushka, beloved one, but the woman knew from personal experience there was nothing to like about that thing unless you were firing it.

A dog paused, looking up from his foraging in the gutter to see if the woman had a scrap for him, but she carried on. She quickened her pace when she heard the call to *Asr*, the afternoon prayer, blare out, scratchy and tinny from a speaker atop the mud-walled mosque at the end of the street. The fighters behind her would be climbing down from the armoured vehicle, unrolling their prayer mats.

She turned right down a narrow alleyway and, away from the vehicles and machine guns, back into the Middle Ages, save for the single-use plastic bags that littered the way. There were no signs for Pepsi or Coca-Cola, no radios blaring, no satellite TV dishes, no vestiges of the twenty-first century. That wasn't all bad, she thought to herself, but the pile of rocks she passed was sticky with blood and hair and the ground around it was stained, all that remained of a woman who had been caught having sex with a married jihadi. The man had been flogged, apparently, but after the stoning the woman had been dragged into the desert, tied by the ankles with a rope fixed to the back of a technical. If she was still alive after being pounded by rocks the last ride of shame would have finished her off.

'*Waqf.*'

She stopped, not daring to look behind her at the man who had just told her to stop. She heard the scuff of his sandals in the dusty street and controlled her breathing.

'*Salaam aleikum,*' he muttered as he came up to her.

Through the gauze covering her eyes she answered, '*Aleikum salaam.*'

He reached for the sack she held and she clutched it tighter. She leaned forward and a couple of dates spilled out of the top. The man laughed and his foul breath penetrated her veil. She looked at the rifle on his back as he bent to pick up the dates. The AK-47 was rusted and dirty, slung so as not to be readily accessible. It would take him seconds to bring it to bear if he needed to use it.

Amateur, she thought.

He stood straight, popping one date in his mouth with dirty fingers and pocketing the other. She stood there and revised her opinion of the man, slightly, when she saw how he looked down at her one foot that was visible beneath the hem of her robe. Her sandal was locally made, simple, grubby, yet her foot, darkened with several coatings of spray tan, was ornately decorated with henna. Maybe he was just a lecherous young man, she thought, or maybe he was making sure there was a woman under the burqa. Either way, the little touch of painting her feet had worked.

He waved her on. She gave a deferential little nod and carried on down the alleyway.

Two more men, both also armed with AKs, walked by her, not sparing the woman in black a second glance. This was why she was here. In this town she could move almost unseen, right up to the ornately carved door set into the deep recess in the mud-brick wall. The guard, who had been given dispensation from praying but nonetheless was reading from a well-thumbed pocket edition of the Qur'an, looked up from the holy book when he realised she had stopped in front of him.

This time she proffered the bag to him, showing him the pile of remaining dates.

'*Shukran.*' He took one and smiled.

Pity, she thought. He had nice eyes. She wondered if he had been one of the men who had raped the girl. She dropped the sack and as the young fighter bent to retrieve it she pulled her right hand from under the folds of her robe and drove the point of the vintage Fairbairn–Sykes commando fighting knife up under the man's ribcage and into his heart. She clamped her free hand over his mouth and pushed him deep into the shadowed vestibule, against the heavy door, and held him, still, until he died a few seconds later. Her black robe absorbed and hid the blood that flowed down over her hand.

She spoke softly, the throat microphone transmitting her voice to the US Navy Seahawk helicopter orbiting out of sight and sound over the desert ten kilometres away. 'One tango down, breaching now.'

'Roger,' came the disembodied voice in her ear. It was Jed Banks, one of the CIA's top men in Africa. Jed was an ex–Green Beret, a combat veteran who had served in Afghanistan, and she felt better knowing he had her back.

She knew the door was locked and bolted from the inside so there was no point in looking for keys on the dead guard. She reached under her robe for the breaching charge she had already prepared in advance. From around her neck she slid forty-five centimetres of detonating cord, with a further length of shock tube attached to a blasting cap on one end and a primer on the other. She peeled the cover off the double-sided tape attached to the det cord and stuck the explosives-packed snake to the door. She backed along the wall and initiated the primer by slapping a metal initiator punch into the primer tube.

The door was shattered, splinters and dust shooting out into the alley. She took a stun grenade from a pouch under her robe and pulled the pin. Before the smoke had begun to clear she was through the door. She had modified her burqa with velcro fasteners and it came apart as she raised the Heckler & Koch MP5 machine pistol, slung around her neck in front of her, with her right hand. On top of the MP5 was a camera, which she switched on. She followed the map of the building in her mind and down the stone-flagged corridor was a door on her right. She tossed the stun grenade inside and as it went off she entered the room, searching for targets.

The eyepiece of her veil, which was still in place, shielded her vision from the bright flash of the grenade, and she saw a jihadi crawling across the floor from his prayer mat towards his rifle. She fired a double tap, two shots in quick succession, into his back, and he fell flat and motionless.

She carried on through to a door on the other side, which she kicked open. She fired into the room, catching one of the two men inside in the shoulder and spinning him around. The second man had his rifle up and was searching for her when she fired again.

Tap-tap. The man fell. She dispatched him with a third shot, between the eyes.

'In,' she said into the mouthpiece, voice calm, heart pounding. 'Three more tangos down. Bring it.'

'Roger,' Jed said. 'On our way.'

There was a door on her right that was not on the plan she had committed to memory. She tested the handle and found it was unlocked. She kicked it open and raised her weapon. It was a storeroom, uninhabited but stacked high with stuff she instantly recognised as being valuable. There were elephant tusks, maybe thirty of them, the ends of the ivory still bloodstained; a dozen rhinoceros horns stacked in a corner; an open sack of marijuana, and a stack of what looked like a dozen small fuzzy tree trunks, each no bigger than a round side table. One trunk was bigger than the others, about a metre tall, and its plastic covering had been partially undone, revealing its rough, diagonal-patterned surface. The camera on top of her H&K would record it all. She carried on.

She had another explosive breaching charge in a pouch on her combat vest. She placed the charge against the locked door that faced her and blew it open.

She knew this would be the hardest target, the final guard who would be standing over the package, a twenty-four-year-old American aid worker, the daughter of a US senator, who had been held hostage for the past six weeks. The man would be ready to kill his captive and die for his cause rather than let her be rescued. She knew she might be too late.

She paused deliberately. The guard would be expecting a force of SEALs to come rushing through the door. She let the H&K dangle from her neck again and closed the folds of her burqa, reattaching the velcro. She drew the Glock 19 from her belt and held it behind her back.

'*Allah-u-Akbar!*' she screamed, then went through the door.

Through the smoke from the charge she saw the guard as well as the woman lying on the filthy bed, her mouth covered with duct tape. The man had his AK-47 up but when he saw the black-clad woman enter he hesitated, as she hoped he would, and lowered his rifle a fraction.

It was enough. She brought her pistol up and fired twice, hitting the man in the chest. She put a third round into his head for good measure, and because of the state of the woman she had come to rescue.

The woman was handcuffed, her exposed skin scored with cuts and pocked with what looked like festering burns, each the size of the end of a lit cigarette. She brought the Glock up again and fired through the chain joining the cuffs. She reached down and ripped the tape from the aid worker's mouth.

The young woman blinked and cowered on the bed. 'Who... who are you?'

'My name is Sonja Kurtz. Don't let the accent fool you – I'm CIA. I'm here to rescue you and kill as many of these fuckers as I can.'

The hostage began to cry, but there was no time for a hug. Sonja grabbed the woman's wrist and pulled her gently but firmly off the bed to the door.

'Come with me.'

Sonja led the aid worker through the rooms, stepping over dead bodies. She had the H&K at the ready again and passed the

Glock to the young woman. 'No safety catch. Just point and pull the trigger.'

The young woman nodded dumbly. At the entrance Sonja peeked out into the street and a hail of heavy-calibre bullets raked the walls either side of her. She had glimpsed the vehicle at the end of the alleyway.

'Technical, blocking the exit,' Sonja said, so the throat mic would pick it up.

'Got it,' Banks replied. 'UAV's on it. Clear to launch?'

'Unleash hell,' Sonja said.

Orbiting above them, out of sight, was a Global Hawk Unmanned Aerial Vehicle, what the media liked to call a 'drone', but in reality a sophisticated jet-powered platform of destruction. At Jed's order a Hellfire missile was launched.

Sonja watched the streak of smoke come out of the sky and the next second the HiLux erupted in a ball of flame and smoke and the machine gun stopped firing.

'We're inbound,' Jed said into her earpiece.

'Copy,' she said.

From the other end of the alley she heard shouting and a mob of armed jihadis rounded the corner. She raised the MP5 and killed the first two. She turned to the woman, just in time to see her faint.

'Shit.'

'Say again,' Jed said.

She bent over and hoisted the woman onto her shoulders. She was malnourished and weighed next to nothing after her period of captivity. 'Package is unconscious and I've got a shitload more tangos than I was briefed. I'm heading to the roof for extraction.'

'Roger,' Jed said. 'We're five mikes out.'

'Copy.' Five minutes could seem like a hell of a long time when people were shooting at you.

Sonja retraced her steps into the house, but followed the corridor to the end where a staircase led to the roof. She held the MP5's pistol grip with her right hand and, at the top of the stairs, shot off a rusted padlock and kicked open the rotting door. The flat rooftop was clear and she laid the young woman down and slapped her face. 'Wake up. Get back in the game.'

The woman blinked once, twice. 'I ... be ...'

'What?'

'Behind you.' The young woman lifted a hand.

Sonja spun around and saw a man in a turban climbing over the low wall separating the roof of this building from its neighbour. She fired twice and the man dropped. There were others coming.

'Give me another Hellfire,' Sonja said to Jed.

'Roger. Target? Location?'

'Fucking anywhere. Danger close. I'm surrounded.'

'Roger.'

Men were emerging like termites from a mound, onto the roofs of buildings on either side of her. She fired until she was out of rounds then ducked down behind the low wall and changed magazines. The young woman, now conscious, had her hand above the parapet and was firing blindly. It was better than nothing.

Seconds later another missile streaked out of the sky and exploded on top of the building next to her, showering her and the package with dust and chunks of dried mud.

'What do we do?' the aid worker asked.

'The choppers will be shot out of the sky if they come into this reception. There are about a hundred more men here than I was briefed.'

The gunfire had fallen away. Men yelled commands to each other. Before the smoke of the missile strike cleared completely, Sonja moved to the edge of the roof and peered over. Another technical was heading down the alley, which was only blocked at the other end by the burning vehicle. The second Toyota's cab roof had been removed so that the whole vehicle was open. 'Come with me.'

The girl crawled to her.

'When I say jump, you jump.'

'You're kidding, right?'

Sonja changed magazines and racked the H&K. 'You want to die up here?'

The younger woman shook her head.

Sonja stood, leaned over the edge of the roof and waved at the men in the truck. 'Hi, guys!'

A turbaned jihadi looked up at the sound of her voice and started swinging his Dushka machine gun up to get a bead on her. She fired first and the man fell into the lap of his loader. The driver reached for an AK-47 on the passenger seat beside him.

'Jump!'

Sonja vaulted over the parapet and landed, hard, in the back of the vehicle, on top of the machine gunner, who was dead. She swung the MP5, smashing the telescoping metal stock into the loader's face. He reeled back and she reversed the weapon in her hands and shot him through the heart.

Sonja turned just in time to look down the barrel of the driver's AK-47. The man was pulling on the cocking handle and even though he had not yet chambered a round she did not think she would have time to bring her MP5 round to get a shot off at him. She lunged at him, but before she could make contact the young woman arrived, from thin air, and landed awkwardly on top of the terrorist.

The driver wriggled and cursed and the aid worker pummelled him with her hands and feet. Sonja pulled her commando dagger from the sheath on her combat vest and managed to slide it into the melee and penetrate the driver's neck. The aid worker screamed and rolled off him.

'Drive!'

'Me?' the young woman said.

'Yes. Now is *not* the time to go all Gen Y on me.'

The woman looked up at Sonja, tears in her eyes. 'But it's a stick shift.'

Sonja rolled her eyes. Jihadis were moving across the roof where she had been. Sonja cocked the machine gun. 'Get behind this and use your thumbs to push the firing mechanism.'

The young woman took her place, and pressed where Sonja had shown her. The heavy-calibre machine gun shook and five rounds whizzed past Sonja's head.

'Like that?' the girl said.

Sonja exhaled. 'Point it at the bad guys.'

The girl swung the long-barrelled gun upwards and opened fire as Sonja pushed the dead driver out of the vehicle and slid behind the wheel. The vinyl seat was slick with blood. She rammed the gear lever into reverse and dropped the clutch. The aid worker nearly lost her balance but she hung on to the firing handles of the machine gun and kept on firing. Two jihadis, hit by the uncontrolled burst, fell to the dusty road and Sonja bounced over their bodies.

Sonja turned hard out of the alleyway and pushed the accelerator pedal into the firewall, heading for the outskirts of the town. She raced upwards through the gears, the engine screaming, but as she passed an intersection she saw two more technicals heading towards her.

'Um, Jed.'

'Yes, Sonja?' He, too, had departed from correct radio procedure and protocols, sensing correctly that now was not the time to admonish her.

'You might want to pick us the fuck up sometime soon or we're going to be kofta meat.'

'Copy that. We have you in sight.'

'How reassuring,' Sonja said as the girl behind her sprayed wild bursts of fire at a Toyota that had latched on to their tail.

Sonja made it out of the town, which was good on one hand because there were no more buildings for terrorists to fire at her from, but bad on the other because the technicals behind her had a clear field of fire ahead. Heavy slugs were thumping into the back of their vehicle.

Sonja looked over her shoulder. The Toyota behind them was gaining on them, but the gunner on board was a worse shot than the aid worker, and had exhausted his ammunition. She could see he was having difficulty loading a fresh belt as the vehicles bucked in and out of potholes and over bumps. Sonja used her knees to steer while she took a hand grenade from a pouch on her vest and pulled the pin. She released the lever and held the grenade in her hand, counting down four seconds before tossing it over her shoulder in an arc that cleared the other woman's head.

The grenade landed on the road and detonated just as the technical behind her drove over it. The blast blew off the right front wheel and the driver overcorrected and the vehicle rolled.

'There's still one coming,' the woman yelled.

Sonja looked ahead and saw the dark, squat shape of the helicopter racing towards her. 'I have visual.'

'Roger,' Jed said. 'You've still got company.'

'I know that. I can't stop. I want you to get over us, lower the winch and get the girl off.'

'We can try and neutralise that technical first.'

'No,' Sonja said. 'The package needs to get out of here. Take her first.'

There was a moment's hesitation. Sonja knew Jed was thinking the same thing she was. This mission had been mounted to save the senator's daughter. She was the priority.

'Roger.'

'Keep firing until you're out of ammo,' Sonja called back to the woman. 'The chopper is going to hover over us and drop a cable with a yellow padded ring on the end. Put your head and arms through it and then tuck it under your arms and hold on. They'll lift you off.'

'What about you?' the girl called.

'Right behind you.'

'Coming in hot,' Jed said.

Sonja saw the Seahawk swing around and come up behind them. She risked a glance over her shoulder and saw and heard the door gunner opening up on the technical behind her. If the gunner hit anyone on board it wasn't the driver, or he wasn't hit badly enough to slow them down. The aid worker fired off the last of her rounds.

Sonja kept the accelerator pedal pressed hard to the floor as the helicopter's shadow settled over her. The girl had climbed into the front of the HiLux and was standing on the passenger seat. Sonja reached up with one hand and grabbed the girl's trouser leg, helping to steady her as she reached for the ring on the end of the winch cable.

A burst of machine-gun fire whizzed past them and pinged into the fuselage of the helicopter above them.

'We're taking fire,' Jed said into her earpiece.

'You think?'

Sonja glanced up at the girl, who was still reaching frantically for the ring.

'I can't do it.'

'You can,' Sonja yelled, 'you have to. Be brave.'

The helicopter pilot brought his bird down another metre – Sonja couldn't help but admire his nerve and flying – and the girl was finally able to get her hands and head through the yellow ring.

'Hold on tight,' Sonja said. There was a pothole coming up as wide as the road and Sonja had no choice but to hit it at speed. The Toyota lurched and the girl squealed as her torso slipped out of the ring.

The machine-gun fire had stopped. Maybe the guy behind her had also run out of ammunition, Sonja thought.

Too soon, Jed said: 'Sonja, the guy behind you has got an RPG.'

'Shit.' She looked back. The gunner had switched weapons and was holding the rocket-propelled grenade launcher on his shoulder. He wasn't aiming at her vehicle, but rather at the Seahawk. The girl had tears streaming down her face as she fumbled with the extraction harness. 'Get that fucking thing over your head, now!'

The girl was crying, but she managed to get into the ring again. In Sonja's experience, it was sometimes helpful if the troops under your command feared you more than the enemy.

The problem was that the helicopter was a sitting duck and the door gunners couldn't bring their weapons to bear on the technical behind her, as it was in a blind spot under the tail rotor. In a split second the man with the RPG would fire. Sonja had no more grenades. She glanced down at the Toyota symbol on the steering wheel. 'I hope you work.'

'Say again?' Jed said. The girl's feet left the vinyl seat next to her.

Sonja stood on the brake pedal. The driver of the technical behind her, no doubt shifting his attention between the Toyota in front and the helicopter above, was a fraction too late reacting and he slammed into the back of Sonja's vehicle.

Just as she'd prayed, the airbag in the steering wheel exploded in her face, which was just as well as she had no seatbelt. The force of the safety device hitting her and the forward movement of being hit from behind knocked the wind from Sonja's lungs, but she fought to control the truck on the loose dirt surface of the road. The Seahawk banked just as the man with the RPG fired and the rocket sailed harmlessly past but terrifyingly close to the departing aircraft. The man with the rocket launcher was catapulted out of his technical over the cab and into the back of Sonja's Toyota.

The two HiLuxes, locked together now, skidded for several metres before coming to a halt. Sonja fought to drag a breath into her tortured chest. Her neck ached but she glanced in the twisted wing mirror in time to see the man who had fired the RPG drawing a knife from a sheath on the belt around his robe.

The man raised the knife and slashed down. Sonja ducked to her right at the last second, reaching for the driver's side door handle, and the man's arcing blade missed her neck and punctured the airbag, which allowed her freer movement. Sonja grabbed her assailant's arm and rolled out the side of the vehicle, taking him with her. She rolled the man over her shoulder, onto his back in the sand by the side of the road, and smashed her fist into his face, three times. His nose shattered and she put a knee on his forearm, forcing him to drop his knife. Sonja scooped it up, punched him again, and drove the blade into his heart.

Sonja quickly scanned the sky. The Seahawk had moved out of range of the RPG, but it was circling back towards her now.

'Jed,' she wheezed.

'On our way. You good?'

'*Lekker.*' She coughed.

Sonja got to her feet and looked around her. The door of the vehicle that had rammed hers was opening and she saw the driver, head bloodied, stagger out. He held up a pistol.

Sonja raised her MP5, still slung around her neck, and pulled the trigger. The firing pin clicked on an empty chamber. She cursed herself for making the rookie's mistake of not counting her rounds. Still, she'd had a lot on her mind. Sonja reached for her Glock, then realised the aid worker still had her pistol.

She turned and ran.

A shot echoed behind her, then another, and a puff of sand fountained by her side.

So this was how it ended, she thought. Out in the desert, in the middle of nowhere, the victim of her own error.

At least the girl was safe.

Sonja thought of her daughter, Emma, about the same age as the aid worker.

'*Allah-u-Akbar*,' the man behind her yelled. He would be steadying himself for the shot, she thought.

She kept running, the sound of the blood pumping between her ears the only noise in the universe. Even the helicopter seemed to be out of range now. Had Jed abandoned her?

Sonja had never run from a fight before, but now the terror overwhelmed her. She wanted to drop, exhausted, and plead for mercy, even though she knew it would do no good.

A Hellfire missile, launched from the orbiting Global Hawk, detonated behind her and knocked her off her feet, sending her sprawling hands and knees first into the desert sands.

*

After their meeting, as tradition dictated, the members of the Pretoria Cycad and Firearms Appreciation Society adjourned to the Bond Cafe in the Pretoria suburb of Montana for brunch.

As a young revolutionary whose party was allied to the Eastern Bloc, Thandi had been busy in training camps in Russia and East Germany learning to kill people and blow things up when many of the James Bond films venerated in the cafe had been filmed. She had only had the time and the money to indulge in the cinema and television much later in her life. She knew that real-life war and espionage were far more brutal and less glamorous than the movies portrayed, but she did catch herself, as she usually did, casting an appreciative eye over the framed picture of a bare-chested Daniel Craig and his sky-blue swimming shorts behind glass as she entered the cafe.

They took their regular dark wood table beneath the firearms display case, between 007's Walther PPK and Christopher Plummer's golden gun. Thandi ordered her usual, the scrambled eggs, bacon and pork sausage. The others all ordered something cooked, except Laurel, the thinnest of them, who had her usual muesli.

'I still can't picture Joanne as a thief and a smuggler,' Laurel said. 'She's no Miss Moneypenny.'

'Moneypenny was one of the goodies, Laurel,' SS said.

'Sure?' Laurel raised her eyebrows. 'What about the Pussy woman?'

'Galore,' Charles said, long and wistfully. 'Honor Blackman. Baddie. Very bad. But good.'

'Stop carrying on like a dirty old man, Charles,' Sandy said. 'You're disgusting.'

'Nonsense, you love it when I talk dirty,' he replied to her.

Thandi shook her head. *Ai*, those two.

Baye looked up from her iPhone. 'Hey!'

'What is it?' Jacqueline asked. A waiter in a black waistcoat and trousers and a crisp white shirt brought their coffees and teas.

'It's Joanne. She's in London. She's been involved in a shootout!'

Laurel put a hand over her mouth. 'They have hijackers in England?'

Baye shook her head. 'No, something we don't have – terrorists.'

'Other than those running the country,' SS said. 'But read on, Baye, read on, girl.'

Thandi bridled at Stephen's comment, but kept quiet. The ANC, South Africa's African National Congress, had been one of the truly great independence movements, but like the ruling party in her own country, it had lost its way. Thandi had for many years been a member of ZANU-PF, the Zimbabwean African National Union Popular Front, but later in life had switched her allegiance to the opposition.

The disastrously corrupt process of land redistribution – taking farms from the whites and giving them to government supporters – had bankrupted the country and done little to alleviate poverty or compensate legitimate veterans of the struggle Thandi had fought for. After failing to change things from within she had joined the opposition party, the MDC, the Movement for Democratic Change.

For a time, under the former president, Robert Mugabe, ZANU-PF had shared power with the MDC and Thandi, whose revolutionary credentials were impeccable, had briefly served as Minister for Women's Affairs in an ill-fated government of national unity. However, once the hybrid government ended, and Thandi went public with her love for her second husband, George Bryant, the ruling party had done its best to marginalise her, painting her as a sellout and a lackey of the whites.

Baye was reading from her phone, telling them how Joanne Flack had shot and killed a terrorist on the streets of London.

'Good shooting,' Charles interjected. 'Centre mass, double tap, I bet.'

Thandi said nothing as the waiter brought their food out, but quietly wondered if Joanne had taken on board some of the things they had discussed on the shooting range. It was always best, her Russian instructors had taught her, to aim for the centre of a person's body, and to fire two shots in quick succession, known to the Western world as the 'double tap'.

Sandy had her phone in front of her as well as she ate. 'It says here that the UK press is calling her a heroine.'

'Thief, more like it,' Baye said.

Laurel stood and was leaning over Baye's shoulder, looking at her screen. 'That's a pretty top Joanne's wearing under that cheap imitation leather jacket.'

'At least we know she's alive,' Thandi said between mouthfuls.

'Alive and in possession of stolen goods,' Jacqueline added.

'Allegedly,' Thandi said. 'Where is she now, girls?'

Sandy and Baye both studied their phones. 'Unavailable for comment or interview,' they said, almost in unison.

Thandi finished the last of her scrambled eggs and bacon. 'Ladies and gentlemen, we have some investigating to do, but first, we have important business to attend to.'

'Hear, hear,' said Charles.

They settled up, separate bills as usual, with each of them contributing ten rand to the communal tip, then collected their handbags and walking sticks and made their way out of the cafe and downstairs to the gun shop and subterranean shooting gallery.

The other members of the society all carried side arms, but Thandi had her personal weapon stored in a safe at the firing range. As she entered, Frans, the young Afrikaner shooting instructor with the cute dimples, greeted her with a hug.

'*Goeie môre*, Tannie,' he said to her.

'It's good to see you, Frans. How is your baby?' Thandi put on her hearing protection and safety glasses.

'*Baie goed*, Tannie, thank you.'

He unlocked the gun rack and retrieved her vintage SKS semi-automatic assault rifle, with its battle-scarred but lovingly oiled woodwork.

'*Dankie*, Frans,' Thandi said, thanking him.

She took the rifle and a clip of 7.62-millimetre ammunition from him, and cocked the weapon and pushed the ten rounds down into the open breech.

Thandi let the working parts fly forward and turned to her friends, who were lining up beside her. 'Let's rock and roll, bitches.'

'Thandi, you are *so* gangsta,' Charles said.

Thandi smiled as she pulled the butt of the Cold War firearm into her shoulder and peered down the old-school iron sights. She held the rifle tight and close to her body, and squeezed the trigger.

Shooting for Thandi was therapeutic; it took her mind off her problems, past and present.

Thandi had been arrested by officers from the Central Intelligence Organisation, the feared CIO, or Charlie 10 as they were commonly known in her home country. She had been beaten and her life, and that of her youngest daughter, also an activist, had been threatened, all because Thandi had dared to run for parliament.

Thandi had eventually been released from prison, but fearing an attempt on her life she and her children and grandchildren had fled Zimbabwe for South Africa, where they all now lived in exile. There had been a change of presidency since then, but her beloved homeland's economy was still struggling and for now Thandi and her family had no other option but to stay and work in South Africa.

Down the line came the pop of pistols being fired. And, she mused, she had friends here.

Laurel was grinning. Sandy, sitting in her wheelchair and peering through the sights of her Ruger Mini-14 rifle, yelped with joy as a round found its home in the bullseye.

Charles looked from his lane to Stephen's. 'SS, open your eyes. You're shooting like an old man.'

'Ha! I'll outshoot you and outdrink you any day of the week, flyboy.'

Baye was motionless, unspeaking, squeezing off methodically aimed round after round at imagined foes. Queen Jacqueline was trying on an American AR-15 for size and Frans stood beside her, giving her instruction as she pumped five rounds in quick succession into the paper target.

Thandi smelled the acrid scent of cordite and heard and felt the reverberation of lead leaving barrels around her. It brought back so many memories, not all of them bad.

She wondered where Joanne was now, and how she was feeling after killing a man.

Thandi applied the safety catch to her SKS and remembered a time when she had trained to kill people like the ones she now called her friends. The temporary buzz of firing rounds down the range was making everyone feel good, but she knew that this, like combat, was just an illusion.

When they had all finished shooting they began pressing the buttons that would return their targets to them, via a high-speed pulley system, from the other end of the range.

Frans walked along the line inspecting their handiwork. 'Best shot of the day is Thandi – again!'

Charles raised his right fist in the air. '*Pamberi ne hondo*!'

Thandi laughed, raised her hand and started toyi-toyiing, dancing on the spot. '*Pamberi ne hondo*,' she echoed, which meant 'Forward with the war'. It was an old slogan from the fighting in then Rhodesia, and the fact that Charles, who had once been the enemy of her cause and people, could make such a joke spoke volumes about him. He was kind, even if he did fancy himself a ladies' man.

They unloaded and cleared their weapons and holstered or slung them before removing their safety glasses and earmuffs. Thandi checked her watch. She needed to get on the road and get to work – she drove her new Mercedes sedan as an Uber car during the day.

'What are we going to do about Joanne?' Laurel asked her as they made their way out of the shooting range and through the gun store.

Thandi looked into Laurel's eyes and patted her on the arm. 'Don't worry, my dear, I'm sure we'll get to the bottom of this and there will be some perfectly acceptable explanation.'

Laurel's face was screwed up in confusion. 'You don't think she stole the cycad?'

'I have no idea, Laurel, but that is what we must find out.'

'*Ja*, we must, hey.' Laurel nodded decisively, though Thandi doubted the pretty woman with the dyed platinum-blonde hair would be of much use.

They went upstairs into the bright Highveld sunshine, towards their respective cars parked in front of the Bond Cafe. Jacqueline came to her as she was opening the door of the Mercedes.

'Thandi, don't take this amateur sleuthing plan too seriously. I think we'd be better off getting Laurel's son-in-law back on the job.'

Thandi said nothing. Queen Jacqueline, she knew, had a habit of saying in meetings what she thought the members wanted to hear, and then quietly going about doing nothing, or sometimes the opposite, once the meeting was over. Thandi had picked up in the past that while not exactly enemies, Jacqueline and Joanne were more likely than any of the others to have differences of opinions on a subject. Thandi sensed there was some historical rivalry between them and in the past had wondered if perhaps Joanne harboured desires of taking over the chair. Why, then, was Jacqueline now asking her to back-pedal in the proposed investigation?

'Of course, Jacqueline,' Thandi said. 'Nothing too serious, but it won't hurt to ask around a bit. Might help the police, don't you think?'

Jacqueline replied with a tight smile and a small nod, then retreated to her Fortuner.

Chapter 4

'Now, kids,' Rod Cavanagh told the group of ten-year-olds, 'this is my favourite part of the museum, the section on plants.'

A couple of the kids groaned, which was normal, but what got Rod's goat was that one of the teachers, a pretty thing in her early twenties, yawned.

The teacher caught him looking at her and snapped into Miss Prissy mode. 'Class, turn to your activity sheets. I want you to find ten plants in this section of the natural history museum that Native American people used for medicinal purposes and write them down.'

The teacher probably thought him an ageing no-hoper. At best she might think he was a volunteer, whiling away his retirement after a successful business career, and not the paid curator he was. The truth was that his ambitions and dreams had been stopped dead twenty-five years earlier. If it wasn't for the love of a good woman, his late wife Betty, he might not even have bothered carrying on with life at all. That union had brought him Jake, which had given him a reason to keep living when Betty had passed.

Rod's phone vibrated. 'I'll leave you all to look around and then we'll move to the Civil War section.'

'Yay,' said one of the kids.

Rod went back to the Stone Age and took his flip phone out of the leather case on his belt. The thing still worked fine so he saw no reason to listen to his son and get a *smart* phone. Jake also ribbed him about the pouch, but it was practical and hand-tooled, two things you didn't see a lot of these days. Rod took out his reading glasses, put them on, opened the phone and saw that he had missed a call earlier, but there was a text message from the same number. He opened it.

Mr Cavanagh, I was given your number by the bureau. I work for another government agency and I need to speak to you as soon as possible.

No name. Rod scratched his chin. He wondered if the man worked for the *other* government agency. OGA was a euphemism often applied to the CIA. The Central Intelligence Agency was usually referred to as 'The Company' in books and movies, so this had more of a ring of importance about it. It had been a long time since he'd been seconded to the Federal Bureau of Investigation and, despite what his son liked to tell people when he'd had too much to drink at parties, Rod had never actually been an FBI agent.

Rod moved to a mammoth skeleton and dialled the number.

'Mr Cavanagh,' said the man who answered the phone.

'Yes, this is he.'

'Thanks for calling. My name is Jed Banks. I work for the government, Mr Cavanagh.'

'Call me Rod. You work for the other government agency I'm thinking of?'

'Yes, Rod.'

'I can't very well ask to see your ID over the phone.'

'No, sir. Rod, I know you worked undercover twenty-something years ago busting an international plant smuggling ring.'

'If you google my name you'll find that information, Jed.'

'I've read the redacted file, Rod. I know about everything, including the shooting.'

Rod paused. He watched the school group through the door leading to the next room of the museum. While the subject of his undercover work did come up from time to time, through discussions with friends, or his son at parties, or some reporter or other somewhere around the world doing a story about species other than mega-fauna that were facing extinction, by and large he tried not to think too much about that time in his life, and the man he had killed.

'I don't know what you're talking about.'

'Sure you do, and you now know that I know more about you than what's on the record. I'm on kind of a deadline here, Mr Cavanagh, and although I hate to sound melodramatic, lives could depend on the shit I need to ask you about.'

'The shit?'

'Plant stuff, Mr Cavanagh.'

'It's Rod, and ask away.'

'I'm emailing you a picture,' Jed said.

'I'll have to go to my computer.'

'You don't have email on your phone?'

'No.'

'OK.' There was a pause, maybe a sigh. 'Can you get to a computer now, Rod?'

'Yes. I'm not a complete Luddite. Hold on.' Rod went into the plant room and saw that the kids and their teachers had already moved to the Civil War gallery. Clearly they didn't need him. He took a short cut through a no-entry door and walked down the corridor to his office. He sat at his desk and opened his email program, noting Jed's address. 'Zambezi at Gmail?'

'A place in Africa I like.'

'I went there once as well,' Rod said, opening the email.

'I know.'

Goddamned CIA, Rod thought. There was no text in the body of the email and the subject line simply read *Files*, of which there were two. He clicked on the first, a JPEG picture. The image was grainy, the light low, but there were clearly a score or more of elephant tusks stacked upright in the corner of a room. The walls looked like mud brick. 'Where is this?'

'That's need-to-know, Rod. You know the drill.'

Also in the frame were some rhino horns. Of more interest to him and, he guessed, the reason he had been called, were half-a-dozen cycads, stripped of their foliage, one of which was taller than the others and partly encased in bubble-wrap plastic.

'Are those trunks what we think they are, Rod?'

'Cycads. And they call that part of the plant a caudex, not a trunk.'

'Is there anything more you can tell us about them?'

'There are plenty of people who know more about those plants than me, Jed.'

'Yes, but none have ever worked undercover for the federal government. This conversation stays between us, Rod.'

Rod felt his heart start to beat a little faster. At his age that wasn't always a good thing and it had been too long since he'd exercised enough, in or out of the sack, to get his pulse racing.

Rod clicked on the photo and zoomed in. He scratched his chin.

'You there, Rod?'

'Yes.'

'I don't want to rush you,' Jed said, 'but you could say this is kind of time critical.'

Rod whistled softly through his teeth. 'There are a couple of rare beauties there – *Encephalartos hirsutus*, aka the Venda cycad, takes its Latin name from its hairy leaves and is very valuable; and, let me see, *Encephalartos lebomboensis*, from the Lebombo hills between South Africa and Mozambique, also worth a bomb. These are almost extinct in the wild, hence their value to collectors.'

'What are they worth?' Jed asked.

'Just like rhino horn these plants are worth tens of thousands of dollars each. The difference between them and the horn and ivory you've got stacked there is that cycads are easier to get hold of – there are no choppers or armed rangers or special forces guys protecting them, as with rhinos – and easier to move because to your average customs inspector in some third-world port those cycads just look like some dumb ol' piece of a plant.'

'What about the one partially wrapped in plastic?'

Rod pushed his glasses up the bridge of his nose and leaned in closer to the computer screen. 'Well, it's keeping good company. It's hard to tell, without its foliage, as it could be one of a couple of species, not nearly as distinctive as the other two variants you've got there.'

'What if I told you,' Jed said, 'that we have intel that someone in that location overheard someone saying, quote: "One of these plants is a female and it's worth millions of dollars"?'

Rod stared at the screen. 'No.'

'What do you mean, "no"? Not possible? You don't get plants worth that much?'

'Well…'

'Rod?'

'I'm thinking,' he said. *Is it possible?*

'Talk to me, Rod. Clock's ticking,' Jed said.

'It's hard to tell from this one picture, and not being able to see it up close, but I guess theoretically it could be an *Encephalartos woodii*, the rarest cycad in the world. There are clones of that plant. They're valuable, but not worth millions, unless… But it can't be, no…'

'No, what?'

'Unless maybe, against all odds, someone really did find a female. It's believed there are no female *woodii*s anywhere in the world. A cycad needs a male and female to reproduce –'

'You can spare us the birds and bees lecture, Rod, but I'm getting a better feel for the value of what we're seeing here.'

'Oh, yeah,' Rod said. 'If I'm right, whoever owns this little mud-brick storeroom is sitting on an incredible fortune, Jed. A female *woodii* would be the most sought after plant in the world and a true collector would pay whatever was asked. Millions, easily.'

'What do people do with plants like this? Don't they need water?'

'They're incredibly hardy,' Rod said. 'They can last weeks, maybe a couple of months without water, and then you just plant them again, water them, take care of them, and their big old spiky leaves will come back in no time. They're survivors, which is one of the reasons they've been around since the time dinosaurs roamed the earth.'

'So they could have been there some time?'

'Yes, sir, but that blood on the root ends of those elephant tusks doesn't look too old to me, maybe a week?'

'Maybe,' Jed said.

Rod didn't know whether Jed knew much about ivory or not, but Rod wasn't only interested in plants. Since his wife had died he'd tried to keep himself as busy as he could, not just in the museum, but learning as much as he could about threats to all facets of the natural environment and trying to do something about it. By virtue of his former job as a US Fish and Wildlife Service investigator he was sometimes called on to give talks about various threats to the environment and he used social media to raise awareness of problems around the world and of stupid decisions made by his own government. 'How else can I be of help, Jed?'

'Any idea who could have stolen those plants?'

'I've been out of the cycad trade loop for a long time, Jed, but I check the net now and again for reports. What else can you tell me about the find?'

'Not much, Rod. Like I said, need-to-know.'

'Yes, and you told me you're calling me because I can keep a secret.'

Rod saw that the second file he had been sent was a video. He clicked on it and saw that the JPEG he'd been looking at was clearly a still that had been captured from a five-second MPEG. The video didn't give him any better views of the cycads, but there was an odd whining sound in the background. He turned the volume up on the speakers attached to his monitor and played the video again. He realised it was not a screeching noise he could hear, but rather a note. He looked at the wall behind the sack.

'Those mud bricks don't look like the interior of a South African house,' Rod said. 'This looks more like the Middle East or north Africa, and I can hear what I think is the tail end of a muezzin's call to prayer from a mosque.'

'So?' Jed said. 'What can you tell me, Rod? I was told you were a smart guy.'

Rod suddenly wondered if this call might be some kind of a test, rather than just a fishing exercise or an agent going through the motions, chasing up a lead he didn't really believe in.

'Mozambique's a base for rhino and elephant poachers and smuggling in general, and they have a strong Islamic community thanks to centuries of Arab slave and commodity trading up and down the Indian Ocean coast, but those mud bricks don't look Mozambican to me, either. There's a gun in the frame, under the camera.'

'You gonna shit or get off the pot, Rod?'

Rod opened his internet browser. Jed was CIA, of that he was sure – ironically the 'OGA' tag was a giveaway because an agent from any other bureau or agency would have declared who they worked for as a means of intimidating or encouraging someone like Rod to snap to and help out like a good citizen. The CIA didn't chase poachers, they hunted terrorists these days. But here, in what was some kind of raid, someone with a gun had stumbled across a room full of ill-gotten treasure stolen from the natural world. Rod typed *terror groups funded by ivory, rhino horn* into the search engine.

He found a link to an article about some attacks on police stations and government buildings by an Islamic fundamentalist group in Mozambique and was wondering if his initial assessment, rejecting that country, might be wrong. The next article mentioned a group called Chengeta, and Rod snapped his fingers.

'Still on the line, Rod?' Jed said through the phone's speaker.

'Mali.'

It was Jed's turn to stay quiet.

'Still on the *line*, Jed?' Rod said, smiling to himself.

'I'm listening.'

'There's a group I follow on Facebook, an anti-poaching group called Chengeta Wildlife – Chengeta's a Zimbabwean word, in Shona, for "take care of". They operate in Mali, training rangers and soldiers in anti-poaching. I read recently that the elephant poaching there is conducted by two rival terror groups, al-Qaeda in the Islamic Maghreb, or AQIM, and Ansar al-Dine, AAD, which is aligned to ISIS. Both of them use ivory to finance their military operations against the government.'

'Could be,' Jed said. 'But there are no rhinos or valuable cycads in Mali.'

Rod was scanning the Chengeta Facebook page while he spoke and found an article from South Africa's *Sunday Times* about Malians involved in organised crime.

'You're definitely right about the rhinos – they were wiped out years ago – and I'm not sure about the other contraband, but there are Malian gangs who operate throughout Africa.'

'Tell me more.'

'I'm sending you a link to an article now.' He forwarded the *Sunday Times* story and hit send. 'Because of the poverty and conflict in their country there are Malians everywhere, not just in Africa,' Rod said. 'They're loyal to each other and their clans and you can have members from the same family at home in Mali, or in South Africa, driving a cab in New York, or studying in France or the UK. They're hardworking and resourceful, but they can also apply this drive to crime. Think of the Mafia spreading its tentacles across the world after the Second World War and apply that to today's world. Chengeta was training anti-poaching rangers in Mali to protect the last of the country's desert elephants, but with China banning the legal trade in ivory the black market is picking up, as are prices for tusks. ISIS and al-Qaeda's affiliates are killing elephants not to line their own pockets – well, maybe partly – but to fund their jihads.'

'I see,' Jed said. 'So the cycads and rhino horn could be coming from South Africa.'

Rod had been skim-reading the article he had just sent Jed. 'Most likely. That piece I just sent you includes some names you might want to follow up. The high-profile Keita family has been linked to organised crime. Moussa Keita, a former politician, recently beat the wrap for some charges on drug importation into Mali and his brother, Rafik, appears to be on the run in South Africa over a gangland murder charge. I'd bet my last dime that the cycads you're looking at have come direct from South Africa and, as you know, that country has the largest remaining population of rhinos in the world.'

'So if, say,' Jed said, sounding like he was theorising, 'you could catch a cycad smuggler, you might be able to get a line on who's moving the rhino horn and ivory as well, and find out who the Mister Bigs of this trade are.'

'Or Mrs Bigs,' Rod said.

'In the Malian gangs?'

'No,' Rod said, emphatically, 'their culture is too male dominated, but in the world of cycad smuggling there are men *and* women involved. We're not talking about down-on-your-luck poor Africans in that trade, Jed – it's more rich white people in South

Africa, Australia, here in the US, and other wealthy collectors around the world, particularly the Middle East and parts of Asia.'

'Rod,' Jed said, 'I need you to fly to Virginia.'

'When?'

'Now. Your son's old enough to take care of himself.'

'You've done your research.'

'I'm sorry for your loss. Your wife, it was...'

'Two years, as you very well know, *Jed*. And yes, my son can take care of himself. I'll send the government a bill for the damage the house parties will cause, but I'll be there. When do I leave?'

'There's already a ticket with your name on it. I'll email you the details now.'

'OK.'

Rod ended the call and looked at the photos of Betty and Jake on his desk. He didn't know how long he would be gone for – he got the sense that if he'd asked Jed he wouldn't have got a straight answer.

If there really was a female *woodii* out there, then Rod wanted to help find it, or stop some terrorists from profiting from it – or doing worse. However, it was more than the lure of a rare plant that had made him say yes to Jed so quickly. The personal guilt he felt over what had happened during Operation Green Thumb had numbed the pain of the government dumping him on the scrap heap. As the years had gone on, however, he had nursed an unvoiced but residual pain at his betrayal. He had messed up, but the operation had been a success and the bad guys had been taken down. He wanted a chance to restore his reputation and make up for the years he had spent languishing away from the front lines of conservation. He thought of all the good he could have done if he hadn't screwed up, if he had continued to rise through the ranks as a Special Agent. This mission might be a way to find some personal redemption.

Rod called Jake and told him he had to go away on business for a while, to a museum conference. Rod had been feeling increasingly isolated and alone since Betty's death. More than once he'd thought about Joanne Flack. Odd that this call from Jed had been about cycads on a day when Joanne had made world headlines. Or maybe it wasn't a coincidence at all.

*

Sonja had slept for most of the flight from Africa to the United States on board a C-17 military transport aircraft. At one point she woke, screaming, still lost in a nightmare, and grabbed the man next to her and put her hands around his neck.

'It's me, Sonja,' Jed Banks had said, over and over again. He had hugged her and soothed her out of the nightmare, but with Jed, she had learned, there was no hidden agenda. That was unusual for a spy. Jed spoke a lot about his wife, Christine, and his two children, from different marriages. He was the sort of guy, she thought, who would even be friends with his ex.

She was at Langley now, sitting in a meeting room, waiting for Jed and some others to arrive. She didn't have her phone with her – it was in a locker at the reception area – and she was feeling bad about not calling Hudson. She played with a pen on the desk in front of her. The door opened and she turned. It was Jed.

'Howzit,' she said.

He grinned. '*Lekker.*'

'Listen to your Afrikaans. You obviously spent too much time in South Africa,' she said.

Jed took a seat opposite her. 'Not enough. I miss it. Christine and I are actually thinking of retiring out there one day, maybe Cape Town. You lived there a while, right?'

She shrugged. 'You're the spy. You tell me.'

He gave her a smile and opened a folder in front of him. 'You doing OK?'

'Sure.'

'That was quite a nightmare you had on the C-17. I thought you were going to kill me.'

She narrowed her eyes. 'You never had a dream about combat, Jed? Two tours of duty with Special Forces in Afghanistan, lots of shit in Africa.'

He leaned back in the boardroom chair. 'Well, who knows what about who?'

'We've got mutual friends.'

Jed nodded. 'No doubt. How's Hudson Brand doing?'

Sonja shrugged again. She and Hudson Brand had an on-again, off-again relationship and he was always on at her to move in with him, although now he seemed to have gone back to his no-madic safari guide ways. Though none of that was Jed's business, she thought.

'You know there was an investigation into his background, go-ing back to his days working for the Company in Angola in the nineties?'

'He told me he got an email, a year or more ago, exonerating him from his unlawful discharge back then. There wasn't anything about compensation.'

'Well, his name's been cleared,' Jed said. 'You called him?'

'He's in Zimbabwe, managing a safari lodge for a while for a friend—the manager took ill. He's busy, and besides, you've got my phone in a locker.'

'You can call or Skype him anytime.'

'Maybe I don't want to, Jed.' She peered over at the papers in front of him. 'I don't think my personal life is agenda item number one for today.'

He shook his head. 'I'm sorry, Sonja. You know, we have coun-sellors on staff if you want to talk to someone.'

She held back a retort. There was a time when she'd scoffed at offers of help or the suggestion that she was anything other than mentally resilient and fit for combat. But shit got to people, of that she was now convinced, and she had sought help in the past. She didn't, however, feel like opening up to a Company shrink. 'How much longer is this debriefing going to take? This is anal, even for the CIA.'

'You got somewhere else to be?'

'Yeah, maybe on holiday, in Zimbabwe, or back in Mali.'

Jed hadn't told Sonja why she was here, just that there was one more meeting he wanted her to attend before they released her and she could fly back to her empty home in Los Angeles. Despite her protestations, however, she was in no hurry to get back there.

Jed raised his eyebrows.

'No,' she replied, 'I'm not serious about Mali.'

'Probably best you don't go back there for a while,' Jed said.

'Probably.'

'Though I do admire the work you were doing there with that Chengeta outfit, training anti-poaching rangers.'

'It was only supposed to be a few weeks.' Sonja fiddled with the pen. She had told herself she was done with fighting the war against poaching, but somehow Africa kept pulling her back. Or maybe it was something else.

'Are you OK for money?'

'Fine. My partner, Sam, was well off.'

'Yes. I'm sorry for your loss, Sonja.'

'I didn't *lose* him, Jed, he was shot dead by a rhino poacher.'

'Is that why you signed on with Chengeta, to train rangers? In Sam's memory?'

Sonja rolled her eyes. 'I'm not some honourable do-gooder, Jed. I'm an American citizen now but I'm not American. I'm not patriotic and sentimental and waving the flag or even doing this for the man I loved.'

He let it rest a moment. 'Then why? Not for money. You were in Mali as a volunteer when we recruited you.'

'You didn't *recruit* me, I agreed to help you rescue a senator's daughter. I don't want to be on the CIA's payroll, or anyone else's for that matter. Yes, I was in Mali as a volunteer. You want to know the real reason I was there?' She had been mulling it over just then, before Jed intruded into her thoughts, and the truth of it coalesced in her mind now.

'Shoot,' Jed said, locking his eyes on her.

'I miss it.'

'What? Africa?'

'No. Combat.'

He looked at her for a few long moments, then nodded, slowly.

She could see it in his eyes, the faraway look, the clenched jaw. 'You know what I'm talking about.'

He didn't nod. 'I knew guys who went back to the 'Stan, for three, four tours, not only because it was their job but because Afghanistan had become the new normal for them; they couldn't fit in at home. One, in particular, was a great operator, one of the best in Special Forces. Even back in the States he was the consummate soldier, well disciplined, motivated, supremely fit, perfect husband and dad. One day he had a fight with his wife, drove off, and shot himself in the head.'

'I'm not suicidal.' She stared at the pen as she rolled it between her fingers, over and over.

'No, but you know, and I know, that you can be fully function-ing – hell, over-functioning – and still have PTSD.'

She looked up again. Jed had been there, killed people, but she didn't see her eyes reflected in his. He could come back, to the States, to his wife, to his children, and carry on like normal. Some people could. Why couldn't she?

'You have a daughter, right?'

She spread her hands wide. 'You know it all.'

'Does she want you to still be doing this shit?' Jed said.

Sonja shrugged. 'She's got a boyfriend, a life. She's an archaeol-ogist. She doesn't get a vote in my life.'

Jed shook his head. The door to the conference room opened.

Glad of the interruption, Sonja turned. A man with a grey crew cut walked in. He wore a white shirt with four pens in the pocket, dark trousers, grey loafers and aluminium-framed glasses. Sonja did not waste money on clothes and accessories, but this guy looked like he shopped at Nerd Brothers. She wondered if he was here to fix a computer.

'Rod?' Jed stood and went to the man and shook hands. 'Good to meet you. This is Sonja Kurtz.'

'Rod Cavanagh.'

He took her hand in a firm grasp and she returned the grip. Sonja liked seeing men surprised when she gave a firm handshake, but Rod just smiled politely. Up close – she had run out of dispos-able contact lenses and didn't have her glasses on – she could see that his broad shoulders stretched his shirt seams and he had nice forearms. Annoyingly, he had a forest of nose and ear hair.

Sonja sat without saying anything.

Rod carried a leather briefcase that, like his ensemble, looked like it had been around since the 1950s. He sat the bag on the table in front of him and undid the buckles.

'Sonja, Rod's joined us because he's an expert in cycads.'

'What the fuck is a cycad?' She looked to Rod, whose eyeglasses seemed to have slid down to the end of his nose through the action of sitting down.

Rod raised his eyebrows and looked at her disapprovingly as he pushed his glasses back into place. 'To the layman a cycad looks like a cross between a palm and a fern, but it's actually more closely related to a conifer.'

'Like a pine tree?'

'Yes,' Rod said. 'They produce cones, like a conifer, often garishly coloured, orange and yellow and so forth, and this, coupled with their increasing rarity, is what makes them so valuable to collectors.'

'Weird.'

Jed picked up a remote off the meeting room table and clicked it, bringing the flat-screen on the wall to life.

Sonja swivelled and saw a still image from the video she had filmed inside the building in Mali. Her heart thumped a little. She remembered the room – she had been through the video during her debrief. Jed had mentioned they were going to call in an expert to try and identify the mini tree trunks she had seen in the room, and which Jed was now indicating with a laser pointer.

'The Venda cycad,' Rod said. 'Venda is in the northern part of South Africa and –'

'I know where Venda is,' Sonja said. 'Is it valuable?'

'Very. Almost as much as one of those rhino horns you can also see in that picture. That's them on the left stacked by –'

'I know what rhino horns are, Rod,' Sonja said. 'I took that video and my late partner was killed by rhino poachers.'

Rod appeared somewhat taken aback. 'Sorry for your loss. I guess I should have known from your accent. You're South African?'

She shook her head. People often made that assumption. 'I was born in Namibia.'

Rod nodded. 'Land of the *Welwitschia* plant. Did you know those plants are thousands of years old and –'

'Um, Rod?' Jed said, nodding to the screen. 'Perhaps you can fill us in a little more on the illegal trade in cycads.'

56

'Sure.' Rod pushed his glasses up again. 'By way of background, cycads date back to the Jurassic period, but they've never been in more trouble than they are today. According to the IUCN, the International Union for Conservation of Nature, sixty-three per cent of all the world's cycads are threatened with extinction. To put it all in perspective, cycads are the most endangered organism on the planet. Three species of cycads are extinct in the wild in South Africa and one in Swaziland, all due to greed. South Africa also has the highest proportion of critically endangered cycads in the world. These plants are in far more trouble than rhinos, though they don't get nearly as much attention.'

'You're saying these plants are actually worth big money?'

Rod looked her in the eye. 'Damn straight, that's what I'm saying.'

'So who's buying them?'

'There are two distinct markets for cycads. The first is in South Africa itself, for traditional medicine. Healers sell strips of bark, just big enough to hold in your palm, which are used as a talisman, a good luck charm to give you protection from whatever you're scared of. That's the small end of the market; a strip of bark will maybe sell for a dollar. However, it's high volume: one report I read suggested nine tons of bark could be sold in the traditional medicine markets in Durban and Johannesburg in a year, so populations of common cycads are being systematically wiped out.'

'That's the small end?' Sonja asked.

'Yup. The big end of town is your collector, and they're the ones who will pay the big money.'

Sonja was surprised. 'How much are we talking?'

Rod gestured back to the image on the screen. 'Size matters to a collector and the value is calculated on the size of the caudex or stem, what you might call the trunk. Collectors pay per seedling or, for mature plants, per centimetre of stem length – the price is generally the same for either. For big, old, shorter plants the dealer might charge based on the circumference of the stem. That Venda cycad on the screen is worth nearly a thousand dollars per seedling or centimetre, so I'm guessing that specimen, at maybe a metre or more, could be worth around a hundred thousand dollars.'

Sonja gave a low whistle. 'Where are these collectors, mainly?'

Rod frowned. 'Everywhere. It's a global market – here in the States, South Africa, Zimbabwe, Australia, the Middle East, Europe – though cycads do favour a fairly temperate climate. The Far East is currently a big market, with China and other Asian economies booming.'

Jed clicked the remote. 'I downloaded a few images from the net so we can see what the actual plant looks like, with its leaves and all.'

Sonja looked at the screen. She thought the cycads, with their spiky green fronds, were quite unremarkable, but she had long ago given up wondering why people paid so much money and were prepared to kill for things as materially useless as rhino horn and ivory. The plants looked familiar and Sonja realised she had seen similar species in the gardens at the Hippo Rock Private Nature Reserve where she and Hudson Brand had stayed for a while. Hudson was the unofficial caretaker of a luxurious house in the reserve, located on the Sabie River, on the edge of the Kruger National Park. Jed was right, she should give Hudson a call, if only to let him know she was still alive, but she was sure he would want her to go to Africa, to see him. She pushed the memories of her time with Hudson, both good and bad, from her mind. She had the distinct feeling this meeting was more than a final chapter in her debrief, as Jed had billed it.

Rod stared at the screen in silence and Sonja saw in his expression the same disillusionment and weary resignation she'd seen in the faces of men and women fighting rhino poachers.

'Rod?' Jed said.

Rod looked back at them. 'Yes, right. So, the trade is worldwide and has been getting increasingly more organised, that is, it's being taken over by organised crime, as the stock of wild rare cycads dwindles.'

Sonja had a question. 'Now that I know what you're talking about, I realise I've seen these plants in plenty of places in Africa. Is it legal to sell them?'

Rod rocked his head from side to side. 'Yes and no. Some species are very common – you can buy them in any garden centre – but the serious collectors around the world want the rare species. To ship a cycad, say, out of Africa, you need permits from the local authorities, and in the old days you needed a permit just to buy a cycad for your own garden. That changed in South Africa in 1994 when the demand for these plants became so great that the authorities simply gave up issuing permits. In recent years you've needed a permit again, but it's like closing the gate after the horse has bolted. There's evidence that the remaining wild stocks of cycads were plundered by dealers and collectors during the no-permit period.'

'But you say the trade is legal, in the same way people want to legalise the sale of rhino horn?' Sonja said.

'Yes, and it's an interesting parallel,' Rod said. 'In South Africa it's legal to sell and export a cycad, even a rare cycad, if it has been propagated in a nursery, *but*, and it's a big but, if the parent of a plant was illegally harvested from the wild, then its progeny are illegal as well. Or, of course, it might have been stolen to order from some national park or reserve. The catch is, there's no way to tell the difference.'

'So you're saying that even though there is a legal trade, and people are *breeding*, or whatever the term is, these plants in captivity, the wild cycads are still being poached?'

'Exactly,' Rod said, adjusting his glasses again. 'I believe it would be the same if the trade in rhino horn was legalised. Dealers get greedy. If you can get a mature cycad from the wild and palm it off, pun intended, as propagated, then you stand to make a small fortune. Also, by encouraging impoverished local people to harvest from the wild a dealer makes a cycad even rarer and, ergo, more expensive. The same would go for rhinos; it would be in the middlemen's interest for the species to be more endangered, or even wiped out.'

Sonja sat back in her chair and shook her head in disgust.

Rod shrugged and spread his hands wide in a gesture of weary resignation. 'The dealers will even try to tell you they're doing the right thing – they'll say that by taking a rare plant from the wild and breeding from it, they're saving the species from extinction. In reality, they're destroying the natural environment in the same way as the small-fry traditional medicine dealers are indiscriminately harvesting plants. In the end, it's all about greed.' Rod let out a frustrated breath and then appeared to remember something. 'Jed,' he said, 'did you get that email I sent before I boarded my flight?'

'I did.' Jed clicked the remote again. 'This is the woman you mentioned in your message.'

A picture of a blonde woman, maybe early fifties, attractive, came up on the screen. Like the plant, Sonja had a feeling she had seen her before.

'Yes,' Rod said. 'Joanne Flack, aged fifty-nine, Zimbabwean.'

Well preserved, Sonja thought, and it clicked where she had seen her – on a television news report. 'She's the woman from London, the one who killed the terrorist.'

'Yes,' Jed said. 'Shot a jihadist down in the street in Chelsea.'

'Joanne Flack,' Rod cleared his throat, 'probably knows more about rare cycads than anyone alive in South Africa, possibly the southern hemisphere.'

Sonja regarded Rod and noticed he was staring at the flat-screen, where Joanne Flack looked back at him with a half-smile. She was pretty, but her eyes were African, a little lost, hardened with sorrow. Sonja had seen those eyes, every morning. 'You sound like you know her.'

Rod watched the screen a couple of beats longer, then adjusted his glasses yet again and looked from Sonja to Jed, and back to Sonja. 'Yes.'

Jed opened the thick file in front of him. 'Joanne Flack was a person of interest in an operation mounted by the FBI back in 1998. She was the subject of surveillance and investigation in connection to an international cycad smuggling ring. Operation Green Thumb resulted in the arrest and imprisonment of eight individuals from South Africa, Australia and the United States. A provincial head of nature conservation was one of the people gaoled in South Africa.'

Sonja glanced at the screen, then at Jed.

'But Joanne wasn't one of those arrested,' Jed said.

Rod spoke without shifting his gaze. 'No, she wasn't. We couldn't prove she was in on it, but her husband was, that's for sure.'

'He was one of the people arrested?'

Rod shook his head.

'Peter Flack, her husband, was a tobacco farmer from a place called Wedza, in Zimbabwe,' Jed said, referring to the file in front of him. 'When President Robert Mugabe let the brakes off his ill-fated land distribution program, farms across the country were invaded by so-called veterans of Zimbabwe's liberation war. In reality, it was mostly party hacks, bureaucrats and military officers who took over white-owned farms and the owners were evicted. Joanne Flack had an impressive and valuable collection of cycads–hundreds of them–on her farm, and before she and Peter were kicked off they managed to dig up and relocate nearly all their plants when they moved to South Africa. Peter Flack, maybe with his wife's cooperation, almost certainly with her knowledge, started selling those plants abroad to collectors.'

Sonja shrugged. 'So?'

'So even in Zimbabwe,' Jed said, 'which was pretty lawless at the time, it was still illegal to ship a cycad out of the country, but she moved her collection without any official export permits. The Flack cycads then started leaving South Africa, bound for collectors in the States, Australia, Dubai, Saudi Arabia, Thailand and Malaysia. All of that trade was illegal.'

'I still don't see the big deal,' Sonja said. She knew a few Zimbabweans, ex–Rhodesian military men mostly, who she had served alongside when she was a private military contractor in Iraq and Afghanistan. Some of them had been dispossessed farmers who had gone back to soldiering in the forties and fifties just to feed their families. 'You had a couple of farmers who had lost everything they had ever worked for and owned and they made a few bucks selling some plants that they'd grown themselves. What's the harm in that, even if they bent the rules? Their government was busy stealing from its own people.'

Rod turned away from the picture of the woman. 'You're right. They wouldn't have come onto our radar, except Peter Flack was also harvesting and shipping rare wild cycads out of Zimbabwe and South Africa. One of his buyers, a collector, was a Mexican-American the bureau and the DEA suspected was involved with the cocaine and marijuana cartels here. We couldn't get the goods on him for his drug deals—he was too clever for us—but we did put him away for a couple of years for plant smuggling.'

'Like taking down Al Capone over tax fraud?' Sonja said.

'FBI tactics 101,' Jed said. 'While the Mexican boss was inside, the DEA was able to infiltrate his organisation and bring it down.'

'So how does the Flack woman fit into what I saw in Mali, and why are we even talking about this?' Sonja asked. 'The French Foreign Legion can go back to fighting AQIM or AAD or whatever acronym of evil is running things in Mali now that we have the senator's daughter out.'

'I wish it were that simple,' Jed said. 'ISIS and AQ took a hammering in Syria and what we're seeing now is that West and North Africa is the new training and breeding ground for terrorists looking to cause harm in Europe and the US. Mali could very well be the new Afghanistan. We've been picking up online Messenger chatter that there's another spectacular in the winds, an attack to rival 9/11, and it will most likely be launched from Africa. We need to get inside the Malian operations and you might have found us the key to the door in that storeroom.'

'The plants?' Sonja said.

'Yup.' Jed took a printout from his folder and slid it across the table to Rod. 'For some time we've been gathering intel about possible links between poaching and terrorism in Africa. We look for wildlife-related crimes that don't fit the normal profile.'

Sonja opened the folder. 'South African Police Service report. Stolen ivory. So?'

Jed nodded. 'The ivory trade is big in other African countries, but not so much South Africa, where the big money's in rhino horn. That report concerns the attempted hijacking of a stockpile of ivory harvested from legally hunted elephants. The ivory belongs to a person of interest to us, a member of the Kuwaiti royal family with a game reserve near Hoedspruit. His name is Prince Faisal al Sabah, aged fifty-nine. He's a bit of a maverick in the family, a bachelor and reputed playboy.' Jed pressed a button on the remote and a picture appeared on the screen of a handsome man in a polo shirt and jodhpurs, standing in front of a horse.

'The Kuwaitis are our friends, right?' Rod interjected.

'So are the Saudis, but Bin Laden was one of them,' Jed reminded them. 'We've been what you might call keeping an eye on the prince, and it seems that recently someone stole two very rare cycads from him. Along with the foiled ivory heist it seems our prince has been having a run of bad luck recently. A poorly paid gardener was fingered for the first plant theft, but the organiser of the planned ivory theft was never identified. A couple of low-level hoods were driving the second plant through Joburg, but we suspect there is someone, or maybe more than one person, close to the prince or inside his reserve who's behind these big-ticket crimes. He let his own embassy know about the plants, but kept the news out of the public domain. The first was a couple of months ago, a Venda cycad, is that right, Rod?'

'Correct. Endangered, worth a lot of money, as I said before,' Rod said.

'Right,' Jed said, 'but the second, two weeks ago, was thought to be extinct. It was a female *Encephalartos woodii*.'

'Holy smoke,' said Rod. 'Why didn't you tell me on the phone earlier that you knew that?'

'Good question,' Jed said. 'We didn't know what it looked like and we wanted independent confirmation of a theory we were working on that it might be the female *woodii* that ended up in Mali.'

'Well, it's the only cycad that someone would potentially describe as being worth millions of dollars and if that news became public there would be the equivalent of mass hysteria in the cycad world. Where does Joanne fit into all this?' Rod asked.

'She worked for the Kuwaiti prince,' Jed said.

Rod's eyes widened.

'There's more,' Jed said. 'We have sources in the South African Police Service. One of them searched their system for recent reports of stolen cycads. There was a report of a plant discovered by some traffic cops twelve days ago. The perps tried to flee from the scene and the detective who recovered the plant, for some crazy reason, handed it over to a bunch of civilians to look after, a cycad lovers' group. The membership of this group, the Pretoria Cycad and Firearms Appreciation Society, includes Mrs Flack.' He nodded to the screen.

Rod hit the table with a closed fist. 'Joanne. What is she up to?'

Jed shrugged. 'We don't know for sure that she was in on the deal with the Malians, Rod, but British intelligence, MI5, has found some fragments of internet chatter that they've linked to the attack on the police officers in London, where Joanne Flack shot the terrorist. The Brits say,' Jed picked up another sheet of paper and read from it, 'that an operative was tasked with kidnapping the, quote, blonde woman, and finding out where she hid the real plant, unquote. Rod? Any thoughts?'

Rod thought for a moment. 'Why would they say "the real plant"...?' He looked up and snapped his fingers. 'Unless Joanne sold them a fake *woodii*.'

'A fake?' Sonja asked. 'Can't a plant fancier tell one from the other?'

'Yes and no,' Rod said. 'When a cycad has all its foliage and, especially, its cones, it's very distinctive, but if you cut all that off, several of the caudexes look the same. Substitution is a common practice in the illegal dealing world. Joanne Flack's husband used a similar MO to get rare cycads out of Africa and had plenty of success. Whoever owns that storeroom you found might be sitting on a cycad worth next to nothing, but my guess is they *thought* they were buying a female *woodii*–a plant thought to be extinct and therefore worth... darn, it's probably priceless. So, to answer your question, Sonja, I was fooled as well, it seems. Jed showed me a picture of a cycad and some elephant ivory in a storeroom in Mali and when he told me that someone had been overheard saying the plant was female and worth millions of dollars, I jumped to the conclusion that it was a female *woodii*. It certainly looked like a *woodii*, but then again, some commercial breeders have produced hybrids from cloned *woodii*s crossed with *Encephalartos natalensis*. They look a *lot* like a *woodii*, but are relatively cheap.'

'Crazy,' Sonja said.

'It gets crazier,' Rod replied. 'Some unscrupulous dealers sell pups, or suckers–baby cycads to you–to customers telling them they're the progeny of rare plants, when in fact they're common. Many pups look alike when they're small and the dealer commands top dollar, but warns the buyer he or she needs to take very good care of the pup or it might not make it to maturity.'

'But if it becomes fully grown then the buyer would know they've bought a fake, right?' Sonja said.

Rod nodded. 'Right. To stop that happening, the dealer puts the pups in a microwave oven before he sells them, knowing this will destroy their cell structure and they will never make it to maturity.'

'Sick,' Sonja said.

Jed cleared his throat and took two printouts from his folder. He slid them across the table to Sonja and Rod. 'Here's some more of that internet chatter from the Brits.'

Sonja read her copy. *The woman is in Chelsea, she visited Kew Gardens.*

Rod looked to Jed: 'The terrorists were tailing her?'

'Yes,' Jed said, then handed them each another sheet. 'You'll see in this next transcript a "woman" was then spotted near the Sloane Square underground station and then the order was given.'

Sonja saw the line Jed was referring to. *I have her in sight. God is great.*

'"God is great" is code for the attack to proceed?' Sonja asked.

'We think so,' Jed said.

'So Joanne was being deliberately targeted,' Rod said, nodding. 'This was a hit disguised as a terrorist attack.'

'Maybe a little of both,' Jed said. He used the remote to bring up the next image. It was a bearded man, lying on his back, dead, with two bullet holes in his chest. A numbered card on a stand was next to a knife that lay by the man's right hand. A second knife, similarly marked, was also visible on the ground in the corner of the enlarged picture. 'This is Jamal Hussein, a Malian-born South African citizen in the UK on a student visa. MI5 don't have much on him and they've reached out to us and the French for help, knowing that we were conducting a joint operation in Mali to rescue the senator's daughter. The French say Jamal had an older brother who was definitely an AQ operative. He was killed last year in a firefight with French Foreign Legion troops backing up the Malian Army. We think maybe Jamal was radicalised to believe he was going to die for the cause, but that his mission was supposedly to target

Joanne Flack specifically. From analysing eyewitness reports and Joanne Flack's statement to the UK police, it seems to us like the two police officers who were attacked were in the wrong place at the wrong time. The terrorist and his backers probably weren't expecting Joanne to fight back.'

'Then they don't know Joanne too well,' Rod said with a snort.

'MI5 is keeping the internet chatter out of the press for now,' Jed said, 'while they carry on their own investigations. We want to talk to Joanne Flack and so does MI5. The police who questioned her after the attack asked her if she knew why anyone would want to kill her and she told them she had no idea. At that point the British bobbies didn't know about the intercepts inferring that Jamal was actually tasked with capturing and interrogating her. Flack told the police she had no connection with any Malians, legitimate or not.'

'She's a cool customer,' Rod said. 'Tough as nails, probably due to growing up during the Rhodesian Bush War and being married to a criminal, and she could cheat a lie detector if she had to.'

Sonja looked at Rod. She noticed how both his fists were balled now and his face was turning a little red, as if his blood pressure was elevated. This woman was pushing some of his buttons, by remote. It was time for her to ask the obvious question. 'What's all this got to do with me, Jed?'

He looked her in the eye. 'We think that one way or another, Joanne Flack can lead us to the Malians who are trading in illegal cycads, as well as all the other stuff you found in that room. I need someone to get close to her, gain her trust and, at the same time, watch out for her, in case these guys come for her again. That was a pretty determined attempt to capture or kill her, and a serious terrorist attack in its own right. Flack is a citizen of Zimbabwe and resident of South Africa so we can't just pull her off the street and question her. Find Joanne and you hopefully find the Malians. Find the Malians and we stop a whole poaching and trafficking syndicate and with any luck disrupt a future spectacular terrorist attack.'

Sonja nodded. 'Makes sense.'

'There's another African angle,' Jed said. 'We've been picking up chatter and information from human sources that there's a terrorist training camp in a remote location somewhere in South Africa.'

Jed clicked the remote and a picture of a crime scene with the Eiffel Tower far in the background came up. 'You all might or might not remember this attack, in which a Malian judge holidaying in Paris was killed by what was believed to be a lone-wolf knife-wielding terrorist a while back. The intel was that the attacker was a Malian who had been living in South Africa and had also been trained somewhere in the Lowveld, the bush. That's your backyard, Sonja.'

'So we find the plant, we find the pipeline to Mali, and we maybe find the terrorist training camp. Simple.' Sonja gave a snort, then looked to Rod. 'What about you? It seems like you know Flack pretty well.'

Rod shook his head. 'She won't talk to me.'

Sonja noticed that Rod had relaxed his hands and was sagging in his chair. He looked suddenly even older than he was; deflated. 'Why not?'

Rod sighed and looked to Jed, who gave him a small nod. 'Because I killed her husband while she and I were having an affair and she hasn't forgiven me since.'

Chapter 5

Joanne Flack joined the immigration queue for returning Zimbabwean nationals and residents at Victoria Falls International Airport. She listened to a gaggle of elderly American tourists complaining about the length of their line and wondered what her similarly aged friends from the Pretoria Cycad and Firearms Appreciation Society were up to, what they were saying about her.

She felt adrift, and scared. She had set all this in motion and she had proved that she was right, that someone would steal the cycad from the lock-up, but it was small comfort. The people who wanted the female *woodii* would do whatever they needed to, in order to get hold of it. However, as with her decision to get out of the UK, she knew that while she was on her own, or in hiding, then she only had herself to worry about. If she was with her friends now, some of them might get caught in the crossfire.

Joanne focused on her surroundings. It was the first time she had flown into the 'Falls' since the new airport had been built by the Chinese. It had a veneer of modernity, but Joanne braced herself for the same old bureaucratic inefficiency she had come to expect in her homeland.

However, instead of an interrogation the man in uniform checked her passport and said: 'Welcome home.'

She smiled back at him. It was good to be back in Africa again, she thought, as she collected her bag from the carousel.

In the arrivals hall she was confronted with a stuffed leopard, mounted in a semi-realistic pose. Joanne wondered if this was really what tourists – other than hunters – wanted to see when they arrived on safari. As if in response to her unspoken question, a pair of smiling Chinese women stopped to pose for pictures in front of it.

A guide in khaki shirt and shorts was waiting, holding up her name on a piece of paper fixed to a clipboard. She went to him.

'Mrs Flack?'

'Joanne.'

'Nice to meet you, I'm Hardwork, and I've heard any joke you can think of about my name.'

'I wouldn't dare,' she said, shaking his hand.

Hardwork took her battered wheelie bag and they went out into the sunshine and fresh air. The sky was clear blue, the horizon blurred a little with dust. It was hot and humid, the air starting to show signs of the rain that was still a month or more away.

'You are from South Africa?'

'Here, originally,' she said.

He smiled. 'Then welcome home.'

Hardwork led the way to a Land Cruiser and loaded her bag. She climbed in, taking the passenger seat next to him.

'How is Zimbabwe?' she asked Hardwork as they set off on the road towards the town and the waterfalls of the same name.

He shook his head. 'Eee, we have some economic problems, but your homeland is as beautiful as ever. You are staying at Matetsi for how many nights?'

'I don't know.'

He swivelled his head and his eyes were wide. It wasn't an answer he was used to.

'My niece, Nikki de Villiers, works there. She's giving me some of her free nights.' She didn't tell Hardwork, but if the transfer from the airport to the lodge wasn't included with Nikki's generous offer then Joanne would have been hitchhiking.

'Ah,' Hardwork said, 'now I understand. You have been there before?'

Joanne shook her head. 'No, but I believe it's very nice.'

'You will love it,' Hardwork promised.

They turned off short of the town of Victoria Falls, left towards the Botswana border at Kazungula. The drive took them along the edge of the Zambezi National Park and the adjoining Matetsi Game Reserve. About forty kilometres on, Hardwork turned right, and after they checked in at a security boom gate they headed through bush in the direction of the river.

Joanne was back in London, in her mind, the blood coming from the male policeman's wound, his gun in her hand. Her heart was beating faster, her vision blurring at the edges. A tide of panic rose up inside her. She had brought all of this on herself.

'Giraffe,' Hardwork said. 'Joanne?'

'What?'

Hardwork pointed. 'Over there, giraffe.'

'Oh, sorry.' She saw it, now, them in fact, a female with a young calf. She felt the calm wash over her, settle her into the car seat. She needed this. She had been so relieved when Nikki had offered to have her stay at Matetsi River Lodge, where she worked as an assistant manager. Nikki had seen her on television and messaged her in England. Nikki couldn't know how grateful she was – Joanne had been worried she would not have enough money to buy food when she returned to South Africa, but Peta had been able to cancel her ticket to Johannesburg and change it to Victoria Falls without having to pay extra. Plus, having somewhere to stay for a few days gave her some time to think about her situation.

It was hot and the Cruiser's air conditioning was struggling so Joanne wound down the window. The smell of the bush was comforting, even though it was dry and most of the trees were bare. While the bush was a balm, her nerves were still jangling below the surface and she held her hands together to keep them from shaking. The attack on her in London was proof that whoever had stolen the cycad from the society's premises was out to get her and had powerful allies. The flaws in her plan were becoming more and more apparent by the minute. Hardwork took a radio handset from the dashboard and spoke softly into it.

A few minutes later he turned off onto a narrower gravel track that led to the lodge. When they reached a dead end and turning circle they saw a man and a woman in matching uniforms waiting for them. The woman held a silver platter with cold towels and presented one to Joanne when she got out of the car. It was cool and refreshing and while she felt like telling the woman she wasn't a paying guest it was nice to soak up their welcome words and hospitality. She waved goodbye to Hardwork and regretted she did not have even a few dollars to tip him; he smiled nonetheless.

The couple led her to a stonewalled entrance with a full-sized mokoro canoe hanging from its bow for decoration. As soon as Joanne passed through she felt a breeze coming off the Zambezi River, which was laid out in all its wild majesty in front of her. It was a spectacular arrival.

Nikki appeared from a bar area on the right, half running to her. She threw her arms around Joanne's neck.

'Aunty, my word, how good to see you. Are you OK?'

'I'm fine, Nikki, thanks.'

Her niece held her at arm's length. 'You're sure?'

'Sure.' Joanne lowered her voice. 'We went through worse things in the war, you know.'

Nikki gave a nod. 'All the same, I bet you're wrecked after your flight and, well, everything that's happened to you these last few days.'

'I'm afraid you're right, there. Thank you, again, for this kindness. I can't tell you how much I appreciate it.' It was the truth, Joanne thought. She couldn't tell her extended family how poorly off she now was. She didn't want people's pity.

Nikki told the man and woman who had met her at the entrance that she would take care of her aunt's check-in, and the staff melted away.

'You know the rules, Aunty – no walking at night by yourself.'

'Yes, dear,' Joanne said.

'I'm serious. I could lose my job if someone catches you wandering about on your own. Besides, it sets a bad example for the other guests.'

Joanne saluted. 'Yes, miss.'

Nikki gave her an indulgent smile.

'I really am grateful, Nikki.'

'Good. I'm pleased to help and it's lovely to see you again. I've booked you in for two nights. I hope that's all right?'

'Perfect, thank you.'

'Will you be flying back to South Africa after that?'

Joanne shrugged. 'Oh, maybe. I'm in no rush.'

'OK.' Nikki smiled and reached out and touched her hand. 'I'll take you to your room now.'

Nikki led her along a pathway through the bush parallel to the riverbank. There was elephant dung everywhere, some of it very fresh, and Joanne hoped she would get some good sightings of the beautiful giant creatures while she was here.

'There's a gym and a lap pool further along the pathway if you're interested in some exercise. I'm sure I don't need to remind you to keep the screen doors closed because of monkeys and baboons,' Nikki said.

'I'll be fine,' Joanne said.

Nikki reached out and touched her again. 'You sure, Aunty?'

'I'm sure.' Nikki's concern was touching, if a little cloying.

'Oh, and no smoking inside, please.'

'I don't smoke any more,' Joanne said, with a tight smile.

'Well, good for you.'

'I'll see you just now.' Joanne sighed as she closed the heavy door behind Nikki. The Western world's rules were colonising Africa, taking the fun out of life, a little more each year – even here in Zimbabwe. Soon the world would be run by self-righteous men with crisply ironed white shirts with pens in their pockets. She stopped, midway to the toilet, and wondered why she had just thought of Rod Cavanagh.

Maybe it was the river, she thought. Or the fact that he would not let her smoke while he was in the same room.

They had been here – not to this luxurious lodge, but to The Kingdom, the hotel-cum-casino next to the more expensive grand old lady, the Victoria Falls Hotel, on one of Rod's many 'business' trips to Africa. She bit her lower lip. He might present like an accountant, but he could be an animal when he wanted to be.

'Bastard.'

She went into the bathroom.

When she was done she opened the screen doors and took in the full dramatic spectacle of the river. She never tired of it. The Zambezi – the name alone was enough to send a tingle down the spine, even for someone such as she, who had seen this view, or something similar, a thousand times or more.

The Zambezi was like a person moving through life. Here the river was young and urgent, rushing towards its fate, which was to throw itself over the black granite cliffs into the Devil's Pool below in a wild, open-mouthed bungee-jumping scream. Downstream, where it became Lake Kariba, it was fat and lazy, middle-aged, languishing like an afternoon fisherman who'd breakfasted on beer. Below the dam, it moved slowly, gracefully, a shadow of its former self before the great flood, but timelessly beautiful nonetheless.

Joanne walked out a side door to a shaded verandah with an enormous day bed. She stretched out, then froze as she heard the crack of a tree branch being snapped, as clear as a gunshot.

Slowly she turned her head, and through the latticed privacy screen she caught a glimpse of wrinkly grey skin. Joanne hardly dared breathe, in case she disturbed him.

The elephant had been there, browsing among the shredded mopane trees, the whole time Nikki and she had been chatting as they walked along the pathway and as her niece showed her the room. They were as quiet as ghosts, these enormous beings, and as angry as hell when they needed to be. Slowly, one vertebra at a time, she lifted her torso up to get a better look.

The bull wrapped his trunk around a higher branch and pulled it down towards him. There, again, was the snapping sound as the tree yielded. The elephant put his prize in his mouth and rotated it, like a human eating corn on the cob, as he stripped off the nutrient-rich bark with his teeth. When he was done he tossed the woody core away.

He went past her field of view, not lumbering but rather tiptoeing on his big padded feet and he made not a sound save for the *whoosh* of air displaced with each flap of his spinnaker ears.

After everything that had happened to her, not least of which her near-death experience in London, Joanne was in a reflective mood. She thought back to her life in Zimbabwe. She and Peter used to sail, a lot. There were the May regattas on Lake Kariba where the men tried to outdo each other and the women drank too much wine in the sun and sometimes slipped away with someone else's husband in the shadows at the edge of the *braai*. They had been good times, she told herself, those days after the war had ended and Mugabe was behaving himself, and Zimbabwe was awash with foreign currency. The labour had been happy – not well paid, but at least they had jobs – and to be a farmer meant having enough money to put the kids in boarding school, go sailing on the lake, and even take the odd trip to Europe.

It all changed, of course. The president and his wife plundered their homeland, the farms were taken over by his cronies and the agricultural backbone of the country was snapped and paralysed.

And yet, she told herself as she watched the elephant move down to the river, there was this. No crooked politician or gang of criminals could rob her or anyone else of the simple joy of seeing a sight as grand as this.

Beyond the elephant, which had stopped to drink at the river's edge, was an aluminium boat with a canopy and outboard and four people aboard. There was nothing unusual about that, except for the hour. Most game-viewing and fishing cruises went out at dawn or dusk to improve the passengers' chances of catching something, with a hook or a camera. But there were no hard and fast rules.

A goliath heron propelled its big body upstream, a couple of metres above the river's surface, and a pied kingfisher spear-dived into the water in search of an elusive little bream.

The bird had the right idea. Joanne, stripped and slid into the suite's private plunge pool. She wanted to just relax and enjoy the view, but that was impossible. Zimbabwe was remote, but if the people who wanted her could track her down in the middle of busy London then perhaps it was not as safe as she had hoped. But where else could she run to?

She had no money.

She had no home.

She had no job.

Her mind returned to the terrible moments in London when the man with the knives had come to her. She was now sure he had been planning on taking her off the street and forcing her to tell him where the female *woodii* was. When she had decided not to go quietly, and called to the police, he had turned his stealthy approach into a full-blown terrorist attack.

Odd.

She could always go back to Faisal and come clean to him about her role in all this. But what if he was part of the problem, if he had engineered the theft of the two rare cycads in the same way she increasingly suspected he had tried to get rid of his stockpile of ivory?

What concerned her most was that the only people who knew about the existence of the female *woodii* were Faisal, herself, and the members of the Pretoria Cycad and Firearms Appreciation Society, with whom she had foolishly shared her amazing discovery when she realised the cycad's identity. Faisal had told her he had no intention of telling anyone else about the plant until he and she worked out what to do with it.

Now she suspected him, or possibly one of her friends, of engineer-ing the first theft from his heavily fortified game reserve and the second theft from the society's lock-up. She could not go back to Faisal, no matter how good he was in bed. At best he would end up breaking her heart, at worst he would have her killed for uncovering some underhanded plot of his to smuggle his priceless cycad out of the country. If he had staged the original theft of the female *woodii* from his own garden, to cover his tracks, then who, she wondered, had stolen the funds from the society and the substitute plant from the lock-up?

Joanne got out of the plunge pool and took a towel from one of the sun beds. She gathered her grimy travel clothes and went into her suite. She showered, blow-dried her hair, did her make-up and put on her white linen pants and a blue T-shirt. She went back to the bathroom and looked at herself in the mirror.

Her reminiscing of Peter brought back a flood of memories of Rod, some good, most bad. The intimacy they had shared had been overshadowed–no, destroyed–by the fact that he had been play-acting all along, turning her into an idiot as well as an adulteress. She wondered if the pictures she had seen of Rod on his Facebook page the last time she had checked were old, or if he really looked that good. She hated that she still spied on the man who had ruined her life.

Joanne walked along the track, again watchful for game, to the communal area where Nikki had met her. On the lawn in front of the lodge, overlooking the river, a table for one had been set under a tree. A couple was having lunch further along the bank. She assumed the single setting was meant for her. A waiter intercepted her and pulled out her chair for her.

Joanne ordered a glass of sauvignon blanc with lots of ice, and while she waited for her drink she got up again and strolled down to the river's edge. At a small wharf, along with two boats bearing the Matetsi River Lodge logo, was another small craft that she was sure was the one she had seen earlier. Looking back at the lodge, Joanne was impressed by how well it blended easily into its surroundings. She couldn't have picked a better spot to hide away and recover from the events of the last couple of weeks.

The waiter was coming with her drink as Joanne walked back to her table. As she sat, a man and a woman in matching khaki safari gear came through the entryway and out onto the lawn. Once her waiter had set her wineglass in front of her, he went to attend to the couple, who he sat near Joanne, at a table for two.

'How you doing?' the man called. His accent was American. He was good-looking with fair hair and a beard turning to grey, solidly built and, like all of his kind, he had perfect teeth. The woman gave a curt nod of her head. Joanne waved to the husband and gave him her best smile.

'Beautiful day, isn't it,' Joanne said.

'Sure is,' the man replied. The woman busied herself looking at the menu.

'Honey, I'm just going to take a look at the river,' the man said. He got up, stretched and walked over to the edge of the lawn.

Joanne sipped her wine and when the waiter came back she ordered her entree and main from the set menu.

'You here for long?'

She looked up into the bearded man's blue eyes. 'A couple of days. You?'

'Same. We want to see the falls.'

'Then you've come to the right place.'

'Guess so,' he said. 'My name's Hank and my wife's Ursula.'

'German?'

'Yes and no—she's from Namibia, but from German stock. I'm from the US of A.'

'No kidding,' said Joanne with a grin.

*

Sonja always used the name of her favourite aunt, Ursula, when she was undercover. The Flack woman was fawning over Jed—Hank to her. Sonja had no claim on Jed, but the cover story was that he was her husband, and here was this woman flirting with him. Sonja had to appear to be the disapproving wife.

She thought about her own life, examining her 'feelings'; her therapist would approve. It had been more than a month since Sonja had seen the shrink. She was sure she was better and, in any case, had only gone at Hudson's insistence.

Hudson.

He was less than a hundred kilometres from where they were now, but he had no idea where she was, let alone that she was in the same country as him.

Hudson Brand was the archetypal safari guide—tall, tanned, handsome as hell and with a side order of danger that was enhanced by the fact that he moonlighted as a private investigator. Women loved him, men wanted to quit their boring nine-to-five jobs and be him. Sonja couldn't make up her mind what to do about him.

He loved her. He'd said so.

She thought she loved him, but hadn't said the words yet.

The last man she had truly, undeniably loved had been killed, probably because he had wanted to prove to her how brave he was.

She felt like she didn't deserve happiness. Love was like a sucking chest wound—it took your breath away at first, hurt like hell soon after, and was rarely survivable.

Sonja sighed. The woman was touching her hair while she chatted up Jed, or vice versa, a sure signal she was interested in him. What wasn't to be interested in? Sonja wondered. He had a great body, hypnotic eyes and great forearms. Other women seemed to be obsessed with men's butts – Sonja wasn't, but she had a feeling she could probably hammer a bent nail straight onto Jed's if she or he had the inclination.

Jed left Joanne, came back to the table and sat down.

'Get her phone number?'

Jed frowned. 'Don't be like that.'

'She wants you.'

'She's lonely, broke, widowed and she was nearly killed in a terror attack.'

'So instead of eating ice-cream straight from the tub and watching *Bridget Jones's Diary* she goes for another woman's husband.'

Jed leaned back in his seat. 'Are you *jealous*?'

'You're my husband, remember, it's my job to be jealous.'

Jed smiled, gently took hold of Sonja's hand and, checking over his shoulder to make sure Joanne was watching, told her in a sickly voice, 'You know you're the only woman for me.'

She smirked at him and took a sip of water. 'So, what did you learn?'

'She's just here for a couple of days, like we thought, staying with her niece. She says she's got no plans, which means she's got no money. I invited her to join us for lunch, but told her I'd ask you if you were OK with that.'

Jed was a fast worker and Sonja was a little surprised, but then again he was a proper spy, unlike her. 'OK.'

Jed turned and waved to Joanne, who stood, picked up her wineglass and walked over to them.

'Hi, I'm Joanne.'

Sonja stood and took the woman's free hand. 'Ursula. Please sit down.'

'Thank you. I don't mean to intrude.'

'Not at all,' Sonja said.

'I hear you're Namibian?' Joanne said to her.

'Originally, yes, but I live in Los Angeles now. That is, *we* live in LA.' Joanne nodded. 'I see.'

Sonja cursed herself for making a silly mistake and then having to clumsily correct it.

'I spend so much time in Africa with work it's almost like we're having a long-distance relationship,' Jed said smoothly, rushing to her aid.

'Right. What do you do?'

'Mining engineer,' Jed said.

'And you, Ursula?'

Sonja smiled. 'Beautician.'

'Forgive me,' Joanne said, appraising her, 'you look very sporty. I picked you for a personal trainer or an athlete of some kind.'

Sonja couldn't help but feel a barb in the comment. 'I like to work out. And you, Joanne?'

The other woman shrugged. 'I'm what you might call in between engagements these days. I usually work as a gardening consultant.'

Sonja raised her eyebrows. 'How interesting.'

'I've worked on a few mines, prettying-up the staff accommodation,' Joanne said, ignoring Sonja's feigned attentiveness and turning to Jed's blue eyes instead. 'Where do you work?'

'All over,' Jed said. 'I'm a consultant. I specialise in environmental monitoring – dust, pollution, that kind of thing.'

Joanne rested her chin on her hand, an elbow on the table. 'Fascinating.'

Barf, thought Sonja. 'I'm interested in redoing our garden in LA. I want something exotic, maybe some palms or something.'

Joanne glanced at her. 'How quaint.'

'What are those plants the dinosaurs used to eat?' Sonja asked.

Joanne sat up and turned her head to face her, ignoring Jed for the first time since they'd met. 'Cycads.'

'Is that what they're called? Spiky-looking things.'

'They're not spikes, they're leaves.'

Joanne regarded her through narrowed eyes. Sonja wondered if she might have spoken too soon, but she definitely had Flack's interest now.

'How odd,' Joanne said.

'Why?' Sonja asked.

'Cycads are my favourite plants.'

'You don't say,' Jed said.

'I do.'

'Well that's a stroke of luck. I want something exotic,' Sonja said, 'out of the ordinary. I've heard some of them are quite rare.'

'Endangered, even,' Joanne said.

Sonja didn't want to dive into asking Joanne Flack if she could source a cycad illegally for her. As it was, she felt she might have been too forward – she had worked undercover in the past, but it didn't come naturally to her. She was more used to full-frontal assaults than sneaking about pretending, and she feared it showed.

'Lunch is coming,' Jed said.

The waiter brought their food and as they ate Jed steered the conversation away from plants and back to small talk.

When they'd finished eating, Jed asked Joanne if she was going out on a game drive or a river cruise – the lodge offered both options – that afternoon.

'A trip on the water, I think,' Joanne said.

'That's exactly what we were planning. See you then,' Jed said.

Joanne left first and then Jed and Sonja got up from the table and walked back to the suite they were sharing. They'd asked for two single beds.

Their luggage had been carried from the boat and left in their room. Jed took a set of keys from his pocket and unlocked two large waterproof Pelican cases that sat between their personal bags. The case had a printed notice stuck to it reading: *Cameras, handle with care.*

They had flown into Victoria Falls, on the Zimbabwean side of the Zambezi River, and, upstream of the falls, they had boarded the chartered boat that had taken them to Matetsi River Lodge. On the way they had made an illegal deviation and stop on the Zambian side of the river at a private property. There a cultural attaché – in reality a CIA man – from the US embassy in Lusaka had met them and handed over the hard-shell cases that Jed was now unlocking.

Jed opened the lids and he and Sonja each helped themselves to a Glock 19 pistol, Kydex holster and four magazines of ammunition. The cases contained other tools of their trade they might need, including two sets of night-vision goggles, tactical radios, and an MP5, the same type of machine pistol Sonja had carried on the raid in Mali.

Sonja checked, cleared, then loaded a Glock and the MP5. She put the spare magazines in the pockets of her cargo pants and clipped the holster onto her belt. Jed armed himself similarly. Sonja held the other MP5 out to him.

'No need for overkill,' Jed said.

Sonja shrugged and put the MP5 back in its case. She checked her watch. They had an hour until they had to report back at the bar and lounge area for the afternoon river cruise. Sonja lay down on her bed, one arm behind her head, the Glock digging reassuringly into her hip. She felt naked without a weapon and when she wasn't carrying one she found herself regularly reaching for the pistol she thought should be there. In the words of her daughter, Emma, she was pretty fucked up.

She closed her eyes, hoping to snatch some sleep. She was tired from the flights and her body had not had time to fully recover from the battering it had received in Mali. It was weird, she thought, that this operation had brought her so close to where Hudson was right now.

Sonja pictured him. Broad shoulders, dark hair with remarkably little grey at the temples, his coffee-coloured complexion, green eyes, crooked smile. He'd taken the job in Zimbabwe not just to help out his friend, Sonja thought, but because she had allowed Jed to talk her into her last mission and thereby extended her time in Mali, where she had been volunteering for Chengeta Wildlife, training anti-poaching rangers. Hudson had told her on more than one occasion that he was happy living in the house at the Hippo Rock Private Nature Reserve on the border of the Kruger Park, working semi-regular shifts as a jeep-jockey, a safari guide taking daytrippers into the reserve from the hotels in Hazyview. He'd said it was as close to a settled, nine-to-five job as he'd ever had and that he liked it and wanted her to feel welcome to share this comparatively easy life with him.

And that had freaked her out.

They had both been wounded three years earlier, taking down an organised crime poaching syndicate, and as soon as she had recuperated she had left South Africa to visit Emma in Scotland. Her daughter was doing her PhD in conflict archaeology – digging up

old battlefields – at Glasgow University. Sonja had been back and
forth from South Africa to her home in LA off and on in the in-
tervening period and as recently as three months earlier had told
Hudson that she would come back to him, but instead she had
gone to Mali, ostensibly for four weeks. She had told herself she
would give up working as a private military contractor – a modern
euphemism for mercenary – for Emma's sake. She had been restless,
however, and had eventually succumbed to the lure of the volunteer
position, training anti-poaching rangers in Mali.

Jed had found her there and recruited her for the mission to rescue the senator's daughter. She hadn't told Hudson why she had
extended her time in Mali, hiding behind the excuse of operational
security, but in truth she was scared of going back to him.

Hudson was a great guy, but try as she might she could not
picture them playing house forever and growing old. Sonja had allowed herself to think that kind of normal life was possible, when
she was with Sam, but then he'd gone and got himself killed making
a documentary about rhino poaching. She liked Hudson – enough
to want him not to die trying to keep up with her, which was what
would happen. He was older than her and his days of getting into
gunfights were over.

So were hers; that was the message her aching, ageing body was
giving her. She sat up and rummaged in her cosmetic bag, where she
found a blister pack of anti-inflammatories and popped a couple.
Sonja wanted to chase the pills with a Klipdrift and Coke Zero, but
they were on duty.

'Want a beer?' she said to Jed.

He looked at her and raised his eyebrows.

Americans – real Americans – could be so puritanical. 'Relax, I'm
joking.'

Jed set down the paperback he'd started reading. 'If we survive
the river cruise you can have a couple of drinks with Joanne to
break the ice. I'm not drinking in any case.'

Sonja sighed. This was a babysitting job and at the same time
Jed was going to work Joanne Flack, to try and recruit her, willingly
or unwittingly as an asset. Sonja closed her eyes and the next thing
she knew Jed was calling her name.

She looked at her watch. It was a quarter to four. She had been asleep for an hour.

'Old soldier's trick, being able to sleep anywhere,' Jed said as he walked through to the open-plan bathroom and began brushing his teeth.

Sonja sat up, glad that Jed couldn't see her wince. She got up, ran a brush through her hair and pulled it back in a ponytail, put in her contact lenses, checked her weapon was concealed, and met Jed at the door. He had a camera bag over his shoulder.

He looked her in the eyes. 'You could probably use another eight hours.'

She felt mildly annoyed that her fatigue was obviously showing, despite her nap. Was he insinuating that she looked old and haggard? 'Just puffy eyes from sleeping. I'm good to go.'

Jed gave a nod.

They retraced their steps to the lounge area of the lodge and walked across the lawn to the jetty where the boats were moored. Joanne Flack was already on one of the craft, along with their guide, who introduced himself as Samson.

'Welcome aboard,' Joanne said to them.

Jed made more small talk, about the weather and what they might see on the cruise, while Sonja scanned the riverbank as their guide cast off and motored out into the fast-flowing Zambezi. Jed was a combat veteran as well, but Sonja felt like she had never come off operations. Her life seemed to lurch from one battle to the next, whether or not there were bullets flying.

'Elephant,' Sonja said.

The guide looked like he was about to contradict her, but saw where she was looking and nodded. 'You have good eyes.'

In her business one had to, or, at her age, have a good optometrist. Missing a target or walking into an unseen ambush was a mistake you only made once in your life, at the end of it.

Joanne readied her phone to take a picture of the herd, which was emerging from the dry bush and taking up positions side by side and commencing to drink. Sonja saw a tiny baby and thought of Emma. She had been a screaming pain in the ass as a toddler and a nightmare as a teenager, but Sonja remembered her now as a newborn baby, freshly hatched, as her mother liked to say. Her feet – she had marvelled at them most of all – were so perfect and rounded, and Sonja would kiss them whenever they were alone. She was so glad Emma was safe.

Sonja looked away from the elephants towards Zambia on the opposite bank of the river. A fisherman was paddling a dugout canoe with the same muscular ease as a crocodile propelling itself through the water by swishing its tail. There had been a croc named Popcorn at Xakanaxa, in Botswana, where her father had worked and where she had spent most of her teenage years. Sonja would toss a slice of white bread, left over from the guests' breakfast table, into the clear waters of the Okavango, and Popcorn would grab it with the tip of his snout. When a fat bream started to nibble on the bait, Popcorn would snap and swallow the silvery fish whole. Sonja had been fascinated by the crocodile's cunning, and by its reflexes. It was, her father had told her, nature's perfect killing machine. Most Africans hated crocodiles; Sonja loved them.

Sonja swivelled her head and caught Flack looking at her.

'Not interested in elephants?'

Sonja forced a smile. 'I've seen a few before.'

Joanne narrowed her eyes.

'Look at the little baby, hon,' Jed said.

'Sweet.'

Joanne went back to watching the elephants, but Sonja could feel that the woman had her suspicions. She worried again that she had gone in too hard, too fast, with her talk of cycads. Sonja didn't like feeling self-doubt.

Another boat was coming down the river. Sonja lifted the compact binoculars from around her neck and focused on it. There was an African guide driving and the two passengers were FAMs, fighting-aged males.

Listen to yourself. She wondered if she would ever be able to look at a view without searching for cover and firing positions, or see or meet a group of people without assessing their capability to do her harm.

She studied the male passengers. One was white and the other looked to be of mixed race, or perhaps Middle Eastern. Both wore safari khaki and looked in good shape. Jed glanced around and Sonja indicated the other boat with her eyes. Samson had opened their throttle in any case, the elephant sighting now over, and Jed followed Sonja's gaze.

Sonja waved at the approaching boat. One of the men raised a hand.

'Is that boat from our lodge as well?' Sonja asked, playing the dumb tourist.

'No,' said Samson. 'There are many lodges along the river, but I do not know this boat or the man driving it.'

'Thought you would have known everyone on the river, Samson,' Jed said.

Sonja's right hand instinctively went to the holster on her hip.

'I do, almost,' Samson said.

Sonja felt her heart rate increase, but she was not panicking. The boat coming towards them seemed to accelerate – she could hear the change in pitch as it approached – but none of the men were making any sudden or unusual movements. A few seconds later the vessel had passed them.

Joanne and Samson were talking, something about birds. Sonja looked back and saw that the driver of the other boat had cut his engine and was now turning, seemingly to follow them.

'Hank?'

He looked over his shoulder and saw what she saw.

Sonja looked through the binoculars again and saw that the man sitting at the front of the other craft was reaching into a bag at his feet.

'Samson,' Sonja said, 'go faster, please.'

'What?'

'Accelerate. Open the throttle. Now.'

The guide widened his eyes. 'But –'

'Do as I tell you.'

'Madam, this is my boat and I –'

Sonja shot her right foot out and kicked the throttle lever forward. The boat leapt away so fast that Samson almost fell back on her, scrabbling to maintain hold of the wheel. When she looked aft again she saw that the man at the bow was holding an M4 or AR-15 carbine—she wouldn't know which until he started firing and she didn't intend to give the shooter a chance to open up on her. Sonja drew her Glock and Samson's next protest died on his lips as soon as he saw the pistol.

Sonja aimed and fired a double tap, and Samson held the throttle as far forward as it would go.

'I *knew* it,' was all Joanne Flack said as she got down on her hands and knees, seeking cover in the bottom of the boat. Jed had his pistol out and was standing at a crouch, over Joanne, trying to get a firing position around Sonja, who was at the back of the boat, kneeling, making herself a smaller target. She fired again.

Sonja's shots missed, which didn't surprise her. She was an excellent markswoman, but both boats were jinking and bouncing. The one following them seemed to be gaining on them, fast, and she now registered the twin fantails of water behind it—the other craft had two outboards, whereas they only had one. She lowered her aim and fired again.

The canvas canopy over her head was stitched with a neat line of holes. The armed man had fired the M4—she now knew it was the military variant—on full auto.

'Stay low,' she called over her shoulder. Beside her, Jed opened up with his pistol.

Another gunman had made his way to the front of the pursuit vessel, this one armed with an AK-47. Sonja heard the distinctive *pop-pop-pop* and two of the heavier 7.62-millimetre slugs punched through the aluminium skin of their hull.

Sonja took another shot. She had the satisfaction of seeing the first gunman stagger backwards, at least wounded if not dead, but the second kept up the volume of fire. His long burst emptied his magazine.

Sonja's first thought was that the man with the AK was less disciplined, expending so much ammunition with one burst, but any hope that this would count in their favour was lost when she felt the boat lose speed so quickly that she had to fight to keep her balance. She looked around and saw that Samson had apparently been hit and was lying on the deck.

The best thing she could do for a wounded comrade, Sonja had been told by a combat medic during her own military training decades ago, was to first kill the person shooting at them.

The boat behind them raced up to them, closing the gap, and Sonja decided it was time to empty her pistol. The gunman was lying low, reloading no doubt, but none of Sonja's bullets hit the opposing helmsman.

'Get down!' Jed, Sonja saw, was admonishing Joanne, who was trying to get to the helm.

'I can drive this bloody thing,' Joanne said to Jed.

Samson was on his back in the bottom of the boat, blood swirling amid the water that was seeping in from the holes in the hull.

Jed seemed to relent, but stepped around Joanne as she climbed into the driver's seat. Jed shielded Joanne's body with his own and probably saved her life because just then the man with the AK-47 stood again and opened fire.

Sonja felt the rounds zing past her, then heard a cry and a thud as Jed toppled over behind her. She screamed, not out of fear, but from a primal release of rage from deep within her.

Chapter 6

Rod was watching CNN in his room upstairs in the stately old two-storey Victoria Falls Hotel when his phone rang.

'Jed?' he said. No one else, other than Sonja Kurtz, had the number for this phone. There was no answer. 'Sonja?'

Rod heard gunfire and someone screaming, not like they were wounded, but more like a wolf baying at the moon or over a kill.

'Hello?'

There were more shots.

'Head for the bank,' yelled a woman's voice. That was Kurtz, he thought.

'Hello?' Rod said again.

He could hear the sudden revving of an engine and what sounded like the slap of water against a hull. That figured, as he knew from their schedule that Jed, Sonja and Joanne Flack should be out on a sundowner cruise right about now. Gunshots, however, were not usually part of the itinerary for a Zambezi River booze cruise.

Rod yelled into the handset, trying to get someone's attention, but all he heard was more engine noise and gunfire. He went to the bedside table and got his notebook. In it he had written the contact number for a helicopter company offering joy flights over Victoria Falls. Jed had said he knew the chief pilot, whose name was Gerry McDonald. Rod reluctantly ended the open line to the boat and called the number.

'Angels One, how can I help you?' said the man on the end of the line.

Rod could hear the whine of an engine in the background. 'Gerry McDonald?'

'Yes, who's calling?'

'My name's Rod. I need to charter your chopper. Now.'

'Sorry, I've finished for the day. I've just done my last flight and I'm shutting down.'

'You can name your price. The company I work for will pay, and people's lives depend on it,' Rod said quickly. 'You know Jed Banks?'

'Jed … yes, I do. Are you with the *Company*?'

'Yes. I'm staying at the Vic Falls Hotel. Where can you collect me?'

'The hotel has a landing pad. I'll call the manager and tell him I'm meeting you there. I'll be there in ten minutes.'

'Make it five.' Rod ended the call. He punched the combination into the small safe in the closet, opened it and took out a Glock 19 pistol. He hadn't fired a gun since the day he shot Peter Flack, more than two decades ago. His mouth went dry.

Rod checked his shirt was covering the firearm as he went downstairs, across the open courtyard, past the diners on the terrace and out onto the manicured lawns and into the heavy heat of the African afternoon. Rod heard the *thwap* of rotor blades and looked up to see a Bell Jet Ranger flaring its nose as it came in to land.

The aircraft settled onto its skids and the pilot gave Rod a thumbs-up. He ran, bent at the waist, and climbed into the co-pilot's seat.

Gerry passed him a headset and took off. 'I take it you're in a hurry.'

'Affirmative,' Rod said into the microphone. 'Banks and two others are taking fire somewhere on the river. They left on an afternoon boat cruise from Matetsi River Lodge. You know the place?'

'Taking fire? Do I need to call the cops?'

Rod thought about that. 'They'll never get there in time. Jed and the two women know how to handle guns and at least two of them are packing.'

Gerry nodded and pushed the nose of the helicopter down to pick up speed. They passed over the waterfalls themselves and he beat a path up the river, low and fast.

Rod saw the upturned faces of tourists on pleasure craft, but none of the boats was taking evasive action. He recalled from Jed's brief that Matetsi was about thirty kilometres upstream of the falls. Gerry covered the distance quickly.

Gerry pointed to the front. 'That's not right.'

Rod saw two boats travelling fast, leaving fat white wakes on the surface of the Zambezi. The one in front was jinking left and right, as if trying to evade gunfire. 'Take her down.'

Gerry looked at him and for a minute Rod thought the pilot was going to baulk at flying his machine into the midst of a gunfight. Instead, Gerry grinned and pushed the chopper into a dive.

'Hold on.'

Rod slid the Glock from the holster on his waist and cocked it.

Gerry levelled out, almost skimming the surface of the Zambezi as he came up behind the second speeding boat. Rod noticed one man crouching, holding an AK-47, and a second with his back against the gunwale, maybe wounded, with an M4 or AR-15 across his lap. The third man, the driver, was concentrating on the other craft, so clearly couldn't hear the approaching helicopter behind him over the roar of his outboard motors. That would change as they got closer.

Rod steadied his hand as he aimed the Glock out the window. He felt a quiver pass up his arm and willed himself to be still. People's lives were at risk, he told himself. Joanne was in trouble.

The distance between the helicopter and the boat rapidly decreased. Rod realised that the best way to stop this chase was to shoot the driver of the boat in the back. Even if the man was a humble safari guide, Rod reasoned, he knew his passengers were trying to kill the people in the boat ahead.

'What do you want me to do?' Gerry asked into his headphones.

Rod's mouth was dry, his heart pounding. 'Hold her steady.'

He took aim, entering the foresight on the driver's back, then lowered his pistol a fraction, aiming at the motors instead. He fired, two shots.

The first missed, but the second found its mark – Rod was surprised. His bullet had gone through the cowling of the right-hand outboard motor and must have damaged it, because the boat suddenly slowed. Gerry wasn't able to bleed off enough speed and in an instant they found themselves abreast with the craft.

The driver of the boat saw them and yelled to his able-bodied passenger, who swung his AK-47 towards them. Rod glimpsed the other man lying in the boat, his shirt bloodied – wounded, as Rod had first thought. Gerry hauled on his controls and they climbed.

'He's firing at us,' Gerry said. 'I can't stay in range of an AK, man.'

'Affirmative,' Rod said, trying to sound like being shot at was an everyday occurrence for him. He looked down as they levelled out again and Gerry swung the chopper into a wide orbit. The boat with Sonja, Jed and Joanne on it had raced ahead and was now pulling into a jetty.

'That's Matetsi River Lodge,' Gerry said.

The pursuit boat veered off, appearing to lose interest, but Rod watched as it carried on past the jetty and then pulled into the shore of the game reserve.

'Can you put me down there, at the lodge?' Rod said.

'Sure.'

*

Sonja knelt by Jed and ripped his shirt open. He had taken a round through the shoulder and, of more concern, another in his side, below his ribs. Samson had been hit in the arm, and had apparently knocked himself out cold when his head hit the boat's gunwale as he fell backwards.

Joanne had already opened the first aid kit and passed some gauze and a bandage to Sonja. Samson had come to and she was bandaging his arm.

Sonja held her hand over Jed's lower wound but the blood had soaked through the dressing and was oozing between her fingers. He was gritting his teeth, trying not to cry out. 'There's a chopper, Jed. We'll get you to a hospital soon.'

A Land Rover with Nikki, the lodge manager and Rod Cavanagh on board sped down the short road to the jetty.

'The chopper's waiting,' Rod called as he jumped down, 'and be quick, because the boat that was following you pulled into shore half a click from here and the surviving gunman got off.'

'Give me your shirt,' Sonja said. Rod stripped and Sonja saw Joanne staring at him. 'Joanne, stop gawking and give me his shirt.'

Joanne went to him, snatched away his shirt and passed it to Sonja, who pressed it against Jed's wound and then took a second bandage Joanne found and wrapped it around his body.

'Sonja,' Rod said, 'let's get you, Jed and Samson on the helicopter.'

'I'm not staying here with you,' Joanne said to Rod, and Sonja could see she meant it.

'No, Rod, you go with Jed and Samson to Vic Falls,' Sonja said. 'The pilot will know a good doctor. Leave me to look after Joanne.'

Rod looked to each of them, then nodded. 'OK, let's get the wounded on the Land Rover.'

They lifted Jed onto the first tier of seats on the game viewer and Samson, with Joanne supporting him, was able to climb aboard himself. The women got in too and Sonja noted how Joanne sat in the back of the game viewer, furthest from Rod, who sat up front next to Nikki. Like Sonja, Rod had his pistol out and was keeping watch in the bush from the direction in which the gunman might emerge at any minute. They sped the short distance to a cleared landing pad, where the helicopter was waiting, its blades still turning.

Sonja held her thumb up to the pilot, who returned the gesture, the military person's all-clear to approach. They carried Jed to the aircraft then Rod and Samson joined him on board. Joanne had got off the Land Rover, but hung back, Sonja noticed.

Sonja took Jed's hand and grasped it. 'You should be fine.'

Jed forced weak smile. 'Should?'

'I never bullshit a bullshitter.'

'Sonja ... where are you going?'

'Let me worry about that. I'll be in touch, Jed.' She stepped back and closed the Jet Ranger's rear door, gave the pilot another thumbs-up, and he lifted off.

Despite her black humour Sonja was worried about Jed. He was one of the good guys. He had been the CIA's senior field man in southern Africa for some time. He'd met his second wife in Zimbabwe and his daughter had worked there as a wildlife researcher. Sonja thought of Jed as an honorary African; he understood not only the politics of the countries he operated in, but also the cultures and the sensitivities. He was a devoted family man and a loving husband; she hoped he would pull through.

But there was work to be done. Sonja went to Nikki. 'As you just heard, there's a man armed with an AK-47 on his way here to the lodge. Lock the place down, send any guests you have out on a game drive and call the police.'

'Who is this gunman?' Nikki asked.

'A poacher, I guess.' It was a convenient fiction. 'Now, I need to take this vehicle.'

'I'm afraid that's not possible without a guide,' Nikki said.

Joanne stepped in. 'Nikki, dear, I'm sorry for all of this. Please do as she says.'

Nikki put her hands on her hips. 'No.'

Sonja held up her pistol and pointed it at Nikki. 'You can tell the cops I stole it, if you like, but I promise you that you'll get it back. Please trust me on this, and don't make me shoot you.'

'Put that bloody gun down,' Joanne said. 'Nikki, you can trust this woman.' Sonja lowered her weapon and Nikki looked to Joanne. 'Are you in trouble?'

'No – yes. Just do as she asked, please, Nikki,' Joanne said. 'We won't hurt your Land Rover. We just need to borrow it for a bit.'

'Joanne, get in the vehicle, now,' Sonja said.

Joanne had turned her face skywards, and was watching the helicopter disappear. She seemed dazed, but she complied. Sonja got behind the wheel, started the engine and drove off. Nikki was left open-mouthed.

Sonja drove as fast as she dared along the access road that led through the Matetsi reserve. She ignored the security checkpoint at the intersection with the tar road, driving straight past the guard, and turned left towards Victoria Falls.

'Where are we going?' Joanne yelled over the rush of air that passed over the open vehicle. She had climbed from the back seat to the one just behind Sonja.

'Somewhere I hope you'll be safe.' There was one place Sonja knew she'd be safe, as much as she dreaded going there. She was more comfortable facing up to gunfire than her personal life.

Another vehicle was coming towards them and Sonja saw it was a South African–registered four-wheel drive. She flashed her lights and waved her right arm out the side of the Land Rover. The other vehicle slowed to a halt and Sonja stopped beside it and took out the key. She could see now from the logo on the car's side that it was a rental.

'Hello, have you seen something?' asked the young man driving, in German-accented English.

'Yes. Your new ride.' Sonja opened the door of the Land Rover game viewer, drew her gun and pointed it at the tourist. 'Please get out of your vehicle and give me the keys.'

His eyes widened. 'You are hijacking me?'

'More exchanging vehicles.' She handed him the key to the Land Rover. 'Do as I say and no one will get hurt. I want you to take this vehicle back to where it comes from, Matetsi River Lodge. The turnoff's down the road.'

'But ... why?'

'No questions. The keys.' The man handed them over and Sonja turned to Joanne. 'Help these people get their luggage out, now.'

Joanne climbed down. The man and his female partner got out. The woman looked terrified. Joanne touched her on the arm. 'Don't be scared. We're in trouble.'

Sonja kept her pistol loosely trained on the couple as Joanne helped them remove the last of their bags, which they piled on the ground. When they were done Sonja took out her wallet and selected her emergency credit card. She gave it to the woman, pressing it into her hand.

The woman read the name on the card and scowled. 'Sonja Kurtz. I will remember you.'

'Whatever. Stay at Matetsi River Lodge a couple of nights, on me. I'll arrange to get your car back to you.'

The woman wiped away her tears, but didn't thank Sonja.

'Come,' Sonja said to Joanne.

*

Come? Joanne thought. This Kurtz woman was a piece of work. Being shot at and seeing Rod again had shaken her world and she didn't know which was worse.

Joanne gripped the handle above the door as Sonja rammed the Cruiser into gear, dropped the clutch and executed a high-speed reverse-turn. It was the sort of manoeuvre police and bodyguards were taught.

When the vehicle was pointed the other way, speeding back towards Victoria Falls, Joanne allowed herself to breathe normally. 'What was all that about? That couple were innocents.'

Sonja didn't look at her, but rather shifted her gaze continually from the road ahead to the rear-view wing mirrors. 'In case you didn't notice, there are people still trying to kill you.'

'You scared them to death. I thought the woman was going to wet herself.'

'I gave them my credit card.'

Psychopath, Joanne thought. 'What are you, CIA? But you're not American.'

'Not by birth, and no, I work for no one. Now.'

'What do you mean, *now*?'

'I mean, I don't know who we can and can't trust,' Sonja said.

'Why should I trust you?' Joanne asked.

'Because I just saved your life and my partner is bleeding because of you.'

Joanne nodded. 'Fair enough. Where are we going?'

'Somewhere safe, close to the Botswana border so we can get out that way if we have to. I'm going to try and find us an aircraft.'

'To go where?'

Sonja looked at her for the first time since the hijacking. 'You tell me.'

Joanne felt her anger rise. 'How the hell should I know what's going on, or who's trying to kill me?'

Sonja checked the mirrors again. She was like a prey animal, Joanne thought, continually aware of danger, and Joanne felt that role didn't sit well with the other woman. No, this one was definitely a predator.

'Think, Joanne.'

Joanne was thinking. She didn't know how much to tell Sonja about the cycad she had stolen or her suspicions. The woman was an ally, for now, but Joanne didn't want to be arrested by some gung-ho CIA agent, or find out later that the US Fish and Wildlife Service was running another sting. The fact was that no matter what her motives were, she had stolen a plant worth millions of dollars and she was in no hurry to give it back. 'I don't know. Maybe it was the terror group whose guy I shot in London. Maybe they want revenge.'

Sonja shook her head. 'Don't flatter yourself. I learned a bit about your precious cycads. This smacks of money.'

Joanne took a deep breath to steady herself. 'I don't know what you mean.'

Eyes ahead, and then to the mirror. 'Bullshit.'

'How should I know?'

'You and your husband were investigated for smuggling cycads out of South Africa and Zimbabwe twenty-five years ago.'

Joanne felt her heart rate increase. Rod Cavanagh had been there in the helicopter. Sonja and the other American, Jed, had been talking to him. 'I was innocent, I was never charged with anything.'

'They're two different things, innocent and not getting caught.'

'What's that got to do with now?' Joanne asked.

Sonja stood on the clutch and the brake pedals and Joanne was thrown hard into her seatbelt as the Land Cruiser's tyres squealed on the bitumen.

Sonja pulled her pistol from between her legs and pointed it at her. 'Get out.'

Joanne looked over her shoulder.

'You worried they're coming for you?' Sonja said. 'You know they will. If I leave you here they'll find you before anyone else does. Get out.'

She shook her head. 'No.'

'You're *innocent*, aren't you?'

Joanne swallowed. 'It's complicated.'

Sonja thumped the steering wheel with her free hand. 'Fuck. I knew it. You're a poacher. Plain and simple, as guilty as any Vietnamese rhino horn kingpin or some poor Mozambican trigger man. I should shoot you myself.'

Joanne held up a hand towards the pistol barrel that was pointed, rock-solid, at the point between her eyebrows. 'No. I'll tell you. At least I'll tell you what I know.'

'Start talking,' Sonja said, her voice icy.

'A ... a cycad went missing; it was stolen.'

Sonja started the car again and accelerated through the gears. They were sitting on a hundred and twenty kilometres an hour, not one below or above the speed limit. Sonja had turned on to the main Victoria Falls–Bulawayo Road, heading south, and she, like Joanne, was no doubt praying they didn't hit a police roadblock in case the tourists had put the word out already.

'It was an incredibly rare cycad from a game reserve owned by a member of the Kuwaiti royal family, near Hoedspruit, in South Africa,' Joanne went on. 'The plant's a female *Encephalartos woodii*. I don't know if you can even imagine how much it's worth.'

Sonja nodded. 'I've been given an idea.'

'Cavanagh briefed you?'

Sonja ignored this. 'So what happened to this cycad?'

'The guy it was stolen from didn't even know what it was until I told him. He's a keen amateur collector. Someone else, however, did understand the significance of the plant and stole it. Or they organised for someone else to steal it to get it out of the country without their fingerprints on it. I don't know. In any case, a couple of wheel men who were transporting it were caught and one of the investigating police left it with a group of cycad lovers that I'm a member of – as is the policeman's mother-in-law. He wisely didn't trust his own people with it. Then it went missing from where we kept it.'

'Did you take it?'

Joanne looked out the window. 'No.'

'Was it going to be sold to someone in Mali?'

Joanne looked back at her and locked eyes with her for a few seconds. Sonja wanted information from her, but Joanne also needed to find out what the CIA knew. She hadn't known what the plant's final destination was going to be, or even if it would be stolen from the society's lock-up. That had been her hunch: that someone close to her who knew where the *woodii* was supposedly being kept would steal it. So she had taken the real *woodii* and replaced it with a more common and less valuable *Encephalartos senticosus*. But when she had learned that the man who had attacked her in London was from Mali that opened a whole new range of possibilities of who was after the plant, and why. She had to draw the information out of the other woman. 'Why do you ask?'

'The Americans have intelligence that some Malian terrorists, or gangsters, or both, thought they had taken possession of a very valuable cycad, but it turned out that what they had was a fake, or rather, a substitute that looked like a very rare cycad.'

Joanne returned her gaze to the bush. 'Yes, well, I wouldn't know about that. If someone stole the rare cycad from our clubhouse and then inadvertently or deliberately double-crossed some gangster terrorists, then they should be chasing the real thief, not me.'

'When did the plant go missing from your group's lock-up?'

Joanne turned her head again. 'The day I left for the UK, nearly two weeks ago.'

'How did you know?'

'I went to check on it,' Joanne said, 'just before I left for England, the afternoon before the flight, as it happens. When I found it was gone I called the president of our society, Jacqueline Smit. She didn't answer so I left a message on her voicemail asking her what was going on. After I got to the UK I got a couple of SMS messages and emails on my South African phone from members of the group asking me if I had taken the cycad. That was crazy. I was framed.'

'So you told your friends, the other members of the group, that it wasn't you?'

'I ran out of airtime on my phone, and since my daughter's husband lost his job, I've had no money coming in and haven't been able to top it up. I'm now virtually penniless. I probably don't have to tell you that highly paid employment opportunities for ageing white women with no formal qualifications other than a self-taught expertise in cycads are few and far between in South Africa. Then, after learning that my daughter's family might soon be on welfare I ended up shooting a terrorist in Chelsea so, no, getting back to the members of the Pretoria Cycad and Firearms Appreciation Society to tell them I did *not* steal the cycad they were supposed to be looking after has not been high on my list of priorities.' The fact was, she did want the help of her friends in the society, but couldn't risk unburdening everything to any of them until she found out which, if any, of them was crooked.

Sonja nodded then did a double take. 'Firearms Appreciation Society?'

'It's a joke, though there's a serious side to it. We were all members of the Gauteng branch of the Cycad Society of South Africa, but we formed a kind of splinter or sub-group when we realised at a conference one year that we all had an interest in guns. All of us, for one reason or another, have had to use them for real, not just target shooting. And we wanted a bit of fun.'

Sonja shook her head. 'Heavily armed little old ladies.'

'And men. And who are you calling old? You're no spring chicken yourself.'

'I'm feeling my age right now.' Sonja turned off onto a gravel road, following the sign to Hwange National Park, Robins Camp. Sonja was racing the sun, off to their right, which was heading for the horizon. 'We've got fifty kilometres to go, through the Matetsi Safari area – hunting lands – before we get to the national park, and we need to enter the park before dusk.'

'I know where we are,' Joanne said, folding her arms.

'None of what you've told me so far explains why you were targeted,' Sonja said.

Joanne was thinking about that as well. Her ruse had been discovered, as she knew it inevitably must, but she'd had no idea that the end recipients of the substitute plant had been terrorists from Mali. 'What do you know about terrorists?'

Sonja shrugged. 'I've shot a few.'

'If I, a Western woman, killed one of their jihadis, spoiling his mission, then it's hardly surprising they would want me killed as payback. That's the predictable response from some dumb misogynist.'

Sonja shook her head. 'Two things I learned serving in Iraq and Afghanistan were that the Western world's Islamic enemies are not dumb, and nor are they predictable.'

Chapter 7

Thandi wanted to go to Joanne's house, where she planned on beginning her informal investigation, but another Uber ride opportunity appeared on her phone. The pick-up was at the Hatfield Gautrain station. It was a risky place to collect passengers, but money did not grow on trees these days, she reminded herself.

She selected the job and made her way to the station. As she approached she saw a couple of metered taxis parked near the entrance. She tapped out a message on her phone to the customer. *Meet me at the Ocean Basket restaurant.*

Where's that? came the reply a minute later.

Thandi sighed. Looking up, she saw a middle-aged man and woman, tourists judging by their large wheelie bags and khaki clothing, striding out of the high-speed train station towards her. The passengers must have identified her number plate as they started waving to her, so she could not avoid them or send them more detailed instructions about an alternative meeting place. She popped the boot and saw through the windscreen that the risk she feared had materialised. One of the metered taxi drivers had got out of his car and was coming towards her, armed with a baseball bat.

Thandi grabbed her handbag and got out of the driver's seat. Her riders were at the back of the car, hauling their bags into the boot. The taxi driver was ten metres away, grinning, close enough for her to see his gold tooth. She reached into her bag and slowly drew out her Makarov.

The taxi driver looked down, saw the gun and froze.

Thandi raised the Russian pistol just a little: '*Hamba la.*'

She saw the driver's fingers rippling on the bat as he weighed his options. She had told him in Zulu in no uncertain terms to go away. Perhaps he had heard of the Zimbabwean granny who had fired two rounds into the right-side tyres of a taxi not far from here, when another driver had tried to intimidate her out of accepting a ride not long ago. The man spat on the ground, but turned and went back to his car.

'Everything all right?' the male tourist asked from behind her as he climbed into her car.

Thandi was able to slide the Makarov back into her bag without him seeing. 'Yes, yes, all fine.'

She got in and accepted the ride, noting that they were going to the Capital Park railway station, headquarters and departure point for the luxurious Rovos Rail train, the Pride of Africa. Thandi pulled away from the kerb, swung the steering wheel and planted her foot, executing a U-turn that left rubber on the road and her passengers sliding across the smooth leather of the back seat.

'Jeez, where's the fire?' the man asked from the back.

Thandi checked the mirrors until she was sure they were not being followed, then said mildly, 'Just want to get you to the station on time.'

'Alive, would be better,' the woman said.

Exactly, Thandi thought. There had been instances of Uber drivers being assaulted by taxi drivers in Johannesburg and Pretoria and their cars being damaged. She wanted to spare this couple the details. 'Where are you from?'

'Australia. Do you drive full-time?'

It was probably the most common question asked of Uber drivers around the world, Thandi imagined.

'I drive most days,' she replied, almost as if from a script, breathing deeply to help the adrenaline subside. She had not been scared of the taxi man; she had been trained to think on her feet. The encounter had almost been fun. 'In the mornings on weekdays I take my grandchildren to school and then pick them up in the afternoons, or take them to their various activities–dancing, karate, gymnastics and so forth – so I mostly drive in the middle of the day.'

'Wow,' said the man, as if he couldn't believe a Zimbabwean grandmother was capable of such miracles. 'This is a nice car.'

Which was code, Thandi knew from experience, for: 'How could someone like you afford to buy a ride like this?'

'Thank you,' she said. 'This is also my personal car, but I own four cars.'

'Seriously?'

Thandi smiled at the man's surprise. Perhaps he thought all Africans were starving Ethiopians who only ate when a troupe of semi-retired musicians tried to rekindle the embers of their dying careers in the name of charity.

The electricity was out again, load-shedding probably, so Thandi looked each way and slowly yet confidently drove through a busy intersection, which had reverted to four-way stop with the traffic lights, or robots as the South Africans called them, blacked out.

'Yes,' she said, answering the tourist's question. 'My son drives when he is not at university and I have a nephew and niece from Zimbabwe who are both also driving.'

'Zimbabwe seems like a real mess,' the Australian said.

She sighed inwardly. Yes, that was true, but how could she explain to this man and his wife on their first-time safari, cocooned in luxury, that Zimbabwe was the most beautiful country on earth, populated by the smartest, most motivated, diligent people on the continent – except that too many of them, like her, were now part of the diaspora. 'Yes, but we have the skills to rebuild our country, when the time is right.'

'You reckon?'

'Yes, I do.' She glanced at him, not angrily, but she wanted him to know a little of what her people had gone through. 'We fought a war, for our liberation, and our government spent the next four decades trying to make itself rich and stay in power. I came here seeking asylum – I once had a senior government position, but I tried to expose corruption. I was in fear of my life.'

He raised his eyebrows, paying attention now. 'Really?'

Thandi nodded. 'But there are no handouts here, and it's hard to get residency, let alone South African citizenship, and the banks won't lend us money. But that doesn't stop us. I joined an association, eleven other women and myself. We all had jobs, mostly lowly paid. I worked as a domestic for a while – I have a degree in business management, but I needed money – and then I worked in a clothing store. The members of the association put in money every week and once we had saved enough the first one of us – we drew lots from a hat – got enough money to buy a car. Eventually, we all had cars. It was a system based on hard work and trust. With my car I started driving, for Uber, and here I am today, with four cars, and my relatives all work very hard.'

'That's amazing.' He sounded like he meant it.

'No,' she replied, shaking her head, 'that is life, especially here in Africa. You must work hard, you must trust your people, you must all pull together. Only then will we succeed.'

The fare ended and the man and his wife shook her hand and a porter took their luggage into the tastefully decorated Capital Park station. Thandi turned off her phone and headed towards Johannesburg. Before hitting the N1, however, she pulled over at KFC and ordered herself a two-piece meal and a Pepsi. She knew she needed to watch her weight and eat healthier food, like Laurel. Perhaps she would sign up for one of Baye's fitness classes. Next week.

Thandi ate her chicken leg as she drove and her thoughts turned to Joanne. If Joanne was innocent, then why had she not replied to the calls and messages that Thandi and her friends had sent to her? It seemed very suspicious, but was silence really an admission of guilt?

Joanne, like her, was from Zimbabwe, and Thandi knew that while their people prided themselves, generally, on being honest and hardworking, the country's economy had been such a mess for so long that even a saint would have found it impossible to live there without bending the rules every now and then. Things were better in South Africa, but, still, so many people lived hand to mouth and that also fed the crime problem.

There were many questions. For one, it was Joanne who had identified the very existence of the female *woodii* cycad. If she had wanted to steal it, she could have done so from the Kuwaiti prince's garden without even telling him what it was, and certainly without breathlessly blabbing the news of her discovery to the other members of the society two meetings ago. Thandi shook her head and started on her delicious chips.

She took the N1 and then the N14 south, towards Roodepoort on the West Rand, the current outer limits of Johannesburg's ever-expanding suburban sprawl. The traffic was light in the middle of the day and she made good time, less than forty-five minutes from Pretoria. At the Cradlestone Mall shopping centre she turned into Hendrik Potgieter, then took the next right.

Joanne Flack lived in a small, newish complex, a gated community. Thandi was a frequent enough visitor that Alfred, the security man on duty, knew her.

'*Masikati*, Alfred,' she said to him in Shona. The other good thing about Alfred was that he was a fellow Zimbabwean, even if he was a Shona from Mutare. Thandi was Ndebele, from Matabeleland on the other side of the country.

'*Masikati, maswera sei*, Mrs Ngwenya?' Alfred said, smiling his customary greeting. Thandi answered that she was fine and they exchanged a few pleasantries, Thandi not bothering to correct Alfred – Ngwenya was her maiden name and she was once more a 'miss'. Bryant had been her last married name, but that was too hard to explain to the security guard. 'Ah, but I am sorry, Mrs Flack is not here. She is in England.'

'Yes, I know, Alfred,' Thandi replied in Shona, 'but she has asked me to check on her garden. You know how important her plants are, yes?'

Alfred laughed. 'Oh yes, everyone here knows how much she loves those strange plants of hers.'

Thandi smiled. 'I just need to check that they have been watered.'

Alfred seemed to consider the regulations for a split second.

'Are you hungry, Alfred?'

'Yes, madam,' he said.

Thandi reached over to the passenger seat for the remainder of her meal. She would have to forgo one piece of chicken and half the chips, which was a little heart-wrenching. However, it did the trick.

'You may proceed,' Alfred said.

Thandi thanked him and drove into the estate as Alfred electronically raised the boom gate. The houses were neat, well kept, mostly Tuscan style and two-storey in earthy colours. Thandi slowed as four children, two white and two black, rolled down the road on an assortment of skateboards, scooters and a bicycle. It warmed her heart to see such simple displays of harmony. If only her own troubled country could find some peace again.

She sighed as she pulled up to Joanne's house. It had three bedrooms, and was plastered on the outside and painted grey. A brick wall hid her garden, which was at the front of the house; the blocks were small so there was very little room out the back.

Thandi parked in the driveway and got out. She went to the steel gate that led to the garden. It was locked, but she could see through the bars and the shade cloth that was snap-tied to the metal bars. It was full of cycads, predictably, given Joanne's love of the plants. Thandi had spent a few pleasant mornings sitting on Joanne's little *stoep* drinking tea and admiring her plants.

They were unlikely friends, perhaps given their very different upbringings, but Thandi liked to think they had more things in common than differences, which kept them together. *So why did you not reply to me, Joanne, or ask me for help if you needed money?*

Growing up, they had been on different sides of a war that had fragmented her country. Joanne had told Thandi her story. Joanne was a farmer's daughter, from Plumtree, and when she had turned eighteen she had married her first boyfriend, Peter, the eldest son of a prominent tobacco-farming family on the other side of the country, at Wedza. No sooner had they tied the knot than Peter had joined the Rhodesian Light Infantry. Conscription was compulsory for white males in Rhodesia at the time, and while Peter could have joined the Rhodesia Regiment and done military service part-time, in six-week blocks over ten years, the regular force, the Rhodesian Light Infantry, was offering young conscripts the option to volunteer to complete all of their service in a full-time two-year block. Peter had told Joanne he was doing it so that he could be with her more in the coming years, though she had suspected, Joanne told Thandi, that what he really wanted was to be in the thick of the fighting.

At about the same time Thandi had left her home in the Bulawayo township of Mzilikazi for the capital, Salisbury, now known as Harare. There she had joined ZANLA – the Zimbabwe African National Liberation Army, the military wing of the Zimbabwe African National Union. ZANLA was dominated by Shona-speaking people, but Thandi and her late brother, Emmerson, had both joined the larger of the two liberation parties, rightly realising that ZANU would eventually gain the ascendency. Little did they know that the party they had pledged to die for would oversee the ruin of their homeland.

From her instructors in guerilla training camps in Mozambique and, later, Russia and East Germany, Thandi learned about using explosives for demolitions, codes and ciphers, surveillance and counter-surveillance, different types of weapons and hand grenades, and the work of foreign intelligence services, such as the CIA and MI5 – that was why she found the Bond Cafe amusing.

Part of her spy training had focused on reconnaissance and surveillance. Thandi liked to think she was good at reading people and assessing situations, noticing things out of the ordinary. These were useful skills given she spent so much time on the roads in Pretoria and Johannesburg – one had to watch the traffic a hundred metres ahead, not just in front, and try to anticipate when something was about to go wrong. She had never been hijacked, touch wood, though she carried her old Russian Makarov pistol with her when she drove. There were better handguns she could buy, but she liked to think that in some small part she stayed true to the revolution and her training.

As she peered through the mesh, taking in Joanne's garden and its reasonably familiar layout, she heard whistling and turned her head.

'Hello, madam.'

She recognised the man by sight, in his blue two-piece overalls, but could not recall his name. 'Hello, how are you … ?'

'Isaac, madam. I am a gardener, for some of these houses.'

'Oh, yes, sorry. I remember, you are from Malawi?'

'Yes, madam.'

'I am Thandi. Nice to see you again.'

He was older than she and he touched his old-fashioned flat cap. 'You work for Mrs Flack, right?'

'I did, madam, but no longer.'

'No longer?'

'Mrs Flack sent me a message, an SMS all the way from *England*, telling me that my services are no longer required. I am sad. She has the most beautiful garden.'

Thandi glanced back towards the cycads. 'She does indeed.'

Isaac nodded. He lowered his voice, as if worried one of the neighbours would hear. 'She said she was sorry, but she could no longer afford to pay me, but that one day she might have enough money to engage me fulltime.'

Interesting, Thandi thought. So Joanne had not bothered replying to Jacqueline or anyone else who had tried to quiz her about the missing cycad and the society's empty bank account, yet it seemed she had been able to SMS her part-time gardener and hint at the hope of fulltime employment in the future ... Did she think she was about to come into a substantial amount of money? Why, then, end his employment claiming lack of funds? It was a puzzle.

Isaac was transferring his weight from foot to foot. He was waiting to be dismissed. Thandi took another look through the gauze.

'How did you get access to Mrs Flack's garden when she was away, Isaac?'

He looked up and down the street then whispered: 'There is a key to this gate, madam.'

'Do you think you could let me in, Isaac? If Mrs Flack cannot pay you, then perhaps I can water her plants.'

Isaac surveyed the street again, then looked down at his shoes.

'Mrs Flack and I are friends. You know me, Isaac.'

He looked up at her and drew a deep breath and she could tell he was about to say no, as well he should.

'You could accompany me, Isaac, show me where the standpipe is and so forth.'

He thought about it briefly, then nodded. Isaac went to the front door of Joanne's house and for a moment she wondered if he would really find the key under the doormat. Instead, he lifted a potted bougainvillea and took the key from under it. Almost as obvious, she thought.

Isaac returned and unlocked the gate to the garden. Thandi could see that it was only the one key, presumably just for the gardener's use, so she would not be able to get into Joanne's house. That would have been too difficult and risky in any case, as Joanne, like everyone in Gauteng, would have an alarm, possibly linked to an armed response unit. Thandi did not fancy coming up against some nineteen-year-old white dude with an itchy trigger finger.

Isaac held the gate open for her and Thandi walked into the garden. It was like a mini Jurassic jungle, minus the dinosaurs. Nearly all of the small yard was taken up by cycads, with neatly manicured green grass in between. Thandi knew that most of these plants had come from Zimbabwe, uprooted from Joanne's farm when she and her husband had been kicked off.

Thandi was fairly sure that Joanne had not gone to the trouble of securing permits to bring these cycads to South Africa, and who could blame her? The government that would have issued the permits had allowed someone to take her farm from her and Joanne had barely had enough time to dig up her plants and move them to Harare, where she lived for a while before subsequently moving to South Africa. Joanne had told Thandi that she was sure she would not have been issued permits and, what was more, she was certain that if she had applied for them, someone would have come around to her house to assess the plants, perhaps casing the house she was renting in Harare with a view to stealing them.

And this, Thandi thought, was one of the greatest quandaries of and threats inherent in the cycad trade. Joanne was the legal owner of her plants in Zimbabwe and, if she was to be believed, had never stolen a plant from the wild. If she had left her cycads in Zimbabwe when she emigrated to South Africa they most likely would have been stolen and/or sold off illegally, so she had *saved* the plants by smuggling them into South Africa, even though she did so without the required paperwork.

Thandi let her finger trail along the deliciously textured, stiff leaf of a cycad as Isaac made for the standpipe and turned on the tap.

Collectors, scrupulous and unscrupulous, were always telling themselves this tale, that the rare plants were better off, safer, in their gardens than they were in the wild. That was, to a degree, true, but what happened when this bountiful gift of God above disappeared forever from the wild? Was that *right*?

Thandi had grappled with similar conundrums in her own life. She had fervently believed in the struggle that she had taken part in as a young woman, risking her life in battle for the freedom of the country she loved. It had been the same here in South Africa; everyone agreed, even most of the whites she met these days, that apartheid was bad, but the ruling powers here and in Zimbabwe had been busy destroying their countries in different ways.

'Must I leave the sprinkler on, madam?' Isaac asked.

She felt bad, taking him away from his other chores, or his taxi ride home to a humble shack in whichever informal settlement he lived in. 'I think we can just give everything a good soaking for now, Isaac. I'll turn it off before I leave.'

Thandi walked along a row of fetching plants, mentally ticking off their Latin names, but stopped when she noticed the soil at the base of one plant. It appeared darker, fresher, than that surrounding the neighbouring stems. Her memory of this part of the garden was one of crowded uniformity, so it struck her as odd that a new plant might have recently been added here. It was slightly smaller than the others on either side of it and along the row.

'Isaac?'

The gardener dragged the sprinkler into place, then stopped and looked up. 'Madam?'

'Has Mrs Flack been doing some work here?'

He straightened up. 'Yes. Mrs Flack decided to swap a cycad for a new plant.'

'Why?'

Isaac just looked at her blankly, then shrugged.

Thandi stretched her arms above her head to ease the tension in her back and looked up at the clear blue Highveld sky, trying to process the sequence of events and understand them. 'What was wrong with the old plant, the one Mrs Flack took from here?'

Isaac shrugged. 'Ah, but I do not know, madam.'

Thandi frowned. 'Do you know what type of cycad it was?'

He smiled. 'Ah, but they all look alike to me.'

Thandi inspected the new plant. It was an *Encephalartos trispinosus*, very common and, for a cycad, inexpensive.

'Did you help Mrs Flack dig up the cycad, Isaac?'

'No, madam. It was already done when I was last here, which was before she left, nearly two weeks ago.'

Thandi nodded. Isaac checked his watch.

'Do you need to go?'

He nodded. 'I must work on Mrs Oberholzer's garden next. She will be cross if I am late.'

'Off you go. I'll finish the watering and lock up. I'll put the key back.'

Isaac seemed to think twice about that proposition for a couple of seconds, but in the end he nodded and handed her the key.

'Thank you, Isaac.'

He touched the brim of his hat again. 'Madam.'

Thandi walked around the garden, though she had no real idea what she was looking for. It was getting hot and there was no shade. She wondered what would happen to these plants if Joanne did not return to South Africa. There were some superb cycads in this garden, and Thandi guessed the combined value of some of the rarer specimens would run to hundreds of thousands, if not millions of rand on the black market.

'What were you up to, Joanne?' she said aloud.

Why replace a perfectly good cycad, whatever variety it was, with a garden variety specimen – literally – just before leaving for the UK?

And how, if at all, did this relate to the loss of the rare cycad from the storeroom at the garden centre where their little group held its meetings, not to mention the theft of the society's savings?

Thandi decided there was nothing more the plants could tell her, so she left the garden, taking care to turn off the water and make sure the gate was locked, then returned the key to its place under the pot plant. She walked up the driveway to where her car was parked and noticed a wheelie bin, out for collection.

Rather, she noticed the tip of a spiky green frond sticking out from under the partially closed lid of the bin.

Just as Isaac had done, Thandi looked up and down the street—she didn't want to be thought of as the type of person who snooped in other people's bins, or like those less fortunate who looked for food. She lifted the lid.

The bin was stuffed with cycad foliage. Thandi withdrew one and inspected it. She had pruned enough of these plants to know how quickly the leaves dried up. And this was not pruning—these cuttings were full length and had been removed right at the base, where they met the stem. Thandi withdrew one of the many whole fronds crammed into the bin. She inspected the foliage and the dry end where it had been snipped from the stem. It was hard to tell exactly, but she guessed the leaves had been removed no more than two weeks ago. There was no scheduled service to collect this type of waste, it was up to the home owner.

The state of the leaves, Thandi guessed, meant this cycad had been stripped of all its foliage around the time Joanne Flack had left for London. She picked up one long, spiky leaf. It looked to her like an *Encephalartos senticosus*. Interesting, Thandi thought.

Chapter 8

'I remember this area from the old days,' Joanne said as Sonja drove hard and fast on the gravel road that led to Hwange National Park, Zimbabwe's largest and best known game reserve.

Sonja heard the nostalgic wistfulness in Joanne's voice. It was a familiar lament, of how things had been. One thing Sonja had learned, though, was that Africa never stood still for long. Things changed. One day a country such as Zimbabwe was the breadbasket of the continent, the next it was merely a basket case. She felt for Joanne; her family had also been affected by the continent's politics, but she was sure the other woman was still holding information from her.

They were close to their destination, but Sonja received a timely reminder of the old soldier's adage that it was easiest to drop one's guard near the end of a patrol or a mission. A great grey shape appeared from amid the tall grass on her left and she had to brake suddenly.

'Sheesh, I didn't see that,' Joanne said as the elephant crossed the road, but not before turning and shaking its head to give them an admonition for speeding.

Sonja waited for the rest of the herd to amble along their way, engine idling. She had found herself becoming increasingly agitated the closer they came to Nantwich Lodge. She didn't know if it was anticipation or fear – perhaps a mix of both.

'You OK? They're just elephants,' Joanne said, staring at Sonja's white knuckles.

'I'm fine,' Sonja replied, forcing herself to relax her grip on the steering wheel. She wanted to tell Joanne that she had grown up around elephants, when her father worked at a game lodge in the Okavango Delta in Botswana, but if she did then the woman would probe deeper, to find out what was wrong with her. 'Just fine.'

'Whatever you say.'

They passed a turnoff to the right to Pandamatenga, a border crossing that led to Botswana. Going by land was an option, but Sonja would either have to cut across country, bypassing customs and immigration, or pray that the couple whose truck they had stolen hadn't already alerted the police, who would then warn the border crossings.

They carried on, the road bisecting a wide open *vlei*, a flood-plain. As they came out of the depression a herd of twenty or more sable antelope bolted, perhaps thinking they were a hunting vehicle. All she saw were the curved horns and black coat of the herd's male disappearing into the golden grass.

Sonja kept up the pace. A few kilometres further on she pulled up at the thatch-roofed entry gate to Hwange National Park and was greeted by a lone Zimbabwe Parks and Wildlife Service ranger on duty. She signed in under the name of Ursula Schmidt.

Joanne signed in as Nicole Kidman.

'Don't worry,' Sonja said, 'we won't be staying around long enough to pay entry fees and show our passports.'

Just through the gate Sonja took a slip road to the right. In her rear-view mirror she could see the ranger waving frantically at her. By rights she should have continued on straight, towards Robins Camp and the nearest parks and wildlife office that could process their entry permits. Instead she followed the sign that read: *Nantwich Safari Lodge, reserved guests only.*

'I remember this place as well,' Joanne said.

'I've never been here,' Sonja replied.

'Nantwich was an old national parks camp, three bungalows overlooking a waterhole. My husband and I stayed here when we were young, just married, and again a couple of times with Peta. It was paradise, but it fell into ruin and was partially burned down. I heard it had been rebuilt as a safari lodge.'

Sonja took a deep breath and gripped the steering wheel even harder. Part of her wanted to keep on driving, to keep running. If it wasn't for Joanne she might have.

*

Hudson Brand heard the growl of an engine being revved hard and sighed. They weren't expecting any guests so this was probably just another curious tourist who had ignored the sign and decided to come down the road to have a look at the lodge.

He got up from the wicker chair on the shaded *stoep* outside the manager's office and living quarters, where he had been alternately dozing and reading a novel about anti-poaching tracker dogs.

Brand put on his faded Texas Longhorns baseball cap and took a look out over Nantwich Dam. You had to keep your eyes open in the bush. There were no fences around the lounge and dining area, which his place abutted, and just a few days earlier three lions had killed a kudu, interrupting lunch for a bunch of awestruck American tourists.

Mishack, the barman, had also roused himself from the far end of the verandah and was making for the door.

'I'll see to it, Mishack,' Brand said.

The late afternoon sun was trying to creep in under the low-hanging thatch roof over the *stoep* and Brand walked out into the soft light photographers lovingly referred to as the golden hour.

He could tell from the silhouette that the vehicle bouncing down the hill–the damn fool was driving too fast for the national park–was a rented camping vehicle. Brand forced a smile; maybe this was a couple of Europeans who had tired of life in a roof tent and were ready to treat themselves to a night of luxury.

The *bakkie* stopped about thirty metres ahead of him, engine idling, and for a few moments no one got out. Brand wondered again if these were sightseers. Sometimes just the sight of him or one of the other staff members was enough for the snoopers to reverse back up the access road and hightail it out of there.

Then the driver turned the key and got out.

Even though she wore new sunglasses and her hair was pulled back under a cap he'd never seen, he knew, immediately, that it was her.

Another person got out of the passenger side and he paid her only enough attention to register she was a woman. His eyes were on the driver, who simply stood there. She put her hands on her hips, looking back at him.

She did not like public displays of affection.

She did not like touchy-feely people.

She did not like talking about feelings.

She did not like talking about the future.

She did not like talking about the past.

She never said the words 'I love you', at least not to him.

Hell, he didn't even know if she really liked him at all, let alone loved him.

He registered movement in his peripheral vision and for the briefest of moments wondered if she might get him killed, if the resident leopard had just decided he would make a nice late lunch. Hudson turned and saw that the other woman had walked from the vehicle to him without him even noticing.

She put out a hand. 'I'm Joanne Flack.'

Her grip was firm, like a man's. 'Hudson Brand.'

'My ... friend here ...'

'Friend?' He wasn't sure she had any.

'Travelling companion, said she knew people here. You?'

'What happened? She get shot in the throat? Not talking?'

Flack ran her hand through her short hair. 'That's not funny, Mr Brand. We have been shot at. That's why we're here.'

He nodded slowly. 'Figures. About the only time I see her is after a gunfight. Come on in out of the sun.'

He returned to the shelter and comparative safety of the lodge. What Sonja was doing he didn't know. He tried to tell himself he didn't care, either. He could only guess at what sort of trouble this woman was in, for Sonja to actually seek help from someone else, but one thing was for sure: it had to be bad.

'Take a seat, Joanne.' Brand gestured to a comfy sofa with a prime view out over the dam, which shimmered in the sun.

Mishack appeared with two mocktails and cold towels and Joanne gratefully accepted both.

'The other lady?' Mishack said.

'She'll be here in her own good time,' Brand said, taking a seat opposite Joanne.

Joanne looked at him. 'So you *do* know each other.'

Hudson gave a small smile. '*Yebo.*'

'You talk like an African with an American accent,' she said.

'That pretty much sums it up. American father and a half-Angolan, half-Portuguese mom. What went wrong?'

She sighed. 'More like, what went right? To cut a long story short, we're on the run.'

'Flack,' he said. He didn't feel the need to catch up on world affairs most days, but a South African guest had shown him a story on his iPad a few days earlier about a woman from Johannesburg who had shot dead a terrorist in London. The name sounded familiar. 'Was that you in...?'

'London. Yes. I came to Zimbabwe to hide but it turns out someone wants me dead and they tracked me here. Your *friend* and her American partner were sent to look after me.'

'Partner?'

Mishack was disappearing into the kitchen. She lowered her voice. 'Yes. The man, named Jed, was shot. He's still in Victoria Falls, hopefully all right.'

'Jed? Six-two, fair hair, beard, good-looking?' She nodded and so, too, did Hudson, his suspicion confirmed. 'Jed Banks, CIA. Who are you on the run from?'

'Several people by now, I expect. There is whoever was trying to kill me – some Islamic terrorists who seem to have taken offence that I, a woman, killed one of their jihadis – and probably the Zimbabwean police.'

'The police?'

Joanne gave a flick of her head and a small smile. 'That vehicle outside; well, let's just say it's a loaner.'

Hudson exhaled. *Sonja.*

'Brand.'

He looked up and there she was, hands on her hips, not smiling. *SNAFU*, he thought: situation normal, all fucked up.

'Sonja.' He got to his feet.

Mishack started to emerge from the kitchen, but Sonja shot him a glance that stopped him as surely as a bullet, and the barman wisely retreated. 'We need transportation, preferably air.'

'I'm fine, thanks, and you?' Hudson said. She didn't crack a smile.

Joanne cleared her throat. 'Is there a ladies' room here?'

'Come, madam,' Mishack said, tentatively appearing again in the doorway, 'I will show you.'

Hudson waited until they had gone, temporarily at least, and went to Sonja. He stopped about a metre from her; that invisible force field of hers was as good as Kevlar body armour. He pointed at the sticking plaster on her right temple. 'You OK?'

'No, Brand. I am *not* OK,' she said in a level voice. 'Someone is trying to kill that woman, and me. They shot Jed Banks and a boat guide on the Zambezi. I need to get her to South Africa. Now.'

'What's she done? Why are people after her?'

Sonja sighed. 'She's involved somehow with the theft of a rare plant and some jihadis in Mali think she double-crossed them – sold them a fake. The Americans think the plant and a whole bunch of rhino horn and ivory are being funnelled to Mali and used to finance a future terrorist attack originating in that part of Africa. We find this bloody plant, we find the trail to the terrorists.'

Hudson flicked his head in the direction Joanne and Mishack had gone. 'She your bait?'

'No comment. And I don't know. I don't want her getting killed before she at least starts telling me the truth about her involvement. This whole operation is a cluster-fuck, Brand, from start to finish.'

He nodded slowly. 'I'll see what I can do. There's a pilot named Andrew Miles staying at Robins Camp, down the road a ways. I've known him for a while. He's what you might call *accommodating*.'

'OK. Just fix it. When's he leaving?'

'He's taking two guests from here south tomorrow, so you're in luck. He'll have a couple of spare seats. You might need to grease his palm is all.'

'Have you got a room for tonight?'

He tried a half-smile again. 'Well, I've got a double bed...'

'I need to stay with the principal, the woman. She's my responsibility.'

'Were you followed?' Sonja's prickliness aside, he needed to think of the safety of his other guests.

'No. And no one knows where I've taken her, not even the company people, so if there's a leak inside they won't find us just yet.'

'All right,' he said. 'Mishack can move your *loaner* car out the back of the staff quarters, other side of the hill. No one driving past or coming up to the lodge will see it.'

She gave a curt nod. 'Good.'

'You want to tell me what's going on?'

'I just told you.'

'I was talking about us.'

Her hands went back to her hips. 'What do you mean, *us*?'

'I mean, I haven't heard from you in weeks and then you show up, you demand an airplane, and you don't even say hi. Where have you been? In Mali all this time?'

'That's classified.'

'*Classified*. Shit. C'mon, Sonja.' Hudson spread his hands wide.

She stabbed a finger at him. 'No, *you* c'mon. I'm gone five minutes and you leave your home in South Africa and take a job in Zimbabwe. Where was I supposed to come... find you?'

'*Home to*, is that what you were going to say, Sonja?'

'I have a home, in Los Angeles. My daughter and I live there.'

He nodded. 'Yes, but Emma is away at university in Scotland and on archaeological digs around the world half the year, like now. She's in France, digging up Western Front trenches.' Sonja lived with him on and off in South Africa, but she didn't seem to think that counted as her home.

'How do you know where Emma is?'

He was incredulous. 'You don't know where your own daughter is, do you?' She didn't answer, just pursed her lips. 'We *talk*, Sonja. On Facebook. You should try it sometime.'

She looked away from him. 'I don't do Facebook.'

He could feel himself getting exasperated. He had told himself he would be cool as soon as he saw her. 'You don't do social media, don't do phone calls, don't do SMSes, you don't do greeting cards or postcards. I didn't know where in the world you were.'

'Ha!' she said, as though she had been vindicated. 'You don't know where I am so you just pack up your *home* and take the first job you can find in another country?'

Like her, he'd been a soldier. He knew the importance of taking the high ground and he could wrest it back from her, no problem. 'Yes, and *I* sent you an email, SMS and voice message telling you I would be here for one month, precisely, filling in for a friend who's on sick leave. Meanwhile I had no idea where you were or when you were coming *home*, Sonja.'

She fumed. 'Well, now I have nowhere to go home to, except America, do I?'

'I'll be finished in a couple of weeks.'

'Sure,' she said, 'if they don't want you to extend. You don't even own that house in South Africa. The owners could come back from Australia anytime.'

That was true. They were at their usual stalemate, within just a few minutes of being reunited. They had tried cohabiting – that was the best way he could describe it. 'Living together' wasn't really a good description for what they had because it seemed to Hudson that even when they were under the same roof Sonja was restless, or hyperactive, or down, or living somewhere in her past.

He couldn't fault her for that. Hudson knew she was suffering from post-traumatic stress disorder, to some degree, even though she wouldn't admit it. He'd been through combat and some tough times himself and had been to a therapist for a while. Sonja pooh-poohed professional help – for herself at least. She had spoken with genuine compassion of friends she had served with in Afghanistan and Iraq as soldiers and contractors who suffered mental illness. She didn't deride them for seeking help, but she was unforgiving of her own troubles.

Hudson wondered, too, if her childhood was as much to blame as her military service for her underlying insecurity and fear of abandonment. Her mother had left Sonja's abusive alcoholic father when Sonja was a teenager and Sonja had elected to stay with her dad, in Botswana, instead of following her English mother to the UK. Eventually, Sonja had seen her father for what he was and had left him to join the British Army, making the most of her dual nationality. She'd had a brief reunion with her father, during a civil war of all things, and then he had died, as had her mother a few years earlier. Sonja loved her daughter, Emma, who seemed like a well-grounded kid, but she had her mother's restless spirit as well, for whatever reason.

There was no way Hudson wanted to forgo Africa and move back to the US. He had lived there as a troubled teenager and couldn't imagine going back to Texas. Sonja knew that and when she wanted to end a fight with the last word she reminded him that she had a house in LA, and that he lived hand to mouth in Africa, by the good grace of his friends who gave him work as a safari guide and by the occasional case that called for his skills as a private investigator. He wondered if deep down she wanted him to dump her, to leave her for good, so that she wouldn't continually be afraid that he would find someone else or some reason not to love her.

'Sonja...'

'Spare me the psychobabble, Brand. I've got work to do. Can you get in touch with this pilot for me or not? Do comms even work out here in this godforsaken country?'

'Sure. Hwange National Park is moving into the twenty-first century now. We've got wi-fi and so does Robins Camp. I'll WhatsApp Thousand.'

'Thousand?'

'Miles. That's his nickname. He's a good guy.'

*

A *good guy*. Hudson was one of those, Sonja thought as she looked at his broad back while he spoke on his phone. He looked great, as always, in his khakis. He didn't seem to age; if anything he looked leaner and fitter than he had when she'd left.

By contrast, she seemed to put on weight if she so much as looked at a cheeseburger or a bowl of fries these days. She found that as she got older she had to work harder than ever to stay in shape.

He could have pretty much any woman he wanted and she knew, from conversations she'd overheard at parties in South Africa when they were living together, that Hudson had a reputation as a ladies' man. Women tourists visiting Africa often fell prey to a malady known as Khaki Fever, where they developed a crush on their typically handsome safari guide, and she'd learned that for a time Hudson's nickname among the guiding fraternity of Hazyview, the town closest to where they stayed, had been 'Malaria'. She wondered if he had been faithful to her the whole time he'd been in Zimbabwe.

She stopped herself. Why the hell should he be faithful to her when she'd given him no indication at all that she wanted to be in an exclusive relationship with him? The truth was, she didn't know what she wanted, and for a woman whose professional life as a soldier had always been about planning and being in control, that was as frustrating as hell.

Sonja bit her lower lip. They'd had a fight, just before she'd left to work as a volunteer in Mali, but the day before she'd flown out they had made passionate love, almost as if they each knew they would never see the other again. She was no prude, but the things they had done that night ... she felt herself start to blush.

Hudson turned around. 'OK. It's a yes from Thousand, although he has to drop two guests in Bulawayo en route. He'll take you on to Lanseria Airport in Johannesburg. You need to think about how you'll get past the customs and immigration people there when you land.'

She nodded and tried to think. Sonja had a fake passport that would stand up to any scrutiny, but Joanne had no travel documents. She needed a new identity or, better still, a way to disappear for a while to take the heat off her.

'What's worrying you?'

Brand must have noticed the look on her face, or, once again, proved he could read her mind. Some couples were like that, weren't they? 'The people after Flack, Hudson, they're good.'

He raised his eyebrows. 'Oh, so it's Hudson now? You must need something from me.'

Sonja carried on: 'Joanne needs to disappear.'

'Better than that,' Hudson said, 'she needs to die.'

Chapter 9

'Die?' Sonja said.

'I might know a way to make her vanish from everyone's radar,' Hudson said. 'Let me make another call while you and Joanne get settled. Mishack can take you both to your room.'

'All right. I want to check the area before it gets dark.'

He nodded. 'I'll bring a game viewer and pick you up in half an hour.'

Hudson went through a door at the end of the dining room, presumably into his office or the quarters he had mentioned.

Joanne emerged from the same door a few seconds later, patting dry her face, which she had washed. Mishack spoke into a handheld radio and a few minutes later a safari guide entered the lounge and introduced himself as Blessed. He led them outside to a tan-coloured Land Cruiser game viewer, open on the sides with a canvas roof for shade.

From the main lounge and dining area Blessed drove them up a hill covered in long, straw-coloured dry grass to the first of three buildings arrayed on a ridge, just below the crest, overlooking Nantwich Dam, which Sonja could appreciate now that she had some physical if not moral high ground after her argument with Hudson. She was a better person when she was working, and as Blessed pulled up outside the thatch-roofed building, she surveyed the terrain with a soldier's eye.

'These used to be three two-bedroom national parks lodges. They were simple, but beautiful,' Joanne said.

'And now they are luxurious,' Blessed said, and opened the door to a room with an ostentatious flurry. 'Now we have three twin or double rooms per building. Welcome to your home away from home.'

Blessed clearly hadn't got the memo that Joanne and Sonja were a couple of fugitives on the run, and if he thought their lack of luggage was unusual he didn't say anything. Sonja ignored the briefing on the location of the shower and toilet and the use of the air horn in case they were invaded by dangerous animals. The only predators Sonja was concerned with carried AK-47s and M4s.

'Thank you, Blessed,' Joanne said. 'I'd give you a tip, but I don't have any money.'

He smiled. 'No problem, madam. I will give you a tip instead – enjoy your stay here.'

Joanne shook his hand and Sonja walked out onto the *stoep*. She looked over her shoulder. 'Blessed?'

'Madam?'

'Is anyone else staying in this building?'

'No, madam, only in the other two. You are alone here.'

'Thank you.'

Sonja didn't think any potential neighbours here were a threat, but if the shit started going down at least there would be no civilians in the firing line. When Blessed had left she sat on one of the twin beds, emptied her pockets onto the side table and took her pistol from the holster clipped to her belt.

'What's happening?' Joanne asked her.

She explained about the call Hudson had made to the pilot, Andrew Miles, and the plan to fly to Bulawayo the next day. 'Brand's got something in mind to help you disappear.'

'You trust him?' Joanne asked.

She unloaded her pistol and began disassembling it. She could do the job while maintaining eye contact with Flack. 'With my life.'

'You two have history, you're close.'

Sonja was a little taken aback. 'How did you know?'

She smiled. 'When I was in the loo I heard you fighting. Acquaintances and just-friends don't talk to each other like that.'

Sonja busied herself cleaning the African dust from her weapon. The repetitive tasks of a soldier calmed her, she found. She looked down. 'Whatever.'

'I'm going to take a shower.'

'Fine.' Sonja finished cleaning her pistol, reassembled it, then unloaded the magazine and the spare and wiped each bullet before reloading them.

While Joanne used the outdoor shower Sonja walked out of their room by the door they had entered. The three accommodation units were set below the crest of the hill and Sonja walked past the swimming pool to the top, about a hundred metres to the rear of the building they were staying in.

On the crest she found the grave of a white pioneer, Percy Durban Crewe. From here she had a 360-degree view, and as she slowly turned and looked, she picked up no sign of human activity save for the gate through which they had entered. On the floodplain below, close to the edge of the dam, was the larger building where she had met Hudson. A small herd of roan antelope, beautiful sandy-coloured animals with striking black and white faces, cautiously approached the edge of the dam; danger lurked everywhere here, more often than not unseen. Off to the right, beyond another small range of hills, were the hunting lands through which they had travelled from Victoria Falls. If she sat up here she would see a vehicle or aircraft coming from miles away. Even intruders on foot would have a hard time staying concealed; the countryside was open and the tree cover that had been there seemed to have been shredded by elephants.

As Sonja walked down the hill towards her accommodation she heard the growl of a vehicle engine and saw that the tan-coloured Land Cruiser game viewer was back, now with Hudson behind the wheel. She met him outside the suite.

'Lovely afternoon for a game drive,' he said from the driver's seat.

Brand could find the bright side of anything and she envied him that. Sometimes her memories, her sadness, threatened to paralyse her. 'One minute.'

Sonja went inside and found Joanne lying on the bed with a towel wrapped around her. 'I'll be back soon. Use the walkie-talkie if you need us.'

'OK,' Joanne said. 'Are you leaving me here as bait for the bad guys so that Team America can swoop in and kill them, and me, as collateral damage?'

Sonja paused and rocked her head from side to side. 'Not a bad idea. Maybe if you can think of anything you haven't told me yet, we won't have to sacrifice you.'

Joanne adjusted herself on the stack of pillows and looked out over the dam. A herd of kudu was tentatively making its way down to drink. 'I've already told you everything I know.'

Sonja doubted that. She closed the door, walked out and got in the vehicle next to Hudson.

He looked over at her. Did he expect a kiss or something? she wondered. 'Well, let's get on with it.'

Hudson nodded, put the vehicle in gear and set off. He carried on in the direction he had been heading, skirting behind her accommodation unit and the next one, then down a steep hill. At the bottom he turned right and Sonja saw a cluster of more modest, but neat dwellings.

'Staff accommodation. It's a big improvement on what was here in the old days.'

'I'm not on a travel agents' familiarisation tour.'

He nodded, getting the message. 'OK. From here, the nearest camp is Robins Camp, about ten kilometres away. We'll go there tomorrow to get the flight out. Early. Be ready to leave here at zero-six-hundred.'

'Roger,' Sonja said. She would keep this businesslike.

Hudson turned right at a junction, driving in front of the staff quarters and following the edge of a wide open *vlei* below the dam wall. 'Off to the left back there is a short cut back to the main road to Robins; this way takes us on an even more circuitous route.'

'Then why are we taking it?' Sonja asked.

'It's pretty.' She frowned at him, but he grinned back. 'I'm joking. This road also leads to the Botswana border. It's not far from here, about twenty klicks.'

'OK.' That was good intelligence. If something happened with the aircraft she could think about cutting cross-country using this road and illegally crossing by road into Botswana. With Jed out of action, Sonja had to think that her plan to get Joanne to South Africa was the best approach. She would be closer there to the scene of the crime and on the trail that fed illegally poached wildlife products and plants into the terrorist organisation. They passed a lone, tall ilala palm tree and then Hudson changed gears as they entered a patch of thicker bush. He slowed down. 'What is it?'

'The lions were spotted around here this morning.'

'Brand, you know I'm not actually here to sightsee or go on a game drive.'

He nodded. 'Yup, I know, but I have a camp to manage and a business to run and my other guests will want to find these lions on their way back to camp this evening or tomorrow morning.'

She folded her arms. However, she now realised she had seen all the roads leading into the camp, which was what she needed to know. She could afford to relax for a little while, but not too long, as Flack was alone in their room.

Hudson leaned out the side of the vehicle, over the open top of the driver's door. 'Yes.'

'What?'

'Lion spoor. It's the three females. They've got four cubs with them.' He drove a little further, then stopped again.

'What now?'

He rubbed his chin. 'Something else. Interesting.'

'Can we get a move on?' Sonja checked her watch. 'It'll be dark soon.'

'Relax.'

'Easy for you to say,' she said. 'No one's been shooting at you lately.'

'No, in fact the last time I was shot at was with you.'

She couldn't hold back a small laugh. They both had scars from that last encounter, which she had hoped, at the time, would be her final gunfight. The problem was, the more time she had to herself, or even alone with Hudson, in the lovely bush house he looked after, the more the memories returned. Hudson was a kind guy and not the sort of man to raise a hand to a woman at all, but when they argued she was scared he would walk out on her, or that if she stayed and kept the argument going he might not be able to control himself. It was irrational, she knew, but her father, whom she had loved for all his faults, had hit both her and her mother.

In her more clear-sighted moments, Sonja knew she'd left because she wanted to spare herself the pain of a breakup and rejection. It was crazy, she was sure of it, but work helped. Hudson had been against her going to Mali to train the rangers in what they both knew was a hot conflict zone. But she had felt valued, even more so when Jed had come looking for her. Jed had been almost apologetic, as if it wasn't really his idea to recruit her, and he had not pressured her, but she realised she had needed to go. By throwing herself into the mission, training beforehand, working on her fitness, getting back on the shooting range, she had been able to keep the bad memories at bay.

And she had avoided having the discussion Hudson had been edging towards.

'What are you thinking?' he asked.

She looked at him. 'Escape plans, fields of fire, cover, the usual stuff.'

He shook his head slowly. 'Usual for someone in a war. We're not enemies, Sonja.'

'No. But I'm stuck with this mission, for now, at least.'

He sat up a little straighter in his seat. 'Does that mean you might come back here when you're done?'

'Trouble is,' she said, honestly, 'I don't know what "done" looks like in this mission, unless I can somehow crack a pipeline between poaching and terrorism. It's a long shot. Flack is lying to me, I'm sure of it. She knows more than she's letting on about who's trying to kill her and why.'

Hudson rubbed his chin with his free hand and steered with the other. 'Maybe she's scared.'

'Given the aim of the guys who were after her, she should be.'

'Terrorist vendetta?' Hudson shook his head. 'I'm not buying it. Money? If it ain't religion – and I don't think this is – then it's money. Or love.'

Sonja snorted. 'I don't think it's love. Spurned or jealous lovers don't use AK-47s and M4s, not even in Africa.'

129

Out of habit, not because she was looking for animals, Sonja scanned the bush around them, looking right to left in a 180-degree arc. It was an old soldier's trick – English-speaking people learned to read left to right and tended to move their eyes in that direction when looking around them, but soldiers trained themselves to look in the opposite direction, which forced the head to move slower and the eyes to work harder and not gloss over details. In the middle of the burned-out *vlei* she spotted movement, a female warthog with two piglets. The mother had raised her head from the fresh green shoots that were sprouting through the black grass ash, and it was that tiny movement Sonja had seen.

The mother took off, her acceleration putting a Ferrari to shame, and her young kept close behind her antenna-like tail. 'What spooked them?'

Hudson looked up, scanning the veld. 'Well, I'll be …' Hudson took out his binoculars, held them to his eyes with one hand and pointed with the other. 'Cheetah!'

Sonja twisted in her seat and saw the blur of spots and the swoosh of the cheetah's long tail, which it used as a rudder as it adjusted its course. Sonja's heart was in her mouth as she watched the chase. 'Run!'

'Who are you rooting for, the cheetah or the pigs?' Hudson laughed.

'Both.' It wasn't true – she was just talking tough. Sonja couldn't bear the thought of one of the little ones being taken. She breathed a deep sigh when the cheetah broke off the chase, admitting defeat, and the warthogs disappeared in a cloud of dust over a low rise.

'Look!' Hudson pointed again, and when she followed his line of sight she saw what he was looking at. Two more cheetah, the same age and size as the first, emerged from the long golden grass at the edge of the burned plain. 'Well, that's some sighting. I saw their spoor on the ground before, but didn't want to get your hopes up.'

'Hah!' Sonja reached for his binoculars and he passed them to her. She had spotted something else and was focusing on an anthill beneath a tall leadwood tree.

'What you got, hotshot?' he asked.

'I'll see your three cheetah and raise you a leopard.'

'No way.'

It was her turn to point. Lying on top of the anthill, the leopard, a big male judging by his size and the girth of his neck and muscled shoulders, had been watching the action on the *vlei*, one big paw folded languidly across the other. He got up, sauntered down from his vantage point, and lowered his body to the ground as he moved towards the three cheetah, who were now reunited.

'He's stalking them,' Sonja said breathlessly. Now she felt fear for the cheetahs. Predators, she knew, not only hunted for food, but also to eliminate their competition. A leopard didn't have a cheetah's speed, but if he could sneak close enough to the other cats through the grass and then pounce, one of the slighter, weaker cats would have little chance of survival.

They sat there in silence, though Sonja wanted to call out a warning as the cheetahs wandered blithely into a patch of thick reed and the leopard increased his pace to intercept them.

A moment later two of the cheetah exploded from cover, running for their lives as the warthogs had a few minutes earlier, the tables turned on them. Sonja's heart pounded and she feared she would see the bulky leopard emerge carrying a dead cheetah by the throat.

Instead the third cheetah bounded out and away.

They waited a while, but there was no sign of the leopard, which had slunk off in search of another victim.

Sonja exhaled loudly. 'We should be getting back.'

'That was something. Do you want me to check on Joanne?'

'I'd rather do it myself.' Her pulse had returned to normal, her mind back on the job. Mentally she chastised herself for letting the natural spectacle distract her.

Hudson unclipped a radio handset from the dashboard. 'Mishack, Mishack, this is Hudson.'

'Go, Hudson,' came Mishack's reply a few seconds later.

'Mishack, can you please check on Mrs Flack and report back, over?'

'Affirmative.'

Hudson drove off from the sighting, not in any hurry from what Sonja could see. She had to admit it was a nice time of day to be out in the open for a drive. The setting sun was red, which magnified and enhanced the layer of dry season dust it was bedding down into. The air was warm and dry but not too hot, and the sounds and smells of the bush were soothing.

'Hudson, Mishack,' said the voice over the radio.

'Go, Mishack,' Hudson said.

'Mrs Flack is fine. No problems, I'm fetching her a cold drink.'

'Copy, Mishack,' Hudson said. 'No unexpected arrivals at camp?'

'Negative, Hudson.'

'Roger, thanks, Mishack.' He turned to her. 'All quiet. Let's stop for a drink.'

She frowned.

'I'll get you back before dark, promise.'

Hudson turned around and they stopped at a spot near the tall lone palm tree she had noticed earlier. That was good, as she knew the camp was on the hills she could see in the distance, just a few minutes' drive away. For all intents and purposes, though, they were alone. Hudson had parked so the sun would set behind the palm.

They got out and Hudson opened the tailgate at the rear and lifted out a cooler box.

'Klipdrift and Coke Zero?'

'How romantic,' she said, 'you remembered. Just a single, OK?'

'Yes, I know you're on duty.'

He poured her a drink and took a small can of soda water for himself.

'You're not drinking?'

'I'm also on duty,' he said.

They stood there, close but not too close. In the distance, a lion began calling.

'I still love that sound,' she said.

'Never gets old, does it.'

She sipped her drink and nodded.

What am I doing? she asked herself. This handsome, kind, big, strong man liked her – loved her maybe – and he had not judged her or criticised her for leaving him to take the job in Mali. They had been living together in a beautiful place and all she could think about, nearly every single day, was how long it was going to last before something happened to destroy their idyll.

She looked at him and she had to swallow hard because he was looking into her eyes now, fixing her with them, like a butterfly to a cork board. Inside she was squirming and...

He came to her and took her drink, setting it on the fender of the Cruiser. He put down his can too, then took her in his arms and held her tight.

'I've got you,' he said into her ear.

She started to wriggle in his embrace, feeling the pull towards him, the heat rising in her, and at the same time the overwhelming sense of being trapped. But he didn't let her go. He held her tighter and said the same words in her ear over and over, until at last she kissed him.

He waltzed her backwards, closer to the vehicle as she fed on him, drank from his lips. She registered him reaching for something. A blanket, which he must have kept in the back of the vehicle. He was Hudson Brand, ladies' man and safari guide, after all. Part of her was annoyed that he'd been doing some planning, but most of her was grateful, and a little amused as he quickly broke from her and did a Sir Walter Raleigh, laying it out like a cloak on the ground, which was stubbled from where some earlier fire had scythed the long grass.

They lay together and she let him undress her, slowly, under the red-gold sky.

The palm reminded her of the Delta, where she had grown up and been happy and then sad, and the Middle East, where she'd experienced the same highs and lows, but she realised, with something akin to a shiver or a shock, that she was home now. It wasn't a place, it was wherever she felt safe.

He was over her now, looking down at her with those big dark eyes that no longer fixed her but rather enfolded her. She felt his fingers on her, and his tongue, and she knew that he more than any man, perhaps even more than poor dear Sam, knew her, inside and out.

She opened herself to him and let him in because she knew that all he had to do was kiss her and she would be ready. Her body, thank God, was not as screwed-up as her mind and it, at least, was happy to live in the moment.

Very happy.

She closed her eyes for a while, just savouring the feel of him, the completeness of him being part of her. It felt so damn good that she wondered why she couldn't make it last. When she opened her eyes again she saw that his had morphed once more. What she saw, what she revelled in, was the look of absolute lust in them.

Sonja arched and drew him in, raked him and bit him, and his grunt of pain and pleasure tipped her over the edge, like she was tumbling, helpless, over the edge of Victoria Falls, and didn't care what was at the bottom.

Chapter 10

Thandi rose early the next morning and dressed before the dawn. Her daughter would be taking the grandchildren to school today. At 5.30 am there was a toot outside her door and she went out to the ageing Volkswagen Kombi.

SS owned the minibus and was behind the wheel. She greeted the others as she climbed in and was welcomed with the smell of coffee from an open flask. Laurel passed her a cup and Baye handed her a box of Ouma rusks. White people's food was not the best, but it was filling.

Thandi dunked a rusk in her travel cup and then screwed on the lid so as not to spill any coffee as SS set off to do battle with Johannesburg's morning traffic.

Thandi oscillated between trying to enjoy the fact that someone else was driving for a change and being terrified every time SS changed lanes. He seemed to think that one used one's indicator after already crossing the white line. Several times he cut off other drivers way too close for her liking and swore at them in Afrikaans. Thandi decided the best course of action was to keep her eyes off the road.

Johannesburg traffic had two speeds – fast and stopped. When it worked it was a sight to behold, a thing of beauty, a 120-kilometre-per-hour humming, rolling embodiment of *ubuntu*, with everyone travelling together as one, watchful and efficient, exciting and forward moving. When it went wrong, of course, it was a disaster.

Thandi reflected, sadly, that she had probably seen more death in her time as an Uber driver than she had in the war. The road statistics in her adopted country did not bear thinking about.

She thought about what she had seen yesterday. 'Laurel,' she said, picking some rusk crumbs off her ample bosom, 'you're a good friend of Joanne – do you know if she sold one of the cycads from her garden recently?'

Laurel tapped a finger against her lips as she pondered the question. Thandi thought that Laurel, although by no means the eldest of them, would have trouble remembering what she had for breakfast, let alone an event of the past week. '*Ja*; no, I don't think so.'

'Think hard, please, Laurel. When did you last visit her home?'

The younger woman's brow crinkled in concentration. 'Well, maybe, yes, but it wasn't this past week as Joanne was in England. I have Pilates on Tuesday and I get my nails done on Wednesdays, so it wouldn't have been one of those days.'

'You get your nails done every Wednesday?'

Laurel blinked. 'Duh.'

'So?'

'So my day for discretionary shopping, or visits to friends, is Thursday, but I went to lunch at Sandton last Thursday while Joanne was away. It must have been the week *before*. In fact, *ja*, I remember I combined a shopping trip with a visit to Joanne that week – we went to the garden centre. How's that for multi-tasking, hey?'

'What did you buy?' Thandi asked patiently.

'Nothing. Joanne bought a granadilla vine.'

'Not a cycad?'

Laurel drew a deep breath. 'Thandi, I might not be some high-flying Uber magnate but I do know the difference between a granadilla and a cycad.'

'Why is the garden centre so important?' Jacqueline asked, turning her head. The Queen had, of course, commandeered the front passenger seat, next to SS. She maintained it was because she suffered from car sickness, but everyone knew Her Majesty was all about status – most of them had bad backs, or arthritis, or at least something wrong with them. Thandi was saving for a double knee replacement.

'Oh, nothing,' Thandi said. 'Joanne didn't talk to you about buying any other new plants lately, did she?'

'No.' Jacqueline returned her gaze to the front. 'SS, watch that *bakkie*. And slow down, we want to arrive in one piece, not a million. You're not actually a taxi driver, you know?'

'Yes, Your Majesty,' SS said under his breath, but Jacqueline heard and folded her arms.

'Thandi?' Baye said from the back of the van.

Thandi turned and saw that Baye had looked up from a copy of *Women's Health*. She paused and brushed some strands of dark hair from her face. 'Are you the self-appointed chief investigator into Joanne?'

Thandi cleared her throat. 'Well...'

'It's all right if you are. Are we all agreed?' Baye craned her head to survey the van.

There was a murmur of 'yeses' and 'ayes'.

'We agreed we would try and work out what Joanne was doing before she left for the UK, yes,' Thandi said.

'She was worried about her son-in-law losing his job,' Baye said.

'Yes, I believe so,' Thandi said.

'Her daughter was supporting her, more or less, apart from the money she earned working on the Arab's game reserve.'

Thandi noticed that Baye's face looked like she had just sucked a lemon. Having fought for the Israeli Defence Force she seemed to harbour some prejudices.

'She had to lay off her gardener,' Thandi said, more to herself than anyone in particular.

'Really?' Sandy, sitting in her wheelchair at the back of the bus, sounded genuinely horrified. 'Poor Isaac. He was a thoroughly decent chap.'

'He's still alive, Sandy,' Thandi said.

'Of course. I just meant that he and Joanne got on very well,' Sandy said.

'So we know Joanne had financial problems. Most of us do,' Charles Borg said. 'It's the economy, you know. The rand keeps falling and even though Joanne's daughter must have had enough to get her to England, one's money just disappears when one travels abroad.'

'*Eish*, that's for sure,' Stephen said, keeping his eye on the road lest he invoke Jacqueline's ire again. 'Do you know how much a beer is in Perth? One hundred *ront*! I'm telling you, when I went to see my son over there I couldn't even afford to get pissed, man.'

Most of them laughed, but Jacqueline frowned at the profanity and Thandi's mind whirred.

From Pretoria the N4 was straight and uninterrupted as it cut through the farmers' fields and the endless blue skies of the High-veld. They slowed a little as they passed Witbank, a sprawling mining town that straddled the motorway and had changed its name to eMalahleni, which meant 'place of coal'. Jacqueline de-creed that they would stop halfway to Nelspruit, to give SS a break and for them all to use the bathroom.

Stephen took an exit ramp and pulled up at one of the fuel pumps at the Alzu service centre. While Stephen supervised the two-man pit crew that set to checking water and oil, filling the tank and cleaning the windows, Thandi and the others eased their tired, cramped limbs out of the Kombi. Charles opened the rear and used the ramps SS had packed to wheel Sandy out.

'Fifteen minutes, people, not a moment more,' Jacqueline commanded.

Thandi took her handbag and walked slowly towards the crowded complex, which consisted of the filling station shop, a cafe and Spur steak restaurant. Once inside she found the place crowded with people, many dressed in the tourist's uniform of khaki tops and green cargo pants with zip-off legs. She heard a mix of languages and had to negotiate her way around a dozen Italians who had clustered in front of the wall-mural map of the Lowveld.

To her great relief there was no queue to get into the ladies' bath-room. When she was done she went to the Mugg & Bean on-the-go cafe and ordered herself a 'serious' cappuccino and a generous wedge of lemon meringue pie for the road. She checked her watch and decided to make the most of the break by walking outside and down some stairs to a viewing platform which looked over the farm behind the service centre.

The animals here were not of the domestic variety, but rather an assortment of game. Thandi could see a pair of white rhinos, a mother and a baby, with their horns removed to deter poachers, twenty or more cape buffalo drinking from a concrete water trough, and in the distance a herd of a dozen sable antelope. Around her, tourists snapped pictures and selfies.

'I suppose the owners of this place think that if they keep their rhinos in plain sight, in the open, that's the best protection for them.'

Thandi turned and saw Charles standing behind her. He sipped from a can of Coca-Cola.

'Sometimes standing in the open is the best form of concealment,' Thandi said, nodding.

'You would have done that, during the Bush War.'

She nodded. 'In civilian clothes we were indistinguishable from our comrades, especially us women.'

'Which made you all the more dangerous.'

She didn't reply, but thought about his words. 'Do you think Joanne was hiding in plain sight – a poacher prominent in the cycad society, and an office bearer as well?'

He shrugged. 'I do know that she went to the garden centre and bought a cycad the Wednesday before last.'

Thandi raised her eyebrows. 'You didn't say anything when we were talking in the van.'

'You didn't ask me. Besides, I don't like to cast aspersions on friends in front of others.' He held up his free hand when he saw her open her mouth to reply. 'Don't get me wrong, Thandi, I think it's good you are trying to find out what happened, and not condemning Joanne outright, but we have to be careful this doesn't turn into a witch hunt. Joanne can be a prickly character, I'm sure you'll agree, and not everyone got on with her.'

She thought a moment, then nodded again.

'Baye and Joanne had that business together, for a while. Do you remember?'

Thandi pursed her lips. 'That was before my time, but I've heard it mentioned. Wasn't it a coffee shop in the mall?'

Charles nodded. 'Yes. Baye put a lot of her late husband's life insurance money into the business and Joanne borrowed some money from her daughter to invest as well. It didn't last.'

'Something about the rents in the mall being too high?'

Charles said nothing.

Thandi looked at him, waiting.

Charles sipped his drink.

'Was there more to it?'

'Like I said, it didn't last–the coffee shop, that is.'

Thandi mulled the information over in her mind. Joanne and Baye had never seemed the best of friends, though they had once been close enough to go into business together.

'I've seen that sort of thing happen before,' Charles said.

'What?'

'Friends going into business. It never works out. You think you have complementary skills–one person is good at bringing in customers, at working the crowd, drumming up business, and the other is good at actually running things behind the scenes. What soon happens is that the partners begin to resent each other, each thinking their skills are more important than the other's.'

Thandi raised her eyebrows. 'Is that what happened with Baye and Joanne?'

Charles shrugged. 'I don't know for sure, but for a while there Baye stopped coming to the society meetings and when she did return she didn't speak to Joanne for some time.'

'But they've been talking since I've known them.'

'Of course,' Charles said. 'It's probably water under the bridge now.'

'Hmmm.'

'Bus is leaving!' Jacqueline called from the top of the stairs above the viewing area.

Thandi and Charles started the walk back to the Kombi. Thandi thought about the information she had learned. Baye might be quicker than some of the others to judge Joanne unfairly. And were Joanne's financial problems also related to her failed business venture with Baye?

She and Charles were last on the bus.

'Have a nice chat?' Baye asked from the rear of the van, fanning herself with her magazine.

'We were looking at the rhinos.' Thandi slid across onto her seat. 'Did you see them?'

'It's risky having them here,' Baye said. 'Anyone could take a pot shot at them.'

'Charles and I were discussing that,' Thandi countered. 'Sometimes it's better to hide in plain view, don't you think?'

Baye narrowed her eyes but said nothing. Thandi looked back to the front of the van as she clicked her seatbelt home. 'All set.'

'Next stop, Nelspruit,' Jacqueline declared. 'Forward, SS, and don't spare the German horses.'

'*Jawohl*, my Queen.'

They all laughed. Except, Thandi noticed as she glanced backwards, Baye.

Chapter 11

Hudson drove Sonja and Joanne to Robins Camp that morning and, to Sonja's discomfort, kissed her goodbye in front of everyone as they boarded Andrew 'Thousand' Miles's twin engine Beechcraft for the first leg of the trip to South Africa.

'How's business, Thousand?' Hudson asked the pilot as Sonja and Joanne seated themselves.

'*So-so*, Hudson. I'm diversifying.'

'How so?' Brand asked.

'I've got a rich American client, a big game hunter doctor who owns a chain of plastic surgery clinics. He's mad about old aircraft. He and I have a fully restored Huey, a UH-1D Iroquois helicopter, Vietnam vintage, that we bought from a collector in South Africa and a Hawker Hunter ground-attack jet aircraft, same type I flew in Rhodesia during the war. We've put them in a hangar in Lanseria and our plan was for me and an old *toppie* named Charles Borg, who still has his chopper licence, to take tourists up in both of them on joy flights. The problem is these old aircraft cost a fortune to maintain. They're on the ground most of the time, so I'll have to take you for a flip next time you're down south.'

'I might take you up on that, but those aircraft sound older than I am.'

'The Hunter probably is. But if you get any rich clients coming through Nantwich who want a joy flight, let me know. My investor's getting nervous. Charles, my other pilot, is virtually destitute, poor guy, so he really needs the tips.'

Joanne leaned forward. 'Did you say Charles *Borg*?'

'Yes,' Andrew said.

'I know him.'

'I'm not surprised,' Andrew replied. 'He does have an eye for beautiful women. Please don't tell him I let on about his financial situation, he's a terribly proud old guy.'

'I won't.'

Sonja noticed that Joanne fell silent, obviously taken aback by this news.

'Time for me to start up,' Andrew said.

'Roger that,' Hudson said to the pilot. He blew Sonja a kiss as Miles closed the aircraft door.

'You didn't tell me Hudson was your boyfriend,' Joanne said to Sonja as they took off from the gravel airstrip and passed over Robins Camp.

'He's not,' Sonja said over the noise of the engines, which were straining as Thousand took them higher. Hudson had been charming over dinner at the lodge, but had not let on there was anything between him and Sonja. She had felt relieved, and when she had returned to the room she was sharing with the Flack woman and gone for a shower, she felt sure Joanne could guess what she had been up to. Apparently, she hadn't.

Joanne had not slept well the night before, no doubt still troubled by the attack on the Zambezi River, and Sonja had decided to stay awake, keeping watch. She was used to sleepless nights and like the soldier she had been she was normally good at falling asleep anywhere. She had counted on sleeping on the flight, even though it would be a short one, but rest eluded her.

Bloody Hudson.

Part of her felt weak for having given into his romantic ploy, stopping for sundowners, but she argued back that sex was a normal human function and she needed it as much as anyone else. But on duty? She thought of Jed and felt guilty for deserting her post temporarily by lying down in the dry grass with Hudson.

But, it had felt so damn good to be with him again.

That was the problem with Brand. She couldn't think rationally, normally, around him. He screwed with her mind just as expertly as he played her body. Sonja wanted to get him out of her head and just sleep for half an hour. She closed her eyes and rested her head against the Perspex window, hoping the thrumming vibrations might lull her to sleep.

Sonja awoke with a jolt as the aircraft's wheels squealed on the tarmac. She yawned and looked at her watch, realising she had slept for no more than ten minutes. Sonja and Joanne let the tourists off the aircraft first. When they were gone the pilot came to them.

'OK, you've got two hours, then I need to leave. That should give you plenty of time to sort your paperwork.' Thousand indicated the terminal building. 'A guy I know, a local fixer, should be waiting to pick you up inside. His name is Boss.'

Sonja and Joanne walked across the tarmac while Andrew secured his aircraft and climbed up on the wing to ready it for refuelling. Inside the terminal there was a man dressed in black suit pants and a white long-sleeved business shirt fraying at the cuffs and collar. He held a piece of paper that read *Mrs Kurtz*.

She went to him and he smiled.

'Get rid of that sign,' she said to him.

Boss looked a little disappointed by her rude greeting, but nodded and stuffed the paper into his pocket. 'I am sorry.'

'Don't be,' she replied, forcing a smile, 'just take us to town. Do you know a Dr Elena Rodrigues?'

'Yes. She is Cuban. Her clinic is in Fife Street.'

'Take us to her.'

They went to his car, a battered old sky-blue Isuzu double cab *bakkie* that had seen better decades. Sonja had specified that they needed a driver with a pickup truck or similar. Sonja and Joanne got in the back seat. Boss drove at a leisurely pace and Sonja drummed her fingers on the door.

Joanne stared out the window. 'I went to school here.'

Sonja didn't reply.

'It was a lovely city.' They entered the built-up area. 'But it all just looks so ... *tired*.'

144

'We are praying that things will change soon,' Boss said from the front, smiling into his rear-view mirror.

'Aren't we all?' Joanne said.

Sonja wondered if she was talking about Zimbabwe or her life.

Boss slowed to a crawl as he carefully negotiated the city's traffic. Bulawayo had the look of a stately old matron, down on her luck, but trying to keep up appearances. The buildings dated either from the early twentieth or late nineteenth century, interspersed with some concrete eyesores from the 1960s. The streets were wide enough to turn a bullock dray, or to squeeze in more parking down the centre line.

Sonja wound down the window and caught the scent of hot buttered corn roasting over a roadside charcoal brazier. A man sat on the sidewalk repairing shoes, a woman dressed for the office carried a bag of mealie meal on her head. Some of the shopfronts they passed were boarded up, others seemed to be clinging on to life like terminal patients hoping for a miracle cure. For all the country's economic woes there was hustle and bustle, and Bulawayo seemed to be pretty much as it had been the last time she had visited it, just making do.

Boss parked outside what might once have been a fashionable apartment block for young professionals, but was now tired and rundown. Not just the windows, but whole balconies were enclosed with rusting burglar bars, and stained sheets served as curtains in several of the flats. On the ground floor was an old shopfront with one frosted window and another pane replaced with a sheet of plywood. The words *Dr Elena Rodrigues, MD* were engraved on a plaque that had been screwed to the temporary window. On either side were vacant shops.

'This must be the place,' Sonja said.

Joanne got out of the car at the same time. 'Many of Zim's doctors come from Cuba, or Nigeria.'

Asking Boss to wait in the *bakkie*, Sonja led the way in. The waiting room was crowded, standing room only. A couple of babies competed in a decibel contest, an old man coughed into a handkerchief and everyone else sat or stood with an air of bored resignation. Sonja went to a reassuringly plump woman behind the counter. At least someone was getting their daily calorie intake. Just audible over the sounds of the patients was something that sounded like clucking.

Eventually the woman looked up from her ageing computer. 'Yes?'

Sonja noted the lack of a polite greeting and, when she peered past the woman, saw the source of the non-human noise. A chicken bobbed its head within the confines of a cage on the floor behind the receptionist. Sonja wondered if it was trying to reach a cardboard box full of vegetables nearby.

'My name is Schmidt. I'm here to see Dr Rodrigues. My friend, Hudson Brand, phoned the doctor.'

The woman looked at her over the top of her spectacles then down at the desk diary in front of her. She picked up the phone, pushed a button, then spoke into the receiver. 'The *American* is here.'

Sonja didn't like the way the woman described her, nor her tone, but held her tongue. In any case, the door opened and a frail-looking, painfully elderly white couple shuffled out. The man wore shorts and long socks up to his bony, knobbly knees and the woman was using a Zimmer frame.

'I will see you next week, Mr and Mrs Byrne,' the woman behind them said.

Sonja took in the dark curly hair, the coffee complexion, eyes made bigger by sunken cheeks. Her black high-heel boots below her white lab coat were scuffed and too big for her skinny legs. She would have looked better with an extra few kilos, Sonja thought.

The doctor raised her thick dark eyebrows, which she had taken some care with. 'Mrs Schmidt? Come in.'

Sonja glanced around her. None of the other patients, some of whom must have been waiting a long time, seemed to have the inclination–perhaps even the strength–to raise an objection. Sonja looked to the receptionist. 'Miss.'

'You will be paying in *Yoosa*–US dollars, cash, yes?'

Sonja nodded.

'Come in, please.' The doctor smiled. She ushered Sonja and Joanne ahead of her, down a hallway where curls of peeling lime-green paint drooped slowly but inevitably towards a cracked linoleum floor. The woman opened the door to her consulting room, which at least smelled of fresh paint. 'Elena Rodrigues.'

Sonja took her hand and introduced Joanne.

'Please, take a seat.' Dr Rodrigues sat. 'Now, which of you is sick?'

'Neither of us, we're here to talk business,' Sonja said.

'OK.' The doctor stood again, reached into the pocket of her lab coat and took out a packet of Zimbabwean Newbury cigarettes. She offered the pack to them, as a reluctant afterthought.

'No, thank you,' Sonja said. Joanne reached for one then pulled back, shaking her head.

Elena went around her desk to a window and opened it, onto an atrium of sorts. Sonja could see discarded, broken furniture outside. Elena leaned against the windowsill. 'This is the only break I will get today, and since I'm not actually treating either of you, well...'

'Fine.' Sonja didn't care if the woman smoked, though the smell of her lighting up stirred an old craving.

'You are friend of Hudson?' Elena exhaled out the window.

'Yes.'

She picked a flake of tobacco off her tongue, then smiled. 'Good friend?'

Sonja didn't like the woman's grin. Hudson hadn't told her exactly how he knew Elena. Her curiosity was piqued. 'Just an acquaintance. I've used him as a private investigator in the past. Purely professional.'

The doctor nodded as she inhaled, then aimed her smoke more or less out the window again. 'Shame, as they say in South Africa. You look like his type.'

Sonja fumed. 'I wouldn't know. How did *you* meet him?'

She gave a little shrug and a reminiscing smile. 'Business and socially.'

Sonja gritted her teeth, took a breath and told herself to be calm. 'When did you see him last?'

'He come to town sometime, you know? Last time I have to give him a check-up.' She seemed to hold back a laugh. 'He is very *fit*, as the English say, yes?'

Sonja clenched her fists by her sides. 'I hadn't noticed.'

'Um,' Joanne interrupted, 'someone said something about business?'

Sonja ignored Joanne. 'Did you socialise with him when he came to Bulawayo last time for his *check-up*?'

Elena shrugged again and reached through the open window to stub out her cigarette on the exterior brickwork. 'What you care? I thought you say you were just, what, *acquaintance*?'

'I don't care.'

The doctor closed the window and put her hands together, even rubbing them a little as she went to her desk. 'OK, you, Joanne, are right. Is time for business, yes?'

Sonja was seething. Hudson was clearly close to this woman and hadn't seen fit to mention it. She wondered why she even bothered.

'I need to get out of Zimbabwe,' Joanne said, filling the void while Sonja quietly stewed. 'Unofficially, if you know what I mean?'

Elena leaned back in her office chair, which creaked. She said nothing.

Sonja forced her mind back on track. 'Brand said you issue fake death certificates.'

Elena put a finger to her lips. 'Not so loud, OK?'

It was Sonja's turn to shrug. 'Can you help us or not?'

'He tell you that?'

Sonja nodded.

It was Elena's turn to screw her mouth up. 'I no know what you talking about.'

'He was very specific.' Sonja unzipped her backpack and took out a fat white envelope. She saw by the way Elena's eyes were drawn to it that she didn't need to say what was in it. 'Hudson told me that during one of his jobs as a private investigator he uncovered a ring of criminals in Zimbabwe who were helping people fake their own deaths and lodge fraudulent life insurance claims. He said you were the doctor who was issuing fake death certificates.'

She folded her arms. 'I have never issued a fake certificate.'

Sonja gave a small smile. Hudson had explained this to her. 'Of course. My bad. The certificates are *real*, you just enter false details.'

The doctor remained tight-lipped.

'There's five thousand US dollars in that envelope.' Fortunately the CIA was nothing if not generous with the emergency funds it supplied operatives in the field; she had been carrying the cash with her in a money belt since she arrived in Zimbabwe.

Elena pushed it away, back towards Sonja and Joanne.

'Sheesh,' Sonja said, 'you can get a person killed for real for less than that in South Africa. Take the money.'

'I no do that sort of thing. Even if I did in the past, is over.' She reached for her packet of cigarettes and started to take another one out, then seemed to think better of it. 'Hudson really tell you I am a criminal?'

It was Sonja's turn to stay quiet now. The silence hung between the three of them.

Elena looked at the envelope, no doubt imagining what she could do with that sort of money.

'I don't have any more,' Sonja said. 'We need to get to South Africa.'

Elena looked up at them, first to Sonja, then to Joanne. 'This is for insurance claim, yes? These companies, they not so easy to fool any more.'

Joanne shook her head, vigorously. 'No, not at all. There are people ... after me. Trying to kill me. I need to cover my tracks.'

'Hmmm.'

Sonja leaned forward. 'I want you to do something else for us.'

'What?'

'We don't want to cover this up, Elena. I want the people who are chasing Joanne to find out she's dead. Do you know anyone on the local newspaper, or a policeman, maybe? They always blab to journalists.'

She thought a moment. 'Both.'

'I'm not a criminal,' Joanne said, pleading.

Sonja wasn't so sure of that, but she added: 'Joanne's telling the truth.'

'Well, I am no criminal, either,' Elena said. 'At least not any more.'

Sonja swallowed. 'Hudson told me to tell you something else.'

The doctor looked up again, her face brightening, and Sonja felt but suppressed another jolt of anger. 'He told me to remind you that he gave you a warning, last time, that allowed you to get across the border to Botswana and escape a certain policewoman, a Sergeant Khumalo, I think her name was, who was after you.'

Elena sighed. It didn't seem to be the message she was hoping for. 'Khumalo got transferred to Harare. She no longer a problem for me. Is why I am back here in Bulawayo.'

Sonja waited.

'Please,' Joanne said.

Elena puffed her cheeks and blew out a long breath. Sonja caught the nicotine in the air and her stomach turned. Elena took up the envelope, opened it and flicked through the crisp bills. 'OK. Just this once. For Hudson.'

Sonja ground her teeth while the doctor filled out the paperwork.

When she was done they all stood and Elena took the US dollars out of the envelope and folded the bills. She reached under her coat and into her blouse and stuffed the money in her bra. She put the certificate in the envelope and handed it to Joanne.

'Here you are. You are dead.'

Chapter 12

Sonja had Boss stop at a small supermarket on the edge of Bulawayo. She had spied the sign she was looking for on the way into town – *Cell phone recharge and coffins.*

The AIDS pandemic had meant roadside headstone carvers, cut-price undertakers and coffin makers were a feature of every town, no matter how small, in sub-Saharan Africa.

'What now?' Joanne asked.

'We need a coffin for you.'

Boss's eyes widened. 'Serious?'

'Yes, Boss, serious. We're going to stay outside. You go in, buy a coffin and six ten-kilogram bags of mealie meal.' She counted off most of her remaining US cash and handed it to him. Now his eyes lit up. 'Hurry.'

They waited and Sonja took Joanne away from the vehicle, to the shade of a mango tree that sprouted from the kerb, so that the store worker who carried the coffin and the maize meal to the truck would not see them.

'Six ten-kilo bags?' Joanne raised her eyebrows.

'Yes, to simulate your weight.'

'You're too kind. You probably should have added an extra bag.'

Sonja ignored the levity. 'You have to help me, Joanne. Tell me what's really going on.'

The older woman put her hands on her hips and looked Sonja in the eye. 'I wish I knew.'

Sonja wasn't buying it. Flack was hiding something, of that she was sure.

'What I can tell you,' Joanne went on, 'hand on heart, is that I did not sell that rare cycad to anyone or send it anywhere, nor did I steal the Pretoria Cycad and Firearm Appreciation Society's bank balance – something else I've been accused of. The theft of the money was obviously part of a plot to frame me.'

'Whatever you say. I don't care about your society's petty cash box, but what we *do* know is that some terrorists in Mali wound up with what they thought was the rare cycad, but turned out to be a fake. Assuming that it was a substitute plant that was stolen from your society's premises – let's forget about what happened to the real female *woodii* for now – who could have done that, switched one for the other and sold the stand-in to the Malians?'

She shrugged. 'Any member of our society.'

'How?'

'There was a key hidden in a pot plant outside the committee room door. We all knew where it was. The only other person who knew the cycad was there was one of the members' son-in-law, and he's a policeman. He's the one who gave it to us for safekeeping because he didn't trust his own station's evidence lock-up. If he was crooked the plant would never have found its way to us.'

'Are you telling me everything?' Sonja asked.

Joanne glanced away for a moment. 'Yes.'

Sonja guessed there was more, but right now she would take anything she could get her hands on. 'Who's trying to kill you?'

'The jihadis – the friends of the guy I killed in London, I suppose.'

Sonja shook her head. 'Think harder. I think this is about money, Joanne, not religion or terrorism.'

It just didn't add up, Sonja thought. She still didn't believe that story, nor in the number of coincidences that seemed to be attached to Joanne Flack. If Sonja was right, and Joanne was lying, and she had in fact stolen the cycad and smuggled a substitute out of the country and into Mali, then who was trying to kill her? If she had fulfilled a deal, had she double-crossed someone along the way? Or was it really, as she maintained, some terrorists with a grudge?

Sonja lowered her voice as Boss and a couple of staff from the store began shifting the coffin and bags of maize meal outside and to the vehicle. 'I don't care if you switched the plants and you have the real *woodii* hidden somewhere, or if you stole it, or whatever. My mission is to pick up the trail between poachers and terrorists, and *you* are going to help me, or I'll leave you on the roadside for whoever it is who's trying to kill me. Understand?'

Joanne gave a small nod.

They arrived at Bulawayo Airport and Boss drove them to the general aviation area and a cargo hangar. Andrew Miles was there to meet them.

'Thanks, Boss,' Andrew said. 'Please unload the coffin and the mealie meal and you can leave us.'

Sonja took her cue and paid Boss. When the driver had gone, she and Joanne helped Andrew load the bags of maize meal into the coffin. Andrew took a battery-powered drill and some screws from a toolbox in the back of the aircraft. When he had finished securing the lid, they loaded it on board.

'Is this scam going to work?' Joanne asked him.

'I've got the paperwork, including your death certificate. I know the guys in South Africa. They're not big on detail and no one's likely to look inside the coffin. If they do they'll probably be happy with the mealie meal.' He laughed.

Sonja wasn't in the mood for joking.

'Make yourselves scarce, please, ladies,' Andrew continued, 'a gentleman from ZIMRA, the Zimbabwe Revenue Authority – customs – will be along shortly to inspect my *cargo*. We'll be leaving in about twenty minutes.'

As Andrew did his pre-flight inspection Sonja led Joanne away from the aircraft and behind a hangar. 'We need to find out who smuggled that cycad out of your garden centre office. If you still maintain you don't know, then I need to find out. I need to get access to your society.'

Joanne drew a deep breath. 'OK. Meetings are only once a month, but the group is all together now, for a few days. They've gone to the international cycad conference. It's being held in South Africa, in White River, near Nelspruit. Do you know it?'

'Yes. I used to live not far from there.' White River, Sonja re-called, was not far from Hazyview, the nearest town to where she had stayed with Hudson.

Sonja took out her phone and called Rod Cavanagh.

'Hello?' he said.

'Rod, Sonja here. How's Jed?' Sonja moved away from Joanne.

'Stable, but the company's put him on a medevac flight out of Victoria Falls. They don't want to risk a long-haul trip, so they're sending him to a private clinic in Johannesburg.'

'So we're on our own.'

'For now,' Rod said. 'Where are you?'

'On my way to South Africa.' She briefly filled Rod in on what was happening. 'How soon can you get there?'

'There's an afternoon flight today. I can make it. There's space, I checked.'

'OK. I'll WhatsApp you the address of a safe house – some peo-ple I know on the West Rand, Johannesburg. The package will be there. You know her…'

'Yes, and she hates me.'

Sonja exhaled. 'I don't care. Get the truth out of her. She's hiding something, probably the real cycad. She's too scared to come clean with me. I tried telling her I don't care about fucking plants, no matter how much they're worth. In the meantime I need to go to White River.'

'The cycad conference?'

'Yes. I'll be in touch.'

She ended the call, and as she approached Joanne, Andrew reap-peared, waving for them to come aboard the aircraft.

*

Throughout the flight to South Africa Joanne talked and Sonja took notes.

Joanne wondered how Sonja would pull this off. She wanted to know, as much as the Americans did, who had smuggled the cycad out of South Africa and how it had ended up in Mali.

'I don't need to pretend to be an expert, more a keen amateur,' Sonja said, looking up from the back of a sick bag – the only piece of paper she could find. It was covered in her notes about cycads. 'Tell me about the group members.'

'Everyone in the society is either ex-military or law enforcement, or they've been in a situation where they've had to defend themselves. They're not young, but neither are they senile. They're street smart and they'll be suspicious of someone trying to get too close to them too soon.'

'Males or females?'

'Both.' Joanne gave Sonja a quick rundown on Charles, Stephen, Baye, Sandy, Laurel, Thandi and Queen Jacqueline.

'Who's the best one to approach?' Sonja asked.

Joanne didn't have to think more than a second. 'Charles. He's a silver fox with a roving eye. Still fancies himself as a ladies' man, even though he'd be old enough, biologically, to be your father.'

Sonja gave a nod and made a note.

'You have something in common with all of them, though.'

Sonja looked up. 'What's that?'

'They all love guns.' Joanne described the post-meeting activities at the shooting range, and gave a summation of how each member had used a firearm in the past.

'So basically we're dealing with a heavily armed bunch of grandmas and grandpas.'

Joanne didn't like to think of herself that way, but she had to agree. 'Yes, I suppose so.'

'Who do I need to watch out for?'

Joanne frowned as she thought about that. 'Jacqueline is the queen bee – she'll be wary of a younger female trying to muscle her way in. Laurel and SS are harmless; Sandy's sharp and cynical and Baye is tough – she's ex–Israeli military.'

Sonja looked down at her notes again. 'You mentioned a Zimbabwean, Thandi Ngwenya?'

Joanne put a finger on her lips and nodded slowly. 'Yes. Be careful of her.'

'Why?' Sonja asked.

'Because she's the smartest of all of them.'

'Tell me.'

'She was a firebrand when she was young, active in the struggle for independence in Zimbabwe. Unlike a lot of her male comrades who were not very well trained she was an excellent shot, a natural leader and intelligent.' Joanne thought about what she knew about Thandi, her background and her personality, and as she related more of Thandi's life she came to the conclusion that Thandi, with her enquiring mind, would be the one in the group most likely to be digging right now, trying to work out exactly what Joanne had been up to. 'She's a former politician and an astute businesswoman.'

'Quite a lady,' Sonja said.

'Yes.'

'You don't think it could have been her who stole the cycad?'

Joanne shook her head. 'Absolutely not. She's a widow twice over, but she manages a fleet of cars now. Even if she was dirt poor, Thandi wouldn't steal.'

Sonja made some more notes. Andrew 'Thousand' Miles looked back from the cockpit and waved to them and Joanne could see he was pointing at two headsets. Joanne and Sonja both put them on so they could hear him as he flew.

'We've crossed the border,' Andrew said, his voice tinny and clipped by the microphone. 'Sonja, now that you want to go to the Lowveld I can put you down at Nelspruit, at the general aviation airfield just out of town.'

'That's fine, Andrew, thank you,' Sonja said.

'And me?' Joanne asked.

Sonja cut in: 'You'll still go to Lanseria. You'll be met there.'

'By who?'

'Rod Cavanagh.'

Joanne's stomach turned. 'Great.'

Sonja continued cramming knowledge about cycads as the flight droned on. Joanne answered her questions, but her mind had switched from the present to twenty-five years earlier, when she had been in love, or thought she had been.

Not with her husband, but with Rod Cavanagh.

Peta had been only five years old and Peter, after whom their daughter had been named, had made it quite clear they did not have enough money to have another child unless something changed dramatically in their lives.

It did. Her husband became a criminal.

Rod, playing the role of Marty Jacobs, a wealthy cycad collector, had come into her life when Joanne was at her lowest ebb, having just moved to South Africa. As well as them having no money, Joanne had her suspicions that Peter had been cheating on her. Rod – Marty – was handsome and charming and the chemistry between them had been undeniable.

Perversely, Peter had even encouraged her to flirt with the American as he tried to lure him into bigger and bigger illegal cycad deals, neither of them knowing that it was Rod who was playing Peter, giving him enough rope to hang himself. Joanne had been angry at Peter for using her as bait and it hadn't been hard for her to fall for the undercover agent's charms, nor his promise of a new life in America sometime in the future if she left Peter.

She had been played by both of them, but by the time of Peter's death she only truly loved one of them.

Chapter 13

Thandi poured herself a cup of tea and took a cupcake from the trestle table laid out in the foyer of the conference centre. The little sweet looked so tiny and lonely in her palm that she selected a friend for it.

'They look delicious.'

She turned and saw a woman smiling at her and pointing down at the cupcakes in her hand. Thandi felt a flush of guilt.

'I won't tell anyone you snuck a second.'

Thandi gave a guilty laugh. The rest of her group were together at the other side of the room, talking and sipping tea and coffee, and Thandi, who had just been to the bathroom in the break between lectures, had been about to join them. 'Excuse me.'

The woman started to move, to give her room, then paused. 'Sorry, can I just ask you a question?'

'Of course,' Thandi said.

'Do you know much about *Encephalartos hirsutus*?'

Thandi smiled. 'The Venda cycad? A little. It's a beautiful specimen.' The woman was attractive, but there was an edge to her, a hardness Thandi couldn't quite put her finger on. She had auburn hair that was greying at the roots, indicating that she didn't agonise over her trips to the salon, and blue eyes. Beneath them, however, was a pair of bags packed for a long holiday. This woman looked tired, though those eyes were alert. She wore a floral pants suit that

Thandi found quite hideous, but then white people were not generally known for their dress sense.

'This is my first conference,' the woman said. 'I'm Ursula.'

Thandi smiled and took the woman's hand. The grip was strong, almost mannish, which Thandi found refreshing. She shot a wistful glance towards her friends, but they didn't seem to be missing her. Thandi did not consider herself an overly sociable person, but these conferences were as much about promoting fellowship and sharing ideas and the love of cycads as they were about technical knowledge and tips.

'Nice to meet you, Ursula. My name is Thandi.'

'I'd like to buy a Venda cycad, but I've heard they're terribly rare and, as a result, very expensive.'

Thandi nodded as she took a bite of one of the cupcakes. She couldn't resist. 'Hm-mm.'

'I'm new to the business so I don't know the ins and outs of the trade yet. Though no one has any money these days, right?'

Thandi swallowed. 'I hope you're not asking me if I know where you can get an illegally sourced cycad?'

The woman held up her hands. 'Oh heavens, no! No, no, no, not at all. My daughter works in nature conservation. She'd shoot me with her pink Glock if she thought I'd bought something that had been poached from the wild.'

This conversation was turning bizarre, Thandi thought. 'A pink Glock?'

Ursula rolled her eyes. 'I know, right? I told her, "Don't be so girly". A gun's a gun and you don't need to be charged more for it because of its colour.'

'Of course.' Thandi was noncommittal.

'Silly me,' the woman said, opening her handbag. 'I didn't mean to come across like some smuggler or anything like that. As I said, I'm new to all this business. Please let me give you my business card.'

As Ursula turned and opened her handbag, Thandi got a glimpse of a Glock 19 pistol inside.

*

Sonja rummaged a little in her bag, making sure Thandi had a chance to see her Glock, then she took out a business card she'd had printed at an instant print place in Nelspruit on the way to the conference.

'Here it is,' she said, handing it over.

Thandi looked at the card. 'You're a private investigator?'

Sonja smiled. 'That's me. Cheating husbands, missing persons, even missing pets.'

'Is that why you carry a gun – for pet snatchers?'

'No, for the husbands.'

Thandi smiled politely and nodded.

'I wouldn't say I'm overly paranoid about living in Johannesburg,' Sonja went on, 'but I'm from Namibia originally and there's not much shooting there. I did serve in the police, though, when I was younger.'

'Very interesting,' Thandi said. She started to turn away and opened her mouth again, as if to excuse herself.

'Are those your friends over there?' Sonja asked. 'Would you mind if I joined you? It's just that, well, I don't know anyone here, except for you, now.'

Thandi pursed her lips, briefly, but Sonja could tell from her smile and her eyes that she was too polite to refuse her. 'Please, do come and join us.'

Sonja followed in Thandi's wake, trying her best to look shy and nerdy, even though she had just forced her way into a group of strangers. Thandi introduced her to the others. Going by Joanne's basic descriptions of them, Sonja could more or less place them as the Zimbabwean woman went around the group.

'Sheesh, I'll never remember all those names,' Sonja lied, having already committed each face and name to memory.

Charles Borg, whom Sonja had recognised from Joanne's description of his leonine mane of white hair and weathered good looks, sidled his way between a couple of the others to position himself next to her. 'Welcome, Ursula, I think you've just lowered the average age of our little section by about thirty years.'

Sonja tittered. 'Hardly.'

'What's an exotic like you doing at a cycad convention?' Charles asked.

Sonja registered Sandy, in the wheelchair, scowling her disapproval.

'Section – that's an army term, isn't it?' she asked.

Charles smiled. 'It is. All of us have something of a military or law enforcement background, either that or we've been in a scrap or two.'

'Ursula was in the Namibian police force,' Thandi said.

Charles raised his snowy eyebrows. 'Is that so? I spent a bit of time in your country back in the old days – along with most of the male South African population.'

'White male population,' Thandi interjected.

Charles raised his right hand in a closed fist salute. 'Apologies, comrade! Thandi served across the other border, in Zimbabwe.'

'On the *winning* side,' Thandi added.

'Stephen was the hero of South West Africa and Angola,' Charles said.

Sonja looked to Stephen Stoke, who shrugged and gave a small smile.

'Not too many war stories, remember, Charles?' SS wiped cream from his fingers on his two-tone shirt and extended a hand to Sonja. 'Howzit.'

'Fine and you?' Sonja said.

'They're being modest,' Baye said. 'SS was a Recce-Commando, and Charlie, who is launching something of an assault on your time and personal space, Ursula, was a helicopter pilot.'

'Hey, still am!' Charles said.

'Goodness,' Sonja said. 'I feel like quite a babe in the woods. Sorry to barge in unannounced.'

Baye waved a hand as if shooing a fly. 'No problem. Charles has a habit of recruiting strangers at these sorts of gatherings. Funnily enough all are female.'

Charles patted Sonja on the arm. 'You're very welcome, Ursula. Oh, and Baye won't tell you, but she single-handedly recaptured the Golan Heights from the Syrians back in '73, isn't that right, Baye?'

161

Baye waved a hand at him. 'Behave, Charles.'

Sonja smiled to Baye who, despite her age, looked lean and fit and regarded her through slightly suspicious, predatory eyes.

'Hello, I'm Laurel,' an immaculately dressed and made-up woman said. 'Do you like cycads?'

'I think that's why Ursula's here, dear,' Charles said to Laurel.

Sonja smiled at them all and sipped her cup of tea. 'Yes, very much so.'

'Where do you live, Ursula?' Charles asked.

'Johannesburg, Randburg, but I travel a lot for work.'

'And where do you travel to?' he asked.

'Iraq, mostly, though sometimes Afghanistan, Syria once or twice, and the less nice parts of Africa.'

'Aha.' He grinned. 'And what line are you in, may I ask?'

'Close personal protection. Bodyguarding, a lot of people call it, though my business card says private investigator.'

The conversations that had started up again among the others petered out, and Sonja felt all their eyes on her. She looked around. 'Have I said something wrong?'

Charles patted her on the arm; he was touchy-feely. 'No, no, no, my dear, not at all. I was wondering, and I'm taking the liberty of speaking for all of us here, if you might be interested in joining our little band of cycad fanciers.'

Sandy snorted. 'That's fast work, even for you, Charles.'

'That sounds lovely,' Sonja said quickly. 'Thank you. I've only recently become interested in cycads, but I haven't ever really had a hobby. My daughter moved out of home after finishing varsity and I found I needed something to occupy me in between work trips. I love the look of cycads, always have, and I'm keen to learn more if you'll take on an amateur.'

'We're all amateurs,' Charles said, 'though some of us know more than others.' He looked around to Thandi, who was watching on, silent since the first introduction, her arms folded across her body. 'What do you think, Thandi?'

Thandi smiled benignly, though Sonja could almost hear the cogs in the other woman's mind spinning. 'Of course, you know everyone is welcome to join our society.'

'As long as they don't mind a bit of gunplay as well, eh?' Charles said. He looked to Sonja. 'Do you shoot often?'

'Twice a week.' Sonja patted her handbag.

'Perfect.' Charles turned his attention back to Thandi. 'Maybe Ursula could join us on our field trip north to look at the sheikh's palace?'

'That is a bit sudden,' Thandi said.

Before Sonja could interject another woman walked towards them from the direction of the bathrooms and joined the group.

'Meet our fearless leader,' Charles said to Sonja, 'Her Majesty Queen Jacqueline Smit the first.'

Jacqueline, whom Sonja also recognised from Joanne's description, gave her a polite smile and extended her hand.

'Ursula here is interested in cycads,' Charles said, 'and is an expert markswoman.'

Sonja could see he was laying it on thick. 'Well, I don't know about that.'

Jacqueline raised her eyebrows and Sonja repeated her cover story, which, like all good fake identities, was based on fact.

'I see,' Jacqueline said.

'We're planning a trip tomorrow, after the conference ends,' Charles said to Sonja, continuing to monopolise her, 'to visit a luxury private game reserve owned by a distant member of the Kuwaiti royal family. He's mad about cycads by all reports. One of our members, well, ex-members – she ran off with our tea money – was supervising the sheikh of Araby's gardens for him until recently.'

'Interesting,' Sonja said, and it was, very, not least because Joanne had not mentioned to her that she had been in the employ of the wealthy Kuwaiti, even though Jed had.

'About that...' Jacqueline said, interrupting Charles. 'I've spoken to the prince's people just now and they're all ready for us tomorrow.'

'With Joanne absent without leave, Ursula could come with us and make up the numbers, right?' Charles said.

Jacqueline frowned and then turned to Sonja. 'I suppose so. I don't see any harm if you'd like to join us?'

Sonja shrugged. 'I don't have anything planned, so, yes, if you all don't mind, I'd love to come along.'

'That settles it then,' Charles said. 'Welcome to we few, we happy few, we band of brothers ... and sisters.'

Sonja looked to each of them and they were all smiling, or at least pretending. If Joanne was right then one of these people was the real cycad smuggler, someone who would be prepared to see Joanne Flack murdered rather than be outed.

'Thank you all,' Sonja said.

It was time for the next session of the conference and the delegates drained their cups of tea and started making for the function room. The others in the Pretoria group started moving and Charles offered Sonja his arm, theatrically. She grinned and played along, for a few steps at least.

Sonja noticed that Baye, the one who had served in the Israeli Army, held back, ushering the others in first. When Sonja let go of Charles's arm, as they entered the room, she glanced over her shoulder and saw that Baye had headed in the opposite direction, further into the lobby, and was talking into her phone.

The next session was, appropriately, an update on the illegal trade in cycads. Sonja took a seat next to Charles and learned in the presenter's opening remarks just how much people would pay for a rare cycad.

These plants, she thought to herself as she looked around and saw Baye sneaking into the room and taking a seat in the back row, were definitely valuable enough to kill for.

Chapter 14

Rod Cavanagh waited at the general aviation area of Lanseria Airport, which was perched on a ridge in the grass-covered hills of Johannesburg's western outskirts. He watched the twin-engine Beechcraft taxi up to the charter aircraft terminal after landing.

Outside a neighbouring hangar Rod saw that two historic aircraft had been wheeled out and a photographer was busy taking pictures of each. One was a Huey helicopter which, interestingly enough, was painted in the olive drab colour scheme and US Army markings of a chopper from the Vietnam era. The other was a sleek military jet painted in camouflage. A sign above the hangar door read *Thousand Miles an Hour Joy Flights*.

The Beechcraft came to a halt and its engines shut down shortly afterwards. The door opened and the pilot, Andrew Miles, Rod presumed, came down the steps and secured the propeller on the exit side. He gave a thumbs-up and Joanne Flack emerged.

Rod felt a tightening in his chest. If she had aged much it didn't show, and she had not grown any less attractive. She certainly didn't look dead, which was what she was, officially, at least.

Miles came to him ahead of Joanne and shook hands and introduced himself. 'Get her out of here, Rod. I'll sort the South African customs and immigration people, but it won't do for an unaccounted-for live woman to be hanging around, all right?'

'Roger that,' Rod said.

Joanne came to them and put her hands on her hips. 'Discussing me like I'm a piece of cargo?'

Miles smiled. 'Well, technically that's exactly what you are. It's been a pleasure, and I mean that.'

Joanne flashed him one of her winning smiles, though her eyes betrayed her tiredness and something of the ordeal she'd been through. She kissed the pilot on the cheek.

'If you ever want to try life in the fast lane,' Andrew nodded to the camouflaged Hawker Hunter jet aircraft parked next door, 'give me a call.'

'I will.' Joanne left Andrew and walked straight past Rod, without even acknowledging his presence.

Rod quickened his pace to catch up to her. He took her gently by the elbow, but she shrugged him off.

'Not even a hello?' Rod said.

She shot him a terse glance as they walked on. 'No.'

Rod nodded. So this was how it would be. 'We've got a safe house not far from here. It's in the Featherbrooke Estate.'

'Near where I live,' Joanne said.

He nodded. 'We figured that if whoever is after you was organised enough to track you to Victoria Falls, then they've probably had your house and anywhere else you'd normally go under surveillance. We might get lucky and catch someone staking your place out.'

'I'm dead, Rod. Haven't you heard?'

He dug into the pocket of his chinos, took out a piece of paper and unfolded it. He passed it to her. 'I read about it just now. That's a printout from BBC World online.'

Joanne slowed to read the article which was headed, *Woman who shot terrorist killed in accidental shooting*. 'Our tame Cuban doctor has done her job well – and fast.'

'Well, I hear she's something of an expert at faking deaths,' Rod said. 'How's your daughter, Joanne? Peta, right? She was just a little girl last time –'

'None of your business, Rod. But I called her from the plane and told her to ignore any reports of my death and not to talk to the press about it. She asked me why, and I made up a story about going into witness protection because of the shooting in London.'

Rod nodded and led her to the vehicle he had hired, a Toyota Fortuner SUV.

'What do we do now?' Joanne said as he unlocked the doors.

'We go to the safe house and you tell me, now or later, who's trying to kill you, Joanne.'

Joanne sighed. 'I've been through that already, with that psychotic Sonja. What makes you think I'll tell you anything I didn't tell her, Rod?'

Rod turned on to the R512. 'You know the answer to that.'

She deigned to look at him now and raised her eyebrows. 'Because we fucked? You think I care about you?'

He shook his head. It had meant more to him than that, but how could he explain, after what had happened? 'No, but I know you, Joanne. And I saved your ass.'

'Hah!' she waved a hand at him. 'You're *not* an FBI agent, or a cop, or some knight in shining armour, Rod, despite what your Facebook friends might think of you, with your seminars about rhinos and endangered pangolins, and your opposition to Trump's plan for oilfields and whatnot.'

That was all recent stuff, Rod thought to himself. Had she been keeping tabs on him on Facebook or had she only recently looked him up? Maybe she wasn't as disinterested in him as she seemed to be. 'I don't pretend to be anything I'm not. At least not since I went undercover.'

'Oh, spare me the sanctimonious bullshit,' she spat. 'You crossed the line, you know you did, by seducing me, and you killed my husband and left a five-year-old girl with no father and me with no money.'

'Your income came from a criminal enterprise, Joanne.' And he hadn't seduced her. If anything it was the other way around. He remembered how she had been – pretty, bored, restless, sexy as hell.

'So that gave you the right to shoot him?'

He exhaled. 'He was going to kill me.'

'Because you were sleeping with *me* and he found out. You screwed your precious investigation just like you screwed me. You ruined my life, Rod.'

'No, *you*...' Rod raised a hand to stop himself, and took a breath. 'So me sleeping with you gave *him* the right to try and kill me?'

Joanne shook her head and folded her arms tight across her chest.

They lapsed back into silence as Rod turned on to the N14, heading south towards Krugersdorp. He wondered if Joanne, like he, was replaying the events of that hot desert morning and the long sultry night before.

In his mind, when Rod thought about that time, the memory always started in the morning, with Joanne sitting up in bed, her hair tousled and the sheet only just covering her breasts.

She had smiled at him.

He tried, as he always did, to hold on to that memory. It had been a split second in time when everything was coming together, when the world – his life, his career, his future – looked full of promise, when anything was possible.

And then he had screwed it all up by shooting Peter.

'You're unusually quiet. You Americans usually like the sound of your own voices,' Joanne said into the silence.

He stared out the windscreen, driving faster than was legally possible in the United States, negotiating the Johannesburg traffic with the precision and concentration of a pilot in an aerial display team – one wrong move, one mistimed manoeuvre, and you were dead.

'I'm thinking about Vegas.'

She snorted. 'Well, you know what they say.'

Rod did, and he wished it was true. He wished he, too, could have stayed in Las Vegas, at that precise moment when she'd kissed him.

Mentally rewinding he saw the two of them at a show, she in the little black dress she'd brought with her from Africa and the heels he had secretly paid for on a delightful, mildly kinky shopping excursion that afternoon. Peter was gone for the day, supposedly visiting an old schoolfriend who had migrated from South Africa. Joanne had known the man in question, and didn't like him, so it had been no surprise when she told Peter that she would go shopping and stay in the hotel instead.

Rod had known that Peter was lying. In fact he knew much more about Joanne's husband than she did; at least he told himself he did. The alternative, that Joanne knew about the extent of Peter's criminal activities, would make her more of an active accomplice than she – probably – already was.

These thoughts had troubled Rod in the early days, weeks and months of Operation Green Thumb. The name was out there now – you could google it and find glowing reports of his involvement – but at the time it had been an undercover sting, a secret joint operation between the FBI and the Fish and Wildlife Service's Office of Law Enforcement that spanned two years in the planning and execution.

For those two years Rod had lived a lie, posing as Marty Jacobs, a property developer cum cycad dealer and collector. The fictitious Marty's passion for rare plants took him to South Africa, newly welcomed once more into the world of international trade and commerce following the end of apartheid and Nelson Mandela's coming to power. As momentous as the change in regime was, it had also opened the door to the export of South Africa's cycads, legally and illegally.

Rod already had some undercover experience as a Special Agent in the Fish and Wildlife Service's Office of Law Enforcement, posing as a buyer in an operation to break up a racket that was smuggling endangered reptiles into the US from around the world. A letter to the department from a botanist about the alleged scale of cycad smuggling had prompted him to start researching the slightly weird plants, and he took it upon himself to get his superiors to mount an investigation.

He read every book and paper he could find on cycads and spoke to legal dealers in the US, to get a feel for which plants were most in demand and to work up a profile of collectors. They could be of either gender, from any racial background, but to be a serious collector you needed money.

Rod remembered Joanne, and Peter, from that time. When he first met them, at a cycad conference in Cape Town, they had just been kicked off their farm in Zimbabwe and were living in an apartment in South Africa. Their farm, he learned, was not some small holding but a vast tobacco estate, the jewel in the area in which they lived, and therefore one of the first symbols of white wealth to fall to the government's ill-thought-out, rapacious program of land redistribution.

Peter and Joanne had a buffer, of sorts, in property. They owned a beachside apartment in South Africa at Umhlanga Rocks north of Durban, and a house on the Indian Ocean coast at Inhassoro in Mozambique, but they were in the process of selling both.

He glanced at Joanne. She had managed to move her extensive collection of cycads, many of them rare and valuable, from their farm into the garden of their house in Harare. By the time Rod met the couple they had been making regular trips to Zimbabwe to fetch their cycads, a few at a time, which they spirited out of the country in a light aircraft. The flights *to* Zimbabwe went from a farm in the north of South Africa, loaded up with black market alcohol, food and any of the other countless commodities and products people needed north of the Limpopo River but could no longer find due to the parlous state of the economy.

The cross-border trade was illegal, but the Flacks and anyone else he spoke to in Africa with connections to Zimbabwe were quite open about breaking the law. It was a matter of survival, and smuggling beer and even flour in a light aircraft seemed, to locals at least, perfectly acceptable.

Rod had come to Africa with clear-cut notions of right and wrong, legal and illegal, and black and white, but this continent had quickly blurred those lines. Joanne, for example, was backloading cycads in the Cessna from Zimbabwe to South Africa without the permits that her own government demanded. Her plants had come from her garden, not the wild (or so she maintained), but without the money Peter was making from collectors and middlemen in South Africa she and Peter might not, literally, be able to eat that week. What Rod learned from Joanne, over several beers and glasses of wine in the course of the cycad conference dinners, was that while their tobacco farm had been profitable, their lifestyle and outgoings had been extravagant.

He remembered snippets of conversations, which had found their way into Rod's surveillance reports.

Rod recalled typing: *JF (Joanne Flack): 'Peter never cared much for cycads, but he's become a real fundi* (expert) *these days.'*

PF (Peter Flack): 'We're saving these plants, even the most endangered of them. I can get you anything you want and, believe me, it will be safer and live a longer life with you in Florida than if some (racially derogatory term deleted) *dug it out of the ground and sold it for muti* (traditional medicine).'

JF: 'You know you don't really mean that, darling. We both know that the rarest cycads need to stay where they are in the wild, or at least here in Africa.'

The profile he had developed of the couple, through his undercover work, background investigations and, much later, wire taps, was that while Joanne Flack had bent the laws of Zimbabwe and South Africa to move her personal collection of cycads across the border, and was prepared to sell them to local collectors (whom she knew and trusted), her husband was positioning himself as a major player in the illegal international trade in endangered cycads. Rod wondered whether Joanne had now moved into that role.

Peter had been an alpha male. He'd been a handsome young airborne officer in the Rhodesian Light Infantry in Rhodesia's dying days. After independence and the end of the war, President Robert Mugabe had courted the whites of his country and encouraged them to stay and make money; Zimbabwe had been a major player in the worldwide tobacco market. The likes of Peter Flack might have lost the war, but peace in their country was kind to them.

Stripped of his farm, Peter was bitter and soon to be insolvent. Cycads gave him access to cold hard cash and a chance to thumb his nose at the governments of Zimbabwe and South Africa, which had made it their business to change Peter's personal world order.

Peter was making money once again. When 'Marty' returned to South Africa six months after the conference, ostensibly for a private holiday, he discovered that Peter had sold the ageing Mercedes he had brought with him from Zimbabwe and replaced it with a new Range Rover. He and Joanne had wined and dined Rod in style and the three of them had gone to Victoria Falls in Zimbabwe and then to a luxury safari lodge in South Africa in the Sabi Sand Game Reserve, which Peter had insisted on paying for. 'I know you'll be one of my best customers,' Peter had said to Rod in a conversation Rod had covertly recorded.

Rod had played along, indicating to Peter that he would soon be in the market for some particularly valuable cycads, once an investment deal he was involved in came to fruition. In particular, a Venda cycad was on his wish list, as was the holy grail for all collectors: *E. woodii*.

There were other marks, or targets, in Operation Green Thumb, including a senior bureaucrat in the Limpopo Province nature conservation department who would be responsible for issuing permits and clearances, but it became clearer and clearer to Rod that Peter Flack was *the* major player in the illegal trade out of South Africa. He tracked deals Peter made, and boasted of, to other buyers, and allowed the semi-rare cycads to leave Africa and make it to their destinations in the US and Asia. All the while Rod was getting closer to Peter and Joanne.

Joanne.

Outwardly they were a happy couple, but little cracks became visible in their relationship the closer you stood to them. Rod could tell that whether or not she was complicit in his illegal dealings, Joanne did not approve of trading cycads without the necessary permits, at least not out of Africa. The permit system had collapsed within South Africa, but on more than one occasion Joanne expressed her personal abhorrence of the way white middlemen and collectors in South Africa were paying poor people from rural townships a pittance to go into the bush and dig up rare cycads from their natural habitats. She would not accept the argument that these endangered plants were 'safe' in the garden of some overseas collector.

Any marriage, Rod reasoned, would come under stress when the family lost its home, lands, and its main source of income, but Joanne wasn't just worried about her change in fortunes. On several occasions in social settings Rod saw Peter, still a handsome brute who kept himself fit, chatting up pretty women while his wife fumed silently in a corner. Rod found himself being drawn to Joanne, at first to learn more about her role in her husband's dealings, but later also out of sympathy.

He knew he was walking on dangerous ground and that his real life, which had been nothing much to write home about before taking this assignment, was melding with his fictional persona.

Rod had learned much of his trade as an undercover operative from his supervisor, Hank, who before moving to the comparatively safe world of Fish and Wildlife had worked at the Drug Enforcement Agency, much of his time undercover in Mexico, where he'd faced the very real prospect of a brutal death if he was uncovered.

'You've got to bend,' Hank had explained over a beer one night, 'to be flexible with your own morals. You see some guy smoking dope or doing a line, you got to understand that you will never bust that dude, or worry about him or her. You got to keep your eye on the prize, man, the big fish.'

Rod had bought into Joanne's version of the law, that it was OK for her to illegally move her cycads from Zimbabwe to South Africa and then sell them to local collectors because she had been disadvantaged, because she was *sure* the plants were staying in Africa. He had believed her when she'd said she'd never taken a plant out of the wild in Zimbabwe, even though her husband was paying others to rape South Africa's bushveld and gouge out the country's natural heritage so he could make big bucks selling to overseas collectors. Peter was his big fish – more like a whale.

Seeing Joanne now, in the present, in the passenger seat next to him, close enough to touch, close enough to smell, still as goddamned attractive and aloof and out of bounds as she had ever been, reminded him.

What a fool he had been.

How he had lost his job, and nearly his life.

He remembered Peter's words, from the recording and subsequent transcript.

'What do you want, Marty?' Peter had asked him when they were alone, at the end of a day's game viewing, smoking cigars outside under the African sky. 'Anything I've got, anything you want, I can get it for you.'

Rod remembered looking over Peter's shoulder right then, through the smoke cloud from Peter's Cuban cigar, and seeing

Joanne in a sleeveless khaki safari dress, simple yet sexy, walking barefoot across the grass.

He had known, then, there was only one thing he really wanted, and the weakness of it, the corruption of his feelings and his principles had eaten him up, just as it threatened to do again now, all these years later.

Her.

Chapter 15

The next morning Sonja was in Stephen Stoke's Volkswagen Kombi minibus, sitting next to Charles who had taken it upon himself to be her personal safari guide as they drove north through the Kruger National Park.

Sonja put up with Charles touching her, occasionally, to emphasise his points. He would lay a hand on her arm, or call her dear, to punctuate his sentences. He was like a lot of older southern African men she had met during her life. They belonged to an era when gender roles were firmly assigned and a little flirting was considered charming rather than sleazy. If a younger man had carried on the way Charles did she probably would have censored him, but Sonja did not find Charles threatening.

Sonja had told Charles that she had spent part of her teens living in Botswana's Okavango Delta, but this hadn't deadened the older man's enthusiasm for explaining everything he could about every bird and animal they saw on their drive.

'And the elephant has a gestation period of ...'

Sandy Burrell, sitting in her wheelchair at the back of the bus, cleared her throat: 'I think we've had enough of the David Attenborough commentary, Charles.'

A couple of the others laughed.

'I was enjoying it,' Laurel said. 'I, for one, am learning a good deal.'

'Poor Ursula might want to snooze; I know I do.' Baye yawned theatrically.

'I think most of us here know as much, if not more, about elephants and the bush than you do, Charles,' said Jacqueline.

Sonja – Ursula – forced a smile. 'I'm just enjoying being back out in the bush. I haven't been to a game reserve for years.'

Sonja was impatient to get to their destination. She had spoken to Rod from her hotel room the night before. He had told her that he and Joanne were in the safe house, but they had not yet gone to Joanne's home to check for signs of surveillance or disturbance.

'She's got a security camera system at the house,' Rod had said. 'We were able to log into it from my laptop. The only thing out of the ordinary she found, on one of the recorded video clips, was a visit by an African woman, a Thandi Ngwenya, from Joanne's cycad lovers' group, who looked around the outside of the house and watered the plants, in the company of a gardener.'

'Yes,' Sonja had said. 'I've met her, and I'm travelling with her and the others. Did Joanne say what Ngwenya was looking for?'

'She said she couldn't tell,' Rod said, then lowered his voice, 'but I'm sure she's still holding out on us.'

'Work on her, however you see fit,' Sonja had said. She didn't think that the Fish and Wildlife Service condoned waterboarding or electric shocks to the genitals, but Rod had some history with the Flack woman and Sonja had to hope he was smart enough to leverage it.

Charles was temporarily silenced and Sonja took a moment to enjoy the simple pleasure of watching a small breeding herd of elephants. In charge was the matriarch, the biggest of the cows, who kept an eye on them while she snapped a branch from a mopane tree and rotated it in her mouth. The rest of the herd was made up of her daughters and their offspring. The peace of their feeding was interrupted only by a short, shrill trumpet blast from an adolescent male, who stomped up the road behind them, towards the Kombi, shaking his head and flapping his ears.

SS, like Sonja, knew it was a mock charge, a teenager showing off his new-found strength and seeing what he could get away with. Laurel, however, shrieked in genuine fear and Jacqueline, for all her regal bearing and supposed bush knowledge, banged on the dashboard.

'Start the engine, Stephen,' Jacqueline commanded. 'Quickly, now!'

Sonja knew that the elephant would back down if they did nothing, but SS was either used to obeying or he knew the pointlessness of resisting their own dominant female. He set off and the young elephant, emboldened by the show of weakness, trumpeted again and followed them for a few more steps.

'My goodness,' Laurel put her hand over her heart, 'that was frightening.'

Sonja had witnessed far worse; as a child she had seen the aftermath of an attack by a fully grown bull elephant on a Land Cruiser game-viewing vehicle. The bull had been in musth, hungry for a mate, and the brash young guide who had been driving should have known to give the giant creature a wide berth. Instead he had taunted the bull, revving his engine and inching closer to give his guests a bigger thrill and better photo opportunity. The bull put his tusks through the tailgate of the truck, leaving the tourists in tears and the guide out of a job. He'd been lucky no one was injured.

That was the thing about Africa – and life – Sonja mused. One minute everything was peace, love and happiness, and the next second people were dying.

Sonja, pretending to look for animals as Stephen drove on, casually studied the group. They'd invited her to dinner last night and had shared some war stories over several bottles of wine. Sonja modestly held back on her own tales, despite Charles's cajoling, and was more intent on learning what she could about the rest of this unusual group. The only member quieter than her was Thandi. Sonja could feel the Zimbabwean woman's eyes on her more than once during the evening. Thandi was assessing her, just as Sonja was sizing up the other woman.

A phone dinged in the bus. Mobile phone reception in the Kruger Park was patchy between the major rest camps, but here and there were pockets of signal.

'My goodness!' Laurel held up her phone.

'What is it, dear?' Charles asked.

Laurel put a hand over her mouth and her eyes were wide as she studied her screen. She lowered her fingers slowly. 'It's Joanne.'

'What about her?' Jacqueline asked, quickly. The leader seemed immediately agitated.

'She's ... she's dead.'

Sonja manufactured a look of bewildered concern, but was pleased the Cuban doctor had done as instructed. Of course, Rod and Joanne would have to be careful as it was quite likely the killers would want to follow up on the media reports and confirm for themselves that Flack was dead.

'Joanne?' Sonja said to Charles.

'Flack,' he said. 'One of our members – well, former members. She put up a black mark, stole a rare plant that was in our safe-keeping. At least, that's what the evidence points to – Thandi's taken on the role of chief investigator. But this ... this news is terrible.'

'Oh dear,' Sonja said. She glanced across the narrow aisle to the row of single seats and saw that Thandi was studying her.

'She was shot, in Zimbabwe,' Laurel continued. 'It's here on one of the Zimbabwean news Facebook groups. Something about elephant poachers who had crossed from Zambia being surprised by a boatload of tourists from a lodge near the falls.'

'What was Joanne doing in Zimbabwe?'

Sonja noted the lack of concern in Thandi's tone. She was playing the role of impartial investigator very well. Or, was the news less of a surprise to Thandi than the others? Was it just a coincidence that Thandi was a political refugee from the country where the killers had chosen to target Joanne?

'What was the name of the lodge?' Baye asked.

'Matetsi,' Laurel said, consulting her phone.

'Joanne has a niece who works there, makes sense she would try and hide up there,' Baye said, 'but this business of a gunfight at Victoria Falls is just awful, and so unheard of.'

Sonja swivelled in her seat to face Baye and asked a question she knew the answer to. 'Did you know Joanne well?'

Baye shrugged. 'As well as any of us, I suppose.'

Sonja could feel the mix of emotions in the confines of the minibus. Jacqueline looked straight out the window, and Charles patted her hand. Thandi seemed lost in thought.

Laurel sniffed into a handkerchief. 'Whatever she did, she was one of us.'

Baye balled her hand into a fist and thumped the windowsill next to her. Sonja casually looked around. Sandy shook her head, perhaps in disgust, maybe dismay.

'We'll never know the truth now, I suppose,' Stephen said, watching the road and the bush, in case an animal leapt into their path.

'The truth is she was a thief.' Sandy Burrell, at the back of the bus, had her arms folded tightly across her chest.

A couple of the others turned to look at Sandy, but no one challenged her. Perhaps having more challenges in her life than the others stripped away the need for her to dance around difficult subjects or sugar-coat them.

'We don't know that for sure.' Laurel dabbed her eyes.

'She disappeared, the cycad disappeared, and the bank balance went with her,' Sandy continued, for Sonja's benefit. 'She didn't reply to anyone's calls or emails, and she snuck back into Africa without telling a soul. We're supposed to think she's a hero for shooting some terrorist, but that was just luck – good luck for her because for five minutes people stopped thinking of her as a thief, and bad luck for the guy wielding the knife. Now she's got her comeuppance.'

'*Comeuppance*?' Charles leaned over his seat back. 'That's a tad harsh, don't you think, Sandy?'

'People are killed every day in this country,' Sandy shot back. 'Joanne was in the wrong place at the wrong time. You know it could happen to any of us, which is part of the reason we all carry bloody guns all the time. She turned her back on us, and worse than that, she betrayed us and spat in our faces. Joanne took advantage of our trust and stole this beautiful, valuable plant that was entrusted to us. Unforgivable.'

Sonja chewed the inside of her lip as she listened to and watched the exchange. Sandy was brutal. *Too* brutal, perhaps?

Thandi, also, was studying Sandy, but not commenting. Sonja wondered whether the same things were going through Thandi's mind. Thandi didn't have the benefit of Joanne pleading her innocence, as she had done to Hudson and Sonja.

Sonja knew from Joanne that Sandy had wanted to travel to the US to undergo some radical new surgery for her injuries and to possibly be fitted for an exoskeleton suit that might allow her to walk again, but she had no hope of raising the money needed. It was no wonder, Sonja thought, that she seemed bitter. How far would Sandy go, Sonja wondered, to pay her medical bills?

They passed a herd of impala and Stephen slowed the bus and turned left into a picnic site called Nhlanguleni. SS pulled up and the passengers eased their stiff joints out into the morning sunshine. Several ambled off in the direction of the simple wooden ablution buildings.

Sonja looked around, her training and instincts kicking in, assessing threats. There was a small building, painted the ubiquitous national parks baby *kak* brown, and a simple log fence demarcating the patch of cleared ground from the grassy bushveld around them. Nothing here to stop a lion, elephant or leopard sneaking or barging in.

'Looking for something dangerous?'

Sonja pivoted and saw that Thandi had come silently up beside her. She reminded herself that this plump lady in sensible shoes had once been a committed revolutionary, a trained sniper. 'It always pays to be alert in the bush. I learned that as a child.'

'Myself also, Ursula, but I suspect the dangers I faced were different from yours, in the Okavango Delta.'

Sonja smiled. She wanted to tell this woman how the PLAN – People's Liberation Army of Namibia – guerillas had attacked her family's farm when she was a child, how she had killed her first man at the age of ten. Sonja held her tongue, though, and smiled, because that story was known by enough people that it might trigger a memory for Thandi. They were of an age.

They looked out over a waterhole, set in an open plain. A big bull elephant was strolling up to drink, tossing his head with each ponderous step, trunk held up to sniff the breeze.

'I am scared of those things,' Thandi said.

'They're OK,' Sonja said, 'as long as you leave them to their business.'

Thandi raised her eyebrows. 'Good advice in general, yes?'

'What do you think about Joanne Flack?' Sonja asked, knowing her curiosity might tip her hand that she was not who she was pretending to be. Their enemy was resourceful and diligent so Sonja thought it worth the risk, to stay ahead of the game. It might have just been a gut feeling, but she sensed she could trust that Thandi was honest.

'What do *you* think?'

'I didn't know her.'

Thandi said nothing and Sonja knew enough about interrogation techniques to know that the other woman expected her to speak now, some more, to fill the void. Instead, Sonja looked at the elephant.

Thandi eventually sighed. 'I don't know what to think. As you gathered from Sandy's little tirade in the bus we – most of us – believe that Joanne stole a rare cycad that we were looking after, and all the money in our society's fund. Her actions, her lack of contact after she disappeared off to England were suspicious, to say the least. And yet I can't believe what happened in Victoria Falls. Zimbabwe is such a safe country for tourists; this is bad news for the nation as well.'

'You said "most of us" believe she stole the cycad. You don't?'

'I believe people are innocent until proven guilty. The case against Joanne is what the Americans would call "circumstantial". Joanne's husband was killed in a police sting operation, many years ago. He was guilty of smuggling cycads. Since I've known her, Joanne has always spoken out against the illegal trade, and was judgemental of anyone involved in it. Also, to empty the bank account and blatantly steal a cycad and run away is not like her. If she wanted to commit such crime, she would have covered her tracks – she was smart.'

'Had she?' Sonja asked.

'Had she what?'

'Committed a crime before?'

'She was from Zimbabwe,' Thandi said, as if that answered the question, but she added: 'Anyone who has lived in my country and says they have never committed a crime is a liar. Things are tough there, as you know, Ursula, and one has to bend the rules in order to live, day to day. Joanne admitted to smuggling some of her own cycads out of Zimbabwe, illegally, when she and her husband were forced to leave, but this commercial-scale trading is different.'

'How so?'

'It's not just about money. We were the closest people Joanne had to family in South Africa. It seems odd she would take our cash reserves. It's not just because that money was ours, you see; it's that it doesn't make sense. The cycad she stole was probably worth millions, if not billions of rand, so why bother taking the cash as well?'

'Travelling money?'

Thandi shook her head. 'She was running out of cash, but she was not completely broke yet. She had a car she could sell, and her daughter had paid for her ticket to London. The son-in-law lost his job, that much I do know, and things were about to get even tougher for Joanne, but why steal thirty thousand rand out of our bank account?'

Why did anyone steal anything? Sonja wondered. Perhaps Joanne Flack was a kleptomaniac, though there was no obvious pattern of prior behaviour. She could see where Thandi was heading – this was not just about the theft of a plant, this was also about leaving a trail as obvious as the passing of a herd of buffalo. Joanne, she'd been told, had been the treasurer of the society and could therefore easily get hold of their money.

There was a sting in the sun now and they drifted towards a shady spot, away from the van, where the others were coming or going from the toilet or snooping inside Stephen's cooler box for something to snack on.

'Why are you here, Ursula?' Thandi said.

Sonja looked her in the eye. 'Because I have nowhere else to be and I'm interested in cycads. I hear this Arab guy has quite a collection.'

Thandi just looked at her, waiting for her to flinch or look away.

'We should be getting back to the others,' Sonja said at last.

'Yes. I am going to the bathroom while I can,' Thandi said, and walked off.

Sonja saw Stephen, sitting on a bench by himself. She went to him. 'Hello?'

He started, flicking his head up to look at her, his eyes wide.

'Sorry, I didn't mean to startle you.'

He shrugged, relaxing. 'It happens. Some things ... like this news about Joanne ... *ag*, they take me back.'

He looked out over the waterhole where the animals were drinking, a view of tranquillity, but Sonja knew the old soldier's thoughts were elsewhere. 'The war? Angola?'

He didn't look back at her, but nodded. 'It's the same, whenever an old comrade dies. You remember all of them.'

She sat down next to him. 'I know.'

He glanced at her and when he saw her eyes she could tell that he knew what she was talking about.

'It's the guilt I feel most,' he said, looking down at his hands.

'That you survived and others didn't?'

'Yes, and other things. Stuff we did. All this talk of smuggling ... plants, ivory, rhino horn; you know, it all happened during the war.'

'A friend of mine served in Angola. He said the CIA was involved in smuggling, to support other anti-communist forces.'

'We would say anything to justify ourselves,' Stephen said, wiping the corner of his eye with a finger, 'but it was all about money. Good people died because of greed. Guilty as charged. Whether Joanne stole that plant or not she was killed because of money. Animal products, drugs, it's all the same ...'

'Drugs?' Sonja asked.

He coughed. 'My grandson, in Australia. All the expats living there, they tell you this and that about how they leave their front doors unlocked and there's no crime and no murder and what-what-what, but this nineteen-year-old boy is addicted to *tik* – ice they call it over there – and now my son and daughter-in-law need six hundred thousand *ronts* to get him into rehab.'

'That's a lot of money,' Sonja said.

He shook his head. 'I'm paying.'

'You are?'

'All those people in Australia and New Zealand and England, they all tell you how there's the big bucks there, how much they're earning, but only your kids tell you how much the cost of living is and that they barely make ends meet. I have – well, had – a place at the coast, an old beach house at Pennington on the south coast. I'm selling it to get the kid off drugs.'

'Stephen, I'm so sorry.'

'*Ag*, forget it. Worse things happened in the war, you know? And now poor Joanne. I don't care if she took the plant or not. We're all guilty of something.'

She put a hand on his back. He stiffened, then seemed to compose himself. SS forced a smile. 'Come. We must get back to the Kombi, or the Queen will have my head.'

They walked over to the bus and it was Charles's turn to take her gently by the arm and lead her towards the low log fence, where they could see that the elephant was now sucking up trunkfuls of water and alternately shooting it into his mouth and showering his back.

Charles cleared his throat. 'Everything all right?'

'Thandi asks a lot of questions. I feel like I'm being interrogated.'

'She's smart as a whip, that one,' Charles said. 'She's trying to work out what happened with Joanne and the missing cycad, but maybe we'll never know, now that Joanne's dead, God rest her soul.'

'What do you think happened, Charles?' Sonja asked. 'Is Joanne guilty?'

Charles lowered his voice. 'We're off to see this Kuwaiti sheikh because Jacqueline, or Thandi, thinks that perhaps Joanne was doing some underhanded dealing with him. However, Thandi's not convinced that Joanne was responsible for stealing the plant or the money. Like you say, she asks a lot of questions. I believe our lady detective suspects one of us.'

'Why couldn't it just have been Joanne?'

'It could have, of course. But even at her little house at Muldersdrift Joanne was sitting on a king's ransom of cycads so it would have been easy for her to get into the international smuggling racket. The permit system's a joke. You can either fool or bribe the authorities into letting you get a plant out of the country by air, or one can drive across the border to Mozambique or Botswana where it's even easier to arrange shipment.

The cycad we were looking after was priceless, and Joanne would have known that taking it would immediately have put a target on her back. This is a theft that couldn't go ignored. The other crazy thing was that it was Joanne who alerted us to the fact that she had discovered the female *woodii* in her Arab prince's garden in the first place. Why spill the beans if she was planning on stealing it all along?'

'Not such a good idea in hindsight,' Sonja said, and Charles could only look sad and nod. There were plenty of reasons why Joanne would not have committed the crime, and yet all the evidence pointed to her having done so. But why, if she was innocent, had she not communicated with at least one of her friends from the society, to tell them what had really happened? 'Who else might want to steal your rare cycad?'

Charles furtively cast his eyes over the rest of the group, still milling about the picnic site, and lowered his voice. 'Any of us could have used a cool hundred million rand, or however much the thing is worth. I know I could. Baye still hasn't forgiven Joanne for "Cafe-gate" as we called it, a business venture between the two of them that ended in tears and debt, so she was probably the least upset that Joanne was accused of acting like a criminal. I've some valuable plants in my collection, but nothing in that range. There's also the matter of ethics.'

'You wouldn't sell your plants illegally or smuggle them out of Africa?'

'There's that,' Charles said, 'but it doesn't just come down to our own plants. Any of us has the knowledge and, I dare say, the contacts to start up an illegal business as a middleman – or middlewoman. You've only got to work the crowd at conferences like the one we've just been to, or get online on some of the chat groups and forums about cycads, and you'll soon find rich foreigners looking to expand their collections. But we don't.'

The elephant bull had slaked his thirst and moved to a bare patch of ground. He snorted up a load of loose earth, raised his trunk and exhaled it over his back. Sonja knew the animal was covering himself in a layer of mud which would dry hard and protect his skin from the sun and parasites.

'Why not?' Sonja asked. 'It's not like it's a crime that hurts anyone, or kills anything.'

Charles nodded to the elephant. 'Because of him. We're friends, at least I assume we all are, because we care about nature and the environment, and if you think digging a plant up out of its natural environment and selling it illegally to someone overseas for a massive profit is less of a crime than shooting that big fellow and hacking out his tusks, then I'm afraid, my dear Ursula, that we may need to part company.'

'I don't think that, not at all,' Sonja said, honestly.

Charles patted her on the forearm again. 'Good, because I'd rather like you to stick around and join our merry band.'

Sonja gave him a smile. 'I think I'd like that.'

Charles sighed. 'I really hope Thandi does not discover that one of us is a criminal, Joanne included. I still can't believe she's dead; at our age it is rather a fact of life, but it never gets easy.'

He turned away and raised a hand to his eye. Sonja saw his shoulders start to shake. She went to him and put her hand on his back. 'Charles?'

He looked at her and she could see tears forming in his eyes.

'Damn it. Sorry, I don't want to blubber in public.'

Sonja put her arm around him. He fished in his pocket for a handkerchief and mopped his eyes.

The others had gathered in a knot and were watching them. Laurel, Sonja saw, had also started to cry again and Baye was comforting her. SS had his hand on Sandy's shoulder, but she seemed to just stare at them, impassively.

'It's all right to grieve, Charles. Really it is.' Sonja was good at giving advice, but, she acknowledged, useless at following it.

She squeezed his shoulder, feeling slightly awkward herself. Her therapist had told her she didn't cry enough and she guessed it was true. She envied Charles his ability to grieve for his lost friend and it pained her that she couldn't tell him that Joanne was, in fact, very much alive.

At least Sonja hoped she was.

Chapter 16

Thandi thought it too much of a coincidence that a gun-toting, cycad-loving bodyguard had pitched up at the conference and befriended them all in a matter of a few short hours.

Charles was besotted with her, but then that was nothing out of the ordinary – his head was turned by every pretty woman he saw.

The question was, who was this Ursula, really? Thandi looked around the bus and thought about her friends and their reactions to Joanne's death. Sandy, angry at the world because of her own situation, thought Joanne had got what she deserved, while SS had withdrawn into himself, as he sometimes did when something reminded him of his time in the army. Baye had reacted coolly to the news of Joanne's passing, but Thandi wondered if part of that was guilt that Joanne had died without them fully resolving the rift between them over the cafe. Jacqueline also seemed lost in her own thoughts, looking out the front window; there had also been the business of her going hot, then cold, on the investigation. As much as Thandi hated to use the word, Joanne's death could be seen as convenient; the investigation could now, by rights, go away, with Joanne commended to the earth cast as the villainous thief who had got her just deserts.

No, Thandi, thought, too convenient, and about as likely as a female private investigator showing up at a cycad conference and hitching a ride to an Arab prince's lair.

Stephen turned off the tar road and pulled up at a thatch-roofed gate flanked by not one but two parallel three-metre-high game fences, each made up of rows of barbed wire interspersed by high-voltage electrified fencing topped with razor wire. The two fences stretched away as far as Thandi could see and were spaced far enough apart for a security road to run between them. In this part of the country it was not unusual to see single game fences, but this was a property where the owner was absolutely determined no animal – or person – would get in or out.

They had left the Kruger National Park via the Orpen Gate and driven past the private reserves bordering the national park and on to the town of Hoedspruit, which serviced the local safari industry. There they stopped for fuel for the Kombi, and for themselves, making the most of the pensioners' discount at the Wimpy restaurant.

None of them had been to the Kuwaiti's private game reserve before, but Charles had struck up a conversation with an electrician at the Wimpy who had worked there.

'Every tradesman in town's worked at that place,' the man had told Charles, and then gave him precise directions. 'That *oke* is loaded.'

An African security guard in a camouflage uniform used a hand-held scanner to record Stephen's registration disc on the windscreen, while a white man in matching fatigues surveyed them from outside the bus.

The guard with the scanner checked his clipboard. 'You are expected. Let me radio headquarters.'

The white man came to the driver's side door and looked into the minibus. He was well built, and there was a hardness to him that didn't look like it had come from too much time in a gym. He went back into the gatehouse. The way he carried himself made Thandi think he was ex-military – ramrod-straight, confident bordering on cocky.

'Maybe don't tell the guard that Joanne's dead,' Laurel said quietly from the rear of the van.

Stephen nodded.

The African security guard went back into the office and returned with a mirror on the end of a long stick. He circled the Kombi, using the mirror to check under the vehicle.

'What on earth is he looking for?' Sandy asked.

'Hidden weapons, maybe?' Baye said. 'This is supposedly a big five reserve, so they're probably looking for rifles that rhino poachers would use.'

SS shook his head. 'No self-respecting shooter would hide a rifle under a vehicle. I bet they're looking for bombs. The only place I've seen this sort of security in Africa is in Kenya, where they have a credible terrorism threat from Islamic extremists.'

'What were you doing in Kenya, Stephen?' Ursula asked.

Thandi cocked an ear. This was news to her, as well. 'Oh, nothing much,' SS replied, 'just exploring a few business interests there a few years ago. Came to nothing.'

Thandi filed that titbit away and wondered what, or who, this Kuwaiti prince was worried about. She was no expert on Islam or Middle Eastern politics, but she did know that the various sects sometimes disagreed with each other and royal families, such as the House of Saud in Saudi Arabia, were hated by the likes of al-Qaeda. Where did the prince stand on such things?

When the guard was done searching under the vehicle he went into the gatehouse and emerged again with his clipboard, which he handed to Charles and asked him to record all of their names and South African ID numbers or foreign passport details.

'Check out the depth position.' Charles nodded his head towards something beyond the Kombi as he finished writing and handed the clipboard to Jacqueline. Thandi noted that Ursula's eyes were already focused on the same point.

'Depth' was a military term for a defensive position further behind the front line and Thandi saw now, looking between Charles and Ursula's heads, a second checkpoint, on the other side of the perimeter road. Another man wearing fatigues and a black baseball cap stood half in, half out of a sentry box. He wore body armour and had an LM5 assault rifle, the semi-automatic civilian version of the South African military R5, slung across the front of his body, ready for action.

'These *okes* aren't messing about with security,' Stephen said.

The man's lips moved and he touched a finger to an earpiece. Thandi thought he had just received a radio message and this was confirmed when the white man re-emerged from the gatehouse.

'You're clear to enter,' the man said. He passed lanyards and visitors' ID cards to each of them through the Kombi's windows.

'This is quite a secure operation your headquarters is running,' Thandi said as the man handed her a card. She noted the name badge perched on a pectoral muscle and added, 'Mr Sonnet.'

He squared his shoulders a little. 'I'm actually head of security, just here at the gate doing an inspection.'

'Well, then, compliments to you.' Thandi smiled. 'It would be a brave poacher who tried to get through this fence.'

'A fence is just an obstacle, ma'am, and any poacher worth his salt can find a way under or over one. Obstacles need to be covered by fire and observation, guns and people, and we have plenty of both.'

'Impressive,' Thandi said. And chilling.

'Patricia Littleford will meet you past the next gate,' Sonnet said to Stephen. 'She's on her way. You'll meet her on the access road, before you get to the tunnel.'

'Thank you,' SS said. A barred sliding gate opened and Stephen drove through to the no-man's-land of the perimeter road. Once the first gate had closed behind them the second opened, and the man in the baseball cap with the LM5 nodded as they passed. Stephen looked back at the rest of them with theatrically raised eyebrows. 'Tunnel?'

A hundred metres down the road a new-model Land Cruiser came around a bend and stopped. The female driver waved to Stephen, beckoning him to follow. He waited for her to execute a three-point turn and then fell in behind her.

Through the bend they drew a collective intake of breath as the ground opened up before them and the Kombi followed the Cruiser down a steep road, now tarred, underground. The woman in the Toyota paused to activate another sliding security gate that disappeared into a recess cut into the wall.

'A bloody tunnel!' Charles said.

'He wasn't joking,' Stephen said as he drove through. The sliding gate closed behind them.

Arc lights illuminated the way as they drove at sixty kilometres per hour past walls sprayed with concrete. Thandi could not believe they were in the middle of the African bush. A sign pointing to an emergency exit flashed past and Thandi caught a glimpse of a red-painted ladder fixed to the wall.

Thandi checked her watch and calculated that they had driven about five or six kilometres when the road began to angle upwards. The Land Cruiser driver stopped to open a final gate – Thandi guessed that these barriers must keep wildlife out of the tunnel.

They re-emerged into daylight and drove around another sweeping bend, where they came upon the largest thatch-roofed structure Thandi had seen in her life. The roofline seemed to go on forever. The long building was not straight but rather contoured to follow the line of the high granite ridge whose edge it clung to. Below them was a seemingly endless vista of Africa, plains and thorny brown bushveld. Here and there sunlight was reflected from the surface of waterholes.

'My goodness,' Laurel said, 'this chap must have some money.'

That, thought Thandi, was the understatement of the millennium.

They pulled up in a car park behind the lodge and a diminutive blonde woman got out. 'Patricia Littleford.' She shook hands with each of them as they climbed out of the Kombi. 'Welcome to Assad Lodge. Assad is one of three hundred words for lion, or lion-like qualities, in Arabic.'

Patricia was pretty, late forties or early fifties, a wiry ball of energy in a khaki skirt and Jonsson workwear green shirt.

'What do you do here, exactly?' asked Charles, ever the charmer, with a smile.

'I'm in charge of interior design for H. E. – that's what we call the prince, short for "his excellency" – but my job was recently expanded to include the gardens around the lodge. Forgive me, but you are all friends of Joanne Flack, aren't you?'

Charles nodded.

'Then … do you know what happened to her?'

Jacqueline stepped forward. 'We just heard the news of her passing.'

'Shame,' said Patricia. 'Terrible. We'll miss her here.' A walkie-talkie clipped to Patricia's belt hissed and a voice came through in Afrikaans. She replied, raising her voice.

Thandi wondered how Patricia and Joanne had got on. Perhaps the woman didn't have time to grieve for a friend.

'We weren't sure whether or not to come,' Charles said, 'but we were all in the Lowveld for a cycad conference so we decided to make something of a pilgrimage here, to see Joanne's work.'

Patricia gave them all a cursory sweep of her eyes and, satisfied, nodded. 'Right, well, I'll show you around, but forgive me, H. E. is in residence at the moment and I have a meeting with him in half an hour.'

'We won't keep you,' Jacqueline said.

'Follow me, please.'

Thandi wanted more time to look around, maybe ask some questions. 'Excuse me?'

Patricia couldn't help a little frown of impatience. 'Yes?'

'Can you please tell me where the bathroom is?'

Patricia pointed to a door. 'You can enter the lodge via the back of the house area there. Go through to the reception lounge; there are bathrooms there.'

'Thank you. Please don't wait for me,' Thandi said.

Patricia seemed in no mood to wait for anyone, and led the group out of the car park and around the outside of one wing of the lodge.

Thandi went inside. Once under the high thatch roof it was immediately cooler. She passed an administrative office and slowed as she noticed a closed door marked *Security*. Before she gave in to the temptation of trying to open it, the door was flung wide and a man in camouflage trousers and a black T-shirt came out, holding an empty coffee cup. A Sig Sauer pistol sat in a tactical leg holster strapped to his right thigh just above his knee.

He looked Thandi up and down and his gaze stopped at the visitors' card hanging from her lanyard. 'Can I help you?'

Around one massive arm Thandi glimpsed a two-tier bank of computer monitors and saw the backs of her cycad-loving friends disappearing out of view, then their faces appearing on an adjoining monitor. 'I am looking for the bathroom.'

The man pointed. 'You're on the right track.'

She smiled. 'Thank you.'

Thandi went through to the open-plan lounge area. There was a long bar made from a single highly polished slab from a big tree. There were glass shelves on the wall behind the bar, but no drinks on display. Thandi smelled sawdust and somewhere nearby was the buzz of an electric saw and the sound of a hammer banging. She walked towards the bar across the polished concrete floor, which was decorated here and there with the skins of zebra and various antelope species.

She went behind the serving area and looked underneath. Out of sight were dozens of bottles – spirits, wine, brand name and craft beers, and a variety of mixers. She went back around to the lounge area and then, for good measure, to the bathroom. Everything looked very new and a power point was hanging from its wires on the wall. The place was not quite finished, which might have accounted for Patricia Littleford's abruptness.

Thandi emerged from the bathroom and looked around. There was no sign of the security man. She checked her watch and decided she could spare a couple more minutes before searching for the group. She crossed the sprawling open space of the lounge area to a bank of windows. The view over the bushveld was stunning. Below and to her left she saw a flash of colour: Laurel's red top and dyed blonde hair.

She heard voices coming from a room and walked there, her shoes clicking on the floor. As she came closer she realised the people were not speaking English, but nor were they talking in an African language. She stopped and cocked her head. French.

Thandi opened a heavy wooden door that pivoted on a central fulcrum. Inside the long, narrow room was a dining table of polished wood, perhaps five metres long. There were packing crates on the floor and straw stuffing scattered about. A man and a woman, both African, stood before a modernistic painting. Two labourers in blue overalls, one holding a drill and the other a spirit level, stood to one side.

'*Bonjour*,' said the woman. 'Er, hello?'

'Hello, how are you?' Thandi said.

'We are fine, thank you,' the woman said in accented English.

'I am just visiting,' Thandi said. 'The painting is lovely.'

'*Merci*. My colleague,' the woman gestured to her companion, who was casually well dressed, 'does not speak English.'

'Is he the painter?' Thandi asked.

The woman smiled, but shook her head. 'Oh no, we are, how you would say, dealers?'

'I understand. You have a gallery?'

The woman shrugged. 'Of sorts. A showroom, in Johannesburg. We have supplied several items for the lodge. We are more of a wholesale business, supplying *objets d'art* to decorators. We specialise in lodges and hotels.'

'I love your taste,' Thandi said. 'I'm currently redecorating and have a friend who is opening a lodge in Zimbabwe soon. Do you maybe have a card?'

'Of course.' The woman went to her handbag, on the dining table, opened it and gave Thandi a business card. 'It would be a pleasure to help.'

Thandi read the card. The name was Elodie Keita. 'That is a lovely name. May I ask where you are from?'

'Mali. Do you know it?'

Thandi nodded. 'You are a long way from home.'

Elodie shrugged. 'Yes, but it is very poor in our country. In Johannesburg there are many of us from Mali. We look after each other and there is money to be made. We just need to be careful we don't upset the local South Africans where we live.'

Thandi nodded. Some South Africans were resentful about immigrants from other African countries who took low-paying jobs. This xenophobic prejudice reared its head occasionally, and had been expressed through violence in the past. Thandi felt for the immigrants who had been targeted–her own people were often singled out–but she knew the perpetrators' anger stemmed from the country's unemployment problem. It was a vicious circle.

'We Malians are good traders, sister,' Elodie continued. 'We can get you anything you need.' The girl gave her a wink.

'I will bear that in mind,' Thandi said.

'This is your first visit to the lodge, yes?' Elodie asked.

'Yes.'

'What did you think of the tunnel?'

'Quite amazing,' Thandi said. 'I haven't been to many private game lodges, but that is the first time I've arrived via underground. Why on earth would someone go to such expense?'

Elodie looked around, as if making sure no one was in earshot. 'The sheikh, his excellency, doesn't want to see or hear any vehicles coming and going when he sits up here on his verandah.'

'That's an expensive way of solving a traffic problem.'

'Very, but money is not really an issue in this lodge.'

They both turned at the sound of rubber-soled boots squeaking on the polished floor of the main lounge. The massive shape of the head of security, Sonnet, blocked the dining room doorway.

'You were on the bus, why aren't you with your group?' Sonnet said to her without preamble.

Thandi was taken aback and somewhat offended by his tone and his directness, even though she was technically snooping. 'I heard noises coming from in here.'

'It is cool, Frank,' Elodie said to the man. 'This lady was just admiring the artwork.'

Sonnet – Frank – looked from Elodie to Thandi. 'I'm sure your friends will be missing you.'

Thandi nodded. 'Of course. I was just on my way, in fact. Nice to meet you, Elodie.'

Sonnet stood aside to let her past, but Thandi could feel his eyes on her as she retraced her steps, back past the bathroom and the security monitoring room and administration office. Thandi glanced up and saw a camera. She should have known that her progress would have been monitored on the screens.

*

Sonja dropped to one knee and pretended to admire a cycad up close as Patricia led the others on a tour through the lodge's garden.

From ground level she saw a motion sensor sprouting from a bed of mulch and topsoil, and on the tree that shaded her was a camera, also probably motion-sensitive. She made a point of not looking directly at it.

'*Encephalartos brevifoliolatus*,' Charles said, pausing beside her and shaking his head in wonder. 'I gave up on my mental arithmetic when I reached thirty million rand's worth of plants in this garden.'

Sonja stood and rubbed her hands together. So, the prince had nearly two million US dollars' worth of plants just in the corner of the gardens they had so far explored. Was that the reason for the electronic monitoring systems? It seemed like overkill, she thought. Anyone wanting to steal one of H. E.'s cycads would first have to scale or burrow under the twin electrified fences which, according to the security director, were covered by observation and people with guns, and then navigate their way through several kilometres of bush teeming with lions, buffalo, elephant and other dangerous game.

She heard a vehicle engine and looked to her left. A camouflage-painted *bakkie* drove past the garden, six men armed with LM5s and dressed in fatigues and webbing gear sitting in the back.

'Anti-poaching patrol,' Patricia said to the group, who were all watching the vehicle.

'We have black and white rhino here, and with the growing market for lion bones in Asia we have to monitor our big cat population now, too,' Patricia said.

'How many rhinos do you have?' Laurel asked.

'That's classified information,' Patricia replied. 'One thing you can be sure of, however, is that his excellency's rhinos are probably the best protected in Africa. Those guys take no prisoners, if you know what I mean.'

Shoot on sight, Sonja thought. Such orders were illegal in South Africa, though in practice if one was part of an anti-poaching patrol, as she had been in her last job, and the group encountered poachers with AK-47s at night, the best form of defence was offence.

'Have you had any incursions by poachers?' Sonja asked.

Patricia nodded. 'About a month ago. A three-man team came in: a scout, a shooter with a hunting rifle, and a protection man with an AK. One of our teams intercepted them. A gunfight ensued and our guys fired, in self-defence, of course.'

'Of course,' Sonja said.

'All three poachers were killed. The cops opened inquest dockets on the deaths, but all our rangers were found to have acted lawfully.'

Thandi bustled up to the group, puffing a little. 'Sorry, I got lost.'

'You've missed a very impressive collection of cycads so far,' Jacqueline said.

'I noticed on my way through the garden,' Thandi said. 'Some real beauties.'

Patricia moved off with the group in tow. Sonja hung back, continuing to check the security measures around the lodge. Charles hovered between her and the group. Thandi stopped to examine a plant.

'What do you think of this specimen, Ursula?' Thandi asked her as she took a handkerchief out of her pocket and mopped her brow.

'Lovely.' Sonja lowered her voice. 'Did you see much of the lodge?'

'I was not exactly sightseeing, but from what I did see it looks quite impressive.'

'As is the security.' Sonja glanced at Thandi. She was fishing. Sonja was sure Thandi was suspicious of her already, so she figured it couldn't hurt to push her a bit. If Thandi eventually found out who she was, and it turned out that Thandi was the person who had set Joanne up, then at worst, Sonja might have to kill her. At best, they might actually be able to work together.

Thandi sized her up. 'Cameras throughout the lodge.'

'And here in the garden, plus motion detectors and camera traps.' Sonja casually pointed to the ground where she had spied another sensor. Thandi nodded.

'The head of security – his name is Frank Sonnet,' Thandi said. 'What do you make of him?'

'Looks military, ex–special forces maybe. Possibly police tactical unit?'

'What's the sheikh so worried about?'

Sonja was wondering the same thing. 'Apart from protecting his endangered rhinos and a fortune's worth of cycads?'

'Yes, apart from all that.'

Thandi was right, Sonja thought. Security was big business in South Africa, as was anti-poaching, but this place was better protected than some military bases Sonja had served on. It was as though the sheikh was ready for war, but against whom? 'Maybe he has enemies. Lots of enemies.'

'Please stay with the group, ladies,' Patricia called from the front. 'We don't want anyone being pounced on by the resident leopard.'

Sonja and Thandi caught up with the others and crowded in as Patricia showed off a water feature with a pond that was bigger than even the most extravagant hotel swimming pools Sonja had seen. Water cascaded down a mini waterfall over granite boulders; Sonja couldn't tell if they were real or fake. Patricia walked between a couple of the big smooth rocks and disappeared. The group followed the path she had taken and saw, on the other side, an actual swimming pool.

Patricia had gone down some stairs into a sunken bar that pool users could swim up to and order their drinks.

'Bar's closed, I'm afraid.' She pushed a button under the bar and an electrically operated awning reached its way across half of the pool to provide shade. 'Impressive, hey?'

'That's a nice bar for someone who presumably doesn't drink,' Sonja said to Thandi. 'Kuwait was a dry country last time I visited.'

'Well,' Thandi said, 'I think his excellency might like to play when he's in Africa. The bar upstairs has enough spirits hidden away to knock out the Springbok supporters' club on tour.'

Sonja thought about that.

'Ladies and gents, I'm afraid I still have a mountain of work to do, so if there are no more questions, we really should make our way back to the main lodge,' Patricia said.

Sonja and Thandi fell into step, side by side, behind the others in the group. As they approached the lodge Sonja could see Sonnet, the head of security, leaning on a railing at the edge of the *stoep*, watching them.

Chapter 17

As they approached the stairs leading up to the wooden deck of the *stoep*, Patricia stopped and drew a sharp little breath. 'Your Excellency...'

'Hello, Patricia, how are you?'

'Er... fine, fine sir, and you?'

Sonja looked up to see a handsome man with thick wavy hair, with enough black left in it to remind her of Omar Sharif in his heyday, dressed in a white cotton shirt, two buttons undone, faded jeans and designer sneakers. He smiled, beautifully. She had dealt with plenty of wealthy people in the Middle East, sometimes providing protection for the wives of oil-rich sheikhs. She knew the men could be, by custom and upbringing, charming, and while some really were, others were putting on a front to hide the excesses and attitudes that afflicted rich men around the world. She recognised Prince Faisal from the picture in Jed's briefing.

'I'm also fine, thank you for asking. I heard you were taking a group of Joanne's friends around the gardens.'

'Yes, I hope that was all right, sir...'

'No problem at all.' He looked over her head to the rest of the group. 'Ladies and gentlemen, perhaps if your schedule would allow you'd consider taking some tea with me?'

Jacqueline cleared her throat. 'Your Majesty, we would be honoured.'

'No need to be so formal. Please, call me Faisal. But I'm afraid this is a sad occasion.'

They climbed the stairs and Sonja saw two tables laid out with fine china, cakes and homemade biscuits, water and juices, tea and coffee. Half-a-dozen domestic staff flitted about adding the final touches.

'I am not sure if the news from Zimbabwe has reached you yet, about Mrs Flack.'

Jacqueline nodded. 'It has, Your Excellency.'

He put two hands over his heart. 'I am so sorry for the loss of your friend. I counted her as one as well and my heart is heavy at her passing.'

Sonja guessed Faisal's accent came courtesy of an expensive education in England. She eased her way through the group to get closer to the prince as he picked up a teapot and began pouring. 'It seems impossible, Your Excellency, that she could die in that way, don't you think?'

Faisal handed the cup of tea to Jacqueline, who, Sonja thought, almost swooned.

'It is incredible that something so random and tragic could happen to such a strong woman,' he replied.

'And so soon after what happened in England,' Thandi added.

Sonja noted how the Zimbabwean woman had also manoeuvred herself closer to the prince, while the others hung back out of deference, respect or shyness. Laurel had been given a cup of tea by a waitress, but the poor thing's hands were shaking so much that Sonja could hear the rattle of china. Frank Sonnet stood at the fringe of the group, watching them all, as if he fully expected that an elderly plant fancier might draw a gun on Faisal at any moment. Of course, knowing this crowd as she did already, Sonja thought that wasn't such a crazy idea.

'Yes,' Faisal said to Thandi. 'That was shocking, the business in London. Joanne was so brave taking on that terrorist. I abhor extremism in all its forms. I enjoyed her company and her knowledge and love of cycads. We spent many a pleasant hour together designing the garden and supervising the planting. I shall miss her greatly.'

Sonja sipped her tea. 'You have a wonderful collection of plants, Your Excellency.'

'Please, call me Faisal.' He smiled at her.

'Did Joanne help you choose your cycads?'

'I am something of a collector myself, so I knew the specimens I wanted here in South Africa. Joanne sourced them for me.'

'You have some very rare beauties,' Thandi weighed in.

The prince nodded. 'Yes, but there are still one or two on my bucket list. These were proving very hard to source, but Joanne told me there was no way I could get one of those unless I went through illegal channels. I hasten to add that Joanne was most adamant that she would not go down that route, and neither would I. As much as I love these plants, I have no wish to fuel the trade in endangered species. If you have time to look around my property here you will see we are devoted to conserving threatened animals, not destroying them.'

'Some people would say that collectors are actually conservationists,' Sonja said, 'that the rare cycads are doomed in the wild and responsible enthusiasts are protecting and propagating endangered plants for the future.'

The prince set down his cup on a table. 'Yes, well, I am not one of those people. I would rather see a plant in the wild than be responsible for taking the last specimen from its natural habitat.'

'I meant no offence.'

His smile was charming, but this time it was not mirrored in his eyes. 'None taken.'

'Did you know Joanne was going to the UK, Faisal?' Sonja asked.

He nodded. 'Yes, she told me her daughter had booked a return ticket for her.'

'She had money troubles,' Thandi said. 'She depended quite heavily on her daughter and recently found out that her son-in-law had lost his job in England.'

'I wish she had told me,' Faisal said, 'but then she did turn down a fulltime position working for me here at the lodge.'

Sonja raised her eyebrows. 'You offered her a job?'

'A fulltime position, instead of the consultancy basis on which she'd been employed, as head of my gardens, a resident horticulturalist. As you've no doubt gathered, I have quite a sum of money tied up in my collection and I need someone who knows what they're doing to supervise the gardeners. The job comes with its own accommodation and a vehicle.'

'And she turned it down?' Thandi could not hide her surprise.

'I'm afraid so. Perhaps if she had said yes she might still be alive today.'

Perhaps, Sonja thought. 'Did she give a reason?'

'No, she did not,' Faisal looked sad, 'and if she had, I think it most probably would have been something that I would keep in confidence, don't you agree?'

'Of course,' Thandi said.

Why would Joanne have turned down the job? Sonja wondered. She would have to ask her. Sonja knew that there were some things money couldn't buy, but Joanne had no family left in South Africa, no prospects, and her source of financial support had dried up. What had stopped her? Faisal was charming and attractive. Was that part of the problem?

'Were you *close*?' Thandi asked.

'That is a very direct question,' Faisal set his teacup down, carefully. 'I don't feel that's something a gentleman should answer. Joanne was an employee, a consultant to Patricia, and we enjoyed each other's company.' He looked at his watch and across the table to Patricia, who had been gravitating closer. 'I have a meeting to attend, so if you will all please excuse me?'

'Thank you, ladies and gents,' Patricia said. 'I hope you've enjoyed your visit.'

The others thanked Faisal and Patricia and made their way out off the *stoep* the same way they had come in, via the tradesman's entrance. Sonja and Thandi hung back.

'Do you think there was something going between your friend Joanne and the prince?' Sonja asked Thandi.

Thandi shrugged. 'Joanne is—was—a good-looking woman. That man strikes me as a bit of a charmer.'

'He's hiding something about him and Joanne.'

Thandi frowned.

'Hurry along, you two,' Jacqueline commanded as she climbed into the bus. 'It'll be after dark as it is by the time we get back to Joburg.'

'Coming,' Thandi called.

Sonja lowered her voice. 'Did you learn anything else while you were off snooping by yourself?'

'I went to the bathroom.'

Sonja just stared at her.

'OK,' Thandi relented. 'Not much. I met some French-speaking people who were decorating a dining room. They said they have a lot of dealings with Patricia on behalf of the prince. He likes African art, exotic stuff.'

'French, you say?'

Thandi shook her head. 'No, French-speaking. They were from Mali.'

Sonja stopped.

'Get a move on,' Sandy called from a window at the back of the Kombi. Charles and SS had already helped load her.

'You look like you've just seen a ghost,' Thandi said to Sonja.

Sonja drew a breath and walked on. Not a ghost, but a few dead people. 'That's interesting,' she said, regaining her composure, 'I've heard Malians are big in organised crime in South Africa.'

'And Nigerians, Somalis, Chinese, Congolese, whites, you name it. Even we Zimbabweans are accused of being criminals. Is there something you're not telling me?'

Plenty, Sonja thought. She paused. It was obvious that Thandi was suspicious of 'Ursula', as well she might be, so perhaps she should start sharing with Thandi. 'I don't suppose you got the names of these Malians, did you?'

'As a matter of fact,' Thandi opened her handbag, 'one of them gave me her card.' She fished it out. 'An art dealer from Johannesburg, Elodie Keita.'

They got into the Kombi and Stephen drove out of the car park and into the tunnel.

Sonja thought about the name Keita. She recalled the briefing Jed had given her in the States. The two brothers involved in the alleged campaign were Moussa and Rafik Keita. Perhaps it was just a common name in Mali, or perhaps not.

*

Joanne was sitting on a couch in the safe house, half-heartedly flicking through a copy of *Woman and Home*, when Rod's phone rang. He answered, said 'OK', and passed the phone to her.

'It's Sonja,' he said.

'Hello?' Joanne said.

'Why didn't you take the job with Faisal?'

'I'm fine, thanks, and you?' Joanne said. The woman was trying to bully her.

'Answer my question.'

Rod was watching her so she got off the couch and walked through to a bedroom, closing the door behind her. 'None of your business.'

'Everything to do with you is my business right now.'

Joanne exhaled and ran a hand through her hair. 'It's complicated.'

'Explain.'

'He ... You've met him?'

'Yes, on a field trip with your cycad society friends.'

'Then you know how handsome he is, how charming, how ... rich.'

'I just googled him,' Sonja said. 'Forty-fifth richest man in the world on the Forbes list.'

Joanne remembered finding the same list and almost changing her mind. 'Yes.'

'You and him – you were an item?'

She felt her cheeks redden, even though Cavanagh was not in the room. 'Yes.'

There was a pause on the other end of the conversation. 'So tell me, why didn't you take the job? He's single.'

Joanne could hear traffic in the background. 'Where are you?'

'Ohrigstad. We're heading back to Joburg, via the Lydenburg Road. Answer the question.'

'All right, all right. Can the others hear you?'

'Of course not.'

'I didn't trust Faisal. He told me that he would never deal in illegal plants, or anything else outside of the law, but I had my doubts.'

'Why?'

204

'Another cycad went missing from his garden about two or three months ago. It was before the *woodii* was taken. None of the gardeners, or Patricia, noticed. You met Patricia?'

'Yes.'

'She's very efficient. Anyway, no one admitted to noticing anything.'

'The gardeners didn't see a hole in the ground?' Sonja asked.

'No, you don't understand. Whoever took the cycad replaced it with another one, a different species, but similar. Some of these plants look very much alike. I didn't even spot it at first, but when I did I went straight to Faisal.'

'What did he say?'

'He was horrified. He ordered a full investigation, and the blame was laid on one of Faisal's senior gardeners, Festus Mtethwe, but I think Festus was framed.'

'What makes you think that?'

Joanne frowned. 'I know it's easy to say "he or she would never steal", but Festus was the sort of guy who would point out any irregularity. He reported a builder once who was taking Mopani worms off the trees to sell for food. Also, he was an old guy – strong, but it would have been a hell of an effort to get the plant off the reserve alone. The security there is hectic.'

'Did you get a chance to talk to Festus, get his side of the story?' Sonja asked.

Joanne shook her head. 'He was released on bail then killed by a hit-and-run driver. The police report said he was walking home drunk from a shebeen, but as far as I knew, Festus never drank.'

'What about the *woodii* cycad?' Sonja said. 'It clearly wasn't Festus who smuggled it out of the reserve. Who else could have got past security?'

Joanne shrugged. 'Maybe the only person none of the security guards would suspect.'

Sonja's eyes widened. 'Faisal? You think it was him?'

Joanne sighed. 'I don't know. Like you say, he's one of the world's richest men so he doesn't need the money, but he's a collector as well, and those people can act crazy. I know he has an extensive collection of cycads back home in Kuwait and he'd joked, or maybe half joked, with me that he'd like to fly his whole South African garden to the Middle East if he could ever get the permits to legally do so. There were other things as well.'

'Such as?'

Joanne's phone pinged with an incoming message. 'Hang on.' She held the phone away from her ear and checked the screen. It was a message from the base station of the security cameras at her home. She and Rod had been monitoring the cameras from an app on her phone. 'I'm putting you on speaker.'

'Be quick, please,' Sonja said. 'Everyone's getting back on the Kombi and I don't have to tell you what a dragon that Jacqueline is. What other things did you pick up on?'

Joanne was only half listening. She opened the app and saw a frozen image from the security camera at her house. It showed a man in her backyard. She clicked on the play arrow in the centre of the screen. 'I have to go,' she said, 'now.'

'Wait!'

Joanne ended the call.

Chapter 18

Rod looked up as the bedroom door opened and Joanne came running out. She went straight past him, across the faux marble floor to the front door.

'Wait, you can't go outside.'

She paused. 'The hell I can't.'

He picked up his pistol and phone off the table. 'What's up?'

'Someone's breaking into my house. I just saw it on the camera.'

Rod bent over his laptop computer, which was also receiving a feed from the cameras at Joanne's house. 'Shoot, you're right. I went to the bathroom, I was only gone a minute.'

Joanne walked out the door, ignoring his excuse. Rod holstered his weapon and followed her outside.

Joanne was already jogging up the street. Rod got in the hired Toyota, started the engine and drove up alongside her. 'At least get in the car.'

She was wheezing already. He stopped, leaned over and opened the door for her. Glancing frostily at him, she got in.

'How many?' he asked.

'I just saw the one.' She had her phone out again and was tapping on the screen. 'He's trying the back door; looks like he's got a tyre lever or a crowbar. He's jemmying it open.'

'Description?'

'Blue two-piece workman's overalls, balaclava. Gloves, I think.'

Rod thought fast, weighing up the pros and cons of calling the police.

'We want this guy, Rod,' she said.

It was the first time she had used his first name since they had been reunited. She was right, as well. If they called the cops and they managed to catch the guy they would not get to question him, and Joanne's cover – having died in Zimbabwe – would be blown if they saw her. Rod could pretend to be a passing citizen, but that would leave a paper trail, and if they missed catching the guy then their enemies would know that they were in Johannesburg. Rod tried to think of what Jed would do.

'We have to take him down ourselves, alive,' said Joanne.

Rod's heart was pounding. Joanne was right.

They drove through the security boom gate of the Featherbrooke Estate after tapping out with an access card, then turned right onto Furrow Road. Joanne's house was in a much smaller complex about half a kilometre further on.

'Pull over here, let me out,' she said before they got to her gate. 'I don't want to be recognised inside.'

'Where are you going?'

'There's a side gate to the estate, a short cut to the Spar.' Joanne pointed across the road to the supermarket and an attendant cluster of stores. 'I've got a key. I'll go in that way and SMS you an entry code; you punch the number into the keypad at the gate and the boom will open. There's a house being built next to mine. I'd say by the way he's dressed that our guy passed himself off as one of the builders.'

'Where will I meet you?' Rod indicated and stopped the car.

'At the building site. Pretend to be checking out the workmanship. Turn right when you enter the complex. My house is 273.'

When she was gone, Rod carried on up the road. His phone buzzed on silent just as he reached the entry gate. He entered the four-digit number in the text message and the gate opened. The security guard looked up from his copy of *The Sowetan* and gave him a languid wave.

Rod drove to the end of the access road and turned right. After a short distance he saw 273 on his left, a two-storey bungalow. He passed Joanne's house and the construction site next door, then parked on the verge.

Two men were using a tile saw, powered by a generator, and the high-pitched whine of the blade made conversation within a few metres impossible. Rod waved to the builders, who nodded in return. Another man was banging in nails on a roof truss above.

Rod looked around and saw Joanne's face emerge from behind a hardware delivery truck. She waved him over. The other builders Rod passed, who were laying some concrete with shovels from a wheelbarrow, paid him no attention.

Rod went to Joanne and she held out her phone. 'I've got a live feed from the cameras. Look, you can see him here, on the camera in the lounge room, snooping around.'

He looked at the screen. The man was opening doors, possibly to bedrooms, and the larger cupboard under the kitchen sink. 'What's he looking for?'

'No idea. We don't all have safes, you know, but people put them in places they think criminals are less likely to look.'

'Do you have one?'

'No,' she said.

'He just walked past your television set.'

'Too big to walk out with.'

'He could just be your garden variety thief,' Rod said, but even as he uttered the words he thought the coincidence was unlikely. 'Looks like a big dude.'

'What are you carrying?'

Rod lifted the hem of his polo shirt to show her the Glock 19.

'What are you wearing under there, a bulletproof vest?'

'Yes, actually.'

'You Americans are such pussies.'

'You can have it if you want. In fact, you should.'

She shook her head. 'It wouldn't fit over my boobs. Do you have a back-up piece?'

'Nada.'

'Give me your gun.'

'Um. No, Joanne.'

'When was the last time you shot?'

'When I was trying to save your ass, flying over the Zambezi River.'

'Before that?' Joanne pressed.

He looked down at the ground.

'The day you killed Peter. Shit. If you pull it you'll be a liability. Give it to me.'

'No.'

'I shoot every week of my life, Rod. I killed a man in London only a few days ago, for goodness' sake.'

'I am *not* giving you my piece, Joanne.'

The blow came hard, fast and completely unexpectedly. She must have made a point with her knuckles, rather than a full fist, because it felt like a wedge had been driven deep into his solar plexus and the driving blow forced the air from his lungs. As he doubled over his shirt rode up and Joanne slid the pistol from the holster on his belt.

'If you get the vest, I get the gun. That's only fair.'

Even before he could stand upright she was running off.

'Go to my place, ring the front doorbell,' Joanne called over her shoulder as she ran to the backyard fence that divided her property from her neighbour's half-completed house.

Red-faced with a mix of anger, pain and embarrassment, Rod looked around him for a weapon of some sort. All he could see was half a brick, which he picked up and held behind his back. He walked briskly around to the front of Joanne's house and rang the doorbell with his free hand.

Rod readied himself for what he expected to happen next. The burglar inside would panic and run out the back door, where Joanne would stop him. Hopefully. If there was trouble he would have to kick the front door in – something that was a piece of cake in Hollywood movies, but a damn sight harder in real life, especially for a sixty-year-old with problematic knees. He wished he had his gun. Goddamned Joanne.

Rod cocked his head. He heard footsteps and the squeak of rubber soles on a tiled floor. Problem was, they were getting louder. He looked down and saw the handle start to turn. He licked his lips, his body tensed, then the door opened.

'Can I help you?' The man in the blue coveralls had taken off his ski mask and was smiling enquiringly at Rod.

Rod cleared his throat. 'I was looking for Joanne Flack.'

The man held his smile. 'She the tenant, *bru?*'

Rod swallowed. 'Um, yes.'

'I'm an electrician. Landlord's sent me to fix some wiring. I hear the lady's been away overseas.'

The jagged edges and remnant mortar on the brick dug into Rod's hand as he clutched it tighter. 'Maybe I'll just come in and check on things for Mrs Flack. She's still got a valid lease as far as I know.'

The man's face looked like it was aching holding the smile. He shook his head. 'No can do, *bru*. Landlord gave the keys to me. I can't be letting in strangers.'

Rod caught a flash of movement past the man's right shoulder, but forced himself to keep his eyes locked on the intruder's. 'Well, maybe we can call the landlord. What's his number?'

The tip of the man's tongue darted out between his lips, like a serpent's.

'Put your hands up,' Joanne said from behind him.

The man didn't turn or say anything. Instead he barged forward, and with his Springbok's build and the element of surprise he knocked Rod backwards onto his ass.

'Stop!'

Joanne followed them out, but the man didn't even look back.

A gunshot boomed from inside and the man sprawled on the front lawn, clutching at his leg.

'For crying out loud, Joanne.' Rod turned to look at her, standing in a classic shooter's pose, left hand supporting the gun in her right, feet apart. 'What is this, the wild west?'

'Yes, it's Muldersdrift. Get out of the way, Rod.'

He looked back to the man on the grass who was rolling onto his side and reaching for his own weapon, at his belt. Rod took two strides towards him and brought the half-brick down on the side of his head before the man could draw. The intruder slumped on the grass, unconscious and bleeding.

Rod went to Joanne, who had relaxed, and snatched his pistol from her hand. 'Quick, let's drag him back inside.'

He went to the man and knelt beside him, pausing briefly to check that the builders next door had not been alerted. Either they hadn't heard the shot over the noise they were making or they had chosen not to get involved, because work seemed to be carrying on as usual. A hedge between the two houses out the front mostly concealed him from the builders' line of sight.

Between them they half carried, half dragged the man back inside Joanne's house. There, Rod turned his attention to the man's injuries. The bullet had passed through one meaty calf. The man wouldn't be running for some time, but the wound wasn't fatal. Rod took the man's gun and put it in the waistband of his trousers, then searched him and found a wallet, a set of keys, and a fold-out knife in a pants pocket. Rod rolled him over, quite an effort given the man's bulk, and pulled his workman's uniform top off. He used the knife to cut it into strips – one to bind his leg wound, another as a gag for when he came to.

Joanne hovered over him. 'Is he going to be all right?'

Rod checked the man's pulse. 'He seems to be doing just fine, for someone who's been shot in the leg and knocked out cold.'

In reality, Rod wasn't so sure about their casualty's prognosis. What he did know, however, was that they had one of the men who were arrayed against them. He had been a Fish and Wildlife Special Agent, not a CIA interrogator, so he wasn't exactly sure how he was going to get information out of this man, but he was their only lead right now.

The man groaned, causing Joanne to take a step back.

'He's coming to,' Rod said.

Joanne dragged a dining room chair out from under the table and the two of them lifted the semiconscious man onto it.

'Find something we can tie him to the chair with,' Rod said.

'OK.'

Rod held the pistol against the man's head. 'Steady now, big guy, don't move and you'll be OK.'

The man shook his head. 'I've been *fokken* shot, man.'

'Yes, well, you only have yourself to blame for that.'

The man seemed groggy, shaking his head. 'Water.'

'Hold your horses, partner.'

With the gun still trained on the man, Rod pulled out the wallet he'd taken from him. When he opened it he saw there was a flip-over cover inside. He lifted it.

'Holy shit,' Rod said softly.

Joanne walked back into the living room with an electrical extension cord, to bind the man to the chair. 'What's wrong?'

He held out the wallet and showed her the ID and badge. 'He's a cop.'

Chapter 19

Sonja's phone rang in the Kombi.

'Ursula?' a woman's voice said when she answered.

'Yes?'

'It's Patricia Littleford from Assad Lodge. Please hold for his excellency Prince Faisal.'

Sonja saw that Thandi was watching her. 'OK.'

'Ursula?' It was the cultured voice of the handsome prince.

'Yes.'

'I'd like you to come back to my lodge, please, if it's convenient for you. I have a business proposition for you.'

She gave a little laugh. 'I'm halfway back to Johannesburg, Your Excellency. I can hardly ask my friend to turn his van around now.'

'Where are you?'

Sonja looked out the window. 'Machadodorp.'

'Have you passed the Wimpy at the Engen service station yet?'

Sonja put her hand over the mouthpiece and turned to Charles, who was clearly trying to eavesdrop.

He pointed through the windscreen. 'Just ahead.'

'Almost there,' she said. He clearly knew his local geography.

'Wait there for me, please. I'm sending my helicopter.'

The others waited with her in the car park of the service station, several of them making the most of an unscheduled additional bathroom stop. Charles had gone for coffee at the Wimpy, having given

214

up warning Sonja about the perils of the white slave trade and what ghastly fate the sheikh might have in mind for her.

Thandi sidled up next to her. 'Why you?'

'Maybe he likes greying brunettes.'

'I wasn't joking,' Thandi said. 'Who are you, really, Ursula?'

'I'm a cycad fancier, like you.'

Thandi shook her head. 'Do you know what you're looking for?'

'Not exactly, no. How about you?'

Thandi shrugged. 'The truth.'

Sonja gave a small nod. 'Give me your phone number, please.'

Thandi told her and Sonja entered it in her burner phone, then sent the other woman an SMS. 'If you don't hear from me, call the number I just messaged you. He'll be able to help you with your enquiries.'

'All very mysterious, but very well.'

They both turned at the sound of rotor blades chopping the cool air where the escarpment rose above the steamy Lowveld. A Bell Jet Ranger, painted glossy black, flared its nose and touched down in a field next to the filling station. Holidaymakers on their way to or from the Kruger Park stopped outside their cars to watch. A child ran after his baseball cap, blown off by the downwash.

With a wave of farewell to the little cluster of grandfatherly and grandmotherly gardeners, Sonja climbed the three-strand cattle fence and, bent low at the waist, ran to the helicopter. They all looked so innocent, so concerned, yet Sonja was fairly sure one of them knew something more about Joanne and the illegal trade in cycads than they were letting on.

She let herself into the rear passenger compartment of the helicopter. The pilot turned and handed her a headset, and when she had put it on he introduced himself as Mike.

'We'll be at the lodge in no time.'

The landscape dropped away below them and Mike showed off a little with a steep dive. She didn't smile. Instead, while Mike was focused on flying, Sonja took her Glock from her handbag, where it had been safely stowed so far, and clipped its holster onto the belt of her pants suit. Having spent much of her life in uniform, wearing the same thing every day, Sonja cared little for fashion, but she could not wait to get out of this hideous outfit and wished now she had bought at least one other change of clothes. She put a spare magazine for the pistol in one pocket of her jacket and slid her Leatherman multi-tool into the inside of her right elastic-sided ankle boot.

Then, taking out her phone, Sonja composed a message to Rod Cavanagh, hit send, and then deleted it from the device's memory. She made sure there was nothing else on the phone that could link back to Rod, Joanne or Jed. She was going back into the prince's lair without any back-up. She wondered what he wanted to see her about so urgently.

Flying down the face of the escarpment they passed over farmland that eventually gave way to wild bushveld. She made out the town of Hoedspruit below, the air force base whose runway also served the civilian airport, and the privately owned game reserves that stretched away to the Kruger Park further to the east. Mike swung north, and soon they were coming in low over the distinctive double security fences of Faisal's property.

Sonja thought of the tunnel below and the money that had already been poured into the rich man's folly. She had dealt with the mega-wealthy in the past, those who had acquired their fortunes by both legal and illegal means. As a child she had seen rich people come to the lodge where her father worked, sometimes with a list of demands and special requests that were almost impossible to fulfil in the African bush. There was a peculiar arrogance, she thought, about those who not only flaunted their money, but expected others to change their behaviour, their routines, to suit them.

Mike brought the chopper down behind the sprawling main building where Thandi had been snooping earlier in the day. The prince himself strode out to meet them. Lurking in the shadows, Sonja noticed, was Sonnet. He had taken down her name and number at the gate and Sonja was at least pleased she had not given a false number, but rather the details of her burner phone.

Sonja gave Mike a wave of thanks and took off her headset. As the rotors above her began to slow she opened the door of the helicopter and stepped down.

The prince, she noticed, dismissed Sonnet with a flick of his hand and the security chief disappeared back inside. Probably, Sonja mused, to the room Thandi had told her about, where another operative no doubt surveyed the bank of security screens. She was sure she would be watched at every step.

'Welcome back,' the prince said over the whine of the helicopter's cooling engine.

'Thank you, Your Excellency.'

'Please, Faisal.'

'OK.'

He took her gently by the elbow and Sonja let him steer her into the cool of the main lodge building, then once more onto the *stoep*, where the table had been re-laid with coffee and tea and a selection of cakes.

'Please join me for something to eat.'

'I'm still full from your last offering,' she said, 'though coffee would be nice.'

'I'll pour.' He picked up a silver pot as she sat. 'I don't need staff bothering us.'

'Thank you.'

'If you're wondering how you will get back to Johannesburg, or wherever you're heading, don't. Mike will take you wherever you wish to go in the helicopter, except perhaps not as far as Namibia.' He laughed.

Interesting, Sonja thought as she took her cup and sipped strong but tasty coffee. She had not mentioned her cover, of having worked in the Namibian police service, within earshot of him. 'I don't live there any more.'

'No, but you did.' He poured coffee for himself and sat, crossing his legs as he took up his cup.

'Yes, I was in the police force there. But how did you know that?'

He smiled and set down his cup. 'Come, now, Sonja, we both know that you were never in the police force in Namibia, nor anywhere else for that matter. However, I'm sure the authorities there would love to question you about some of your antics in your home country.'

Sonja glanced around as if looking for the person the prince had just addressed. Him knowing her real name had momentarily caught her off guard. She knew this man was more than just a spoiled playboy – or he had resources akin to the CIA. That meant he could also have tracked Joanne Flack's movements from London to Zimbabwe. They were still alone, though she could feel the cameras on her. 'You have me confused with someone else. My name is Ursula –'

He cut her off. 'I've been reading about you, Sonja.'

'You're mistaken.'

He shook his head. 'No, I'm not. Rather than the police, you served with the British Army, specifically the very secretive 14 Intelligence Company, also known as The Det, a detachment in Northern Ireland made up of male and female soldiers conducting surveillance on the IRA. The idea behind the unit was that the Irish republicans would be less suspicious of females loitering around their haunts than men – the same way you thought I wouldn't be concerned by a bunch of little old men and women who fancy plants. I applaud your use of a ruse, though you're not as good as you think at covering your tracks.'

She said nothing, and took another sip of coffee. It seemed Faisal was content to keep talking and show off his knowledge. As far as she could tell he was carrying no concealed weapons, but men with guns were just a shout or a sudden movement away.

'You worked as a private military contractor, a mercenary, in a number of countries and, inevitably, your photo is stored on more than one database. You had a security pass issued in 2004 in my country, Kuwait, at the Camp Doha military base, en route to an assignment for the UN as a bodyguard in Iraq. Facial recognition software is very good these days, Sonja. What are you doing here?' he asked.

She set down her cup, slowly. 'I could ask you the same thing, Faisal. I'm African, you're not. And don't forget, *you* just flew *me* here.'

He finished his coffee and brought his hands up, fingertips touching as he regarded her. 'You are an American resident these days. What brings you back to Africa?'

'Cheap booze.'

He laughed. 'Very good. I know your former employer, Julianne Clyde-Smith. She speaks highly of you. I told her I was considering recruiting you to run an anti-poaching operation for me. She told me you were the best, but that she doubted you would take such a job.'

'Clever lady.'

He nodded, his face serious again. 'Yes, very. What happened to Joanne Flack?'

'You read the news for yourself. Killed in a gun battle between poachers and security forces. She's probably trending on social media now.'

'You're here because of Joanne.'

Sonja picked up her cup and took another sip. 'Are you asking questions or telling fairy tales, Faisal? I thought you brought me here to offer me a job.'

'I did.'

Sonja waited for him to say more, but this time he was content to sit in silence.

Sonja looked out from the *stoep*. The setting sun was gilding the bush and all looked peaceful and quiet. Soon it would be dark, and the night belonged to predators.

The stand-off between them drew on, the only sound a cape turtle dove whose repetitive call told them to *work harder*, or *drink lager*, depending on the mood.

Faisal looked pointedly up at the nearest wall and Sonja saw he was looking at a security camera. The prince leaned forward, into her personal space, his elbows on his knees as he seemed to casually cup his chin in his hands. However, he kept his fingers by his mouth and Sonja realised he was hiding his moving lips from the camera.

Faisal whispered: 'Did she tell you about her and me, our relationship? Is that why you got yourself invited on the cycad society visit?'

Sonja also lowered her voice and looked away from the camera, out at the sunset. 'I don't know what you're talking about.'

'Why did you come here to my place with that group of old plant lovers? Do you think I'm involved in the illegal trade in cycads? If you do, then you're wrong. My father, from whom I inherited a love of these plants, was guilty of buying cycads on the black market, but when he came to understand more about the plight of the wild populations he changed his tune. He instilled in me not only a love of nature, but a strong desire to protect it, in its natural habitat. It's what we're doing here with big game – rhinos, sables, wild dog and other species, providing a safe haven where they can breed and be protected.'

He sat back, perhaps having decided he would reveal no more secrets. Interesting, Sonja thought, that he had covered his lips when he talked about Joanne and he being close.

Faisal spread his arms wide. 'Look around you, and at me. Do I strike you as some turbaned Taliban or ISIS jihadi? Do you think I'm an Islamic fundamentalist terrorist supporter?'

No, she did not. But why, she wondered, had Faisal raised that idea with her? She decided to bait him a little, to see if he would bite. 'Osama bin Laden came from a very wealthy Saudi family.'

Faisal chuckled. 'Have you seen my booze cabinet? Your Zimbabwean friend took a peek when she was snooping about. My head of security showed me the camera recordings. She's also trying to find out what happened to Joanne.'

'Also? Who else wants to know?'

'Aside from you? Me.'

'As her employer.'

Faisal nodded, slowly and deliberately, as if for the camera. 'Yes, as her employer.'

'She was killed,' Sonja said. 'She was shot in a gunfight.'

'So it says on the internet. But I only believe half of what I read online.'

Sonja leaned back in her chair. 'Why am I here?'

'I need someone who knows cycads.'

She scoffed. 'There are plenty of people who know more than me. Trust me.'

He nodded. 'Walk with me. Please.'

They both got out of their chairs and Faisal motioned to the stairs leading down to the garden. The sun had almost vanished. Sonja followed him. Frogs were croaking nearby.

When they reached the ground level he led her not into the grove of cycads where the group had toured earlier in the day, but down a gravelled path that led to another parking area. Waiting for them was a Land Rover game viewer, but not the standard Defender model. This, by the look of it, was a late model Discovery 4, a top-of-the-range SUV, whose roof had been sliced off. A ranger dressed in khaki shirt and shorts opened a rear door.

'Thank you, Isaac, but I will drive.'

The ranger nodded and closed the door. 'Yes, Your Excellency. The keys are in the ignition and the fridge is stocked.'

'Thank you, Isaac.'

Faisal led Sonja around to the front passenger door and opened it for her. 'Allow me. The view is better from the front seats. It's more luxurious than an old Defender, but it doesn't have the elevated seats in the rear, at least not yet.'

Sonja thought it ostentatious to butcher such a vehicle, but kept her thoughts to herself. Faisal got behind the wheel and drove off.

'Will your bodyguards follow you?' she asked.

He shook his head. 'They have explicit instructions to leave me alone when I drive off by myself around the reserve.'

'Or if you have company?'

He ignored her raised eyebrows. 'My perimeter security is state of the art.'

'So I noticed.'

He scanned the bush as he drove, perhaps deliberately not meeting her eye. 'So, you were snooping earlier today?'

She also looked away and pointed to a herd of elephants moving slowly across a grassy *vlei* in the distance.

'Beautiful creatures, are they not?' Faisal turned off the gravel road, braked, and turned a dial to select one of the automatic terrain response modes for off-road driving. He moved off, more slowly this time, on a course she could tell was designed to intercept the elephants.

'Yes,' she said.

'You come to my lodge dressed like a little old lady, but I know you are a warrior.'

'Whatever you say.'

Faisal navigated his way between some trees and parked so that they had a ringside seat to the approach of the elephants. The old cow at the front, the matriarch of the herd, raised her trunk to sniff the air, and if she caught the scent of Faisal and his vehicle then she did not regard him as a threat because she carried on towards them.

He lowered his voice. 'I want you to work for me.'

'Why? I'm only an amateur cycad enthusiast, a newcomer.'

He shook his head. 'No, you are neither. You are not a cycad collector and nor are you a newcomer. You are experienced in the arts of war and interrogation. That is why I want to employ you, but it must be in secret.'

'Why in secret? Why not use your own security people?'

'You have a friend who is a private investigator, a Mr Hudson Brand, yes?'

Sonja said nothing and tried to stay calm. If the prince wanted to rattle her with how much research he had done, then it was working.

'You don't deny it,' he pressed.

Sonja said nothing, and worked to keep her anger in check. She drew a breath. 'What's your point?'

'My point is that sometimes people don't go to the police, or even their own security people, if they want something investigated discreetly. I would like you, perhaps with the help of your friend Hudson, to find out what happened to Joanne.'

'Why?'

'We were friends.'

'Close friends?'

He looked out at the elephants. The matriarch was close enough for them to hear her stripping the bark from a slender mopane branch with her teeth. The old cow's belly rumbled as she communicated with the rest of her family. A young male, boisterous and curious, lifted his trunk and shook his head, ears flapping, in their general direction. Sonja knew that for all the youngster's posturing he was not a threat. Was the prince?

'Joanne died, Your Excellency.'

He nodded. 'So you say, but the circumstances, you will agree, are out of the ordinary, even for Africa.'

'I'll give you that,' she said. 'Zimbabwe is a very safe country for tourists.'

'And that business in London, just a few days earlier, with the extremists. They were from Mali, I believe.'

'So I read,' she said. 'What's your connection with Mali?'

'I don't have one. If you are asking if I had dealings with terrorists, with al-Qaeda in the Maghreb or its offshoots, then no, most certainly not. Such people despise my family and bring shame upon my religion.'

'You have Malians working for you, I believe.'

He looked taken aback, then nodded. 'Ah yes, the people your Zimbabwean friend was talking to, in the dining room. Artists, interior decorators, not terrorists. I am sure you spent enough time in the Middle East to know that not all Muslims are suicide bombers, Sonja.'

There seemed little point in trying to maintain her cover now. The man clearly knew who she was so if he was innocent, she needed to recruit him to help her.

'I try not to stereotype my enemies, wherever I am.'

'I'm not your enemy, Sonja. I need your help.'

She raised her eyebrows. 'So what do you want me to do, exactly?'

'Go back to Zimbabwe, to Victoria Falls, to England if you have to, right back to before Joanne left Johannesburg for London. Find out for me, please, what went wrong, how this tragedy happened.'

'You're convinced it's all related, not just an unfortunate train of circumstances?'

'No more than you are, Sonja. Come now, it's why you visited Joanne's workplace, isn't it? To see the lair of the potential terrorist mastermind?' He smiled and its perfectness was infectious.

'She was supplying rare cycads to you.'

'Yes,' he said, without hesitation, 'with permits and only from reputable dealers, and from a deceased estate. But–'

'But?'

He held up a hand. 'Allow me to finish, please, Sonja. If Joanne had offered me an illegal cycad I would have asked her why she was so desperate that she needed to break the law to make money. I would have *given* her money.'

'Yet she didn't ask you for any, even though her son-in-law had lost his job and her lifeline of cash from abroad was about to dry up. Pride?'

He shrugged. 'Perhaps, but she was a very forthright person. With no British pounds coming into her bank account and no family left here in South Africa, why would she not have accepted my standing offer to come and live here, and to work for me fulltime?'

Sonja remembered with some discomfort that she had not received an answer to this question.

The elephants filed past them, one almost close enough for Sonja to reach out and touch. The sheikh seemed mesmerised, but perhaps his love of wildlife was just an act.

'It will be dark soon. You'll stay at the lodge tonight.'

It didn't seem like a question, but nor was Sonja ready to leave just yet. She had more questions of her own for the prince.

Chapter 20

Joanne poured a half bucket of water over their prisoner's head.

The man had passed out again and had been showing signs of regaining consciousness as they tied him to the chair, but now he came to fully, coughing, spluttering – and crying.

Almost immediately he started sobbing. 'Let...let me go.' He sniffed as tears rolled down his face.

'Sheesh, what's wrong with you, man?' Joanne asked. 'Is the pain so bad that you have to cry like a baby?'

He shook his head, his body still heaving. 'No. I don't know.'

Rod cleared his throat and held up the wallet and identification he had taken from their captive. 'You're a police officer?'

The man sniffed again. 'Yes. And you're going to prison for holding me against my will.'

'What were you doing in this house?' Joanne asked.

'Investigating.'

'Where's your search warrant?'

'I thought I heard someone crying for help from inside.'

'Bullshit.' Joanne raised her hand as if to strike him, but the man didn't even flinch. He kept on crying, though. 'I saw you sneaking around in the backyard with a ski mask on. Cops on legitimate investigations don't do that.' Joanne looked to Rod. 'Why the fuck is he crying?'

Rod shrugged his shoulders.

'Con—' the man drew a deep breath to try and still himself. 'Concussion. It's a side effect sometimes. I'm going to *fokken moer* you two.'

'You're talking big for someone who's tied up and sobbing, buster,' Rod said. 'Now tell us the truth, what were you looking for?'

The man looked up at Rod, still weeping, but silent.

'Do something,' Joanne said.

'Like what?'

'I don't know. You're the CIA. Waterboard him or something.'

The man sniffed through his tears and tried to laugh. 'Who, this pen-pusher?'

Rod took her elbow and ushered her out of the lounge into the kitchen. He spoke to her in an urgent whisper. 'Do *not* say that again. Anyway, I'm not CIA, I *was* Fish and Wildlife Service, and we don't torture people, not even when they do really bad stuff.'

'I'd stick with pretending to be CIA if I were you. You're good at lying—it's the only way you can get laid.'

'Stop it. What are we going to do with him?'

'I don't know, but I do know he was not on a legitimate investigation. OK, fair enough if the police wanted to search my house because they think I'm dead, but they'd still need permission from someone, maybe my daughter or my landlord, and they wouldn't send a man in disguise to break in. What the hell would a cop want at my place?'

Rod took the man's wallet out of his pocket and emptied the contents on the kitchen counter. 'Let's see what we've got here.'

Joanne helped him sort the credit cards, two-hundred and fifty rand in notes, and other pieces of paper.

'There are some cash slips here.' She held them up to the light so she could better see the pale print. 'The Bond Cafe, Pretoria. Hey, that's where my friends and I have brunch after our meetings and where we go shooting. Do you think he was following me?'

'Could be,' Rod said. Joanne handed him the slip and he checked it. 'And whether he was watching you guys on official or unofficial business, it looks like he was planning on claiming his cheeseburger and Coke on expenses.'

Joanne found a business card. 'Drycleaners, at Clearwater Mall. That's close to here, on Hendrik Potgieter. Maybe he lives and works near here.'

'Let's go ask him some more questions,' Rod said. 'You want to be the good cop or the bad cop?'

'Bad. Very bad.'

They went back to the lounge. Joanne stood in front of him, hands on her hips. 'Now's the time to start chirping, *bru*. Where are you stationed?'

'*Fokof*,' he said.

Joanne kicked him in the leg, where she had shot him.

The policeman howled, tears still rolling down his cheeks.

Rod put a hand on her shoulder. 'Hey, take it easy. This guy's a hard-ass. I'm sure he can take a lot of pain.'

'Let's see, shall we?'

Rod stepped between her and the man and bent so that his mouth was close to the man's ear. 'She's crazy. Someone has tried to kill her, a couple of times. Now, tell us where you're based. We'll call your station, and once we corroborate your story that you're here on official business we'll get your fellow officers to come collect you. OK, buddy?'

'You *fokof* as well, *buddy*,' the man said.

'Now look, Officer –' Rod checked the ID, '– Lindeque, I'm sure we can all take a deep breath and discuss this like adults, without the cussing.'

Lindeque seemed to be getting his tears under control, Joanne noticed. He snorted. 'I'm going to cut your cock off and stuff it down your throat, and make it look like suicide.'

Joanne scoffed. 'You talk big for a crybaby.'

'*Poes*,' Lindeque spat at her.

Joanne punched him in the nose and Lindeque screamed. The tears returned.

'What was that all about?' Rod asked.

'He called me a very bad name,' Joanne said. She leaned over the policeman, whose nose was bleeding. 'Now, what were you looking for?'

'When–' he spat blood onto the tiled floor, '–when are you going to let me go?'

'Your people tried to kill me at Victoria Falls and you shot one of this man's colleagues.' Joanne drew her pistol and placed the tip of the barrel between Lindeque's eyes. 'I'm inclined to kill you to send a message to your employers.'

Rod coughed. 'Um, maybe we need to ratchet this down a notch.'

She looked at him and she knew this was no longer an act, at least not for her. '*Um*, no, Rod, I think it's time to ratchet things *up* a couple of notches.'

'You shouldn't use his real name,' the man said, sniffing noisily.

Rod looked from him to her. 'He's right, you know. He'll be better able to identify us.'

'Sure,' she said. 'That would be an issue if I was going to let him live, but think about it, *Rod*. We've shot, cuffed, bound and assaulted a serving police officer.'

'Whoa there,' Rod interjected. 'I didn't do any shooting or assaulting.'

'Apart from hitting me in the head with a *fokken* brick,' Lindeque interjected.

'Oh, right, yes.'

'So my point,' Joanne pressed the pistol hard enough between Lindeque's eyes to tilt his head back, 'is that we need to kill this prick. Sadly, honest cops die far too often in South Africa. This will be just one more body to be found. I'm going to kill him, Rod.'

'No,' the man called out, 'no!'

'Yes,' she said. 'Unless you tell me, right now, what you were looking for.'

'I can't.'

Joanne lifted the pistol and fired a shot into the ceiling. Plaster rained down on the prisoner's head. Rod swore. Joanne slammed the butt of the pistol grip into Lindeque's temple then returned the now-hot barrel to its place between his eyes, pushing even harder than before. She felt the blood lust rise in her, as horrifying as it was pleasing. She thought of the dying policeman in England, the man coming at her with two knives, the thugs on the boat on the Zambezi River who had shot Jed and were determined to kill her.

'Fuck you,' she said, taking up the slack on the trigger.

Rod put a hand on her arm. She swung the pistol and pointed it at him.

He raised his hands. 'Take it easy.'

'Don't touch me again. These people tried to kill me.' She returned the pistol to the bridge of Lindeque's nose. 'You've got to the count of three. Three, two –'

'OK, OK – it was a plant!'

'What?' Rod said.

'Call her off, man,' Lindeque said to Rod.

'Talk first, and quickly,' Rod replied.

'I came to look for a plant. All right, maybe I should have got a warrant or permission from the landlord, but,' his eyes flashed up to hers and he paused a second, 'whoever lives here is supposedly dead. She's a criminal who double-crossed some Malian gangsters and when they found out they'd been ripped off they sent a hit squad to get her. So, I didn't think it would matter.'

'Why did you sneak in the back way,' Rod asked, 'dressed as a builder?'

'This is Joburg, man. Someone would have called armed response if they'd seen a strange *oke* trying to get in through the front door.'

'Bullshit,' Joanne said. 'In Joburg most people wouldn't have done anything. What plant were you looking for?'

'A cycad. Ugly-looking thing, just a trunk, really, probably wrapped in plastic.'

Joanne swallowed. Rod looked at her then back to Lindeque. 'Why?'

The policeman exhaled. 'We caught a couple of guys, a few weeks ago, who had this plant they were planning on smuggling out of the country and it was supposed to be worth, like, a billion rand or something. It was moved from the evidence lock-up because the detectives in charge thought it would go missing. Turned out it *did* go missing, but the lady who lived in this house stole it and then she died, killed in Zimbabwe by poachers or something. Like I said, I came to look for it … to take it back to the evidence locker.'

Joanne laughed. 'Sure.'

'You have to let me go,' Lindeque said.

'So you can come back with your police friends and arrest us? I don't think so,' Joanne said.

He looked to Rod. 'Please. There are people – kids – depending on me.'

Joanne looked down at his hand. 'No wedding ring.'

'I'm divorced, but the kids stay with me today. They'll be waiting for me, missing me, tonight. You can't do this to them.'

'You should have thought about that before you decided to moonlight as a break-and-enter man, Lindeque,' Joanne said. She nodded towards the kitchen, as a signal to Rod. 'Don't go anywhere, Lindeque.'

She and Rod left the lounge room. Joanne lowered her voice. 'What do you think?'

Rod shrugged. 'He's playing the dumb hired help. He hasn't given any indication he actually knows who you are.'

'No, but that means nothing. He could just be a good actor. If we let him go he *will* find a way to bust us, or worse. Also, he'll be able to tell his superiors that I'm alive and well and in Joburg.'

'Yes.' Rod filled a kettle with water and switched it on. 'You're right, of course. We need to keep him on ice, but how long before his friends or business partners come looking for him? And there's that business about the kids. You think that's legit?'

'Who knows?' Joanne said. 'We need to check him out, find out if he's really working alone or if he's part of all this – whatever it is.'

Rod took out three cups and spooned instant coffee into them.

'You're making Lindeque a hot drink?' she said incredulously.

'I'm the good cop, remember? Besides, he's been knocked out and shot. We need to keep him conscious and treat that wound properly. I'll do it. You can electrify his nuts later.'

Joanne poured and added milk, her hand shaking, and three sugars for the cop while she thought about what to do next. This was what she wanted, to find out who was behind the thefts, attempted and successful, from Faisal's reserve. The man they had was a foot-soldier and what she had done had set in place the chain of events that had led him to her, or vice versa. There was a difference, though, from theorising who was behind all of this to having to deal with a real live human being, who bled real blood. They were close now, and she had to steel herself to carry on and not just fall apart.

Rod's phone and rang and he answered it. 'OK,' he said, then passed it to her. 'It's Sonja.'

'Yes?' Joanne said.

'You need to tell me what was going on between you and his excellency the Sultan of Swing,' Sonja said.

'Where are you?' Joanne said quietly into the phone.

'His lodge. He's put me in a guest suite for the night.'

'Be careful.'

'Why?'

'I can't be sure we can trust him. I think he could be lying about not wanting to trade in illegal cycads.'

'Do you have evidence?' Sonja asked.

Joanne sipped her coffee. Rod took his cup and the one for Lindeque through to the lounge room. 'Like I was telling you before, another rare cycad was stolen from his garden, before the *woodii* was taken.'

'I know. So?'

'You've seen the security there; it's like Fort Knox. How would you get it out?'

'He told me this already; he was open about it and said he'd ordered a full investigation. You think a Kuwaiti prince is smuggling plants out of his own garden all by himself, with no help? I'm guessing he'd spend more on a new suit than what he'd make from selling a cycad.'

'Collectors are strange people,' Joanne said.

'So what,' Sonja asked, 'you think he sold it to another collector?'

'I think he might have done, yes.'

'Why wouldn't he let you in on this?'

'Because he knows how I feel about the illegal trade in cycads, and that I'd leave if I found out he was breaking the law.'

'So? Why should that worry him? He could get another cycad expert.'

'Not one who was sleeping with him.' Joanne heard soft footsteps and turned around. Rod was standing in the kitchen doorway, staring at her. She felt her cheeks redden and walked through the kitchen into an adjoining scullery and kicked the door closed behind her.

Sonja had not replied, so Joanne carried on. 'There's more. You know he's had that game reserve for a number of years; the lodge and the tunnel and stuff are recent additions.'

'And?'

'And other members of the royal family, foreign diplomats, big businesspeople from around the world go there to hunt. Faisal's justification, and it's not without merit, is that while the reserve is big it's a finite space, so it has a limited carrying capacity for big game, especially elephants. There have been elephant hunts there, more like culls, where they killed ten or twenty at a time, whole herds. He said there were already too many elephants on the reserve when he bought the place a decade ago.'

Sonja nodded, feeling a moment's sadness. 'I suppose that was the only option – killing.'

'Yes, that's the problem with elephants,' Joanne said. 'Endangered or near-extinct across most of Africa where they're persecuted, and causing a problem through over-breeding where they're protected. The prince could have afforded to relocate some elephants, even though it's hellishly expensive, but you literally can't give away elephants in South Africa.'

'What happened to all the ivory from the dead elephants?' Sonja asked.

'That's the sixty-four-thousand-dollar question, or rather the million-dollar question. It was all stored in a vault, in the original lodge building, but when the building work got underway in earnest, Faisal had plans for an even bigger safe. I saw crates of ivory being moved – not from one room to another, but off the property. Faisal told me it was being moved to a Limpopo Parks Board storage facility, but I did some snooping. I managed to get a look at the paperwork when a truck came to pick up the crates – they were headed to OR Tambo Airport and the crates were marked as "wooden handicrafts".'

'You confronted Faisal?'

'Of course. He denied any knowledge of trying to smuggle the ivory out of the country and called in the police. Detectives arrived, from a special wildlife crimes unit, and the driver of the truck was arrested. It seemed the driver was carrying a duplicate set of paperwork and he made the mistake of sticking the new waybills on the boxes before he left the reserve – I saw them as they were being loaded. Not exactly a criminal mastermind, but then any cop will tell you that it's the smart criminals who are the hardest to catch. The detectives were trying to find out who the driver was working for, but they never did.'

'Why not?'

'The driver died in custody, in a lock-up in Johannesburg, murdered by another prisoner in a fight over something.'

'Convenient,' Sonja said. 'Why do you still suspect Faisal?'

She paused to think. 'It's hard to put my finger on it. He's a charming guy, he says all the right things, he's handsome, and when something's wrong, like the theft of a plant or a shipment of ivory nearly being hijacked he's, like, implacable. Nothing upsets him. You're right about him having so much money that these deals are more like pocket change to him, and so it's not going to hurt him if he's robbed, but I'd expect him to at least show some emotion.'

'What about the people who work for him?' Sonja asked.

Joanne thought for a moment. 'Patricia Littleford needs her job. She's got three kids and her husband left her, but I don't think she's crooked.'

'Why not?'

'She's just not the type.'

'You really think there's a "type" when it comes to criminals?'

'Maybe. I guess not.'

'How about Sonnet?' Sonja asked.

'He's like a smart Neanderthal. He looks like an ape, but he's cunning.'

'What's his background? Military?' Sonja asked.

'Yes, and police. I heard him bragging a couple of times to his underlings about some big cases he supposedly solved, so I'm assuming he was a detective.'

'Where?'

'Joburg, I think.' That got Joanne thinking.

'Did anyone else know about the ivory shipment, outside of Faisal's people?'

Joanne paused. 'Yes. I mentioned it at a meeting of the cycad society. We were discussing poaching of cycads and wildlife and the subject of elephants and ivory came up.'

'And they all knew about the existence of the rare cycads?'

'Yes,' Joanne said. 'The female *woodii* in particular was an exciting discovery that I told the society about, before the plant was stolen. It was stupid of me, but the news was just too enormous to keep to myself. In our world this discovery was nothing short of a miracle. I swore the prince to silence, but went and blabbed away myself. I just never thought that could be a dangerous thing to do; not with my friends.'

The silence hung between them for a few seconds, then Sonja broke it. 'The prince said he would have given you money if you needed it. Why didn't you go to him? I know your financial tap was turned off when your son-in-law lost his job.'

Joanne eased the scullery door open a crack. Through the kitchen doorway she could see that Rod was holding the coffee cup to their prisoner's lips. She closed the door again. 'Faisal is handsome and rich, and even though he's about the same age as me he's not looking for a wife. He wanted me as his concubine here in Africa. I like him, but I'm not a whore, and as I was saying, I'm not sure I can trust him one hundred per cent.'

'He never married?'

'No, he's the original playboy, and not looking to settle down. For all I know he's got a girl in London, or New York, or Paris, or all of the above – wherever he likes to hang out when he's not at his game reserve. He doesn't seem to spend too much time in Kuwait. He really loves his cycads, which is why he's here so often.'

'OK, let me talk to Cavanagh.'

234

'Hold on.' Joanne went through to the lounge and gave the phone to Rod.

Rod nodded and went back into the kitchen where he could talk in private.

'You're a detective, Warrant Officer Lindeque?' Joanne said to the bound man.

'I'll be anything you want me to be.'

She thought about slapping him, or kicking him, and realised how easy it was for a normal human being to become a torturer. However, she realised that there was probably nothing she could do to make him tell the truth.

Instead, she sat on a couch where she could keep Lindeque in sight, and started googling the phone numbers for South African Police Service stations in the local area.

The operator at Krugersdorp SAPS told her in a bored voice that she had never heard of a detective named Lindeque. Joanne enjoyed the sight of her captive licking his lips nervously as she made the next call in front of him.

'Oh, so you say Warrant Officer Lindeque used to work at Roodepoort?' She raised her eyebrows, watching him squirm. 'Must I try Florida SAPS instead?'

He rolled his eyes.

Joanne called the Florida station, located up the hill from where they sat. 'Could I speak to Warrant Officer Lindeque, please?'

'Sorry, he's on leave for two months,' the woman on reception said.

'Thank you.'

Joanne ended the call. 'Seems you've been moonlighting, Lindeque. Care to explain?'

He narrowed his eyes. 'I'm going to tell whoever I send to kill you to take their time with you.'

She gave a little laugh. 'Do you know an ex-cop named Frank Sonnet?'

'*Fokof,*' Lindeque said, though Joanne thought she caught something in his body language. He had started, ever so slightly, at the mention of Sonnet's name, and now she could see the muscles in the side of his face strain as he clenched his jaw shut.

Joanne had a thought. She called the Florida station a second time and apologised to the same officer for calling again. Joanne asked the woman if she remembered a Frank Sonnet working at the station sometime in the past.

'Yes, he left about a year ago, I think.'

'Thank you,' Joanne said. She looked at Lindeque. 'This is fun, isn't it?'

Joanne mentally replayed her conversation with Sonja and thought about the business of the ivory shipment that had very nearly been diverted out of the country. She hadn't been at Faisal's reserve when the police from the Endangered Wildlife Unit had come to investigate. If Faisal was crooked, and the investigation into the ivory was just a sham that he covered up, then perhaps he had tried the same tactic with the two cycads, making it look like someone else had stolen them to cover his attempts to smuggle them out of the country. If he had sold the *woodii* to a bunch of Malian terrorists then maybe he was guilty of more than just smuggling; perhaps he was backing Islamic extremists? Maybe, Joanne thought, the *woodii* had actually been a donation to their evil cause?

She used her phone to google the EWU and found a number of hits about arrests of rhino horn smugglers, along with articles about pangolins, vultures and ivory being illegally traded and/or smuggled out of South Africa. The head of the unit, Colonel Fanie Theron, was quoted in several stories, so she narrowed her search to him. Theron, it seemed, had left SAPS and was now working with an NGO that specialised in disrupting international traffic in wildlife products.

Joanne found a Johannesburg number for the organisation, called it, and told the person who answered she was the South African correspondent for *The Times* of London, and was looking to interview Theron, urgently.

'That should prompt him to call me back,' she said to Lindeque as Rod re-entered the room. She updated Rod on Lindeque's leave status.

'Our contact,' Rod said, referring obliquely to Sonja, 'agrees we should keep him on ice for a while.'

'Maybe she should interrogate him?'

'She?' Lindeque smiled. 'Maybe I'll like that.'

Joanne shook her head. 'I don't think so. She's more likely than either of us to slit your throat if you don't talk.'

Joanne's phone buzzed. 'Hello?' It was Theron. 'Mr Theron, thanks so much for calling back. I'm phoning to find out if you were aware of an incident at a private game reserve in Limpopo Province last year, with a shipment of a million dollars' worth of ivory that was almost hijacked and diverted to OR Tambo Airport?'

Theron paused. 'Um, no, I'm sorry, I can't recall that incident.'

'The ivory was from elephants that had been legally hunted on a reserve owned by a member of the Kuwaiti royal family. I believe detectives from your unit investigated.'

'As you would appreciate,' Theron said, 'the vast majority of our work in the unit's last few years was devoted to rhino poaching, so I'm sure I would remember an incident involving that much ivory, especially if it had been owned by a royal, and therefore a legal shipment.'

'Of course. I'll double-check my facts and get back to you. Thank you for your help and enjoy your day.'

Joanne studied Lindeque, who glared back at her. She SMSed Sonja. *Don't alert Sonnet, but ask Faisal the name of the detective who investigated the failed ivory heist.*

Chapter 21

'Let's make a deal,' Lindeque said.

'I'm listening,' Joanne replied.

Rod stood in the corner of the room, arms folded, watching the two of them. Lindeque seemed to feel increasingly cornered the more Joanne investigated, which was good, but he wondered if the policeman was serious about wanting to bargain.

'You let me go, give me the plant I'm looking for, and when I come for you – I won't even bother wasting ten thousand rand on a hit man, and I won't rape you before I kill you.'

Not serious, then, Rod thought.

Joanne moved closer to him and slapped Lindeque's face.

He shook his head. 'Is that the best you've got? Pathetic.'

Joanne looked around her, as if searching for a weapon.

'Cool it,' Rod said softly.

'Yeah, listen to the boss,' Lindeque said mockingly.

Joanne raised her right leg and delivered a high kick into Lindeque's chest, which sent the detective toppling helplessly back onto the floor. He gave a high-pitched scream. The fall knocked the air from his lungs and he seemed to struggle for breath. Joanne stood over him, a foot either side of his chest, hands on her hips, seeming to enjoy the moment.

'I'd piss on you right now, but I think you'd probably enjoy it too much.'

The policeman coughed and forced a grin and she stamped down on his chest. Lindeque spluttered and howled.

Rod went to the bound man as Joanne stepped to one side, looking satisfied with her footwork. Rod heaved Lindeque's chair back upright.

'Take my advice, buddy,' Rod said into Lindeque's ear, 'shut your mouth before she kills you.' He took a scarf that Joanne had earlier fetched from her bedroom and tied it around Lindeque's mouth as a gag. He took Joanne by the elbow and ushered her back through to the kitchen. He shut the door behind them.

He felt a rush of emotions. He was shocked by her callous cruelty, but he understood the man was trying to get to her. It was her smile, though, as she looked down at her victim, that had pressed another button. His mind flashed back to one of the times in a hotel in Vegas, where they had played around, experimenting, taking turns at tying each other up.

'What, Rod?' She was looking at him, straight in the eyes.

'You... you enjoyed that.'

She held his stare. 'I've been fucked over by men all my life. My father was a drunk who did nothing and told me I was imagining things when I told him the pastor used to touch my sister and me; my husband was a criminal; and you ruined my world. That prick in there,' she jabbed a thumb over her shoulder, 'violated my home and I'm pretty sure his comrades tried to kill me at Victoria Falls. So, yes, Rod, evil person that I am, I just enjoyed getting a little payback. What are you going to do about it?'

He kissed her.

She didn't put her arms around him – he had just leaned forward, no touching – and she kept her lips resolutely closed at first. Just as he felt them start to soften and open she seemed to have second thoughts. Joanne recoiled back into the kitchen bench and slapped him hard, in the face.

'Goddamn you, get off me.'

He held up his hands. She was breathing heavily, but those eyes stayed locked on him. 'Sorry.'

'Fuck.'

'Sorry.'

'Stop saying sorry, Rod.' She grabbed two handfuls of her hair and screamed.

239

'What's wrong?' he asked softly.

Joanne thumped the kitchen benchtop. 'I didn't want this to happen!'

'What?'

She came at him, kissing, clawing, pushing into him, so hard he had to step backwards to stop from tumbling over. His glasses were knocked to the floor and he felt his heart rate, already elevated from his first move, redline.

He remembered her as if it were yesterday, the taste of her mouth, the way she kept her eyes open all the time, the smell of the same shampoo. So many years. Even as he kissed Joanne he remembered his wife, Betty, and the soft, simple love that had held them together. He could not, would not, let himself compare the two of them. Joanne overwhelmed him.

In his sorrow and grief when Betty had passed, he had chastised himself for thinking of Joanne. He hadn't for years, well, not often. And then she had returned to his thoughts and sometimes his dreams. He hadn't had the courage to contact her or search her out via Facebook, but when Jed Banks had called and asked him about cycads he had known, without a doubt, that whatever the CIA wanted would lead him back to Africa, back to Joanne, and back to this.

She was touching him through his pants, the way she liked to, getting him ready even before they were undressed. Even in the heat of passion she liked to tease, to take control a little. He was OK with that, as he knew the tables could be, would be, turned at some point. Rod thought about their captive, in the lounge room.

'What about...'

Joanne stepped away, brushed her hair from her eyes and straightened her blouse and skirt. 'Wait here.'

She left the kitchen and Rod moved to the door. Lindeque was sitting peacefully, eyes closed, probably not sleeping but regaining his composure after being assaulted. Joanne had gone to a bedroom and returned with a pillowslip. She crept up behind the bound officer and slipped the hood over his head.

'Hey!'

'Shut up or I'll go find the iron and straighten you out.'

That was enough to silence him. Joanne beckoned Rod with a crooked finger, and as she walked she slipped off each of her sandals in turn. By the time he caught up with her, in the doorway of the master bedroom, she was unzipping her skirt and letting it fall to the floor.

He came to her and undid the buttons of her top. She kissed him as she shrugged the flimsy garment from her shoulders and stood there, dressed only in bra and pants. He dropped to his knees and kissed her stomach as she wound her fingers in his hair, her fingernails digging into his scalp.

'Kiss me.'

She put a foot up on the bed, and he buried his nose in lace and did as he was told.

He thought of her dominating the prisoner and it drove him over the edge. He stood, put an arm around her waist and half carried, half threw her onto the bed.

'Yes,' she said.

He slid her pants off as she undid her bra, impatient for him, and he came to her.

The feel of her was like coming home as they met, again, after all these years. Although they were both single now there was the same feeling of illicitness, the same danger as when he had been undercover and she was one of his targets, maybe even the prime suspect. He had known it was wrong back then and it was probably a dumb thing to do right now, but, the hell with it, Rod thought. His life since his last trip to Africa, both at home and at work, had been one of following the rules, of a continual feeling of having to atone for the wrongs he had done. And here he was committing those same sins all over again.

He didn't know if Joanne was innocent, or what crimes she might have committed. As before, in this moment he didn't care. All he wanted was to lose himself and his cares in the glorious depths of her.

She drew him in, hands and legs and ankles urging him closer, deeper, telling him, without words, to let go of himself. She was like a predatory plant, a Venus flytrap, beguiling and beautiful, and he was the insect, the drone, drawn to her beauty and danger. *Swallow me*, he wanted to beg, *devour me, take away my will.*

He had wondered, after Operation Green Thumb was over, what he would have done if he had found out that she, not Peter, was the mastermind behind the smuggling ring.

In fleeting secret thoughts, almost too dark to be allowed to surface, he asked himself if he would have let her go, or worse, if he would have left the department to be with her.

He knew she had hated him when it was all exposed, when her husband was dead and the rest of the cycad smuggling ring, many of them her friends, had been convicted and either fined or imprisoned. Joanne had told him he should rot in hell and that she would never speak to him again. He'd told himself he didn't want to see her either, but that was a lie.

If she had aged, he couldn't feel it. Sunlight streamed in through an open window, bathing their bodies. He slowed and paused above her.

'What?'

He smiled down at her and shook his head. 'Nothing. I just don't want this moment to end.'

'Well, I liked that moment a few moments ago. Giddy-up, cowboy, or whatever you people say.'

The words were there, hanging just inside him, threatening to spill out of him, just as they had been on the day he killed her husband. *I love you, Joanne Flack.* Instead he simply nodded and began moving again.

She was right, it was a perfect place in space and time. They were together. The arousal was there, sparking just as easily as it had all those years ago. If he could capture this feeling, this moment, this perfect glide path, he would.

'Yes,' she whispered, and half closed her eyes. That's how he knew she was close.

He hadn't thought about protection and neither had she, though she was too old to conceive. It was the story of their lives, this risk-taking of theirs.

Though he knew it was futile, he couldn't help but revisit the 'what if'; if only she had got back in touch with him after it was all over last time. He wouldn't have met his wife, or had his son, neither of which he regretted at all, but their lives could have been so different.

Joanne grabbed him by the buttocks and drew him in deeper, harder, and the surprise and force of it were too much for him and he surrendered to the pure, terrible joy of it, the eruption emptying him of whatever thought it was he had been thinking.

After a while he rolled off her and she turned her head, cheeks red, her chest rising and falling as she smiled at him. Joanne reached out a hand and laid her palm on his belly. 'I missed you.'

'I did too. For a long time. And then lately, more often,' he said, the words tumbling out, his brain still not engaged enough to dissemble.

'Because of your wife?'

He nodded. 'She died. Cancer.'

'I know.'

'You do?'

'There's a thing called Google, Rod. People get drunk and search for stuff they shouldn't, stuff they occasionally regret.'

He let that sink in, his senses returning enough to remind him that sometimes it was better not to answer.

'Phew,' she said, 'I'm not as fit as I used to be. That was exhausting. Excuse me.'

Joanne got up, taking the top sheet with her as a wrap, and went to the en suite bathroom. Rod looked around the bedroom for his clothes. He dressed, but found he was missing a sock. Joints creaking, for he, too, had found the ferocious bout of lovemaking more than a little tiring, he got down on all fours and looked under the bed.

Rod could see his errant sock and was about to grab it when he noticed something else. The object was packaged up in bubble wrap and looked to be an odd shape. It was cylindrical and about half the length of the bed. To reach it he had to lie down flat on his belly and stretch as far as he could. He couldn't get under the bed completely, but managed to reach far enough in that his fingers touched the plastic wrapping. He couldn't quite get purchase on it, so he tried pushing it instead. The object rolled a few centimetres towards Joanne's side of the bed.

Rod hauled himself to his feet and scooted around to the other side. Lying down again, he reached under and found he could now grasp the package, which he rolled free of the bed.

Even before he began unwrapping it he could tell what it was. 'Holy smoke...'

*

Joanne finished in the bathroom. She could hear the builders next door still banging and clanging away.

She opened the door and drew a sharp breath. Rod was lying on the floor next to the bed, face down. He had started to dress – he wore his shirt and trousers, though his feet were bare.

Her first thought was that Rod had found the hidden cycad and she tried to think what she would tell him. 'Rod...'

He didn't answer or move.

She felt suddenly like she'd been punched in the chest. The holster at his belt was empty. She had left her weapon – Lindeque's silenced pistol – on the bedside table, but it was gone.

'Looking for this?'

Joanne turned her head at the sound of the voice. Lindeque stood in the doorway, grinning through a mask of dried blood, most of which she had inflicted on him. He had his pistol in his hand, pointed at her, and by his side was the caudex of the missing *Encephalartos woodii* female cycad, still swathed in bubble wrap.

'I didn't get time to look under your bed before,' Lindeque said, 'but your boyfriend discovered your hiding place – I must say that was an obvious choice. Sorry, I had to put two shots into his back. Curiosity got that cat.'

She looked at Rod again and saw how still he was. It was true. He was dead. A sob rose in her throat. 'You've... you've got what you wanted. Now go!'

He laughed. 'You're kidding, right?'

Joanne felt worse than vulnerable as she clutched the sheet to her breasts. There was no way she could get past him, nowhere for her to run, other than back into the bathroom, where he would corner her and gun her down. Joanne looked at Rod again.

She had lost him a second time, and this time, forever. Her legs felt like they were about to give way. Never in her life had she felt more like her age.

Lindeque laughed. 'The noise you two were making – *jislaaik* – I thought he was stabbing you, not fucking you. Get dressed.'

She glared at him. 'And if I don't?'

He shrugged. 'I suppose I'll kill you as well.' He gestured to the collection of pictures on the wall. Most of them were of her daughter, Peta, from when she was a baby through to her wedding and a few more recent snaps. Joanne was in some of the pictures. 'I only just realised that you're definitely Joanne Flack. I guess they'll want you alive, once I tell them you're not actually dead, but I'm sure my people won't mind if I bring them your head in a box, either.'

Joanne put on jeans, a T-shirt and her sandals.

He ushered her out of the bedroom. Lindeque had obviously been able to free himself of his bindings; Joanne guessed that the electrical cord had come loose when her anger had got the better of her and she had kicked him over onto his back. It was her fault.

Tears of hopelessness gurgled up inside her. Grief for Rod would come later. For now it was the terrible realisation that she had brought all this on herself that was threatening to undo her. Rod was dead; she would be killed soon. The fact that she had hurt this oaf would only make things worse for her.

'You should have killed me,' he said as he prodded her in the back, moving her towards the front door. When she stopped he gagged her with the same scarf she had used on him. It was wet from his saliva and that made her retch, provoking more laughter from Lindeque. 'Oh, yes, I am so going to enjoy this.'

He reached around her and opened the door then shoved her forward, the fronts of her thighs painfully colliding with the lowered rear bumper of the Fortuner as he pushed her inside, face first, and tied her hands behind her back and bound her ankles. Lindeque closed the rear of the vehicle so she could not wriggle out and returned a few minutes later, huffing and puffing as he hauled the heavy cycad stem up into the space next to her.

Lindeque started the engine and drove off. When she felt the turn, pause and acceleration that told her he'd found her keys and the swipe card that opened the security boom gate, she knew she had no chance.

She thought about what had just happened with Rod, the feel of him, the smell of him, still so familiar after all these years. Joanne had come so close to telling him the truth: that she had always loved him.

Now it was too late.

Now she would die alone.

Chapter 22

There was a knock on the door of Sonja's luxury suite. When she opened it she saw Patricia, holding a clutch of garment bags.

'H. E. thought you might like to get changed for dinner.'

'What's wrong with what I'm wearing?' In fact, Sonja disliked the outfit intensely and so did Patricia, judging by her pursed lips.

'Nothing,' she said diplomatically, 'but he's a bit old-fashioned. He will have smartened himself up.' She held up a brown paper gift bag. 'And there are some extra toiletries and amenities from the lodge gift shop, in case you needed them.'

'OK, thanks.' Sonja took the bags and Patricia turned to leave. 'Patricia?'

'Yes?'

'Does he keep women's clothing here just on spec?'

'The prince likes to entertain and has guests from around the world. Few bring enough formal clothes or cocktail wear, so he decided it would be nice have a selection on hand.'

Sonja nodded and closed the door as Patricia left.

She laid the garment bags on the king-size bed, which was made up with starched white linen. The decor was safari chic, not animal skins and wind-up gramophones but enough dark wood to give a feeling of yesteryear, and contemporary art to remind visitors that Faisal had excellent taste. Either that or he had very good decorators.

Sonja stripped and wrapped a towel around her then walked through to the bathroom. There was a choice of bath, indoor shower, or outdoor shower. She chose the latter as it was mild outside, the night sky pricked with a couple of early stars or planets. Sonja turned on the hot tap and hung her towel while she waited for the water to warm up.

Once in, she closed her eyes and tilted her face up to the large showerhead, which delivered a rainstorm of soothing water. She thought about what Joanne had told her about Faisal, fancier and collector of women and plants. Perhaps she would play along with his game and dress for him. She would get nothing out of him by antagonising him.

Sonja lathered some shampoo into her hair then rinsed it out and reached for the conditioner, but her fingers were still slippery and the bottle fell from her hands. As she turned and knelt on the shiny, smooth pebbled floor she caught a flash of movement in her peripheral vision.

Slowly she turned.

The snake was arranged into the form of a two-metre question mark, its girth as thick as her wrist. The reptile's body colour was a mix of olive and grey, and the head, as it rose up to greet her from less than a metre away, was coffin-shaped.

Black mamba.

It was the first snake she had learned to recognise as a child, living in Botswana's Okavango Delta, because it was one of the deadliest and most dangerous creatures in the bush. She remembered tiptoeing past a tree that led to the staff accommodation where she and her father lived, scared because everyone in the camp knew a mamba lived there. She would see the snake occasionally, or her father would point it out at night as it slithered through the bush or climbed trees in search of bush babies or birds. A couple of times it had reared up, raising its head high above the long grass. Its beady eyes had sized her up as it languidly decided whether or not it would kill her that day while young Sonja stood her ground, her heart trying to smash through her ribs.

Sonja froze, naked, dripping water, one knee on the floor, her arm half reaching for the bottle of conditioner, which lay next to the snake. How the hell had it got there? She looked up by rotating her eyes rather than risking a movement of her head. There was a tree, a jackalberry by the look of it, but it hardly overhung the shower. Perhaps the thing had just slithered over the wall.

She knew that if she kept still, as she had when she was a child, the snake, while inquisitive, would be unlikely to strike at her. If it had been a Mozambican spitting cobra it would already have expectorated a stream of blinding venom into her eyes. Instead, it watched her, its head moving slowly, slightly, from side to side, its forked tongue darting in and out, detecting her scent.

Sonja lowered her eyes and saw that the creature was holding its ground. She tried to slow her breathing. Mamba bites, if not treated or misdiagnosed and treated incorrectly, would kill. If she was bitten she would need immediate attention, but she wondered how long it would take someone to find her. As far as she knew she was the only guest at the lodge and her bungalow room was a good hundred metres from the main lodge. Patricia would be long gone.

She looked around her for a weapon. Nothing.

Sonja had closed the door leading back into the suite, so both she and the mamba were trapped in the shower area. Unfortunately, the snake was between her and the door. It retreated a little and lifted its body, nearly two-thirds of its length, along the wall. Sonja used the time to edge further back and slowly pull her towel off the hook beside the showerhead. She wrapped it around her right hand and arm.

The polished concrete surface of the wall was too slippery for the snake to gain purchase and climb out of the arena, so it lowered itself to the floor again and resumed its malevolent, beady-eyed vigil. It began to bob and weave its head, as if it was becoming impatient.

Sonja had heard many campfire stories about these snakes. Her first boyfriend, Stirling, a safari guide, had told her that some of the common beliefs about black mambas were false. Others, such as its deadliness, were true. Mambas had a reputation for being aggressive and, according to legend, unlike other snakes they would attack rather than try to escape when disturbed. Sonja knew this to be untrue, though the caveat was that they might attack when cornered. This one had nowhere to go, but she told herself that as long as she – and the reptile – remained calm, there was no reason for it to strike at her.

She focused on her breathing. She just had to wait. Would they ring if she didn't show for dinner? Probably. If someone came to her suite and then tried to enter, would that disturb and provoke the mamba? Maybe.

Sonja looked up at the walls, just as the snake had. She could see nothing on which she could stand to get up and over the wall before the snake panicked. If it struck it could reach her easily from where it was, on the other side of the shower area; she was just a couple of metres from that darting tongue and the fangs inside the inky-black mouth which gave the black mamba its name.

Stay cool, she told herself. *And stay still.*

Then something fell from above, taking both Sonja and the mamba by surprise. She saw that a section of tree branch had landed next to the snake. It reared up and Sonja, who could not help but flinch, dived to one side and rolled on the cool wet floor as the mamba struck at her. She lifted her arm wrapped in the towel and the mamba bit down on it.

She felt the power of its jaws, surprisingly strong for a comparatively small head, and prayed the fangs wouldn't penetrate the towel. She shook her arm and the snake's whip-like body jerked as it released and reared back, ready to strike again. The towel unravelled, fortunately, and Sonja was able to toss it over the snake. The creature wriggled and bucked under the fluffy white shroud.

Sonja stood and darted further away from the danger. This snake was beyond provoked now. She saw that the showerhead was mounted at the top of a copper pipe that ran up from the brass taps. The simple fittings had been left partially exposed rather than recessed into the wall to give a rustic effect. Sonja grabbed the narrow pipe with both hands and, juiced with adrenaline, she ripped the fitting from the wall. She had to bend the pipe hurriedly back and forth a few times, all the while watching the snake flailing under the towel.

As she continued to work at the metal Sonja looked down again and saw the towel moving towards her. The snake's head emerged from the covering and lifted up, the towel falling away.

She looked into the black mouth, saw the fangs ready to plunge into her body, and with a yell of anger and frustration and one more mighty heave the shower pipe and head snapped off. She swung the plumbing down in a slashing arc just as the mamba struck, and knocked it sideways. It slithered away and Sonja reached down and grabbed the towel again. She hurled it like an unfurling cape and it landed on the snake once more as she advanced on it and struck down, again and again, with all her strength. The snake was still writhing, but now she was between it and the door. She ran and slid open the glass door. Just as she closed it the mamba, emerging from under the towel and moving with the speed of a startled impala, struck at her, its head and fangs rapping against the glass. Sonja, exhausted, slid to the cool polished floor. Venom dripped down the pane as she tried to regain her breathing.

Eventually, she got up and went to the garment bags still strewn on her bed. She looked at her handbag and considered getting her Glock out and shooting the snake.

No. It was a living creature and all it had done was react to the danger it perceived. Sonja unzipped the first bag and took out a simple little black dress, which she shimmied into. She walked barefoot back to the sliding door and looked at the snake. Still tormented, it slithered back and forth. There would be a ranger somewhere at this lodge who would have the special tongs and a bag with which to catch it and release it. It seemed her blows with the copper pipe, as vicious as they had been, had done no more than annoy the mamba, and for now it was safely corralled in the outdoor shower area.

Sonja brushed her hair, then, with no shoes to match the dress, put on her riding boots again. She was no fashionista, but according to her daughter Emma it was apparently acceptable to wear boots with a cocktail dress these days.

Instead of taking the path to the main lodge she walked through the knee-high dry grass between her suite and its neighbour, to the rear of the shower enclosure. Sonja studied the ground. It was dark, but she could just make out the crisp indentations of footprints.

The spoor looked to have been made by a man, fairly tall given the size of the one clear track she could see. The deep and chunky tread pattern came from a boot, military style, not a sneaker or sandal like some of the staff wore.

Circling the unit she returned to the path and made her way to the lounge area.

Faisal was there, along with a couple of servants. He wore a slimly tailored black suit, which would have been overdressed, Sonja thought, except his white dinner shirt was open-necked and, as was the current fashion, he wore shoes with no socks. Even his five o'clock shadow looked elegant.

'Good evening,' he said, smiling. 'I hope you were able to get some rest.'

'Hardly.'

'Really? A drink? Champagne? I have a nice Billecart that I have flown in from France.'

'I'm more of a spirits girl.'

'Excellent. I can offer you a superb bourbon from the Taconic Distillery in upstate New York, their Dutchess Private Reserve is the best I've ever –'

Sonja turned to a woman clutching a silver tray, waiting to take her order. 'Klipdrift and Coke Zero, please.'

'Of course, madam.' The waitress retreated.

The prince cleared his throat. 'Sit, please.'

Sonja joined Faisal on a pair of canvas and leather armchairs that had the look of old British colonial campaign furniture, though each would have required a separate bearer to carry it.

'Was something not to your liking?' he pressed.

'The black mamba was an interesting shower companion.'

'Oh dear, I should have said something.'

She raised her eyebrows, then told him what had happened. 'You'll need to send someone to remove it from the shower, and the shower will need to be repaired.'

'My head of security, Frank, informed me this afternoon that he had seen a large mamba between two of the suites. He was going to get one of the safari guides to catch it and release it away from the lodge. I wonder if it's the same snake.'

'This one would have eaten any competition in the neighbourhood, trust me.'

'I'm very sorry for your ordeal, however you strike me as a woman who knows how to look after herself in a dangerous situation.'

Sonja sipped her drink. 'Do you have security cameras around the suites?'

'Not inside the suites or the shower areas, goodness, no.'

'I mean around the outside of each unit.'

The waitress came and topped up Faisal's champagne and gave Sonja her brandy and Coke.

'The security and safety of my guests is paramount,' he said.

Noting that the prince hadn't actually answered her question, Sonja took a sip of her drink and chose her words carefully. 'Perhaps you'd take a look at the footage from around my suite this evening. You might get a good look at a snake.'

Faisal narrowed his eyes slightly. 'Perhaps I will.'

'I'm curious,' she said.

'Yes?'

'Why all the security? The double fences, the tunnel, the cameras?'

'Many of my guests are rather well off. They're considered targets for abduction and ransom in many countries. Also, world politics at the moment – I'm sure I don't need to tell you – are unstable. New enemies can arise anywhere, anytime.'

She fixed him with her gaze. 'Yet with all those security measures still you can't stop a load of ivory from almost disappearing from under your nose.'

He crossed his legs and straightened the fabric on his trouser leg. 'You're well informed. Has Patricia been talking out of school?'

'Let's just say you're not the only one who does their research.'

'I was lucky that Joanne Flack was on the ball and detected the fact that the driver who came to collect the ivory was premature in changing the shipping manifests. But I thought you were new to the cycad society. You wouldn't have known Joanne?'

'People talk,' Sonja said. 'To tell you the truth I heard about it from one of the other members; Joanne had related it to her.'

'I see.' He visibly relaxed, appearing to have bought her story. 'Yes, as I say, I was lucky. I had my security procedures reviewed. You might also have heard that a rare cycad was stolen from me before this latest incident with the *woodii*.'

She nodded. 'Also odd, given how tight your security is.'

He waved a hand in the air. 'Perhaps. Like hiding in plain sight, sometimes the easiest way to steal something is to boldly walk out with it. One of the gardeners was found to be the culprit, and dismissed.'

'What was his name?' Sonja already knew about the gardener, from Joanne, but didn't want to let on, as she wanted Faisal's take on the theft.

'Festus Mtethwa.'

'It's nice that you know the names of your staff.'

Faisal gave a small laugh. 'Not all three hundred of them, I assure you. However Festus I employed especially, poaching him from Julianne Clyde-Smith's game reserve, in fact, as he was an expert on cycads. Clearly he, more than any of his underlings, was aware of the missing plant's value.'

'What happened to him?'

'He was arrested and charged by the police, however he died before his first court appearance. He was run over by a car at night, near his home in Acornhoek. I heard he had been drinking heavily.'

'I see.'

'Yes, a terrible business,' Faisal said. 'I really liked him.'

'Was he loyal?'

The prince crossed his legs. 'Yes. Up until the moment when he stole from me.'

'You didn't think that odd?'

He shrugged. 'A little, because he seemed genuinely happy here, but it's like those articles one reads about national parks rangers in the Kruger who have worked in the system in the cause of nature conservation for decades and are then caught for rhino poaching. The lure of money will eventually corrupt some people.'

'You don't seem too worried.'

'Don't I?' He leaned forward. 'If Festus was suffering some hardship, an ill child, school fees, whatever, I probably would have afforded him some assistance, just as I would have helped Joanne. I had already offered her a fulltime job with remuneration that anyone in this country would have found more than adequate.'

Sonja smiled. 'So you said. Perhaps the position came with conditions that she didn't like.'

He raised his eyebrows. 'What are you insinuating?'

'Oh, nothing. Perhaps she just didn't want to be cooped up here out in the bush, that's all. I'm sure she enjoyed her work.'

'Yes, she did, as far as I know.' The prince leaned forward, looking perplexed. 'What are you investigating? Or, rather, who are you investigating? Me?'

'You're the one who brought me here, Your Excellency. I was on my way back to Johannesburg before you summoned me. What do *you* want to know?'

'As I said, I want to know what really happened to Joanne Flack. Poachers do not shoot innocent tourists–if that's what Joanne was–and nor do they generally operate in broad daylight.'

'Do you think Joanne was a criminal? A poacher?' Sonja suspected Joanne knew where the missing *woodii* cycad was, though she did not think she had stolen it from Faisal in the first place.

Faisal sat back in his chair and sipped his champagne. He set the glass down. 'I would be lying to you if I said the thought had not crossed my mind.'

'Why were you suspicious?'

He grimaced. 'I don't know. Small things, big things. I did some research into her, or, rather, I had her vetted, as I do all my key employees. Did you know her husband was killed during the course of an undercover operation to bust a cycad smuggling ring?'

Sonja said nothing.

'I'll take that as a yes. While she was never convicted, the word in cycad collecting circles was that her husband was guilty, as were several of his close friends in the plant world who subsequently went to prison in the US or faced heavy fines–but you know all this. I wondered when the cycad went missing from here if she might have been involved somehow.'

'Why?'

'Even though she never asked me for money outright I could tell she had fallen on hard times–little things like saying she needed a new pair of shoes, and when I suggested she buy some or I buy them for her she told me she would rather spend the money on food. Security here is, as you have observed, tight, but more than once I allowed the helicopter to ferry her to and from Johannesburg. Her luggage was never checked, of course.'

'Yet she raised the alarm about the ivory shipment,' Sonja said, 'and your missing plants.'

'Who are you working for? The South African government? The Americans? You live in Los Angeles these days.'

She would not confirm her identity to him, but it was clear that Faisal knew plenty about her. He hadn't mentioned the CIA, so perhaps he thought she was a Fish and Wildlife investigator, like Rod had been. He might not know what agency she was working for, but he knew she was law enforcement and if he was asking her all these questions it meant one of two things – he was a criminal despite his magnificent wealth and wanted to know how much she knew about him, or, perhaps, he was innocent and genuinely needed her help to get at the truth. Joanne knew Faisal, intimately, and she was suspicious of him. Perhaps he was working with someone in the cycad society, who stole the decoy cycad from the lock-up? If Faisal was guilty of trying to smuggle out ivory and cycads then it looked likely he was doing it to fund Islamic terrorists in Mali. He didn't need money, but perhaps by having his valuable goods allegedly stolen and then shipped to Mali for the terrorists to sell he was helping to fund the extremists in their struggle without leaving a money trail to himself.

'OK, don't answer me,' Faisal sighed, 'but, yes, Joanne uncover the plan to re-route the stockpiled ivory, from a secure storage area to OR Tambo Airport and then, apparently, to mainland China via Hong Kong. That would seem to indicate that she was not in on the plot. I'm innocent in all of this. If I wanted to move ivory or plants out of this country, I would do it in a more professional manner than enlisting – or even framing – a truck driver and a gardener. My money does not put me above the law, but I do have a brain and I doubt Joanne is our thief.'

'So it would seem,' Sonja agreed, 'on both counts.'

'If we are being honest, I thought later that perhaps by outing that plot she was actually setting up an alibi for herself, putting herself above suspicion.'

That would have been convoluted, to say the least, Sonja thought, though perhaps, in the prince's mind, a smuggler of cycads would draw the line at ivory smuggling. Sonja still had her own doubts about Joanne. It seemed that every time she talked to her she revealed something new, but Sonja still had the feeling the older woman was holding something else back.

'You are thinking,' Faisal said.

She nodded.

'Perhaps we should continue this over dinner.'

He stood and indicated the way towards the dining room on the far side of the sprawling deck. A Mozambican nightjar gave its long, chirring call, like a little motor puttering away. Somewhere in the distance a hyena whooped.

'I love the sounds of the bush,' Faisal said as they entered the dining area and took their seats, 'even the sound of danger can be soothing, don't you find?'

It was a weird way of putting it, but she agreed. He was handsome and likeable, but Sonja had met plenty of killers in her time who would make good dinner party guests.

'Did you hear about the terrorist incident in Australia, at the Sydney Opera House today?' Faisal asked.

'No.' She'd had no time to check her phone for news. Faisal recounted how a Colombian man and his bodyguard had been stabbed to death in front of the first man's wife, before police had shot the killer dead.

'The killers – a man and a woman – were from Mali.'

'As were the ones in England.'

'Yes,' said the prince. 'Al-Qaeda in the Islamic Maghreb has so far contained its jihad to its own country, fighting their government and the French armed forces, who have intervened to prop up the president. They have kidnapped foreigners in Mali in order to help fund their struggle through ransoms, and their poaching and organised crime syndicates are also linked to the terrorists. Perhaps with the fall of the Caliphate in Syria this West African sideshow is now becoming the extremists' main game?'

Sonja was well aware of all this, but she said nothing.

A waiter appeared, and Faisal asked him to bring their meals, as per the set menu. A sommelier presented a bottle of red wine to the prince, who nodded. The man opened and decanted the wine and poured a glass for each of them. Sonja could see Faisal was drumming the fingers of one hand on the white linen tablecloth until the wine waiter left.

He went on, 'The man who attacked Joanne was also Malian and there was an earlier incident, a few weeks ago, where a Malian judge who was very vocal in his opposition to extremism and organised crime in his country was killed in what appeared to be a lone-wolf terrorist attack in Paris. These recent attacks are the first incidents of the militants targeting foreigners on foreign soil.'

'What do you know about the man and his bodyguard who were killed in Australia?' Sonja asked.

'Perhaps a random attack, perhaps not,' Faisal said. 'I googled the name of the first victim and it turns out he was a prominent businessman in Colombia, with close ties to the government there. However, I also have a cousin who is the head of police in my country. I asked him if he had any intelligence on the man.'

'And?' Sonja asked.

'And he is suspected of being the head of one of Colombia's largest cocaine cartels. The Americans have become more and more successful in recent decades at thwarting the flow of cocaine into their country –'

'So Europe is now a bigger market,' Sonja said.

'Exactly.' Faisal nodded. 'And do you know which country one of the major routes for drug importations from South America into Western Europe runs through?'

Sonja knew the answer already. 'Mali.'

Sonja watched Faisal, waiting for him to continue. If he was crooked, as Joanne suspected, why was he assembling the pieces of this puzzle for her – even though her mind was working at the same speed as his? Was he simply trying to draw out whatever she knew, such as the fact Joanne Flack was still alive?

'Sonja ... We can work together on this. I am at risk here, despite all of my security.'

'You were talking about Mali?' she said, wondering where he was going with all this.

He waved a hand in the air in submission. 'As you probably very well know, Mali is a staging point for drugs and wildlife products such as ivory and rhino horn – and even plants – destined for users in Asia and other parts of the world. Malians have tight family bonds which, like the Sicilian mafia, make them a formidable force in organised crime. The country has vast tracts of empty desert and remote, abandoned airstrips which are perfect places for cargo aircraft, ageing passenger liners in the main, to fly drugs in from Colombia and other parts of South America. From there the drugs are taken on caravans – camel trains – through the desert to ports on the Mediterranean where the narcotics are shipped to Europe. The local al-Qaeda and Islamic State franchises take a cut of the trade, just as the Taliban does in Afghanistan, and when not fighting the government, their jihadis are killing off Mali's desert elephants or acting as middlemen between Africa and Asia for ivory, rhino horn and cycads.'

'What about the Malians you have supplying artwork for your lodge?'

He nodded. 'I've had them under surveillance for some time and have had their company investigated. So far there is nothing to connect them with any organised crime activities. They are legitimate dealers in art and antiquities from central and west Africa.'

'If their presence is a coincidence and you can't connect them to your missing cycad or the plan to hijack the ivory, then why are you so interested in a possible Malian connection to the cycad trade, and what happened to Joanne Flack?'

Faisal steepled his fingers together on the tabletop. 'There is a link between the terrorist attacks in Paris, London and Sydney, and, I am sure, the men who killed Joanne.'

'What is it?' Sonja asked.

'If I tell you, I need to know that there is a purpose to me revealing this information, that you will help me follow up on it, that your – people – will use the information to protect the innocent and not overreact.'

'I don't understand,' Sonja said. 'I don't have any "people".'

Faisal sighed. He leaned across the table to an almost intimate distance and put his right hand by his mouth. He whispered: 'Please, Sonja, drop the act. This is important for world security.'

Sonja mirrored his gestures and body language. 'Are we being recorded now?'

'Possibly.'

'Tell me what you know,' she whispered.

'You agree to my terms?'

Sonja gave the slightest nod.

'The link between the three attacks, and possibly some others, is that the people responsible all received instruction in a Darul uloom in Johannesburg.'

Sonja thought back to cultural awareness briefings she'd had on deployments to the Middle East. 'A Darul uloom – like a place of higher study for Islam. A kind of finishing school for young people who've received instruction at a madrasah.'

'Yes. Kind of. The Darul uloom is located in Mayfair, just west of the Johannesburg CBD. You know the area?'

She did. 'It has a high proportion of Muslim immigrants, from Somalia and all over Africa. Mali as well?'

'Yes. I recently received notification that one of the imams had been giving inflammatory talks, directly in support of al-Shabab and some of the terrible attacks they've carried out in Kenya. There was a suggestion that he was also actively recruiting young people for the organisation.'

'What did you do?'

'I used my influence to have the imam removed, but I've just found out there is another leader, from Mali, who set up a so-called youth group for young men and women from his country. The people responsible for the Sydney and London attacks had attended that program.'

The prince paused and Sonja knew it was time for her to ante up. 'All right. There's a good chance your two missing cycads ended up in Mali, in a storeroom full of ivory, rhino horn and other loot, all of it destined to be sold to finance Islamic State in the Maghreb.' She decided to hold back on the fact that the female *woodii* had been substituted with a fake.

He tapped the table. 'I knew it.'

Sonja leaned forward and put her hands to her mouth to make lip-reading difficult. 'So tell me, what's the connection between the smuggling and the terror attacks, other than the fact that one is used to fund the other?'

'It goes further than just financial support. The two are enmeshed. The information I had is that the man who was running the youth group is one Rafik Keita, a Malian, but he is also the brother of a reputed organised crime lord, Moussa Keita.'

'I've heard of them,' Sonja said, recalling Jed's initial briefing. 'You think they're in business together?'

Faisal nodded, also continuing to shield his mouth. He lowered his voice even further. 'Moussa Keita is reputed to be the king of the transnational drug trade through Mali. He makes regular trips to South America, including Colombia. I don't think Moussa's brother Rafik is simply training young men and women to be jihadis.'

'What then?' Sonja asked.

'They're being trained to be hitmen and women for the Malian mafia. Rafik Keita has disappeared – he's on the run, facing a murder charge for a gangland killing in Johannesburg. That leaves me very exposed and that is why I am reaching out to you and your American employers, Sonja.'

'Yes, but why?'

'Because I funded this whole terrorist training school.'

Chapter 23

Stephen Stoke pulled up outside Thandi's house. Laurel was the only other member of the group who still needed to be dropped off.

'Stephen?' Laurel said as Thandi opened the Kombi's sliding door.

'Yes?'

'Why don't I get out here? Thandi can give me a lift, can't you, dear, and that way SS doesn't have as far to drive.'

'Of course,' Thandi said. 'I'm more than happy to.'

'Super,' Laurel said as she offloaded her wheelie bag. They both said goodbye to Stephen, who drove off.

'You sure you don't mind?' Laurel asked.

'Of course not.'

'Thands?' Laurel said.

'Yes, Laurel?'

'What do you suppose happens to someone's plants when they die?'

'What do you mean?' Thandi had other things on her mind, such as what Prince Faisal wanted with Ursula that was so important he'd sent his helicopter for her.

'I mean Joanne's plants. What will happen to her cycads and all her lovely indoor plants, now that she's, well, you know? The ones in her house won't last long.'

'Hmm, well, I suppose her daughter will have to decide what to do with the house and the cycads. It's distressing for us, but it will be terrible for Peta having to come over and sort out her mother's affairs, and I rather fear she might not have the money to do so.'

Laurel frowned. 'I wish we could help.'

Thandi opened her garage with a remote, went in and reversed her car out. She left her bag in the garage and Laurel loaded hers into the boot of Thandi's Mercedes.

'I gave Joanne's plants a quick water the other day, but they're probably due for another one,' Thandi said. 'We'll drive right past Joanne's house on the way to yours, so we can pop in and water the outdoor plants at least.'

'Good deed for the day, check,' Laurel said. 'But wait, how did you get in? We don't have a key to her garden.'

'I know where she hides it.'

Laurel looked at Thandi in wide-eyed awe. 'You're very good at this detectiving, Thands.'

Thandi drove from her place onto the N14 and then took the Hendrik Potgieter exit by Cradlestone Mall and Furrow Road to Joanne's estate.

'What do you make of Ursula?' Thandi asked Laurel as they stopped at the security gate. Alfred, the Zimbabwean security guard, popped his head out of the booth, recognised Thandi, smiled at her and raised the boom gate.

'That pants suit of hers is atrocious,' Laurel said as they drove through. 'It's not even retro-chic. It looks like the curtains I had in my flat in Hillbrow back in 1972.'

'I mean as a person, Laurel.'

'Oh.' Laurel pouted. 'Nice. Could use a professional hair colouring, though. I suspect she does it out of a bottle.'

Thandi sighed as they turned down Joanne's street and drove past similar-looking Tuscan-inspired houses.

'Look!' Laurel stabbed a finger out the window as they approached Joanne's house. 'The door's open!'

Thandi felt a tiny jolt in her chest as they pulled into the drive. She opened her handbag and took out her Makarov pistol.

'Seriously?' Laurel said, looking at the gun.

'This is Joburg, right?' There was more feeding Thandi's concern, but she didn't feel she needed to burden Laurel with it. 'Perhaps you should stay in the car, dear.'

'No ways, *sisi*, I've got ya six, girlfriend.'

'This is no joking matter, Laurel. Besides, your ghetto accent is appalling.'

'Whatevs, as the young people say.' Laurel smiled broadly. 'I'm here for you in any case. Shall we go take a look?'

Thandi got out of the car and racked her Russian pistol. She held it loose by her side. Laurel nodded to Thandi that she was ready.

They moved forward slowly, approaching the house to one side of the open front door, and as Thandi came closer she lifted her pistol in a two-handed grip. Thandi knew that Joanne rented the house and she wondered if the most innocent excuse for what they were seeing was a visit by the landlord. Had he or she walked here? There was no vehicle parked outside. The building site next door was unoccupied, the workers having left for the day. A light came on and they both froze. Thandi looked up and realised it was a motion-sensitive security light.

No one came running out, and the illumination allowed Thandi to spot something on the ground.

'What do you see?' Laurel whispered.

Thandi knelt and inspected a half-brick lying on the driveway. 'This looks like blood, on the brick and on the concrete here.'

Laurel went to the open front door.

'Be careful,' Thandi murmured.

'Hello?' Laurel called. They waited, but there was no answer.

Thandi moved past Laurel and entered the house first. An almost-forgotten feeling, the rush of adrenaline through her body to her extremities, made her catch her breath as she looked around quickly. Her swollen knees were forgotten, her senses alive as they had been forty-five years earlier when she had first gone into battle.

In the middle of the living room was a dining chair lying on its back and a length of electrical cord. There was a stain on the carpet. Blood. Thandi's pulse quickened. She moved across the room, checking the kitchen, which was clear, save for three coffee cups. One, she noticed, had a pink lipstick stain on the rim.

Laurel scooted past Thandi and went to the first bedroom. The door was open.

'Thandi!'

Thandi came up behind her friend and saw what she saw. The room was in disarray and there was man lying face down on the ground. Thandi went to him and put her fingers to his neck. 'He's alive.'

As if on cue, the man groaned and Thandi, surprised, recoiled.

She could see that the man had been shot, twice in the back, but there was no sign of blood. She carefully rolled him over and unbuttoned his shirt.

'A bulletproof vest,' Laurel said, looking over her shoulder.

The man blinked and reached, slowly, for his head.

'Looks like you fell and knocked yourself out,' Thandi said to the man. 'Who are you?'

The man blinked a couple of times. He looked groggy and, when he spoke, sounded American. 'Rod. Who the heck are you?'

'Me first, Rod. What are you doing here? Who shot you?' Thandi crooked an arm under Rod and helped him sit upright.

He put his hands to his chest, then reached around to feel his back.

Thandi looked up to Laurel. 'Maybe get him a glass of water?'

Laurel gave a curt shake of her head. 'I want to find out what he's doing in Joanne's house.'

'Joanne...' he said.

'Yes. This is the home of Joanne Flack,' Laurel said. 'Why are you here, Mr Rod? Who sent you?'

'Joanne...'

Thandi frowned, trying to control her impatience. 'Who else was here?'

'Joanne—' He coughed and winced. 'Joanne's dead. In Zimbabwe.'

He was rubbing his head again and becoming more lucid by the second. Thandi wasn't sure, but she guessed she might get more out of him by pressing him now, while he was still dazed. Thandi pointed her pistol at him, between the eyes. 'I think you're a thief, and you'd better tell me what's going on, or I'll call the police.'

'No cops,' he said, eyes suddenly wide. 'Police. Lindeque.'

Thandi looked back to Laurel, who just shrugged.

Rod coughed again and reached around and gingerly felt his back. Thandi guessed he must have felt like he'd been struck a couple of times with a cricket bat wielded by the likes of Henry Olonga.

'Who...who are you?' he asked, and it was as if he was seeing her clearly for the first time.

'We're friends of Joanne Flack, Rod. What are you doing here in this house? Who else was here with you?'

'A man broke in. He's the one who shot me.'

Thandi thought of the chair and cord in the living room. 'You restrained him?'

Rod nodded. 'He got away. He took...'

'There was a woman here,' Laurel said from behind. 'I saw lipstick on a coffee cup. Who was she?'

He blinked up at both of them. 'Aw, hell. It was Joanne.'

Thandi whistled. '*Eish*. She is alive?'

'I sure hope so,' Rod said. 'The guy, Lindeque, took her.'

'I *knew* it,' Laurel said gleefully. 'I'd recognise Joanne's shade of coral pink anywhere!'

'Who is this Lindeque?' Thandi asked.

'A cop. A crooked one. He came here looking for the cycad,' Rod said.

'What cycad?' Laurel asked.

'I'm not a hundred per cent sure, but I think it's the rare one a local cycad society was looking after. It was here all along.'

'I knew it again!' said Laurel. 'And that's *our* society you're talking about.'

But Thandi still wasn't convinced. It made no sense for Joanne to steal the plant, hide it in so obvious a place as her own house, and then fly off to the UK. The smart thing would have been to offload it as quickly as possible. Another idea dawned on her. 'I do think Joanne took the *woodii*, but I don't think she was the one who stole the plant from the storeroom,' she said slowly.

Laurel goggled at her, a look of complete incomprehension on her face. 'What do you mean? It sounds like you're talking about two different plants.'

'I am,' said Thandi simply. 'I think Joanne knew that the *woodii* was likely to be stolen by someone else – a person who knew its true value and would have been paid a fortune for it. She substituted a common variety from her garden, lopped the leaves off it and wrapped it in plastic so that it would look like the same plant. That means Joanne suspected one of us.'

Rod rubbed his head again. 'How did you figure that out?'

'There's a new cycad in Joanne's garden, and her bin is full of cycad leaves.'

Rod nodded. 'She was so scared she couldn't trust anyone.'

Laurel pouted. 'Not even us in the cycad society?'

'Especially not us,' Thandi said. This man was not a threat to them, she decided.

Rod rolled carefully onto his side and with Thandi's help was able to stand. 'We think the cycad Joanne substituted ended up in Mali, in the possession of some terrorists who realised it was not what they were expecting. She hid the real *woodii* here, under this bed, in fact. Maybe she didn't expect to need a better hiding place because she hoped the switch wouldn't be discovered – or not quickly, anyway.'

'Where's the cycad now?' Thandi asked.

'Lindeque, the crooked policeman, has taken it, along with Joanne.'

'Oh my goodness,' Laurel said. 'This is all too much to take in.'

'Keep it together, Laurel,' Thandi said. Laurel looked like she was about to start crying at any moment. 'We've got to find Joanne.'

'Who from our group could be so corrupt?' Laurel asked.

'And dangerous,' Rod said. 'I think Joanne had a solid lead on who it was, because whoever did steal the substitute cycad was out to capture or kill Joanne. There would have been big money involved, and Joanne double-crossed the thief. His or her buyers would be baying for blood.'

Laurel sat down on the bed. 'This is terrible. But at least Joanne's alive.'

'For now.' Thandi shook her head. She had to think. Criminals, she knew, needed motive and means. None of the members of the

Pretoria Cycad and Firearms Appreciation Society were strangers to firearms, but who had a motive?

Thandi thought back to the last meeting of the society. Jacqueline had been the most strident advocate of Joanne being expelled from the society. Sandy, too, had been quick to judge and there was bad blood between Baye and Joanne over Cafe-gate. Charles and Stephen had defended her, but if someone wanted to deflect suspicion away from themselves, that would be the way to do it. As for Laurel, she had trouble knowing what day of the week it was. 'You say this police officer's name is Lindeque?'

Rod nodded. 'From Florida SAPS, yes.'

Thandi turned to Laurel. 'Isn't your son-in-law based there?'

'Yes,' Laurel said. 'I wonder if he knows this Lindeque fellow.'

Thandi wondered more, like whether maybe Laurel's son-in-law, James, was in cahoots with Lindeque. It had been James's idea to bring the cycad to his mother-in-law's society to look after it, as James purportedly didn't trust his fellow officers to look after something so valuable in their evidence locker. Had the move been part of an elaborate plan for James and Lindeque to then steal the plant themselves and pin the blame on Joanne? 'Could you call James, please, Laurel? Ask him about this Lindeque character.'

'Sure, good idea,' Laurel said. She took out her phone and dialled, looking at Thandi while she waited. 'You're for sure like a proper detective, Thands. This is exciting, except for poor Rod here being shot and Joanne being kidnapped.'

Thandi turned to Rod. 'The vehicle Lindeque stole – whose was it?'

'A rental, Toyota Fortuner.'

'Give me the registration.' Thandi took a pen and a pocket notebook out of her handbag and wrote down the details and a description.

'Hello, James, darling,' Laurel said into her phone. 'Yes, I'm fine, thanks. I'd like you to have a word to Miss Ngwenya, you know, from the cycad society?'

Laurel passed the phone to Thandi, who dispensed with the pleasantries as quickly as she could. She asked James if he knew an officer named Lindeque.

'Hennie, yes,' James said. 'One of the detectives, a Warrant Officer.'

'We have information that he may have been up to something illegal, James.'

There was a long pause. 'Yes?'

Rod came closer to Thandi and whispered to her: 'Lindeque said he was on leave.'

'James, this Lindeque was apparently on leave. Is that right?'

More silence.

'James?' Thandi tried again. 'This is very important. Someone's life may be at risk.'

'He's not exactly on leave, not technically, at least.'

'What, then?'

'He's under suspension, Miss Ngwenya.'

Thandi whistled through the gap between her front teeth. '*Eish*, James, what did he do?'

'Nothing's been proved, Miss Ngwenya, so it's really not appropriate for me to say. He's innocent until proven guilty.'

'Of course.' A crooked cop, for sure, she thought. 'Thank you, James. Just hold the line for a moment, please.'

'Sure, hundred per cent,' James said.

Thandi lowered the phone, holding it against her ample bosom to mask her voice, and looked to Laurel and Rod. 'We could report the rental vehicle as stolen and get James to get the police to look for it.'

'Good idea; he'll be able to help,' Laurel said. 'He's a very clever boy.'

Thandi switched her eyes to Rod, who shrugged. Laurel seemed to realise something.

'Hang on, what are you thinking?' she said, raising her voice. 'That my James might be in cahoots with this Lindeque criminal? That's preposterous. James is the one who *gave* us the cycad to protect, remember? He was the one who was suspicious that one of his fellow officers might steal it from the evidence locker. We all know there is corruption in the South African Police Service but it is most certainly *not* most officers, and definitely not my son-in-law!'

'I'm sorry, Laurel, I hear what you're saying,' Thandi said.

'Make the call,' Rod said. 'We're running out of time and, let's face it, the bad guys have Joanne anyway.'

Thandi lifted the phone to her ear again and gave James the vehicle's details. She decided not to tell James that Warrant Officer Lindeque was driving. 'The man driving is armed and dangerous, James, and he may have a woman hidden somewhere in the vehicle.'

'I'll do it right away, Miss Ngwenya,' James said, 'and I'll call you if I hear anything.'

Thandi gave James her number then ended the call and gave the phone back to Laurel.

'You've got a car?' Rod said to Thandi.

'Affirmative.'

'We need to find Joanne.'

An obvious statement, Thandi thought, but this man was not thinking straight. 'We've got no idea where he's taken her. Where would we start looking?'

Rod gingerly rubbed the back of his head. 'Someone wants Joanne alive, otherwise Lindeque would have simply shot her, like he did me, and taken the cycad. Who would want both the plant and Joanne?'

Laurel, who had been on the sidelines of the conversation, stepped in. 'That bloody Arab prince.'

*

Sergeant James Benson called the car rental company and gave them the details of the stolen Fortuner.

'We have a tracker on the vehicle,' the young woman who had taken his call said. 'I'll alert our tracking company. Must I give them your contact details as well?'

'Yes, please,' James said. After ending the call, he went to the station kitchen and made himself a cup of coffee. By the time he returned to his desk his phone was ringing. James answered it.

'Sergeant Benson?' a man said.

'Yes, that's me, howzit?'

The man told him that the Fortuner had been located, not far from where they were, near the Lion and Elephant Park. James scribbled down the precise GPS coordinates then left the building and ran to his car.

It only took him fifteen minutes to get to where the Toyota had been abandoned on the edge of the road. A SAPS *bakkie* was parked next to the stolen vehicle and two uniformed officers were questioning a teenage boy. James flashed his ID at the officers and they exchanged greetings. 'What have you got?'

The senior officer rubbed his chin. 'Ah, but this is a strange one, Sergeant. This boy said he saw a helicopter land just by here in that open patch of ground. He said the driver of the car and a woman with blonde hair got out and then they got into the chopper and it took off. He says the helicopter was painted all black and the *ou* loaded a big, heavy log wrapped in plastic into the helo.'

'Bizarre,' James said, shaking his head. He called Thandi Ngwenya.

Chapter 24

Sonja banged her cutlery down on the dining table. 'What do you mean you financed a terrorist training cell?' Talk had been suspended while waiters topped up their drinks and cleared away their entrees.

The prince held up a hand. 'Not knowingly. The Kuwaiti government supports development and community projects all over the world. Unemployment is rife in South Africa and I recommended to the government that we support the youth group at the Darul uloom in Mayfair as it seemed to be doing good work in diverting young people away from crime and helping them find pathways into employment or study. Unfortunately, the group was hijacked by an extremist cleric from Mali.'

'How did you find out about the extremist connection?'

'From the media, believe it or not. The *Sunday Times* did a feature on young South Africans who had been recruited by ISIS to fight in Syria and how they were returning home following the Caliphate's demise. The school I funded was mentioned, as was Kuwaiti involvement.'

'I see,' Sonja said.

'I made it my business to find out more. I went to Johannesburg, undercover as it were, with a protection officer, and talked to some of the young men who attended the school. They said the Malian imam was preaching the need for jihad. Naturally, they were wary about talking to outsiders. I found out that Moussa Keita's brother,

Rafik, had recently returned from Syria, where he'd been a member of ISIS. Rafik had been a member of Ansar al-Dine, the local ISIS affiliate in Mali, before he went to Syria, but AAD merged with another group and Rafik defected to AQIM – al-Qaeda in the Islamic Maghreb – when he returned home. It was Rafik who set up the youth group and he continued recruiting and training impressionable young men as would-be terrorists even after I had the imam removed. I think Rafik moved his training program underground when the police took out a warrant for his arrest.'

Sonja could see where his logic was heading. 'You think impressionable, devout young men were indoctrinated and trained to carry out suicide attacks, but then let loose in Paris, London and Sydney not to carry out random attacks, but to kidnap or assassinate specific people.'

'Exactly,' Faisal said. 'The Malian judge in Paris, Joanne Flack in London and the Colombian drug lord in Sydney. All of those attacks were carried out by young men who had been members of Rafik Keita's youth group.'

'That's quite an operation, and as evil as it's well thought out.'

'Agreed,' Faisal said. 'Western police forces will write the attacks off as terrorist-inspired, yet by targeting foreign nationals while they're travelling overseas there's less likelihood of France, the UK or Australia taking offshore retaliatory action.'

'And it's hard for even the best bodyguard to prevent a surprise attack by a committed jihadi in what's otherwise a benign environment.'

'Let's go out onto the *stoep* for some fresh air.' Faisal dabbed his lips with his serviette and stood. He slid Sonja's chair out for her.

They walked to the edge of the balcony and Faisal leaned forward, his elbows on the railing. Sonja joined him. The deck overlooked a man-made waterhole. At night-time, like now, it was floodlit. A duiker, a dainty little antelope, was nervously approaching the water, stopping every few steps to look around and sniff the air. Sonja and Faisal were close to each other as they watched the animal, and she sensed he wanted to say something to her away from the cameras again.

'I've told you all this because I need your help,' he said in a whisper.

'How?'

'As you know, I asked you here to find out the truth about Joanne, but it's also a bit more than that. I'd like you to investi-gate the same things Joanne was concerned about: wildlife products – cycads and ivory – being funnelled out of southern Africa, out of my very reserve, to fund a terrorist organisation –'

'I'm –'

He held up a hand to silence her. 'Spare me the cover story, please, just listen to me. Even though we are a conservative Muslim country, Kuwait has not been spared the horrors of terrorism. Our famous Al-Sadiq mosque was attacked by an ISIS suicide bomber, killing twenty-seven people, and like many Western nations we, too, have had the problem of dis-affected young people leaving to join the extremists in Syria. My extended family is routinely warned about plots to kill us, even here in Africa.'

'Is there a specific threat against you now, from ISIS or one of its splinter groups?'

'Yes and no,' Faisal said. 'Our security services have picked up some online chatter about a big terrorist attack being planned, originating somewhere in West Africa, but I think you know this.'

'Why would I know?'

'Because the Americans conducted an operation in Mali re-cently; a hostage was freed. My people say there is word filtering out that a female operative was involved, and that it was she who rescued the kidnapped woman, a US senator's daughter. I am fairly sure, now, that female operative was you.'

Sonja said nothing, looking out instead over the waterhole where the duiker had at last gathered the courage to drink.

'Al-Qaeda in the Islamic Maghreb needs that rare cycad to re-plenish its coffers. That plant was stolen from my garden. Even I only recently learned just how much it was worth – although being a female *Encephalartos woodii* it's probably priceless. It was part of a collection I bought from a deceased estate in Nelspruit and had transplanted here. I thought it was something else, something more common. Joanne worked out what it was and it was just after she positively identified the *woodii* that it was stolen.'

'So what are you worried about, other than your two missing plants, one of which is apparently priceless?'

'I, too, have been asking questions,' Faisal said, 'and the more I learn and the more I think about this, the more I believe some of my people are involved.'

'Like who?'

'Pretend to kiss me.'

'What?'

'Just do as I say.' Faisal put his hands on either side of Sonja's face and drew her mouth close to his, so that they were almost, but not quite kissing.

*

'*Fok*. What's he saying?' Sonnet said to Delport, whose job it was to man the monitoring screens as well as install, adjust and maintain all the security cameras and sound-recording equipment in the lodge.

Delport held his hands flat against his headphones. 'I can't tell. The microphones are sensitive, but he's speaking so softly I can't hear. He's kissing her now, in any case, the dirty dog.'

Sonnet shook his head. He had no time for insults and didn't care about the prince's love life – he had eavesdropped and spied on his employer enough to know he was a playboy of note. He needed to hear what the prince was saying to Sonja Kurtz and work out exactly how much she knew. It was a bad sign that his employer had been consciously trying not to be overheard.

Sonnet's phone vibrated on silent in his shirt pocket. He took it out and checked the screen. It was Lindeque. 'Sheesh, *boet*, where are you?'

'In the chopper. I've got Flack and the missing cycad. Thanks for sending the bird for me. We got out just in time. I could see the uniformed guys on their way just after we took off.'

'You can tell me when you get here how you fucked up,' Sonnet said. He was annoyed that the targets had got the drop on

Lindeque, but pleased his former partner in the police service had then managed to escape and bring Joanne Flack with him. However, the fact that she was alive and not dead in Zimbabwe, as they had first heard and hoped, complicated things. Sonnet had no way of knowing exactly how much his enemies now knew. Americans meant that the CIA, or maybe some other agency, was investigating cycad smuggling. The prince had brought back Sonja Kurtz; he was either suspicious of her or wanted to have sex with her and Sonnet could not blame him on either count. If she was in cahoots with Joanne–and it seemed likely, unless the former mercenary had changed her name and taken up gardening as a hobby–then at least they would be isolated from each other and unable to communicate. Sonnet believed he could still keep the operation intact if he acted quickly and decisively.

'Tell me about the guy with her at the house.'

'Like I said, American,' Lindeque said, 'CIA, I suppose, but kind of old for a field agent. He knew his plants, though–he's the one who actually found the cycad. Flack had hidden it under her bed, of all places. Who does that?'

Sonnet ignored the question. 'The American's dead, right?'

'I put two bullets into his back and he didn't get up. That dead enough for you?'

'One in the head would have been better.'

'I was in a hurry, man,' Lindeque said. 'What did you tell the prince about the chopper?'

'I said the wide area surveillance system had picked up human movement on the north perimeter, poachers trying to get in. He authorised me to send the helicopter.'

'OK. We should be at your location in less than ten minutes. What do you want me to do with the woman?'

'Take her to the tunnel. I want somewhere we can question her where it won't matter how much noise she makes. We need to find out just how much she knows about our operation and our undercover operative.'

Lindeque lowered his voice, as if he didn't want the woman inside the helicopter with him to hear. 'And when you finish with that?'

'We kill her,' Sonnet said. 'We can't very well let her live, now, can we?'

He ended the call. Sonnet was still annoyed at Lindeque's amateurish behaviour, allowing himself to be captured by a woman and an old man, but they might still be able to get out of this mess with their cover intact.

'She's taking a call,' Delport said.

Sonnet put his phone back in his pocket and looked at the computer screen. Sonja was walking away from the prince, who continued to lean on the deck railing. Kurtz proceeded down the wooden stairs to ground level, and the waterhole beyond. The duiker which had been drinking took fright and, true to the English translation of its Afrikaans name, dived out of sight, into the night. 'Keep a watch on her. Radio me if you see anything unusual. I'm going to try and get close enough to her to hear what she's saying.'

'Affirmative,' Delport said.

Sonnet inserted an earpiece and turned on his portable radio. He left the monitoring room and hastened quietly out into the inky darkness. He drew his Glock. There was danger in the African night, but Sonnet knew that apart from him the most dangerous predator in this patch of jungle right now was the one with the auburn hair and shapely legs talking on her phone.

He made his way past the cycad garden and through the acacias and mopanes that screened it from the waterhole. He watched his footfalls, careful not to step on any dry twigs.

'I'm not sure, Rod,' Kurtz was saying in a hoarse whisper.

She was trying to be quiet, Sonnet thought as he dropped to one knee and strained to listen.

'You think he might bring her here, to the prince's reserve?'

Sonnet swore under his breath. Sonja was getting word from someone that Lindeque was bringing Joanne Flack to them, but how? He slid his phone out and tapped a quick SMS to Lindeque. *Who is Rod?*

'OK,' Sonja said.

Guy I shot. American, Lindeque replied.

Sonnet swore again. Clearly, Lindeque had failed to kill the American. His incompetence might cost them dearly.

'The prince is worried,' Sonja whispered. 'He thinks the Malians might be planning a jihadi attack on him.'

Sonnet nodded to himself. As head of Faisal's South African security he was copied into the intelligence reports from the Kuwaiti government to the extended royal family. It was a fact that high-profile figures from the kingdom were often touted in terrorist chatter as likely targets for Islamic State and other extremist groups.

'Joanne's friends from the cycad society...' Sonja began. Sonnet cocked his hear, straining to listen, when Sonja was interrupted. 'Oh, you're with Thandi now? Good. Tell her who I really am and what I'm doing. She's smart, maybe she can help you.'

'Shit,' Sonnet whispered to himself. He wished the mamba had killed Kurtz, or taken her out of the game, as he had intended. The very fact that she'd been summoned back to the reserve and lodge meant that the prince was worried, if not about her then about a plot against him. This was like a game of poker, Sonnet thought – he had to decide if it was time to bluff or to fold. The latter option was not simply a matter of running away, however; it would be nothing short of a small-scale war. He hoped that he could hold off escalating things to that level.

'You need to get me what information you can on a guy called Frank Sonnet, ex-police, from Joburg, Rod. Ask Thandi as well, she might have her own contacts.'

'Shit,' Sonnet whispered.

'OK, bye,' Sonja said.

Sonnet knew now there was no other option. He needed to stop Kurtz from further meddling in the affairs at the lodge. He called Rafik Keita and told him it was time to go to war.

Chapter 25

Rafik Keita was a devout man. A veteran of many battles in Syria, he was a true believer, unlike the decadent Kuwaiti prince, Faisal, who owned the land on which Rafik and his young lions were secretly camped.

It often brought a smile to his face, the knowledge that they lived here, under the very nose of a man who would denounce them to the South African Police Service or the hated American CIA just as easily as he would take a white whore to his bed or destroy his mind with hard liquor. The prince was a degenerate.

It didn't matter that what Rafik was doing here was principally about money and the furthering of his brother Moussa's business empire, nor that he was hiding from the South African police, who wanted to arrest him over the murder of a Nigerian rival in the Johannesburg drug trade. He slept well knowing that the money-making ventures his work protected were, ultimately, funding the struggle against the infidels. That was why he worked so hard training his lion cubs and preparing them for martyrdom.

A real lion called somewhere in the bush, less than a kilometre away judging by the volume of the mournful two-part call. Rafik made his rounds of the six tents, waking the three men in each.

'On your feet,' he commanded. 'Full uniform, weapons and kit. Now!'

They roused themselves and struggled into their camouflage fatigues. Some cursed in Arabic, the language they shared, as they tripped over their gear or fumbled to find headlights. He heard the click of metal on metal as men fitted magazines to their AK-47 assault rifles and the slick sliding of oiled working parts as they pulled on cocking handles, chambering rounds.

'Look lively, men,' he said. 'Tonight we may see some real action against our true enemies.'

Rafik himself carried a .22-calibre rifle fitted with a bipod, suppressor and telescopic sights. It was not a big-calibre weapon, no use against dangerous game, but tonight he would need accuracy for his mission, and the relative silence the suppressor provided.

His lions may not, in fact, be needed, but they were his insurance policy, and every one of them was ready to die at his command.

The lions emerged from their tents, equipped and dressed, and sorted themselves into two ranks of nine, facing him.

'You two.' Rafik pointed to the recruits whom he considered to be the bottom of this pile of potential martyrs. One's fitness was substandard and the other was a dullard, little more than a mouthy street hoodlum. 'Go back to your tent and change into civilian clothes – jeans and dark T-shirts will do.'

He addressed the others while he waited. 'Tonight we may have to do battle with the non-believers.'

There was some whispering.

'Silence!' They stilled themselves. All eyes were on him. 'Tonight we go on an exercise. We will drive through the reserve in three vehicles and then we will patrol, in silence, to a lodge building. You are to be ready for any eventuality, even the possibility of combat. Do you understand?'

'Yes, sir!' they answered in unison. The two he had dispatched to change returned dressed as he had ordered.

They organised themselves into three sections and mounted up in a trio of camouflaged Toyota HiLux four-by-fours. The vehicles bore the logos of an anti-poaching unit, with pictures of endangered rhinoceros, and while the Toyotas and the men's uniforms were the same as those of rangers who did, indeed, conduct anti-poaching operations on Prince Faisal's reserve, Rafik's men were not here to protect anything.

From the air – via satellite if the Americans ever had the brains to think of such a thing – their encampment would look like any other on an African game reserve established to train and house an anti-poaching unit. The truth, however, was that these impressionable, idealistic, slightly naive young men from half-a-dozen different African nations had no idea where they were, other than somewhere in South Africa. They did not know that a Kuwaiti prince owned this land, nor that the man's rich, debauched friends and relatives partied at the lodge they were about to patrol to. They knew of the presence of dangerous game – their training was conducted in the full knowledge that lion, elephant, buffalo, rhino and leopard patrolled at large around their camp – but these men cared nothing for big game or its protection.

Each had been smuggled into the reserve, blindfolded, in the dead of night, in the back of a truck bearing the logo of a fruit and vegetable supply company.

They knew Rafik only as 'sir'. They lived a Spartan existence, and their training and lectures and religious study were focused on one aim: to die the holiest of all deaths in the advancement of their beliefs. Some had graduated from the basic military training provided here on the reserve and had travelled to distant lands. Rafik had shown them printouts – since computers, phones, internet and other electronic means of communication with the outside world were banned – that showed the work of their classmates in Paris, London and Sydney, where non-believers had been hacked to death.

This was what they dreamed of, the only form of release any of them would ever know, or ever desired, from the hot, inhospitable bushveld where they were trained.

Of course, not all the young men were serious about wanting to sacrifice their lives. Some had been eager to volunteer, but the rigours of life in the bush had proven too much for them, or the reality of taking part in an impending suicide mission had sunk in and scared them – or both. These youngsters were not sent home to their families but rather taken to a remote corner of the reserve by Rafik, where they were told transport would be waiting to take them home, and dispatched with a bullet to the back of the head. Hyenas and other predators and scavengers took care of the bodies.

Rafik had food, arms, ammunition, explosives and the components he might need to assemble suicide vests. By and large the recruits were keen and strong, eager to undertake training in firearms, unarmed combat, demolitions and extra religious studies provided by him.

While the internet and television were banned, Rafik ensured his lions received a daily dose of propaganda in the form of copied videos from Syria and Mali, and other fronts in the war against the infidel, showing valiant victories on the field of battle. It did no good to let the recruits know that the Caliphate was in its death throes – even if the Americans and their allies did win on the ground, the war would continue for a thousand more years through lone-wolf and small-scale attacks around the world.

All the lions needed to know was that they would play a role, that they would take the fight to the enemy, and that they would cleanse their souls in blood en route to paradise.

As they drove through the reserve, Rafik kept a wary eye out through the lead HiLux's windscreen in case the grey bulk of an elephant loomed. At the same time he watched the satellite navigation device and listened to the reserve's radio frequency. The prince was in residence, so security was stepped up and the radio control room was monitored twenty-four hours a day. There were no guests, so no game-viewing vehicles would be going out in the morning, unless his excellency himself decided he wanted to go looking for animals, but Rafik did not plan on being out during daylight hours if he could help it.

'Leopard!'

Rafik looked to the right and saw the curled tail and rosette-dappled coat of the big cat disappearing into the undergrowth on the right side of the road.

'Not too fast, Bilal,' he said, placing a hand on his young driver's arm. He did not want the boy to waste both their lives in a driving accident.

Rafik could see from the sat nav that they were getting close to the lodge. He told Bilal to pull over and the other vehicles stopped behind them. Rafik took a pair of night vision goggles from the glove compartment and got out. At his signal the lions debussed. He led them, single file, into the bush.

He adjusted the goggles' harness on his head and turned on the device. 'No talking, and remember, if we come across a real lion, the one who runs dies.'

He glimpsed smiles in the dark. Some of these men had been here for several months. They were restless, eager for action and glory. Even the most dedicated spirits could wane in the face of boredom. Tonight, Rafik hoped, there would be action. However, if things went badly, they needed to be ready to relocate their entire operation at a moment's notice. His men were ready to die, but Rafik served not only God, but also the false but very necessary idol – money.

'I said *quiet*,' he hissed to a youngster, a recent recruit, who was whispering to a friend. 'I will kill the next man I hear.'

They set off into the night.

A Scops owl trilled its high-pitched call and a baboon, perhaps disturbed by the nocturnal creeping of a predator, cried *wah-hoo* in warning. The bush glowed a luminous green through his lenses, the ambient light of the fingernail moon and the stars intensified by the night vision device. He caught a glimpse of movement ahead and held up a hand to halt the men behind him. Rafik raised his rifle, suddenly acutely aware of its paltry calibre, then breathed easier as half-a-dozen impala took fright and leapt away from them.

Rafik led them on cautiously, stopping every few paces to listen to the sounds of the night and check his direction on the wristwatch GPS he wore.

A real lion called in the distance. Rafik paused again, then set off, but when he turned, as he habitually did when patrolling, just as he had taught the men, he saw that the next of his recruits was some twenty metres behind him, too far away. Rafik waved to the man, but he shook his head.

Annoyed, Rafik retraced his steps. 'What is it?'

'You said to stay still if there was a lion,' the boy whispered.

Rafik shook his head, then reached out with his left hand and slapped the youth, hard, across the face. 'If you are *close* to it. If

283

you are looking in its eyes. That thing is more than a kilometre away. Get moving.'

He led them, aware just how cosseted they had been, for all their talk of killing and dying. Virtually all of them were town boys. He hoped he had trained these young lions of his well enough to acquit themselves well in a proper firefight. There was a difference between crawling under barbed-wire obstacles and firing rounds from an AK-47 for the benefit of propaganda videos – and they had done their fair share of that – and actually fighting and facing live, incoming rounds.

They moved through the bush and up a small rise. At the crest, Rafik dropped to one knee and held a closed fist over his head. The men behind him mimicked him. Below, he could see the lights of the prince's lodge.

*

Sonja walked back up the stairs to the deck and found that while she had been taking the call, two men had joined the prince. Faisal leaned against the railing, where he'd been before, a tumbler of whiskey in his right hand.

'Sonja, please meet Hassan and Ali, my personal protection officers.'

The bodyguards nodded to her. They looked Kuwaiti, like their employer, and both were dressed in jeans and lightweight short-cropped bomber jackets that no doubt concealed shoulder holsters. Sonja wondered where they had been hiding.

'Hassan and Ali travel with me wherever I go; it is a requirement of my family, though when I'm here in South Africa they have an easy time of it,' he said, reading the question in her eyes. 'I thought I should bring them on duty now.'

Sonja took a deep breath. It was time to level with the prince. If he was crooked then he would know, already, what she was about to tell him. 'Probably just as well. Joanne Flack is alive – at least she was at last contact – but someone's kidnapped her.'

Faisal looked genuinely surprised. 'What?'

Sonja nodded. 'It's true. She wasn't killed in Zimbabwe, though someone did their best to finish her off. She was staying at a safe house in Johannesburg, but when she discovered someone was breaking into her home she went there and confronted the man. It was a policeman by the name of Lindeque. Ring any bells?'

Faisal put a hand to his brow, as if thinking, or overcome by the rush of news. 'I don't know. This… this is incredible news. Where is she now?'

Sonja shrugged. 'My people don't know. The policeman got away and took Joanne with him. He's in the wind. The authorities have been alerted to keep an eye out for them, but it's believed he escaped in a helicopter.'

'A chopper?' He shook his head. 'I can't believe she was alive and didn't contact me.'

Sonja put her hands on her hips. 'Did it ever cross your mind that she might suspect you of being involved in a crime?'

He looked her in the eye. 'No, it did not.'

'She uncovered a plot to hijack a load of ivory you happened to have in your safe and fly it out of the country, and then two of your most valuable plants went missing right out from under your nose.'

Faisal looked to Hassan and Ali, and with a tiny flick of his head they retreated, not out of sight, but out of earshot. The prince lowered his voice. 'Sonja, I can assure you that I have more money than one man – one small city – could ever hope to spend in his life. I do not need to smuggle ivory or plants.'

She nodded her head. 'That's what I thought. However, we both know collectors will go to extreme lengths to get the plants they want.'

He frowned. 'If it's legal, I own it; if it's not, it's not worth the damage to the reputation of my family, my house or my kingdom to get involved with it. Trust me.'

She thought she did, so why didn't Joanne Flack? In her own lifetime Sonja had come across extremely wealthy people who were still criminals. It wasn't just money that drove them, but also the thrill of risk and the fact that for some people there was no such thing as 'enough'. But did that extend to royalty?

'Excuse me,' Faisal said to Sonja. He spoke to Hassan in Arabic and the man replied, nodded and left. 'I've asked him to search the security files on the computer system, to call up the incident reports from the ivory and the cycad investigations. The case of the missing *woodii* is still open, and it seems worth revisiting the theft of my Venda cycad. Who knows, perhaps this man Lindeque's name is mentioned.'

'Good thinking,' Sonja said. She had been going to ask him to do the same thing. She heard footsteps and turned around.

Frank Sonnet came up the stairs.

'Where have you been?' Faisal asked.

'Forgive me, sir, I was checking around the lodge and heard a voice out in the bush.'

'That would have been me,' Sonja said.

'Frank, tell me,' Faisal began.

Sonnet braced up, as if standing to attention. 'Yes, sir?'

'Do you know a policeman, a detective, Warrant Officer Lindeque?'

Frank nodded. 'Yes, I do. I used to serve with a man named Hennie Lindeque. In fact, he's helped me on occasion investigating things for you.'

'Is that so? How come I wasn't told of this?'

Sonnet smiled. 'I employ twenty people here, sir, and, with respect, I'm sure you don't know all their names. I make it my business to keep an ear to the ground in the local community and have various sources there that I make use of. I can't bother you with all the details.'

'Has Lindeque been working for you lately?'

Sonnet nodded again. 'Yes, sir. Following Joanne Flack's death I asked Hennie to carry out some investigative work in Johannesburg, to check on her last known movements and to have a look around her home.'

Faisal raised his eyebrows. 'Really? And you didn't think to tell me?'

Sonnet coughed into his hand. 'Well, sir, the investigation was outside the framework of the law. I told Lindeque to check out Joanne's house, but he did so out of business hours, without a search warrant.'

'I see.'

'Sir, I think Hassan and Ali would be best employed escorting you and the lady inside. Further to my earlier report about possible poaching activity one of our patrols has definitely picked up a breach of the perimeter fence. Where's Hassan, sir?'

'In the security office,' Faisal said.

'We might need him here now, sir. I'll radio the control room.'

Sonja saw Faisal start to object, but Sonnet had stepped away and was already making the call. She felt a chill run down her spine, the way it did just before an ambush or a contact.

'Faisal,' she said quietly.

He turned to her. 'Yes?'

'Come with me.'

'Not yet. I need to talk to Frank.'

Sonja heard the zip of an incoming round just as Sonnet spun around and fell to the deck. She grabbed Faisal by the arm and propelled him away from the edge of the *stoep* towards Ali. 'Get him out of here!' she yelled at the bodyguard.

Sonja felt the air displaced beside her head. For a supposedly professional bodyguard Ali was slow to act, so Sonja grabbed Faisal again, this time by the collar of his shirt and, using her body to shield him, ran with him towards the dining room.

Hassan appeared from the corridor leading to the security room. 'What is it?'

'We're taking fire. Sonnet's hit. Look after the prince.'

Sonja turned back towards the deck, but dropped to her belly and leopard-crawled across the smooth polished concrete floor and then out onto the wooden boards. Sonnet was on his back. Sonja made it to him and he looked to her, grimacing.

'Where are you hit?'

'Arm.'

She looked him over quickly. He had his right hand pressed to his upper left forearm, the fingers wet with blood. 'You'll live.'

A round smacked into the timber railing less than a metre above their heads.

'Maybe not for long. Is the prince all right?'

'He's fine,' Sonja said.

She rolled over onto her back, raised her pistol and, one after another, shot out the two lights closest to them.

'You're paying for that.'

Sonja smiled. 'I think your boss can afford it. Move on three. I'll cover you.'

Sonnet nodded.

'One, two... three!' Sonja rolled onto her side and emptied her magazine into the darkness as Sonnet crawled towards the dining room. She ejected the empty mag, slapped a new one into the pistol, and slithered after him. As she hadn't been fired on while crawling towards Sonnet she guessed they were out of the shooter's line of sight in the dining room, off the deck and *stoep*.

Once inside, Sonja took a large white linen serviette off the dining table, wrapped it around Sonnet's arm and knotted it tightly. 'That will keep you going.'

He had his pistol drawn. 'Come with me.'

Sonnet led her through the dining room and down a corridor she hadn't been in before. 'There's a safe room along here.'

They passed a cellar and the entry to the kitchens and came to a room with a stout door which, on closer examination, was made of steel and covered with slatted decorative timber. Sonnet punched a number into a PIN pad and pushed the door open. Ali and Hassan greeted him with raised firearms.

'Relax,' Sonnet said.

Sonja looked beyond the protection officers to the prince. 'Are you OK?'

'A little shaken, yes, but unhurt. Frank, are you all right?'

Sonnet looked down at the makeshift bandage. 'Can't feel a thing, yet.' He looked to Sonja. 'I'm going to the control room. Stay here.'

She shook her head. 'The prince has his protection detail. I'm not one for sitting still. I'm going to find this fucker.'

'Sonja...' Faisal began.

'I'll be fine.' She saw a cupboard on the far wall of the safe room, which was also furnished with armchairs, a bar fridge, a computer monitor and a flat-screen television screen. 'What's in there?'

Hassan opened the cupboard, revealing a small but well-stocked armoury.

'May I?' Sonja asked.

'Be my guest,' Faisal said.

'Sonja, I really do think you should stay here in the safe room. This isn't your fight,' Frank said.

She selected an American-made M4 assault rifle and three spare thirty-round magazines of ammunition in a green canvas shoulder bag. The fully automatic military rifle was illegal, but Sonja guessed that smuggling arms into the country in the diplomatic pouch was one of the perks of being a minor royal. 'It's my fight as soon as someone takes a shot at me.'

Sonnet looked to the prince, who simply shrugged. 'I don't think Sonja is the type of woman who takes kindly to unsolicited advice from men.'

'Not from anyone.' She loaded the rifle before taking a pair of night vision goggles from the cupboard as well.

'How many men do you have?' Sonja asked Frank.

'Myself and three others here or off duty around the lodge; Hassan and Ali; and eighteen armed anti-poaching rangers at their camp, about a kilometre from here. I'll stand them up now. Some of those men and the prince's helicopter are investigating a reported breech of the perimeter fence earlier. I assumed it was poachers. I'll have more men deployed.'

'Good.' Sonja looked from Sonnet to the prince. 'Who's out there in the bush shooting at us?'

'Could be a poacher who slipped past my men,' Sonnet said. 'They use silenced weapons sometimes when they're hunting rhino.'

Sonja shook her head. 'You need a .375 or a .458 calibre to take down a rhino. If you'd been hit with either of those rounds it would have taken half your arm off. Smaller calibre means less noise and you need to be closer to the target.'

Faisal's eyes widened. 'An assassin?'

Sonja shrugged. 'You tell me, Your Excellency.'

'My family and I, sadly, have no shortage of enemies.'

'I'm going out,' Sonja said.

Sonnet gave her a handheld radio. 'Take this.'

She turned to Faisal. 'Stay here. I'll be back.'

Hassan puffed his chest out. 'We are in charge of the prince's security, not you.'

'Enough,' the prince commanded. 'This is not the time for some kind of turf war or dick fight.'

Sonja gave a small, surprised laugh. 'Well said.'

'Good luck, Sonja,' Faisal said.

Sonja yanked back the M4's cocking handle. 'Good hunting, you mean.'

Chapter 26

Sonja felt slightly more relaxed once she was in the dark of the bush, away from the lodge and its lights, even if a little black dress was less than ideal combat clothing. She was a creature of the night, a predator, and there was no way she was going to lock herself away in a panic room.

She had her suspicions about Sonnet, but whatever he was up to it was undeniable that he had just taken a bullet that was meant for Faisal. Whether that shot had been deliberate or accidental was unclear, but it muddied the waters somewhat. Sonja replayed Sonnet's movements – he had walked up the stairs to the deck and been shot just as he passed the prince. As she had told the others, a shooter needed to be close to get a good shot with a small-calibre weapon, though a rifle was better than a pistol. The wound in Sonnet's arm looked like it had been made with a .22 or similar. With a pistol you had to be almost close enough to feel the target's breath to kill with a .22 – the bullet was best fired into the back of the head, where it bounced around inside the skull.

She moved to the front of the lodge, careful to stay just beyond the cone of light that illuminated the waterhole. The shooter would have been less than a hundred yards away. The question was: was he still here?

Sonja stopped and listened.

Animals made noises when they moved, though, oddly, it seemed the bigger the creature, the quieter it was. Elephants made barely a sound, unless they were eating and then the snapping of tree branches gave them away. By contrast, she remembered hearing something stomping, rattling, thrashing and chewing outside a tent on a childhood camping trip in Namibia and being surprised when she poked her head out of the zippered door to see a porcupine.

Then Sonja heard a sound: the scuff of a boot through leaves. She dropped to one knee and brought the M4 up, not into her shoulder but tucked under her right arm, half propped against her chest. The rifle was to military spec, with a night aiming device attached to the side of the barrel. She switched on the NAD and, through her night vision goggles, was able to see the laser sight beam.

She saw movement.

Sonja shifted so she was partly shielded by a leadwood tree. Its trunk would stop a .50-calibre round. She waited and was rewarded with the sight of a young man, dressed in jeans and T-shirt, carrying an AK. It was hard to tell in the dark, but he appeared to be of mixed race. He sported a black beard.

She waited as the man came closer. His movements were slow, but rather than being deliberate he appeared unsure of where he was going. He turned and whispered something over his shoulder. Sonja couldn't hear the words. She adjusted her aim so that the laser was on the man's back. His comrade came into view, just over his shoulder. He was also dressed in civilian clothes and carrying an assault rifle.

'Sonnet,' Sonja whispered into the radio the security chief had given her.

'Go.'

'I've got two tangos,' she said, using the military term for targets, 'males, in civvies carrying AKs.'

'Not friendlies,' Sonnet said into his radio.

'Roger that.' The first man turned back towards her and Sonja painted him with the laser. 'Drop your gun!'

The man raised his rifle and Sonja saw he meant to use it. She squeezed the M4's trigger twice, her torso absorbing the recoil, and the man fell to the ground. His comrade fired a wild burst of three rounds; he was clearly scared or inexperienced, walking around with his weapon set to full auto. Sonja shifted the laser but was not able to get a good visual on the man, who turned and sprinted away from her.

Sonja got up and ran forward. She paused to nudge the man she had shot with the toe of her riding boot. He was dead. Sonja took off after the other man.

'One tango KIA and I'm in pursuit of the other, heading...' She looked up into the night sky and identified the Southern Cross, 'southwest, over.'

'Roger,' Sonnet said. 'Be careful. The chopper's inbound and I'll vector him to your location.'

'Affirmative,' Sonja said, her breath coming in ragged gasps. Thorny acacia branches whipped and scored her bare arms and legs. As much as she hated to accept it, she knew she was also getting too old for this kind of shit and certainly wasn't dressed for it.

Adrenaline carried her forward, and she realised that despite her huffing and puffing she never felt more alive than she did at times like this. She was a hunter and this was what she had been bred for.

Sonja cast her eyes downwards and confirmed she was hot on the trail of the man who had fired. The grass was flattened and branches where bent in his direction of travel.

'*Saeiduni!*'

Sonja stopped and listened. She had heard a man's voice ahead.

'*Saeiduni!*'

She was by no means fluent in Arabic, but had spent enough time in the Middle East as a private military contractor to pick up some basics. The man was calling out for someone to help him. He called again, from the same location; he was stationary, lost maybe.

Sonja crept forward, rifle up, the pinpoint of her laser sight probing the darkness for targets. Somewhere in the distance she heard a new sound, the *thwap* of helicopter blades cleaving the night air.

She ignored the noise and froze when she saw the silhouette of a man, a rifle by his side. Watching her steps she moved closer and took aim, placing the illuminated green dot of the laser over the back of the man's right leg, in the rear of his kneecap. She fired. He screamed.

Sonja ran forward. The man had dropped his rifle and was clutching at his shattered knee as he howled and writhed in the dirt.

Normally she aimed for the centre mass of the target's body. She never shot to wound, but she needed this one alive and in pain. Sonja picked up the fallen rifle and tossed it a couple of metres away, out of reach. 'Shut up.'

He half rolled and looked up at her, tears already streaming down his face. She saw now that he was younger than she had thought, perhaps still in his teens. 'Who are you?'

'Don't kill me,' he whined.

'Poacher?'

He shook his head.

'What, then?'

'Please, please,' he said, 'I need a doctor. Get me out of here, please.'

'Take off your shirt,' she ordered. He complied, clearly in pain every time he moved. The man spoke English with an accent – South African crossed with South Asian, she thought. 'Wrap that around your knee and tie it tight. Where are you from? Where is your family?'

He sniffed. 'Mayfair. I don't want to be here any more.'

Sonja nodded. He was from a part of Johannesburg with a high concentration of Muslim people.

Sobbing now, he did as she told him. 'Can you help me get home?'

'Talk fast. What are you doing here?'

The boy blinked and swallowed, and jutted his chin up at her. It seemed like he was trying to show some resolve. Sonja took a pace towards him, her rifle still pointed between his eyes, and raised her foot. She began to lower it down on his injured leg and his resistance crumbled. 'No! Please!'

Sonja removed the pressure from his leg. 'What are you doing here? What was your mission?'

'It's a training exercise. We were to approach the lodge, to provide cover, for …'

'For what?' She raised her foot again.

'Will you help me?' She could see the genuine pleading in his eyes.

'Depends on what you tell me. You were to provide cover for the sniper, yes?'

The boy seemed to hesitate, but as she moved the rifle barrel a few centimetres closer to his face he gave a small nod.

'So tell me, who is the sniper, and what are you doing here on this property, if not poaching?'

'Training.'

'Training for what? For fuck's sake, don't make me shoot you again, we haven't got all night.'

His lower lip trembled. 'Training for the war, but I don't want to go any more. I would have left here, but we're pretty sure that the recruits who don't make it are killed. We're, like, prisoners, miss.'

'What fucking war?' Sonja was losing patience with this snivelling excuse for a man, and she was concerned for the prince's welfare if there were more of these clowns out in the bush. They might not be the best-trained foot-soldiers, but they were carrying automatic weapons.

'Jihad.'

Sonja exhaled. 'How many of you are there?'

The man stared up her, once more trying to muster some vestige of dignity through defiance. She kicked him and he squealed. 'Eighteen.'

'You're what, training for global jihad here on the reserve?'

'Yes.'

'Under the nose of a member of the Kuwaiti royal family?'

The young man shrugged, then groaned and clutched at his knee again. Sonja could see that the makeshift bandage was already soaked through.

'What about security, the anti-poaching rangers working on the reserve?'

'They stay away from where we are. If any poachers wander into our area we have the power to kill them, like. One was shot last month.' He jutted out his chin again, as if this tough stance on poachers might endear him to a white woman. 'We buried him where we killed him so there was no investigation.'

Sonja shook her head. It was bizarre, but this was Africa. She'd heard of illegal goldminers working underground almost side by side with legal miners; pirates hijacking ships full of luxury cars; and she herself had once been recruited to join a black-ops anti-poaching unit whose secret mission was to assassinate poaching kingpins. Truth was stranger than fiction on this continent. 'You're coming with me,' she decided.

'You will help me escape, keep me safe?'

'If you keep singing, yes. Tell me about this so-called war you've been training for.'

'I have had enough. I wanted to go home. We are trained to kill people, using knives. Our fighters have already carried out success-ful attacks.'

'Where?'

He grimaced, aware he had already said too much.

Sonja stood on the young man's wounded leg.

'Stop!'

'Where?'

Tears rolled down his face and his breath came in sobs. 'In Paris, London and Sydney, but the *Shahid*, the martyrs, were all killed. I don't want to die. Please ...'

Sonja took the precaution of taking off the man's belt and using it to bind his hands, then slung her rifle, dropped to one knee and hoisted him across her shoulders in a fireman's carry. As she straight-ened, adjusting him on her back, she heard the *whoosh* of air being displaced next to her cheek and the thud of a bullet into flesh and bone. The young man's body jerked and she dropped to the ground again, the would-be jihadi landing hard on her. When she rolled him off her she saw that a bullet had entered his left eye. He was dead.

Leaving him where he lay, Sonja crawled through the under-growth as fast as she could on all fours, then popped up, sprayed five rounds on full automatic in the direction the silenced shot had come from, and ran again.

Every few paces Sonja felt another bullet whiz through the trees near her. She was breathing heavily. She wondered if the man shooting at her also had night vision goggles. He was unnervingly accurate, even though she was a running target.

The noise of the helicopter's blades and engine intensified in her ears, but she didn't dare pause to look up in case she tripped over a root or rock. She felt the rush of wind from a downwash and a brilliant white light flicked on, coning her in a beam from above.

Sonja had to switch off her night vision device – the lenses had been seared by the sudden burst of illumination, perhaps even ruined, as too much ambient light caused havoc with such things. She slid the harness off her head and waved angrily at the pilot above. He continued to hover, moving slowly forward. Still holding the goggles, she drew her free hand across her neck to signal him to 'cut' the light, but still he kept her lit up like Times Square.

Sonja stopped, raised her rifle and fired two rounds, close but not on target. The pilot finally realised she was serious and banked away.

The lodge was close now, a hundred metres off to her right. The helicopter was circling, its searchlight still stabbing and scything the dark bushveld below as the pilot brought the aircraft around again. God help her, she thought, she would shoot the bloody thing down if he lit her up like that again.

Sonja paused and took cover behind a stout tree. The searchlight was following the path she had just taken. She caught sight of a flash of movement and fired two quick rounds at a fleeting figure. Sonja was rewarded with a cry of pain. The chopper pilot settled into a hover, turning his machine from left to right, searching the ground below. In his beam she saw a man on the ground. He wasn't dead, but he was not in a good way, either. Sonja saw her chance and darted off through the darkness towards the beckoning lights of the lodge.

She took the stairs two at a time to the wooden deck. She went first to the security room and kicked open the unlocked door. There was no one inside. Sonja checked the bank of monitor screens and saw no movement on any of them.

Heading back out onto the deck she tracked towards the dining room, where the unfinished desserts and drinks still sat – the staff had obviously gone to ground. Down the corridor she came to the panic room. Sonja knew she would not be able to enter without the PIN, but hoped there would be some sort of intercom via which she could communicate with the prince.

She slowed, peering over the open sights of the M4, and stayed close to one wall of the corridor. When she reached the heavy door to the panic room, however, she saw that it was open.

Drawing a breath, she once more used her foot to enter and raised the rifle, ready to fire.

There was no movement inside, just the bloodied bodies of Hassan and Ali. Of Faisal there was no sign other than his half-empty whiskey tumbler.

'Shit.'

She went to each of the prince's bodyguards in turn, placing fingers on their necks. Neither had a pulse. Sonja looked around. On the floor she counted four spent casings, all nine-millimetre. A handgun. She checked the men again and found that their concealed pistols had been removed.

Sonja lifted the radio to her mouth and spoke quietly. 'Sonnet, this is Kurtz, over.'

There was no reply. She tried again.

'Where are you?' Sonnet replied at last.

'Where are *you*?'

She thought about what she had seen earlier. Sonnet had the code for the entry to the panic room as, presumably, did the prince and his bodyguards. Who else? No one, she thought. And then there was the business of the terrorist training camp on the property – Sonja did not think Sonnet was a fool, so the camp had to have been operating with his knowledge.

Sonja keyed the radio again. 'I caught one of your men. Since Hassan and Ali are dead, I'm thinking that the inside man is you, and that you got a sniper with a peashooter to wing you deliberately, to make it look like you tried to save the prince's life.'

Silence.

Sonja went to the armoury cupboard at the end of the room while she waited for Sonnet's reply. There were no weapons remaining. All that was left was a smoke grenade, which she took and put in her bag.

She keyed the radio again. 'I'm coming for you now.'

He laughed. 'With what, one rifle? Against many, many armed men.'

'You, your goon from the monitoring room, plus sixteen second-rate wannabe jihadis. I killed one and the sniper shot a stool pigeon I wounded before I had the chance to finish him off. I'd say that's a fair fight.'

The radio hissed again. 'This isn't your war, Sonja. You can leave now. No hard feelings.'

She heard the helicopter pass low over the lodge, above her head, on its way to land somewhere nearby. 'I think I'll stick around a while. This is just starting to get interesting.'

'Have it your own way,' Sonnet said. 'But it's only a matter of time before we find you. There's no one coming to rescue you, and I've got Joanne Flack. How badly do you want her?'

Sonja didn't answer or rise to his bait. The fact was that Joanne Flack meant very little to her.

'Don't want her alive any more?'

Sonja held the radio up to her mouth again. She would need to get moving. 'I know now that it's you who's been moving cycads, and tried to steal the ivory off this reserve, under the prince's nose. Joanne was on to you, which is why you and your Malian business associates tried to have her killed.'

'Whatever you say.'

'I know about the Malian mafia, how they're moving anything of value – drugs, people, wildlife products – across Africa to support the jihad and line their pockets. I also know about the Darul uloom in Joburg where your friends recruit their impressionable young men. They're brought here, to the reserve, where they're indoctrinated with terrorist propaganda and trained to carry out suicide attacks. I don't know what's more evil, training these fools to be terrorists, or using them as organised crime hit men.'

'Nice theory. You can take it to your grave.'

She knew she was right. Sonnet and his Malian partners were filling the boys' heads with jihadi rubbish, but really using them to wipe out their gangster rivals. The would-be terrorists would have thought they were being sent to kill random Westerners, not the business rivals of their recruiters. It was sick.

Sonja made her way from the panic room down the corridor. The hallway led to another exit onto the rear of the lodge. She was just in time to see the helicopter touching down, but it was on the far side of an open-front carport that housed a dozen late-model Land Rover Defender game viewers. She was about to cross the driveway to the vehicles to get a better look when the growl of an engine made her duck back inside the lodge.

The truck that roared past her was a brute of a thing, an RG-32 Scout mine-protected vehicle. Designed and built in South Africa, the armoured four-wheel drive had been used by the Americans and a few other coalition allies in Iraq and Afghanistan, which was where Sonja had seen the type. On its roof was a .50-calibre heavy machine gun on a ring mount—Prince Faisal might have been a stickler for following the letter of the law when it came to exporting cycads, but it was clear he valued his own security over South Africa's gun laws. A shield hid the gunner from view.

The RG-32 swung around the end of the garage and accelerated away, a throaty roar emanating from its Steyr engine. Sonja knew she would need an anti-tank weapon to stop that beast.

She forced herself to breathe deep and slow as she assessed the situation. She was in the middle of an eight-thousand-hectare game reserve, surrounded by dangerous wild animals and an even deadlier force of soldiers, most of whom would not hesitate to give their lives to achieve their mission. The troops arrayed against her had air support in the form of a helicopter, an armoured vehicle, electronic monitoring sensors and heavy weapons.

She, on the other hand, had an assault rifle with, by her count, seventy-eight rounds of ammunition left.

Sonja heard voices. She darted out across the access road to the garage and peered into the first Land Rover she came to. 'Damn.' It was too much to hope that the game viewers would have keys.

The sound of men calling to each other was getting louder and coming from the far side of the lodge. Sonja saw a man in camouflage, carrying an AK-47, poke his head and torso tentatively out of the corridor she had just exited at the rear of the lodge. He looked left and right. Sonja could shoot him, but that would give her position away immediately. She could see another man, perhaps two, crouching behind the first.

The Land Rover was open-topped, allowing better game viewing, and the front driver and passenger's doors had also been removed, giving the vehicles a more rugged, military air to them. Sonja stayed low, working her way along the side of the Defender and reached up into the cab. The truck she was beside was pointing straight at the entryway opposite, across the access road.

Sonja pressed the clutch in with one hand and knocked the gear lever out of first and into neutral. She released the handbrake and then moved to the rear of the Land Rover. Anchoring her boots on the rough-surfaced concrete she put her back into the tailgate and heaved. The vehicle started to roll, silently.

The man in the doorway was looking off to his left, towards the noise and the dust cloud being generated by the helicopter, whose engine was still running as it sat on the helipad. He didn't see the two tons of vehicle gathering momentum as it rolled over the ramp at the entrance to the garage.

Men yelled and ran back down the corridor to the deck as the big four-by-four smashed into the rear of the lodge. Sonja heard a scream and saw that the first man she had seen had been pinned against the brick wall.

In the ensuing chaos Sonja made good her escape without firing a shot, running down the access road and into the darkness beyond the lights of the lodge while the would-be jihadis tried to regroup and recover from their shock.

Sonja paused, took out her phone, and composed an SMS to Rod. She didn't dare make a call and talk in case there were scouts out in the dark.

Jihadi training camp based on prince's reserve. Prince taken captive by Frank Sonnet, head of security. I suspect Sonnet is behind cycad and other smuggling. Enemy force—now 15 men with automatic weapons, plus armoured vehicle with .50-cal machine gun. Chopper has arrived, strongly suspect JF on-board. Need reinforcements asap.

Sonja hit send. She needed to find where Sonnet was holding the prince and Joanne and try to work out her enemy's next move. It felt good knowing who her foe was; the next time she met Sonnet he would see her war face.

Chapter 27

'Shoot,' Rod said, checking his phone messages.

Thandi guessed that in America this must be a swear word. 'What is it?'

'It's from Sonja.' Rod had explained to Thandi who Sonja really was and the purpose of her mission. 'She's walked into World War Three out there on the game reserve. Turns out the head of security is the big man in the poaching racket.'

'Sonnet. I didn't like him from the moment I met him,' Thandi said. 'And Joanne?'

'Sonja thinks she's just arrived, by helicopter.'

'And the prince?'

'Seems he's been taken captive. She needs reinforcements.'

Laurel, who had been moving about Joanne's house, re-joined them. 'I've watered all the plants, Thandi.'

Thandi drew a breath. 'Well done, Laurel.'

'Have I missed anything?' she asked.

'There's a war starting on the prince's game reserve and Joanne may be there.'

'Gosh.' Laurel turned to Rod. 'Can you get some US Marines?'

Rod looked at her blankly. 'From where? If I call the US embassy in Pretoria without official authorisation they'll think I'm a crackpot.'

'We can't just sit on our ... arses ... and do nothing,' Thandi said. She could count on the fingers of both hands the number of times she had used swear words in her life, but it seemed appropriate at the moment. 'I'm going to call the others. We need a means of getting out to the Lowveld quickly, though.'

Rod snapped his fingers. 'I have an idea where we can get a helicopter.'

'Where?' Laurel asked. 'I'd love to go on a helicopter.'

'Andrew Miles, the guy who flew Joanne from Zimbabwe, has a vintage helicopter.'

'Yes,' Thandi said, 'I know it. In fact one of our members, Charles, flies it sometimes.'

Thandi took out her phone and went to WhatsApp. She scrolled until she came to the Pretoria Cycad and Firearms Appreciation Society group and typed a message urging everyone to contact her as soon as possible. Within seconds Stephen called.

'Thandi, howzit?' he said.

'SS, we have a situation, as the Americans would say.' She explained the predicament.

'I can't believe all this—Joanne being alive and what-what-what. And you say we're off to a gunfight? Count me in,' he said. 'Should I get the Kombi ready? The gun cases?'

'Yes. We're going to Lanseria.'

In quick succession, Baye, Charles and Queen Jacqueline all called in, all equally as astonished as SS had been. Thandi's mouth was dry from explaining and answering, but she was buoyed by her friends' responses. They all agreed to come with her, on whatever this mission would be, and Thandi told them to come armed and ready to help their friend.

It appeared that whatever Joanne had been up to, she was most definitely in trouble. As exciting as this all was, and as relieved as she was that Joanne was alive, Thandi still believed, as Sonja and Joanne did, that one of their number was a traitor, and if this was the case then he—or she—would probably reveal themselves at some point on this trip.

Her phone rang again and she checked the screen. 'Sandy, how are you?' Thandi said.

'Fine and you? What's happening?'

Thandi went through her briefing again. She drew a breath, thinking about how best to conclude.

'I'm in,' Sandy said, pre-empting her.

'Sandy, thank you, but...'

'Spare me your pity, Thandi. Do *not* tell me that I cannot come simply because I'm in a wheelchair.'

Simply? Thandi stayed silent.

'You say you're getting a helicopter?'

'Yes,' Thandi said.

'Then get me into it and strap me in. I can provide top cover with my Ruger Mini-14 and a scope.'

Thandi hadn't thought of that. In the guerilla war she had fought, the enemy had always had air superiority, and she had learned to fear the Rhodesian K-cars, or 'Killing Cars' as they'd called their Alouette helicopter gunships. Ironically, her late husband had been one of those pilots she had feared so much. Sandy was an excellent shot and her disability would not stop her from being their airborne guardian angel.

'OK. SS will pick you up. Laurel and I will meet everyone at Lanseria Airport as soon as possible.'

Thandi ended the call, briefed Stephen about Sandy, and checked with Rod.

'Andrew Miles is in,' he said. 'I've promised him the US government will pay for his time and fuel in due course and he says he's happy for Charles to take the Huey.'

Thandi drove and they went back to her house where she quickly changed into black jeans and a long-sleeve turtleneck top. She went to her gun safe and took out her trusty old SKS semi-automatic carbine, the one she fired when she was at the indoor range, and an AK-47 she had smuggled into South Africa when she fled Zimbabwe, fearing for her life. She had brought the SKS home from the firing range because she needed to oil its woodwork, something she liked to do in the evening in front of the television, while watching her favourite soap operas.

'Shame,' Laurel said, hands on hips and shaking her head, 'don't you have anything from this century, not manufactured in some tractor factory in the former Yugoslavia, Thands?'

'I'll take the AK,' Rod said, accepting her spare weapon and fitting a banana-shaped magazine of thirty rounds. Thandi loaded a green canvas satchel with spare magazines for the AK and several boxes of ammunition.

'This is all I have.'

Laurel pouted. 'Let's go to my place. I'd rather get my AR-15.'

Rod looked at his watch. 'Laurel, I'd suggest you take what's on offer.'

Thandi took her Makarov out of her handbag and held it out to Laurel. 'Very well,' Laurel said, taking the pistol, 'but I do feel a tad underdressed.'

'Maybe the others will bring more guns,' Thandi said. 'But Rod's right, we must go.'

Thandi drove fast down the N14 towards Lanseria while Rod loaded the spare magazines for the AK-47. Thandi glanced in the rear-view mirror at Laurel, who sat in the back seat inspecting the Makarov. The other woman looked nervous. 'Are you all right, Laurel?'

She looked up, eyes big. 'I'm OK, Thands. I'm just so worried about Joanne. Wouldn't it be terrible if now that she's alive she dies again?'

'Be brave, Laurel and … keep it together.' Thandi nodded to the pistol in Laurel's hands. 'The trigger pull is heavy, dear, so squeeze hard.'

Laurel's lower lip trembled, but she nodded. 'Yes, Thands.'

'Good girl.'

*

Rod was thinking about Joanne and the brief time they'd spent together, reconnecting. He felt sick to his stomach that after all this time they had both realised they still had feelings for each other, and now she had been snatched away from him.

Thandi was impressive. She handled her Mercedes like a race car driver, nudging a hundred and sixty kilometres, clearly breaking the speed limit, but driving with safe, single-minded determination to get them to Lanseria as quickly as possible.

They turned into the airport. A Kulula flight took off as they pulled into the general aviation area, where Andrew Miles had established his new joy flight business. On the apron in front of the hangar was the American-made UH-1D Huey helicopter, in a drab olive colour scheme with lurid red and white shark's teeth on the nose.

Andrew walked out wearing a one-piece military flight suit that matched his chopper.

'Rod.'

They shook hands, again, and Rod introduced Thandi and Laurel.

'Ladies.' Andrew smiled. 'Welcome. I hear you're heading to a hot LZ.'

'Possibly,' Thandi said.

Stephen Stoke's white Kombi pulled up outside the hangar and the rest of their team climbed out, with varying degrees of slowness. SS went to the rear hatch, opened it, and laid down the ramps to accommodate Sandy's wheelchair.

Charles got out of the Kombi, went to Andrew and shook his hand.

The two men walked over to the Huey and Charles ran his hand lovingly over the nose. 'Hello, my lovely.'

'Take care of her, hey,' Andrew said. 'Bring her back in one piece.'

Charles nodded. 'Affirmative, *boet.*'

Miles turned to Rod. 'Just how much shit are you guys flying into?'

Rod looked him in the eye. 'Plenty. A numerically superior force, hostiles with at least one armoured vehicle and a .50-calibre machine gun. The people we're going after are armed and trained for war.'

Miles rubbed his chin. 'That kind of hardware could take my dear old Huey out of the sky and I don't think my insurance covers anti-aircraft fire.'

'We're in a jam if we can't use your chopper,' Rod said. 'I'll go out on a limb and say Uncle Sam will cover any damage.'

Miles looked sceptical. 'I gave up trusting governments a long time ago. If whomever you're up against has got a .50 cal then they're breaking the law, a weapon like that is illegal, even in South Africa. I may have a plan.'

'What do you mean?' Rod asked.

'Come with me.' They followed Andrew past the helicopter and into his rented hangar. Baye and Thandi tagged along.

Andrew's Hawker Hunter sat as sleek and as poised as a leopard ready to launch itself at its prey. Painted green and brown camouflage, its swept wings and smooth lines were more retro 1950s cool than modern computer-driven killing machine, but there was no doubting this was an aircraft made for war.

Andrew rested an arm on the black barrel of a cannon that protruded from under the nose. 'This isn't just for show.'

'What kind of gun is that, thirty-millimetre?' Baye asked.

Andrew nodded. 'Yes, an ADEN cannon. It came with the aircraft, which I bought from a guy in Qatar, and while it was rendered inert for export, I know a guy who used to work on these aircraft during the Rhodesian Bush War and he got it going for me.'

Stephen raised his eyebrows. 'And ammo?'

Thousand Miles smiled. 'I met a Shona guy in Zimbabwe who used to fly Hunters when they were still airworthy, in the 1980s, and he told me about a stash of thirty-millimetre ammunition at the Gweru air base. You can buy anything in that country for US dollars. I had an idea that I might take especially wealthy clients out over the ocean somewhere and let them fire off a few rounds.'

Rod shook his head. 'All highly illegal, I'm sure.'

Miles shrugged. 'If your enemy has a heavy machine gun, then take a cannon to the gunfight. The fact is this little business venture of mine is going out backwards, even with support from my wealthy partner. I'll send you a bill, Rod, and hope your people come through. I'd rather go out fighting than having the bailiffs repossess my jet and my Huey.'

Rod looked to Thandi, then back to Andrew. 'It could be useful just to have you doing a low-level pass, like a show of force, if it looks like we're in more trouble than we can handle.'

'We're already at that point,' Thandi said. 'If Charles flies the chopper, and Sandy's in an airborne sniper's position, then that means there are just five of us on the ground to take on a force of fifteen or more armed men. Let's face it, most of us are nearing our best-before date – we're going to need all the support we can get.'

'OK, Thousand,' Rod said, 'you've got your answer. Uncle Sam will cover the Hunter's fuel bill along with the Huey's if any of us survive this.'

Andrew grinned. 'Hell, I'll do it just for the fun of it. I've got to load the ADEN, but you guys must leave now-now – that's immediately for you, Yank.'

'The Huey's got a top speed of just over two hundred kilo-metres per hour,' Charles said. 'It's going to take us two hours to get out to the game reserve and by then I won't have much fuel left.'

'I've got a pal at Hoedspruit,' Andrew said. 'Tienie Theunnisen, who does game capture with a helicopter. I'll let him know you'll need fuel and you can top up there. It'll only take me half an hour to get to where you are, but I can only stay on station for maybe ten minutes. I can't very well land a Hunter jet in the Lowveld and beg for some gas.'

Back outside, Rod called them all into a huddle and they synchronised watches. 'Andrew, you load your gun and I'll give you a call when we're about to go in.'

Andrew grinned. 'Roger that.'

While Andrew took Charles to help him load the Hunter's cannon, Rod, Thandi and the others unloaded an assortment of weapons and gear the society members had brought with them in the Kombi.

Stephen hauled out two black plastic bin bags and opened them. 'I found this stuff in my garage.' He laid out an array of canvas and nylon tactical vests, ammunition pouches, belts, water bottles and packs. 'Some of it's gone a bit mouldy.'

'Like some of us,' Baye said, selecting a vest and tightening the adjustable straps to bring it down closer to her size. 'The smell of this stuff reminds me of the army.'

Laurel found a camouflage hunting shirt from a pile of old clothing and put it on over her own white T-shirt, knotting the tail tight around her midriff. Even in cast-off military gear she managed to look attractive and stylish, Thandi thought, as she cocked her SKS and pushed a clip of ten rounds down into the magazine.

Charles emerged from the hangar and climbed into the pilot's seat of the Huey. He began flicking switches and checking gauges. The engine started to whine, and the big blades began to slowly turn.

Rod looked to each of the committee members. Stephen was smearing his face with black boot polish; Baye's mouth was a crooked scar of a smile as she cocked her LM5, a South African knock-off of the Galil assault rifle designed for the Israeli Defence Force she had served in. Thandi adjusted a set of chest webbing and gave him a sombre look and a nod. Sandy, who had been busy cleaning her Mini-14 rifle, finished reassembling the weapon and fitted a magazine. She gave him a thumbs-up.

Rod did a quick headcount then looked around. 'Where's Jacqueline?'

The helicopter's engine was winding up to full speed, the smell of burning aviation gas hanging in the air, the downwash of the rotors blowing around them. Jacqueline emerged from around the corner of the hangar, an Uzi submachine gun in her left hand and her phone pressed against her ear. Judging by her choice of weapon it seemed that Jacqueline, like Thandi, had an illegal stash as well. She ended the call and slid her phone into the pocket of her green cargo pants. She wore a matching safari shirt.

'You with us?' Rod called above the high-pitched whine of the Huey's turbojet engine.

'I am the *leader* of this society, I'll have you know,' Jacqueline replied haughtily as she joined the others.

Then start acting like it, Rod thought to himself. Charles was giving them a thumbs-up, indicating it was time to board the helicopter.

Stephen pushed Sandy's wheelchair to the open side of the cargo compartment and together he and Rod lifted her up into the chopper. They climbed inside and moved her from the floor into what would have been the right-hand side door gunner's position, facing outwards, and strapped her in. She smiled broadly at them.

'This is the most excitement I've had for years,' she yelled into Rod's ear as he tightened her seatbelt.

Rod held out a hand to help Thandi climb in, and Laurel boarded from the other side. Baye took the left-hand side gunner's position. Jacqueline walked around the shark's teeth nose to the co-pilot's side, opened the door and got in next to Charles. Rod boarded last, and took two headsets hanging from hooks and passed one to Thandi.

'I hear you,' Thandi said to him when he gave a radio check.

'Just got clearance from the tower for our "joy ride",' Charles said to them via the intercom.

Rod felt his stomach try to fight gravity as they lifted off. Charles kept the nose down as he followed the runway for a while, gathering speed, and then they were away.

Stephen, seated with his back against the padded rear bulkhead of the cargo compartment, had carried aboard a large picnic basket, which he now opened. He began passing out plastic mugs. 'Coffee and rusks, anyone?'

Rod gave a nervous laugh, but winced with the pain it caused his fractured ribs. He looked out at Johannesburg's sea of lights and shook his head. This was crazy.

Chapter 28

Joanne was scared.

A hessian bag had been placed over her head and she stumbled and fell, grazing her knees as Lindeque dragged her out of the helicopter. He grabbed her by the back of her T-shirt, tearing the fabric as he lifted her to her feet again and frog-marched her forward.

From the landing pad she was shoved into a vehicle, an open-topped game viewer, she guessed, because it was cold and windy as they started moving. The helicopter ride had been long and she had felt claustrophobic, deprived of her sense of sight.

'Where –'

Lindeque shook her. 'Shut up.'

She sensed the vehicle moving downhill and the rush of wind was replaced with the sound of the vehicle's engine and exhaust echoing back at them from the walls. They were in a tunnel. Joanne realised then that she was on Faisal's game reserve. Did that mean he was involved after all? After a couple of minutes, the vehicle stopped and she was manhandled down by Lindeque and someone else.

There was a room underground, she recalled, a bay built into the tunnel wall. She had never been inside, but she was sure that was where they took her. A door closed behind her and the hood was pulled from her head.

'Sonnet.' She blinked at the sight of him. So *he* was the inside man. Joanne realised that there must be a connection between the prince's head of security and someone in the society.

Lindeque and an African man undid her handcuffs and then re-attached them to a ring on the wall. Lindeque went back out into the tunnel.

'What is this?' she asked him. 'Your private torture chamber?'

Sonnet smiled and shook his head. 'No, it's a first aid room, and there's a shower and toilet behind the other door. You've just been manacled to the towel rack.'

'It's you. You're behind all the poaching,' she said to him.

'No, Joanne, you're wrong. *You* are the one who stole the prince's plants and tried to hijack the ivory. That was clever of you, raising the alarm – did you know we were about to arrest the driver and that he would have spilled the beans on you? Is that why you launched your pre-emptive strike?'

'Don't be ridiculous,' she said. Lindeque walked back into the first aid room, straining under the weight of the still-wrapped *woodii* cycad. Joanne glared at him. 'Why did you bring me here?'

'For the same reason I broke into your house,' Lindeque said, 'to find evidence, or, in this case, to get you to confess to being the brains behind the cycad smuggling operation.' He patted the cycad. 'The prince takes his plants very seriously.'

'Where is he?' Joanne said. 'I demand to see Faisal. He'll vouch –'

Sonnet held up a hand. 'We know all about your liaisons with the prince. Now that he knows you're a criminal I don't think he'll be coming to your rescue, Joanne. Anyway, we've got a bit of a situation here.'

'What kind of situation?'

'There's been an attack on the reserve, by some fundamentalist terrorists. They're possibly the same people you've been helping to fund with your sales of smuggled cycads. I think everyone – the Kuwaiti government, the South African police, the CIA – is going to thank me when I explain to them that you're the one who has been bankrolling an African terror organisation that's been responsible for killings around the world.'

'A terrorist tried to kill *me*!'

'There's no point in screaming, Joanne,' Sonnet said. 'Please try and keep a civil tone.'

'*You're* behind this,' she looked to Lindeque, 'you and this thug.'

'Stop being hysterical,' Sonnet said in an oily voice. 'All I need you to tell me is why you stole the cycad that had been entrusted to your little plant fanciers' society and substituted it with a fake. Did you do it for the money or to lay a trap for someone?'

'Fuck off.' Joanne narrowed her eyes, trying to read his real motive. He knew why she stole the *woodii*, because she suspected someone else was about to do just that. Sonnet, she believed, was fishing, trying to find out if she knew which one of her friends was his accomplice.

Sonnet gave an exaggerated sigh and then flipped open the velcro-fastened flap of a black nylon pouch on his belt. He took out a taser, held it up and pressed a button.

Joanne flinched at the sight and sound of the white arc of high-voltage electricity.

'Please, Joanne. Torture is not nearly as fun to administer or as easy to resist as it seems in the movies.' He came closer, holding the device just a few centimetres from her face, and pressed the button again.

'Bite me, Frank.'

He pushed the taser into the side of Joanne's neck and pushed the button.

She screamed.

Sonnet grinned. 'OK, so I lied. It's a little bit fun.'

*

Sonja moved as quickly as she could through the bush without making a sound. All her senses were on full alert. Her phone vibrated in her pocket.

She took it out and looked at the screen. Hudson was calling her on WhatsApp. She pressed the button to ignore the call, then sent him a quick message. *Busy.*

She could see he was replying to her straight away. *Don't give me that. I'm in Joburg. Where are you?*

Sonja exhaled. It was his private investigator's training, she presumed—he was tenacious. She didn't want to scare him, but by the same token there was no reason why she should hide what she was doing from him. Besides, there was nothing he could do to help her. She tapped the screen again: *Can't talk. JF has been kidnapped and I'm looking for her.*

Where?

He was infuriating. Rod was on his way, supposedly with reinforcements, but he was still more than an hour out, according to his last message. It would not hurt for Hudson to know where she was, in case the whole operation got into trouble. She sent him her location by dropping a pin. *Satisfied?*

Shit. Do you have back-up?

Inbound. Geriatrics in Miles's ancient chopper. All under control. Leave me the fuck alone.

That silenced him, but then she worried she had upset him. She sent a final message: *x. Next time you're on Facebook with Emma tell her I love her.*

She hated social media, and the fact that Hudson and her daughter talked more on that banal platform than she did with either of them was a running joke that secretly hurt her. She felt that Hudson would also grasp her other meaning, that she hoped he would take care of Emma, or at least keep an eye on her, if something happened to her. It was a longstanding arrangement they had.

WTF. You're in trouble, he messaged back.

She put the phone back in her pocket and resumed her mission, ignoring the device when it vibrated again.

*

Hudson Brand willed the Uber driver to go faster, and for the Johannesburg traffic to miraculously part for him. Sonja had mentioned Andrew Miles in her SMS to him so he had called the pilot and found out more about the air support Miles was providing to Sonja's mission.

He had decided to fly from Victoria Falls in Zimbabwe to Johannesburg and had left Mishack in charge of Nantwich lodge. Hudson wanted to track Sonja down—he was worried about her and there were things that had to be said. He'd been as guilty of running away from their issues as she had.

Hudson kept checking his watch as they crawled along and was almost tearing his hair out by the time they finally passed the scene of an accident between a truck and a car. The driver was able to speed up on the N14 and Hudson breathed slightly easier once they took the exit onto the R512 towards Lanseria Airport.

He directed the man to the general aviation area and thanked him as he got out.

Andrew Miles, wearing a G-suit over his flying overalls, was doing a pre-flight check around his sleek but ageing Hawker Hunter. He ran a hand along the glossy panels, almost lovingly.

'Hudson, nice to see you. Lovely night for flying.'

Brand shook his hand, and shook his head at the same time. Sonja was on some rescue mission and Andrew 'Thousand' Miles was preparing to fly through the small hours of the night to provide close air support to a helicopter insertion force made up of a bunch of geriatrics, and everyone was carrying on like they were going on a goddamned picnic.

'Thousand, what the fuck is going on?'

He smiled and shrugged. 'You'll have to ask the CIA that. Wait a minute, aren't you CIA?'

'That was another lifetime ago.'

Andrew checked his watch. 'You got here just in time. I was just about to climb aboard and leave without you. Come, let's get you suited up.'

Hudson followed the pilot into the hangar and an office that doubled as a changing room. Miles gave him a quick look up and down and selected a flying suit off a peg. 'Slip into that. Quickly, now.'

Hudson took off his boots, safari shirt and shorts, unclipped his .45-calibre Colt model 1911 pistol and zipped himself into the flying suit. He took his gun from its holster and slid it into a pocket on the right-hand side of his right leg below the knee. Andrew then helped him fit a G-suit.

'Tell me,' Hudson said, 'won't the South African Air Force have something to say about a military jet aircraft flying around at night.'

'For sure, the radar station at Mariepskop would pick us up long before we get to where the action is, and they would scramble a couple of fighters and shoot us down, but,' he gave a theatrical wink, 'I know a guy. There's a certain general who I taught to fly, after Mandela came to power, and I've called him to let him know I may have to make an emergency dash in the Hunter tonight. He knows me and he loves flying in my old kite. He's got eight children and I told him a wealthy client in Joburg may need to fly to Lowveld tonight for the birth of his child. He's arranging clearance on the promise that I'll let him take the controls some time.'

Brand shook his head. 'Only in Africa.'

Miles checked the G-suit was fitted snugly, adjusting a buckle. 'Normally you'd have to have a check-up from a doctor, but I'm assuming you're not about to die.'

'I'm fine,' Hudson said. Andrew gave him a helmet and oxygen mask and they walked back out to the Hunter.

They climbed up onto the wing. 'You ever parachuted?'

Hudson nodded. 'I was a US Army Ranger, airborne.'

'OK, at least you know how to land.' Andrew leaned into the cockpit and touched two loops that protruded from the top of one of the seats. 'This is the primary method of ejecting—we call it the face-blind handle because it's above your helmet and behind you, out of sight. Reach up with both hands and pull down when you hear the command to "bale out, bale out, bale out". Only you Yankees say "eject". There's a secondary ejection handle, between your legs. When you leave the aircraft and the main parachute comes out, the seat will fall away. However, and this is important, under your butt and behind your knees is a dinghy pack, in case you bale out over water. It's in a fibreglass pack and you have to undo the release catch, here, to let it drop and swing below you on a fifteen-foot lanyard. If you don't do this and you land on the pack you'll probably break your legs. Got it?'

'Sounds like it might be safer to stay with the aircraft.'

Andrew laughed. 'You're not far from wrong. I ejected once during the war—it's not something you do recreationally. OK, climb aboard and let's get you strapped in. We're on standby now from your girlfriend.'

317

'Roger that.'

Andrew got into the cockpit and buckled up. 'Tell me again why I'm taking you along on this flight? You're not going to be able to do anything to help the people on the ground.'

'It's better than sitting on my ass here in Joburg doing nothing. Can you put me down after you've done whatever you need to do?'

Andrew frowned. 'Maybe. Depends on my fuel status. I've only got enough for about ten minutes over target. I could declare an emergency maybe and put down at the air force base at Hoedspruit. That'd be the closest airfield to where we're going that's capable of handling the Hunter.'

'That'll do just fine,' Hudson said.

Andrew explained to Hudson what was happening with his other aircraft, the Huey helicopter, then called his friend Tienie Theunnisen and arranged for a fuel top-up.

'He's not suspicious or concerned about filling up your chopper in the middle of the night?' Hudson asked.

Andrew shook his head. 'Tienie flew special ops missions during the Border War. He's a good *oke* and he doesn't ask questions.'

Hudson checked his phone. There were no new messages from Sonja. There was nothing much he and Andrew could do just now, except wait.

*

Rod thanked Tienie for the fuel and waited until the last of the team had re-boarded the Huey. Most of them had used the re-fuelling stop as a chance to go to the bathroom. Rod calculated that the average age on board the helicopter was more than sixty years.

'Wish I was going with you, wherever it is.' Tienie shook Rod's hand as Charles powered up the engine again.

They lifted off from the farm, Charles plotting a course for the prince's reserve with the help of Jacqueline, who had an old-school paper map spread across her knees. Rod noticed Jacqueline also had her phone in her hand, but the ancient Nokia was neither new nor smart enough to support a navigation app.

Rod's phone vibrated with a message from Sonja. *Suspect JF is in the access tunnel. 10-plus tangos guarding entrance by lodge. In OP now, going for CTR.*

Rod showed the message to Thandi. 'Tunnel?'

She nodded. 'There's a road access tunnel that runs from near the main gate all the way to the lodge. It's maybe five kilometres long. "CTR" – close target reconnaissance?'

Rod nodded. 'I think that means she's going in.'

'Where do you want me to set down?' Charles asked over the intercom.

Jacqueline was still studying the map on her lap. 'Thandi, do you remember when we passed the staff quarters?'

'I do.'

'There was a football field, hey?'

'Yes, that's right. Charles, I think it's about a kilometre from the main lodge if I remember correctly.'

'I remember now,' Charles said. 'Sounds like a good enough LZ to me.'

'Approach from the north, Charles,' Jacqueline said, 'that way you'll be approaching from the opposite direction to the main road and over bushland. Less chance of security spotting us.'

'Lift your feet up, everyone,' Charles said, 'I'll be brushing the treetops on the way in. Ten minutes to landing.'

Rod sent Sonja a message saying they were going to land on the football field, and giving their estimated time of arrival. He looked to all of them in the chopper, making eye contact to get their attention. 'Lock and load, everyone!'

*

Sonja dropped to the ground at the sound of an oncoming vehicle. A beam of light swept over her head, and when the vehicle passed she could see it was the RG-32, trundling along a gravel game-viewing road. A man standing in a hatch was swinging a handheld spotlight and the gunner behind the .50-calibre machine gun was rotating his turret left and right to follow the illumination. They were looking for her.

She moved towards the tunnel entrance and spotted two men standing guard. Sonja needed at least one of those men to be somewhere else.

She doubled back towards the lodge, realising that would be the last place they would be looking for her now. When she got to the building she moved as silently as a stalking leopard, up the stairs from the cycad garden and onto the deck. She kept her M4 up, the tip of the barrel searching for targets as she made her way back to the dining room.

The candles were still burning in their silver sticks on the polished leadwood table. She took one, hurried quietly back outside to the deck and held the flame up to the overhanging thatch roof. This was a beautiful, traditional form of African roofing, but it was also highly combustible. Within seconds the dry grass was smoking and flames began crackling. Sonja went back downstairs through the cycad garden and returned to the tunnel entrance beyond the car park.

By the time she got there the burning roof was lighting up the night sky. As she hoped, the two sentries had seen the blaze. One was talking into his radio and the other was running towards the lodge, no doubt in search of an extinguisher.

This was what she had wanted.

Sonja slung the M4 over her shoulder and took her Leatherman out from where she had hidden it, inside her elastic-sided boot. She opened it to the wickedly serrated blade and crept forward to the bush.

She waited until the lone guard was looking away from her and then darted forward. She put her left hand over his mouth from behind and sawed the blade across his neck, severing his windpipe and his carotid artery. Blood flowed over her hand and arm as she held on to the dying man and lowered him to the ground. She dragged him into the bush.

Sonja wiped her hands on the dead man's uniform, noticing it was the same camouflage the reserve's anti-poaching rangers wore—yet more proof of Sonnet's complicity and how the terrorists had been able to literally blend in. She put away her Leatherman and headed into the tunnel. Her heart pounded and adrenaline powered her legs as she ran.

Ahead of her the brightly lit tunnel seemed completely empty, until she heard the echo of a scream. She slowed her pace, her rifle and all senses raised and ready for action. There it was again, a woman, in agony. That meant Joanne was still alive, for now. Sonja knew that few people held up to torture very long so she had to find her, and quickly. Sonja was sure that once whoever was holding Joanne had extracted the infor-mation they needed, they would kill her. It was what Sonja would have done.

*

Joanne hung from the handcuffs and chain securing her to the wall, the pain in her lacerated wrists nothing compared to the tremors that rocked her body as a result of the repeated tasering.

Sonnet came closer to her and she flinched, involuntarily, fearing another shock. He smiled and reached out. She recoiled, but he merely smoothed some stray sweat-dampened strands of hair from her eyes. He leaned in and put his lips close to her ear.

'Just tell me who it is, Joanne. We know you hid the real cycad under your bed in your home in Johannesburg – your late boyfriend saved us the inconvenience of a thorough search – and that you sub-stituted it with a common garden variety. Pun intended. Who took it, and who sold the fake cycad on to the bad guys?'

They were still fishing to see if she knew who the insider was, but the reference to Rod finding the cycad had sapped what little strength she had left. She had tried to deny her love for him after the sting operation that had left her a widow and her daughter without a father. Try as she had to maintain her anger at his du-plicitousness, she had thought of him more than once over the years. He'd come back into her life, and while she had put up a veneer of hostility, it had quickly crumbled. Joanne realised that she had loved Rod, just as strongly as when they were younger and she had talked of leaving Peter. And now Rod was gone. Her grief turned to anger. She glared at Sonnet. 'It was me. I'm the smuggler, the thief.'

He shook his head. 'No, I think you're a good girl, Joanne. I think you took the rare cycad and hid it for safekeeping while you played amateur sleuth. You knew the substitute cycad was going to be stolen, didn't you?'

She shook her head. 'No...' Her mouth was parched. 'No, I just wanted to rip off the people I was supposed to sell the rare cycad to. I double-crossed them.'

Sonnet laughed. 'You're neither that evil nor that smart. Why are you protecting the real smuggler?'

Joanne glared at him. 'You claim to be working for the prince, in his best interests.'

'I am.'

'And you resort to torturing an old... a woman of advanced years. What would he think of that?'

'The prince doesn't care about you, Joanne. You were just a plaything for him. Now you're no better than a common criminal. In parts of the Middle East they would cut your hands off for stealing, or stone you to death for being a whore. Torture's not un-common where he comes from.'

'I'll go to the press.'

Sonnet shrugged. 'I doubt it.'

She didn't believe for a moment that Frank was still loyal to the prince, even if he had once been. 'Bring Faisal to me. If I see him, in person, and he confirms that you're working for him, I'll tell you and him everything you want to know.'

Sonnet shook his head. 'He's in lockdown. There's something of an insurrection going on here at the game farm. Armed men are running around everywhere. We're going to get him off the prop-erty as soon as we can.'

Rubbish, Joanne thought.

'You've got your cycad back. You can let me go.'

Sonnet smiled. 'Nice try, Joanne, but no. The *prince* has got his cycad back, you mean. It will go straight back into the garden. And, since you won't tell me who you think really stole the substi-tute and sold it to the Malians, then I'll just get the South African police – my friend Warrant Officer Lindeque here – to charge you. We'll see how long you, a still reasonably attractive woman, last in Johannesburg's women's prison.'

'Go to hell.'

Sonnet turned to Lindeque. 'Take her pants off. Let's give her a taste of what the prison guards and the other prisoners will have in store for her.'

Joanne's eyes widened. Sonnet was a criminal but she had thought she could barter and negotiate and outfox him. His use of the taser showed he had a sadistic streak, but a small part of her had reasoned that as he had not cut or burned her, there might be a way for her to do some kind of deal with him and talk her way out of this. Her blood turned cold. He was going to rape her.

'You wouldn't dare.'

Lindeque grinned in anticipation as he reached for her legs. 'I shot your boyfriend in the back, you think I'm above rape?'

She kicked out at him, swinging from the cuffs even as they cut further into the bloodied skin of her wrists.

'Feisty. I like that. So will the other inmates.' Lindeque laughed.

There was the sound of gunfire from outside and Joanne screamed for help as loudly as she could.

Chapter 29

Sonja had rounded a bend in the tunnel and seen a man in camouflage fatigues guarding a steel door set into the wall. The man saw her and raised his AK-47, and Sonja dropped him with a double tap, two rounds to his chest.

Having lost the element of surprise she sprinted to the door. Finding it locked, and no keys hanging from the belt of the man she had just killed, she fired at the lock. The door held fast, her rounds ricocheting off and flying around her in the confined space.

Sonja was about to search the sentry's pockets for a key when she heard a truck engine and turned to see the RG-32 armoured car approaching. The observer in the open hatch who had been using the spotlight above ground saw her and tapped the gunner on the shoulder. The man slewed his turret around.

Sonja flicked the M4's selector to automatic and sprayed five rounds at the vehicle, but the spotter had ducked down inside. Her bullets pinged and zinged off the gun shield and the thick armoured body of the vehicle and its bulletproof glass windscreen.

She ran.

Fat .50-calibre machine-gun slugs chased her, pocking and ploughing the tarred road at her heels and bouncing off the tunnel walls. Each round was the size of a small Cuban cigar and a hit from one of those, she knew from her combat experience, would take off one of her limbs. This was not a weapon to mess with.

The driver, having recovered from the shock of being fired on, accelerated. The tunnel had been dropping but now started to climb, and Sonja had a brief respite from the gunner as she ran uphill, moving out of the enemy's line of sight. The RG-32, however, would catch her in seconds.

Embedded into the right-hand wall just ahead of her was a set of red steel rungs, a ladder leading to an emergency exit, she hoped. She slung the M4 around her neck, reached up and started climbing. Above her was a manhole cover, but she would not reach it before the armoured car got to her. It was screaming towards her now.

Sonja held on to the steel rung with her left hand and with her right grabbed the M4's pistol grip and pointed the rifle towards the machine gunner, who was already turning and angling his barrel up to finish her off. But the turret was open-topped and the man was now exposed, his shield offering no protection from above.

Sonja fired fast and wild, emptying her magazine as the assault rifle bucked in her one-handed grip. It was a pray-and-spray tactic. Bullets hailed harmlessly down on the roof of the truck, but one round found its mark and the machine gunner screamed and fell down into the bowels of the vehicle.

Sonja didn't hang around to see if the man was dead or wounded. She climbed higher, reached the manhole, and tugged on a red handle marked *Emergency Use Only*. She figured this qualified.

The hatch swung down and Sonja could see it led to a narrow tubular chute, a tunnel to the surface with more rungs. She climbed higher and higher, now into darkness. Below her she heard the idling engine and braced herself for the stream of hot lead that would follow her up this warren as soon as a replacement got behind the machine gun.

The bullets didn't come, however, and she heard the engine note change as the RG-32 drove off.

Sonja scaled higher and higher until she came to another hatch. She heaved on the handle and smelled fresh bush air and saw stars above her in the black African night sky.

Climbing out she stopped, listened and looked around her, taking a moment to catch her breath. Given that she had been near the dip, the deepest part of the tunnel, Sonja reasoned that she must be about halfway along the five-kilometre length of the subterranean roadway. She had two-and-a-half klicks to go to either get out of this crazy game reserve or back into the fight.

However, Sonja had only one direction in her internal compass. As she ran towards the lodge and certain danger, she took out her phone and dialled Hudson.

'Sonja? What's happening?'

She could hear the whine of an engine in the background as he spoke to her. 'Complicated,' she gasped. 'I just wanted to say, take care of Emma.'

'I got your message. We're coming. Andrew can be there in thirty minutes in his jet fighter, but because of fuel we've only got about ten minutes time over target. Do you need air support?'

'Get out of that aircraft. He doesn't need a passenger.'

'Sonja, this is not the time for an argument,' Hudson said. 'Andrew's going to drop me at Hoedspruit when he's used his fuel. I'll come to you as soon as I can. I'm not going to have you lose your life over a plant.'

'It's not just a plant, it's a whole jihadi-inspired hit squad on the loose here. Tell Andrew there's a chopper here. If we haven't disabled it by the time he gets here then he needs to. I don't want these bastards getting away from here with Joanne, if she's still alive. Is Andrew ready to fly?'

'We're sitting in the cockpit as we speak,' Hudson said.

'OK. Tell him to stay on standby for now. Maybe we can do this without the jet.'

'I want to be there, with you.'

'Don't go all chick flick on me, Brand.'

He gave a small laugh. 'You're a pistol.'

'An assault rifle, at least. Take care, Brand.'

'No, you take care.'

She paused. She needed to go, to get into the fight, but she didn't want to hang up. There was silence on the other end of the line. Sonja wondered if she should say something.

'Sonja ...'

'Yes?'

'I love you.'

Sonja heard the distinctive heavy *thwap-thwap* of a Huey's blades chopping the night air. 'I have to go.'

She ended the call and started jogging towards the designated landing zone.

*

Joanne was able to get back on her feet, relieving the pressure on her bleeding wrists, as Lindeque backed away from her at Sonnet's urging.

He had only got as far as undoing her belt and the top button of her jeans, but still she felt vulnerable and scared of what had nearly happened to her. The gunfire from outside, aimed at the locked door judging by the sound of the clanging, had interrupted their perverse plans. Sonnet was talking on a radio.

'Come, now,' he said into the handset.

Joanne had caught the tinny voice on the other end of the transmission talking about a woman who had got away via an escape hatch in the tunnel.

Sonnet's phone beeped and he checked the screen.

'We've got to go to the staff football pitch. There's a chopper on approach. Those old fogeys from the Pretoria cycad society are coming to look for the woman.'

Joanne felt quietly elated and surprised that her friends were coming to her rescue. It made her wonder who the other woman was, who had been firing at the locked door. Perhaps it was Sonja Kurtz. If so, then Sonnet and his cronies were in for the fight of their lives.

Sonnet came to her and removed the handcuffs, then re-affixed them behind her back. He marched her to the door, which Lindeque unlocked. When they emerged into the tunnel an armoured car was waiting for them. The two men lifted and pushed her up into the truck then climbed in after her. Joanne saw the body of another guard, dressed in camouflage, lying on the roadway in a pool of blood. Someone was already causing havoc.

Joanne saw the .50-calibre machine gun in the turret and a young man with a wispy black beard behind it. Inside the vehicle, slumped on the floor, was another body, and blood was spattered around her on the walls. Joanne swallowed back bile. The problem was that Sonnet knew exactly where the helicopter was about to land, and this confirmed what she already knew: that one of her friends was a traitor. She didn't know how long she could have held out against the torture, but it was all academic now. Joanne sat with her back against the armoured side wall of the truck as the driver engaged the gears and accelerated through the tunnel.

The vehicle emerged from the tunnel and instead of turning towards the main lodge it swung towards the staff quarters. Through a thick glass window Joanne saw that the roof of the lodge was burning fiercely. Employees were milling about and Sonnet, standing in the observer's hatch, waved and yelled at them to get back inside their single-storey accommodation blocks.

The vehicle came to a halt in the trees that lined the open cleared area that served as the football pitch.

Joanne heard the approaching chop of rotor blades. She needed to do something. In the turret the gunner was sighting down the barrel. Lindeque had a pistol in his hand, and was nominally covering her, but in fact he was staring out the vehicle's windscreen, looking for the approaching helicopter. Sonnet was still standing in the observation hatch, talking on a radio.

She looked out the side window and saw figures in fatigues moving among the trees. She counted ten, maybe twelve men, all armed with rifles and all taking up ambush positions.

'Hold your fire,' Sonnet said into his handset. 'Wait until they're on the ground and all out.' He lowered the radio and addressed the man behind the gun. 'When everyone's out, you take out the helo.'

'OK.' The man blinked repeatedly, and Joanne saw sweat blackening the underarms of his uniform shirt. He flexed his fingers on the handles of the big machine gun. He was keen, maybe scared, but definitely nervous. She saw how his thumb rested on the firing button between the handles.

Sonnet did not want to shoot the helicopter out of the sky, Joanne realised, because she was now sure his undercover business partner was on board.

'Here they come,' Lindeque said.

Joanne looked around him and saw a wave of dust, leaves and dirt sweep towards them in advance of the helicopter's rotor blades. The chopper came in tail down, nose up, as the pilot bled off speed. Joanne could make out Laurel and Sandy's faces in the open doorway on one side.

She pushed herself up out of her seat, momentarily unseen by anyone in the truck, and launched her body towards the gunner. Her face collided with the man's thigh and she bit down, as hard as she could, on his leg.

The gunner screamed and accidentally pushed the firing button. The heavy machine gun bellowed to life as a burst of bullets, including three glowing red tracer rounds, arced through the sky towards the helicopter.

From around the vehicle men opened fire with AK-47s, mistakenly thinking that if the big machine gun was firing then that was the signal for them to open up as well. Joanne hung on to the man's leg, worrying it like a Jack Russell shaking a rat to death.

Sonnet was screaming at the gunner and the men around him to cease fire, but the ambush had been sprung too early. The helicopter pilot pulled up and she saw the skids flash over her through the open hatch, just before the gunner's frantic kicks and a punch in the side of her head from Lindeque knocked her to the floor of the vehicle.

Sonnet would have attacked her as well, she thought, except someone on board the helicopter was firing down at them out of the side door and the men around her were ducking for cover.

'Fuck!' Sonnet was livid. 'Get to the lodge,' he barked at the driver. The vehicle lurched off. Joanne didn't want to antagonise them, but she couldn't hold back a smile as she watched the security chief's fury.

He staggered through the cramped interior of the moving armoured vehicle, slapped her, abused Lindeque, and ordered him to blindfold her.

She felt the hard jab of a pistol pushed into her temple as Lindeque tightened a rag around her eyes. She could smell Sonnet's breath as he spoke. 'I don't care if you tell me what you know, I'm going to kill you. But first, I'm going to dangle you like bait in front of your friends so I can kill them as well.'

Joanne's sense of elation at saving the helicopter disappeared.

*

Rod felt the thump of bullets slamming into the tail boom of the helicopter as Charles pulled it up and then into a sickening turn that threw him against the back of Jacqueline's seat.

Someone had ratted them out. The bad guys were there waiting for them, in ambush, even though they'd blown it.

Rod called Sonja.

'What happened?' she asked him, without preamble. 'I heard gunfire. I was close.'

'You tell me what happened,' he said. 'They were waiting for us.'

She thought for a moment. 'Seems like Joanne was right to suspect someone in her plant society. You must have a traitor on board.'

'Roger that.' He looked around them and saw that Thandi was doing the same thing. Sandy and Laurel pumped a couple more rounds down at the disappearing enemy. They were all on edge.

'Rod, these jihadis that have been training on the prince's reserve, it's all a sham. They're cannon fodder being told they're going to die for Allah, but they're really being used as hit men for a Malian organised crime gang. Sonnet's involved in it. I'm telling you this in case I don't make it out.'

'Hold on. We're coming,' Rod said. 'I'll call you back.' He turned to look at his companions. 'Everybody OK?' He received a thumbs-up from all of them, though it had been a lucky escape. He spoke into the microphone of his headset, which was connected to Charles, Jacqueline and Thandi via the intercom. 'What now?'

Charles was scanning the ground ahead. 'We came over a clearing on the way in – I keep an eye out for open spaces in case we have to put down in an emergency.'

'Can you put us down there?'

'Looking for it now,' Charles said.

'We've lost the element of surprise,' Jacqueline said. 'I wonder if we should just pull back and leave this to the police.'

'We're sure the police are involved in this,' Rod said. 'And Sonja thinks Joanne's still alive – for now at least.'

Rod and Thandi made eye contact and he wondered if she was thinking the same thing as him: that Jacqueline might have other reasons for wanting to turn back. Had she tipped off their enemy about the time and place of their touchdown? He had seen Jacqueline on her phone just before they left Lanseria. Whoever the spy was, if there was one, he or she had very nearly just ended up in a crashed and burned helicopter.

Rod called Sonja again.

'I see you,' Sonja said into the phone. 'I'm about five hundred metres closer to the lodge than you are.'

'This is the spot,' Charles said via the intercom.

'We're landing here,' Rod relayed to Sonja.

'Roger. I'm going after their helicopter. RV at the lodge.'

'Will do.' The burning building would be a hard landmark to miss for a rendezvous place.

'Tell Andrew to scramble. We're going to need his air support since it's just us against that armoured car, and maybe twelve or more tangos.'

'I hear you,' Rod said. 'We're landing. Out.' Sonja was reducing the odds against them, but they were still outnumbered.

'Thirty seconds,' Charles said via the intercom. 'Good hunting!'

Rod and Thandi took off their headsets as Charles brought the Huey down fast. They all released their safety belts and edged their way closer to the open side doors. As soon as the skids touched down they were half climbing, half stumbling down onto the ground. None of them was nineteen any more, but Rod still thought they were a force to be reckoned with.

His own ribs protested as he slid his butt off the edge of the cargo floor and his feet touched ground. He looked inside and checked they were all out, save for Sandy and Charles. He gave the pilot a thumbs-up and Charles lifted off. Sandy gave him a wave.

The noise of the helicopter's jet engine and the swirling cloud of dust gave way a few seconds later to the sounds of the African night. A Scops owl chirped from a tree nearby and frogs croaked out their nightly singalong.

Jacqueline took out her map and pointed north. She needn't have bothered, as the burning roof of the lodge cast an orange glow on the horizon in that direction. Jacqueline set off.

'Stephen, you take point,' Rod said.

SS nodded, but 'Queen' Jacqueline put her hands on her hips. 'This is my society, Rod'

'Yes, and this is my mission. Besides, as a commander you don't lead the way. This isn't the First World War, Jacqueline.'

'This is no time for arguing,' Thandi hissed.

Baye muscled her way into the group. 'I'll take point. My eyesight's better than Stephen's. At least I've had laser surgery.'

SS gave a grunt and pushed his thick glasses up his nose. 'I suppose you have a point, Baye, but I'll go number two and keep an overwatch on you.'

'That works for me,' Baye said.

'What is this?' Laurel asked in a low voice. 'Democracy in action?'

Jacqueline cleared her throat. 'Very well. Lead on, Baye. If you want to get killed first, then be my guest.'

'Let's just get a move on,' Thandi said.

*

Sonja saw the spotlight atop the RG-32 sweeping the bush to either side of the gravel game-viewing road that led close to the spot where the Huey had touched down. If the vehicle and its machine gunner caught the oldies in the open, they would be toast.

The vehicle's departure from the football field had, however, given Sonja time to return to the lodge, which was now well and truly ablaze. The radiant heat from the fire was warm on her bare arms and legs even a hundred metres away as she skirted the remains of the luxurious building and moved around the garage to where the helipad was.

Mike, the prince's helicopter pilot, stood by his machine, shifting his weight from foot to foot and smoking. He was keeping an anxious eye on the fire. Sonja saw him raise a radio to his mouth with his free hand and speak. He ground out his cigarette and climbed into his aircraft.

Shit, Sonja thought, he'd just been given an order to take off. Sonnet probably wanted the pilot's help to find the assault team.

Assault team. She shook her head. They were a bunch of grand-mothers and grandfathers, plant fanciers who liked to shoot paper targets on the weekends.

Sonja ran forward, her M4 in her shoulder, but she was acutely aware that she was running low on ammunition. She emerged onto the helipad and Mike, who had already started the engine, looked up from his instrument panel and spotted her.

She had no idea how the pilot was involved in all of this, whether he was just following orders or if he was in with Sonnet. She fired a warning shot over the spinning rotor blades, but Mike ignored her and started to lift off. Sonja lowered her rifle slowly and fired into the engine above him.

Still the chopper rose. Sonja sprinted towards it just as the pilot dropped the nose. She ducked, narrowly avoiding being hit by the aircraft, quickly slung her rifle, and grabbed the right skid as it brushed past her.

Clinging on, Sonja fought to hold tight as Mike lifted off and started to turn. She needed two arms and hands to hang on, so there was no question of her bringing her rifle to bear. Plus, if she sim-ply shot the pilot through the floor of the cockpit he would crash, probably killing her as well.

She had to hope that Mike didn't know she was there. Summon-ing all her strength, Sonja heaved her body up and hooked one, then the other armpit over the skid, then hauled a leg over. Mike levelled out, having gained some altitude.

The helicopter was gaining speed, the slipstream snatching at her dress. The chopper was a Bell Jet Ranger, a civilian model with all its doors on and closed. Thinking that there was nothing like the di-rect approach, she dragged herself to her feet and, standing on the skid, grabbed the handle of the co-pilot's door and opened it.

Mike swore as she swung the M4 towards him.

'Return!'

He shook his head. Sonja raised the M4 one-handed and pulled the trigger. A round flew just inches from Mike's face and out the other side, penetrating a Plexiglass window.

'You'll kill us!' he yelled back.

Sonja nodded. 'If I have to. Land this fucking thing.'

Mike nodded, then threw the helicopter over into a violent turn. The force of the bank caught Sonja off-guard and gravity snatched her body off the skid into thin air. There was no way she could hold on to the door with just one hand so she had to let go of her rifle, which tumbled away into the trees racing past just metres below.

Sonja managed to get two hands on the door, but the g-forces made it feel like her arms were about to be ripped from their sockets as she swung on the open door. But Mike couldn't hold such a steep angle on the bank for long, and as he started to level out, no doubt planning on trying again to shake her off, she lifted herself once more, muscles straining, and got her feet inside the cockpit. Cold fury overtook her. This man was no innocent bystander – he had just tried to kill her. Sonja didn't care what happened to him as she launched herself into the cockpit and across to the pilot's seat.

Mike tried another violent manoeuvre to throw her off balance, but Sonja got to her knees on the co-pilot's seat and delivered a hard, fast punch to the side of his head. He tried to ward off her next blow with the one hand he could free from flying, and started to go for a pistol he had in a shoulder holster, but Sonja was on him like a wild dog on a kill, punching and scratching at him.

She reached across his body as he fought to keep control of the helicopter and drew his pistol. She held it against his head. 'Take us back to the lodge and land this fucking thing now or I'll kill the both of us.'

'All right, all right! I'll land it now that you've got control of my aircraft.'

'What?' It suddenly clicked and Sonja looked down and saw that Mike had been pressing the transmit button on his controls. He was broadcasting a message to someone – Sonnet, most likely.

Sonja looked out of the side window of the Jet Ranger and saw that while the pilot was apparently following her order to return to the lodge, he had taken his time to turn the helicopter around and, in the process of their fistfight, had lost a good deal of altitude.

The dark bush below them was suddenly lit up by a beam of white light angled upwards. For an instant Sonja wondered if this was what it must have been like to be a World War Two bomber pilot coned by searchlights. She held up a hand to stop from being blinded, kicked open the window and fired blindly at the RG-32 below. 'Get us out of here, he's going to shoot us down!'

Mike smiled and shook his head. 'No ways, he's my *boet*. He'll just want to talk to you, to negotiate. Put on a headset and hear him out.'

'You idiot! He's not your brother, he's a killer.' She pointed the pistol at the pilot again. 'Get us out of here!'

Sonnet would want to take her out of this fight, at all costs. The stupid man was hovering now. Sonja buckled herself into the co-pilot's seat, preparing for the inevitable.

'He's going to kill you!' she continued.

Mike started laughing, but stopped when the first of the .50-calibre slugs started smashing into his aircraft. 'Brace, brace, brace!'

Chapter 30

Baye stopped and raised a clenched fist above her head. Next she gave a thumbs-down hand signal.

Rod was no soldier, but he knew from the basic training he had received at Quantico many years ago that she had just signalled that she had seen the enemy.

They all stopped and dropped to one knee, except for Rod and Jacqueline, who crept forward to Baye. She pointed, then raised two fingers. Rod made out the silhouettes of two men wearing peaked caps and carrying rifles. They were looking in the direction of the heavy gunfire that had just broken out. They had all heard and briefly glimpsed the lodge's helicopter flying over. Rod knew that Sonja had been trying to disable the chopper and he wondered what had happened to her. It had been a while since he had heard from her.

'Can we get around them?' Rod whispered to the two women.

'Let's backtrack,' Jacqueline said.

Baye shook her head. 'I say we take them out.'

Two choices, Rod thought, suddenly feeling the weight of command in a war-like situation. The easiest thing would be to wait here and see what the men did next, but that was the 'do nothing' option and they were here to rescue Joanne and, hopefully, bust an international smuggling ring and a terrorist/organised crime training school.

Having taken on the role as leader he knew he had to make a decision. Then circumstances made it for him. The crack of a breaking branch or something similar behind him sounded as loud as a gunshot, and may as well have been, as one of the two men they were watching looked their way. He shouted something in a foreign language, perhaps Arabic, and swung his AK-47 towards them.

Baye was quicker than the man and fired a double tap, which dropped him. His friend, however, let off a burst of fire in their general direction as he dived for cover in the undergrowth.

Stephen got up, as quickly as his creaking knees would allow. 'Cover me, Baye!'

Baye stayed put on one knee, firing into the bush where the man had disappeared, as SS leapfrogged past her.

They were advancing on the enemy, seizing the initiative like a couple of pros, Rod thought. 'Laurel, Thandi, push right, try and outflank these guys,' he called. 'Jacqueline, with me!'

Rod took out his phone as he ran and hit Charles's number, which he had programmed into the device.

'What's happening down there, Rod?' Charles answered.

'We're in a contact. Two men, one down.' Rod was breathing heavily, his ribs aching with every gasp.

'We're on our way. Another chopper lifted off from the lodge, but it was shot down a few minutes ago by the armoured vehicle; no idea what's going on.'

'Shit,' Rod said. 'Sonja was trying to take that aircraft down.'

'Well, their own guys did that for her.'

'I'm worried. She might have been on board,' Rod said.

'I'll see if I can do a pass and check for survivors.'

A burst of gunfire erupted from Rod's front, shredding the vegetation around him.

'You bastards!' Laurel fired half-a-dozen wild shots from her pistol towards where the gunfire had come from.

Rod sought cover behind a tree. 'Get down, Laurel. And save your ammo.'

'Bastards!' she continued.

Rod spoke urgently into the phone. 'Charles, we're pinned down here, can you come take a look? I'll turn my flashlight on and off like a strobe. Fire's coming from our west and north, but Baye and

Stephen are somewhere up ahead, so watch out for them; Thandi and Laurel are pushing right of my position.'

'Roger. Rolling in.'

*

Charles pushed the Huey over into a steep turn. Off to his right was the burning wreckage of the other helicopter. Sandy was strapped into the door gunner's seat on that side. 'Any sign of survivors?'

'Not that I can see,' Sandy replied into the intercom. 'Look out, Charles, there's the armoured car. Nine o'clock!'

Charles banked again, this time away from the fat, glowing red balls of tracer that chased them across the night sky. Luckily their destination, the bush where he could see the winking of Rod's torch, was out of range of the RG-32 – for now.

'You see the strobe, the torchlight?' Charles said.

'Got it.'

'Hunt north and west of there for targets.'

'Affirmative,' Sandy replied.

Charles levelled out, low and fast, the skids of the big troop carrier almost skimming the treetops. 'There's Rod.'

'I see him,' Sandy said.

Charles glanced over his shoulder and saw Sandy peering through the sights of her Mini-14.

'Bring me around again, Charles,' Sandy said, 'I've got eyes on two of them.'

'Roger.'

He banked and turned and heard the crack of the rifle behind him, shots fired in quick succession.

Charles had left the line open to Rod and the American came back, his voice animated. 'That's good. She's keeping their heads down. Baye and SS are advancing.'

Charles could hear more gunfire, this time over the open phone line, and then Sandy started up again as he circled.

'More targets,' she said into the intercom.

Her rifle barked twice more.

*

'Someone's shooting at us!' Thandi screamed.

A bullet smacked into a tree trunk next to Thandi, but instantly she knew it had not come from the gunmen they had just been trading shots with.

Thandi looked up at the Huey helicopter above them. Another round hit the ground next to her. 'It's Sandy!' She knew Rod was in contact with Charles and she called to him: 'Tell the chopper to cease fire, for goodness' sake!'

Laurel and Thandi hugged the ground at the base of a stout jack-alberry as they heard Rod giving the order.

'Bastards!' Laurel yelled.

Thandi scanned the bush ahead of them for the man who had been shooting at them. 'He's gone to ground or run away.'

'Affirmative, Thands,' Laurel said. 'Should we go forward?'

The rush of fear and excitement was coming back to Thandi. The sound of the helicopter petrified her. She remembered a terrifying morning spent hiding in thick bush and granite boulders in the Eastern Highlands of Zimbabwe, near the border with Mozambique, playing cat and mouse with a Rhodesian gunship. She closed her eyes tight, then screamed when she felt a hand on her.

'Thandi, it's just me,' Laurel said, recoiling. 'Are you all right?'

She blinked. It was, in fact, Laurel, and not some long-dead comrade whose body had been eviscerated by fire from above. She made an effort to pull herself together. 'We must push forward.'

'You sure?' Laurel asked.

Thandi heard the hesitation and knew that Laurel probably wanted her to say no, she was not sure she wanted to advance, and that they should back away from danger. But she couldn't. 'Our comrades need us, Laurel. We must do this.'

She drew a deep breath and stood. At least Sandy had stopped firing at them. The chopper was orbiting away from them, hopefully looking for more targets. Thandi couldn't help but wonder if Sandy had targeted them deliberately.

'Are you thinking what I'm thinking?' Laurel whispered as they moved through the eerie darkness.

Thandi said nothing, scanning ahead instead.

'Sandy,' Laurel said. 'What if she knew it was us? What if…?'

'She's the traitor?'

Laurel nodded. 'You know she needs that operation, and even with the fundraisers we've held we all know we'll never beg enough money to send her to the US.'

That exact thought had just crossed Thandi's mind, but she also knew that combat was a crazy, confusing business, and friendly fire accidents and casualties were one of the many sad realities of war.

But Jacqueline, too, had been acting oddly. Thandi recalled the phone call she had made away from the others, before they took off. Thandi had already deduced that someone had tipped off the bad guys about where Charles was going to land the helicopter, further proof that there was a traitor in their midst.

'Thandi, look out!'

Thandi turned towards Laurel, realising her showreel of memories had made her lose concentration. Laurel raised her gun hand and fired twice, the bullets passing no more than a couple of metres in front of her.

'Bastards!'

Thandi looked left, towards where Laurel was aiming, and saw a man retreating. Laurel's wild-west style of shooting seemed to have scared him.

'This is getting dangerous,' Laurel said. 'Thandi, let's regroup.'

Shaken by the thought that her lapse had almost cost them both their lives, Thandi could only nod. Laurel took her by the arm and led her back the way they had just come, to Rod and Jacqueline.

'What's happening?' Rod asked them. Jacqueline popped up from behind a fallen log and fired a three-round burst from her Uzi.

'Thandi's having a little moment,' Laurel said, 'and we were taking too much fire. I'm sorry, Rod.'

He shook his head. 'Don't be. We're outgunned. Baye and Stephen are pinned down up ahead. They can't even fall back, and –'

'Stephen's hit!' Baye yelled.

*

Sonja unbuckled herself from the co-pilot's seat of the crashed helicopter.

Mike, the pilot, had done a pretty good job of auto-rotating and bringing the chopper down in a controlled manner, but his luck had run out. While she had survived the crash unscathed the branch of a dead tree had pierced Mike's side of the fuselage as he crashed. The pilot was dead, impaled horribly on the limb. Good, she thought, with grim satisfaction – she would have finished him if he'd still been alive.

She took her phone out from her bra, under her now ripped cocktail dress, and called Cavanagh. He didn't answer.

Sonja reached over, checked Mike's body, and found his pistol. There was gunfire, plenty of it, about a hundred metres to her west. Rod and the other oldies must be pinned down, she thought.

The Huey circled around, looking for targets, she guessed. Sonja heard the heavy, slower *thunk* of a .50-calibre machine gun. The armoured car was searching for targets too.

Sonja dialled Hudson again.

'Sonja, are you OK?' he asked as soon as he answered.

'Not exactly. Tell Miles to spool up that museum piece of his. I need air support, now.'

'On our way.'

Sonja headed towards the gunfire and into the fray. The Huey swooped low overhead and she hoped no one on board took a shot at her. She needn't have worried.

The RG-32's searchlight flicked on and stabbed the night sky, coming to rest on the helicopter. The pilot tried an evasive move, but the glowing tracer rounds followed it, painting an oddly beautiful display of light and movement that ended in the big fat body of the lumbering old aircraft.

Sonja heard a shout of elation ahead of her and brought up her stolen pistol. There was a lull in the gunfire on the ground as shooters on both sides probably watched the helicopter and the fire and smoke blossoming from its jet turbine engine.

Undistracted, Sonja carried on through the bush. She saw two men looking skywards and shot the nearest with a double tap. He fell to the ground, and as the man next to him rose on one knee from behind the tree where he had been sheltering, Sonja fired again. The first round found its mark, but when she pulled the trigger a second time the pilot's weapon, perhaps poorly maintained, jammed. Sonja ran towards the men she had just shot.

The first man she had hit was dead, but the other was only wounded, in his right arm. He brought his rifle up to fire, clearly surprised to see her still charging towards him. Sonja twirled the pistol in her hand, holding it by the barrel and brandishing it like a club. He pulled the trigger of his AK-47 but the bullets flew wide.

Sonja brought the butt of the pistol down on his forehead and shoulder-charged him and pushed him up against a tree, body to body so he could not bring his rifle to bear on her. She rammed a knee up into his groin and he screamed and punched the side of her head. She ignored the pain and laid into him, using her pistol, hands and fingernails to gouge and beat him into submission.

The man may have received some training in hand-to-hand combat, but he was clearly unprepared for the violent, blisteringly fast savagery of her attack. Sonja drove a fist into his face, three times in quick succession, to knock him out. When he was down, her chest heaving, she dropped the jammed pistol, picked up his AK and shot him in the head.

Her face streaked with blood and nostrils flaring, head reeling from the blow she had taken, she stripped the man of his spare magazines. She hoped he might be carrying a grenade, which she could use on the RG-32, but she was out of luck. She put the ammunition in the bag still slung over her shoulder and headed into the gunfight.

*

'Covering fire!' Rod yelled, and fired his rifle.

Baye, probably the strongest and fittest of all of them, was staggering towards them, rifle in one hand and Stephen draped across her shoulders in a fireman's carry. Even though he had a beer belly SS was not a big man, but carrying him single-handed was still a mammoth effort.

'Bastards!' Laurel yelled, and fired her pistol again.

They heard a command in Arabic and the volume of enemy fire slackened off.

'Pull back,' Rod said as Baye reached them.

'The … the armoured,' Baye panted, 'the armoured car is just ahead. I saw it shoot down the chopper. Charles and Sandy …'

They had all seen it go down. Rod needed to focus on whom he could save. This fight was fast turning into a rout. He gathered those who were in earshot around him, making the most of the lull in the battle.

Baye kept Stephen on her shoulder.

'How are you doing, SS?' Rod said.

'Strong, like a bull,' Stephen croaked, but winced as he tried to smile.

'He's hit in the right upper leg,' Baye said, 'I've bandaged him as well as I can. He'll live, for now, but he can't walk.'

'The bush is too open here,' Rod said. 'That truck's going to mow through these trees like they're weeds. We passed over a creek line on our way in, maybe three hundred yards behind us. We've got to get there. With luck we can cross it and the vehicle won't be able to follow us to the other side.'

'All right,' said Thandi, seeming to recover all of her senses. 'Baye, can you manage?'

Baye nodded. 'I think it will hurt my back more to bend over and put him down for now. I'm good.'

Thandi looked around the group. 'Where's Jacqueline?'

At that instant the gunfight started again, with the rattle of automatic fire and more shouted commands in the language none of them understood.

'That sounded like Jacqueline's Uzi,' Baye said. 'I'd know the sound of that weapon anywhere.'

'Jacqueline, pull back!' Rod yelled. The firing continued.

'We've got to get to her. She can't hear us,' Thandi said.

Baye swayed and dropped to one knee, her face deathly white. Thandi went to her. 'Baye, what is it?'

'I'm … I'm OK, I told you.'

Thandi helped her ease Stephen from her shoulders and immediately spotted the problem. 'You're hit as well, Baye, in your arm.'

'It's nothing, just a graze,' Baye said.

Bullets started zinging closer to them, shredding trees and leaves.

Laurel checked her pistol, unloaded it and slapped a fresh magazine of ammunition into the butt. 'Thandi?'

'Yes, Laurel?'

'You help Baye with SS. I'll go and find Jacqueline and bring her back with me.'

'Laurel ...' Rod began.

She squared up to him. 'Rod, the reason I look like such a hot Sandton babe is because I go to the gym five days a week. I'm not as big and strong as Baye, but I can run faster than any of you. Cardio is my thing. I'll find our Queen and bring her. All right?'

'OK,' he said.

Laurel nodded and jogged off. Rod and Thandi shouldered Stephen's weight, and with Baye covering their rear they fell back towards the thick riverine vegetation of the watercourse.

'I'm coming to get you, you bastards!' they heard Laurel scream as they retreated into the bush.

Chapter 31

Sonja followed the sporadic sounds of gunfire and the rumble of the RG-32's engine. In between the gunshots was the crack of breaking trees as the armoured car smashed its way through the bush.

She realised that she was following in the wake of the enemy advance and that Rod and the others must be retreating. As she crested a low rise she saw by the light of the full moon that the action was moving to a thickly wooded line of vegetation that marked a stream or river. It would be sensible for the small force on foot to move into deeper cover, which would slow the advance of the RG-32. The high revving note of the engine told her the vehicle was already struggling.

'Push out to the flanks, ahead of us,' a male voice called through the bush. She recognised it as belonging to Sonnet, the security chief. 'Use your men as a screen for the vehicle. Find them and we'll finish them with the .50.'

Sonnet knew what he was doing. Sonja knew that one of the tenets of armoured warfare was that tanks and other heavy vehicles needed to be supported by infantry. If that RG-32 got stuck in thick bush the pensioners might find a way to swarm in and take it. The men ranging ahead and to the flanks would keep Rod and the members of the cycad society on the run.

Sonja was gaining on the attackers and, lightly armed and scantily dressed as she was, she was moving faster than the armoured car. She glimpsed it ahead of her, through the trees, ramming and almost mounting a stout tree, which eventually toppled under the mighty weight of the vehicle and the force of the engine. Sonnet was sitting on top, next to the gunner in his turret, probably to maintain a good view. He was cocky, seemingly unconcerned by any threat posed by the people he was chasing.

The closeness of the vegetation, and the fact that Sonnet and the man behind the gun were focusing their attention to their front, allowed Sonja to sneak up on the RG-32 from behind. She moved into the shadow of the vehicle, close enough to be out of sight if Sonnet bothered to look behind him. The behemoth had slowed to a walking pace.

Sonja moved to the left side of the vehicle and looked through a thick armoured glass window. Inside she saw the driver, peering intently through the windscreen, and a man and a woman sitting on opposite sides of the vehicle from each other. They had hessian sacks on their heads, but Sonja was sure she was looking at Joanne and Prince Faisal. The body of the man she had killed had been tossed out somewhere.

The RG-32 smashed through the trees in its path and a patch of relatively clear ground allowed the driver to speed up. Sonja slung her stolen AK-47 and, reaching up, grabbed a door handle and held on. Again her arms took the strain of her body weight, but soon enough the vehicle slowed to traverse a washed-out gully.

'Target front!' Sonnet called out.

The man behind the .50-calibre machine gun opened fire. Sonja used the noise and the slowing of the vehicle to make her move. She opened the left-hand rear door and climbed inside the vehicle. She put her mouth close to the hood Joanne was wearing and said softly. 'It's Sonja. Say nothing. Run.'

Sonja grabbed Joanne by the shoulder and propelled her out the door. As she fell, Sonja ripped the hood from Joanne's head.

Next she grabbed the prince's arm, and as she was dragging him out of his seat, the driver looked around.

'Hey!'

Sonja grabbed a heavy green metal box of .50-calibre ammunition. She swung it around and slammed it into the side of the driver's head.

'Go!' she yelled at the prince as she pushed him out the side door, yanking off his hood in the process.

Sonja followed Faisal out, then paused by the open door and reached into her bag for the smoke grenade she had taken from the prince's armoury in the panic room. She pulled the pin and tossed the canister into the vehicle.

The gunfire from the turret had stopped. The driver had raised the alarm. Sonja unslung her AK-47, got it as far as her hip and opened fire, spraying rounds at the men on top of the vehicle.

Sonnet pulled a pistol from a holster on his belt and turned awkwardly at the waist. He started firing and might have drawn a bead on her, but red smoke from the grenade started billowing up out through the hatch and enshrouded him, obscuring him and his view. Sonja followed her charges back into the thick bush they had all just passed through.

'Get rid of that bloody grenade!' Sonnet yelled at his stunned driver. 'Turn around, turn around!'

Sonja urged Joanne and the prince onwards. Behind her she could hear the RG-32 making hard work of turning around amid the trees.

'I didn't think anyone would know where I was,' Joanne said.

'You can thank Thandi and your pals, if they survive tonight.'

Joanne nodded. 'The guy behind the machine gun is a police detective called Lindeque. He and Frank Sonnet are in cahoots. They're the ones who've been trying to smuggle the treasures out of this game reserve.'

Sonja looked to the prince, who nodded. 'Joanne's right. He was doing all this dealing under my nose and it seems he's been training his own private army as well. We should call the police.'

'The nearest station's fifty kilometres away, with only a handful of cops,' Joanne said. 'We'll be dead by then.'

'We need the cavalry, and a landmark to guide them.' Sonja looked around and saw a pillar of smoke rising to her east. 'That must be the downed Huey.'

As she took out her phone the .50-calibre heavy machine gun opened up again and a hailstorm of lead erupted around them.

*

Sandy Burrell undid the safety belt in the side gunner's position of the helicopter and fell to the ground. Disoriented, she hadn't realised the Huey was on its side. Her wheelchair was nowhere to be seen. She dragged herself through the dirt using her fingers and elbows.

'Charles,' she coughed. 'Are you OK?'

There was the sound of electrical wires sparking and shorting out and she could smell burning plastic as she propelled herself, inch by inch, towards the front of the chopper. Smoke was rapidly filling the cockpit. Sandy got to the pilot's side door and could see Charles slumped against it, his face a mess of blood. He was either dead or unconscious.

If fire spread through the wreckage and it exploded, she would be dead. At the rate she was moving she thought that even if she tried to haul herself away now she still wouldn't outdistance the blast radius. She reached up for the door handle and turned it.

The door opened and Charles fell out of the cockpit, onto her paralysed legs.

She twisted, trying to sit up, and cradled his head in her lap.

'Charles, please talk to me.'

She felt for his pulse. Sandy had never told Charles, but she was fairly sure she loved him. He was so handsome, so debonair with that white-lion mane of his, and his cravat and sports jacket and his pick-up lines. He couldn't walk past a pretty woman of any age without making her smile with a compliment and it always seemed that he was the centre of female attention at any gathering. She had long understood that she could never be with a man like that, and, to protect herself, she had always been ruder to Charles than she was to most other people. If he knew how she felt and then rejected her, as she was sure he would, it would crush her. But now, when it seemed like they'd run out of time, she wasn't sure that mattered any more.

She felt his heart beating, weakly. He opened his eyes.

Charles forced a smile. 'I'm in heaven. It's an angel.'

She tried to laugh, for his sake, but tears rolled down her cheeks.

The smile disappeared from Charles's handsome though bruised face. 'Sandy...'

'Yes?'

'I'm trying to move, but I can't. Touch my legs for me.'

She moved her hands over his body, something she'd only ever dreamed of doing, to his thigh. She pinched it. 'Feel that?'

He swallowed. His lower lip started to tremble. 'Nothing. It might be my back.'

Sandy looked around her. The smoke, now acrid and black, was getting thicker. It was coming from under the cockpit control panel, which was now just above them.

'You made it this far,' Charles said. 'Get away from here now, as quick as you can, my dear, before this thing blows up, or we're both cooked.'

'No.'

'You have to, Sandy. You can save yourself. I think my arm's broken as well; I'm done for, my girl.'

My girl. It was such a common, old-fashioned South African-ism, and Sandy thought Charles had probably used it on every second woman he'd ever met. Yet he had just said it to her, for the first time since she'd known him. 'I'm staying with you. Charles...'

'Yes?'

'I'd...I'd rather die than go to our meetings knowing you weren't going to be there.'

She held her breath.

Charles blinked at her and said nothing for a few seconds. Sandy thought she might die from embarrassment, if the burning heli-copter didn't incinerate her first.

'Sandy...you never seemed to care, never seemed to like me, but ever since I met you I've thought you are the smartest, bravest, most inspiringly beautiful woman I've ever met. I just never knew how to get through to you.'

She kissed him. His lips still worked. Just fine.

When they broke apart Charles blinked again. '*Sjoe*. You're a good kisser as well.'

Sandy held him tight.

'Go, my love. Save yourself,' he said.

My love. 'I'm not going anywhere.'

Flame blossomed from the instrument panel and began spreading through the cabin. Sandy kissed Charles again as she felt the fire start to scorch her cheeks.

'Sandy,' he croaked again as their lips parted.

'Yes, my love?'

'I... I love you, Sandy.'

'Me too. I mean, I love you, Charles.'

The heat was becoming unbearable. The fire was almost at Charles's legs, though his flight suit would give him a few minutes of respite before the flames took hold.

'There's a pistol in my shoulder holster.'

'I don't understand, Charles.'

He looked up at her and she saw yet again how beautiful his blue eyes were. The realisation dawned on her.

'I think you do, my love. It'll be quicker that way.'

*

Laurel crept through the bush as quietly as she could. The RG-32 had ceased firing towards the creek line where Rod, Thandi, SS and Baye were holed up. Through gaps in the foliage Laurel could see the vehicle ponderously negotiating a U-turn.

Her first priority was to find Queen Jacqueline who, as the Americans would have said, had gone off reservation. Laurel was worried that she knew why and her fears were confirmed when she saw Jacqueline, ahead of her, kneeling behind a cluster of granite boulders, tapping something on her ridiculously ancient Nokia phone, her Uzi slung over her shoulder.

'Jacqueline, are you OK?'

Jacqueline turned to Laurel and looked up from her screen. Her right hand dropped to the pistol grip of the Israeli-made submachine gun.

Laurel swallowed hard. She had Thandi's Makarov pistol held by her side. 'Jacqueline, talk to me. What are you doing? Who are you messaging?'

Jacqueline just stared at her, though Laurel noticed she was slowly raising the Uzi at the same time. 'Are you alone, Laurel?'

'Yes. We need to get you back to the others. They're in the creek line. It's better defended. Please lower your weapon, Jax. You know the number one rule of the shooting range: don't ever point a gun at someone –'

Jacqueline did just that and finished the sentence for good measure, '– unless you mean to kill them.'

Laurel held up her left hand. 'Jax, please, don't. It's OK. We can talk this through.'

'No!' Jacqueline pulled the trigger.

Laurel was trying to take aim with her pistol when she felt a kick in her left shoulder. She saw Jacqueline's look of wide-eyed surprise that turned to dread when she realised she had either emptied her magazine or her gun had jammed. Even as Laurel felt her torso spin from the hit she was firing a double tap.

Jacqueline dropped to the ground, two rounds in her chest. Laurel rushed to her and fell to her knees. She hadn't even registered pain from her own wound. She took Jacqueline's hand, which had just opened to let her phone drop into the grass. Laurel felt the tears brim in her eyes. 'Oh Jacqueline, why, why did you do that?'

Chapter 32

The vintage jet fighter streaked through the empty night sky, the flat, open South African Highveld plummeting away below them to the steamy subtropical Lowveld.

Andrew pushed the nose of the Hunter down, following the contour of the terrain.

'We're about ten minutes to time over target,' he said into the intercom, his voice tinny in Hudson's ears.

Hudson would ordinarily have enjoyed the thrill of flying in this retro war bird, but he was too worried about Sonja to savour the moment. He scanned the ground ahead of them, hoping to make himself useful.

'Fire on the horizon,' he said after a few minutes.

'You've got a safari guide's eyes. That should be where we're heading if I've got the GPS coordinates right,' Miles replied.

'I'll call Sonja,' Hudson said.

Thanks to a modern re-fit, Miles could use a mobile phone in the cockpit, with an audio feed to their headphones. Hudson punched in Sonja's number.

As soon as she answered, both Hudson and Miles could hear gunfire.

'What, Brand? I've kind of got my hands full here.'

He heard the *pop-pop-pop* of an AK-47 being fired.

'We're inbound.'

'I sincerely fucking hope so.'

He gave his head a little shake. 'Less than five.'

'Roger that,' she said. 'Can Miles hear me?'

'Affirmative,' Andrew said.

'Northeast of the burning lodge there's what's left of your Huey.'

Hudson glanced at Miles and saw the older man grimace. 'Go on.'

'Looks like it's also burning now. That's where we're heading and we've got the RG-32 armoured vehicle hot on our heels. You see that truck, you light it up, Miles. Copy?'

'Um, how close are you? What's your position?' Miles asked, his voice fighter-pilot calm.

'*His* position, in a couple of minutes, will be up my arse, Miles. Don't worry about me, just smoke that fucker.'

'Roger,' Miles said.

'Sonja ...' Hudson began.

'Do *not* tell me you love me again, Hudson. I need to change magazines so I don't have time for girl talk. Bye for now.' She ended the call.

'That was sweet,' Miles said.

Hudson shook his head. At least she had called him 'Hudson'. Maybe she did love him.

'Hudson, have you ever flown a plane before?'

'Sort of. A buddy of mine in Zimbabwe had a Cessna. He used to let me take the controls sometimes in mid-flight.'

'OK. If I get hit by that .50-cal in the attack run then you need to pull us up and to the left. We're going to come in low, ten-degree dive angle, and I'll open fire at five hundred feet. We'll be at two hundred feet by the time I start pulling out and there's a real risk of us being hit by ricochets from our own rounds. I'll climb out to the left because the rifling of the cannon is clockwise, which means the rounds will ricochet off to the right if they bounce off that mini tank down there. If I'm a goner, climb to five thousand feet and bale out. Got it?'

'Sure.' Hudson pointed. 'There's your burning Huey ... and tracer fire. That's coming from the RG-32. There's your target, Thousand.'

'Seen. Goodbye insurance no-claim bonus.' Miles pushed the Hunter into a shallow dive and Hudson held his breath.

*

Thandi peered around the trunk of a big tree and looked down the open sights of her SKS. Again a collage of memories from the liberation war tried to distract her, but instead of the panic she'd felt at the sound of the helicopter, now a sense of calm washed over her.

The man she could see wanted to kill her and her friends. This is what war came down to, at its most elemental. The people on the other side wanted you dead, and you wanted to protect your friends. She drew a breath, steadied herself, released half the air from her lungs and squeezed the trigger.

The man dropped to the ground.

Baye was ten metres to her right and she, too, fired. There were no cries of elation or anger. Even Stephen, with his leg bandaged, was lying behind a log taking his time with well-aimed shots.

Those hours of practice on the Pretoria shooting range were paying off. This battle had changed from a wild melee to a contest between a squad of young men, charged with testosterone but short on marksmanship training, and a group of friends who had all not only seen combat, but were also expert shots.

Baye, SS and Thandi were settled into the bank of the dry creek bed and the trees there, nourished year round by underground water, were big and stout, providing excellent protection and concealment. Their attackers were losing their nerve and had gone to ground. Every time one of them was brave or stupid enough to put his head up there was a very good chance he was going to end up with a bullet in it. Rod crawled to Thandi's position.

'They've lost the initiative,' he said to her.

Thandi nodded. 'Yes, but with only three of us able to walk, and Laurel and the Queen missing, it would still be suicidal for us to try and advance on them.'

Rod's phone buzzed in his shirt pocket. He took it out and checked the screen. 'Sonja's got Joanne and the prince. She says Miles is inbound, in the Hunter.'

'Good.' Thandi saw movement and took a snap shot. She wasn't sure if she had hit the target or not. 'The armoured car has turned around, so the air attack may distract these guys.'

'I need to get to Joanne. I'll go by myself if I have to,' said Rod.

Thandi stared at him. 'Is it worth risking your life over?'

He nodded. 'It is, Thandi.'

Someone fired a quick volley of three shots. 'Bastards!' yelled a high-pitched voice.

Thandi glanced at Rod. 'That will be Laurel.'

'Covering fire!' Rod called.

Thandi, SS and Baye all fired at the spots where they'd last seen targets. From off to their left, crashing through the trees, Laurel sprinted to the creek then dropped to her knees and slid down the bank to land next to Rod and Thandi.

Her face was striped with tears and dirt. Her whole upper body was heaving.

'Laurel, what is it, dear?' Thandi reached out her free hand and placed it on her shoulder. 'Did you find Jacqueline?'

Laurel seemed to be in shock now. Her bottom lip quivered and she didn't seem able to speak. Dumbly, she reached into her pants pocket, pulled out a phone and handed it to Thandi.

Rod kept his eyes on the perimeter. 'What is it?'

'Jacqueline's.' Laurel sobbed and sniffed. 'Mess–messages.'

Thandi went to the message history and scanned the entries. 'My gosh. This is giving away all our movements, how many of us there are, what arms we're carrying, and where Charles was going to land the Huey. There's even a message here saying we've pulled back to the creek line. The other person is telling the sender to join them at the armoured car because he's about to "finish your friends off". Where did you get this, Laurel?'

'Jacqueline.'

'Where is she now?'

'I...I...' Laurel howled.

Thandi wrapped an arm around her.

'...I killed her, Thandi. She shot me.'

'Goodness.' Thandi was momentarily speechless. She noticed blood on Laurel's top. 'You're such a mess I didn't realise you'd been shot, dear. Your shoulder–let me see to it.'

Rod looked back at them. 'Laurel, I know you're hurt and that you've just been through hell, but you made it back here. Can you get up again? We need to take the fight to these guys, to link up with Joanne and Sonja.'

Laurel took a deep breath and, with her good hand which still held Thandi's pistol, wiped her eyes. 'I can. I want to kill these bastards, Rod.'

Rod nodded. 'Then patch her up, Thandi, and let's do this.'

*

The smoke from the burning Huey helicopter obscured Sonja, Joanne and the prince from Sonnet's view. The machine gun rounds kept searching for them, but the RG-32 was firing blind now and a patch of thick vegetation had once more slowed it to a crawl.

Joanne heard a scream and ran ahead of the others. Sonja had put a bullet through the chain securing her handcuffs, which she now wore as two heavy bracelets. She ran around the wreck of the chopper and saw Sandy lying on the ground, cradling Charles in her arms. Sandy was screaming with pain.

The fire seemed to have started in the cockpit and while Sandy and Charles were lying below the epicentre of the blaze, the heat was already scorching their skin. Joanne could see how Sandy was covering Charles's face and head with her torso, and therefore taking most of the heat herself.

The rear-most bulkhead of the chopper hadn't been engulfed yet. The helicopter was on its side, so Joanne had to hoist herself up by grasping one of the skids, and climb up the underside of the fuselage to get inside. Once there she saw what she was looking for: a fire extinguisher clipped to the padded bulkhead wall. She took it and jumped down and ran around to her friends. There she emptied the extinguisher into the instrument panel and soon the fire was out.

Joanne looked down at them. Sandy kissed Charles on the cheek.

'Maybe I should have saved some of this foam for you two lovers, to cool you down,' Joanne said. 'Looks like you need to get a room.'

Charles smiled up at her. 'It took a lot for me to get this one's attention.'

Faisal arrived at Joanne's side, breathing heavily. 'Can I help?'

'They're OK, alive at least,' Joanne said.

Charles tried to smile. 'It's good to see *you* alive as well, Joanne. I take it from this appearance that you and his excellency are officially good guys?'

Joanne nodded and glanced to Faisal. 'I stole the *woodii* from our storeroom because I was fairly sure it was going to be taken again, by someone in our society. I hid it for safekeeping, and a substitute I planted was stolen, but now the real bad guys have the real *woodii* again.'

Faisal's eyes widened. 'Really? You didn't think to give it back to me instead?'

Joanne didn't have time to feel embarrassed. 'I wasn't sure about you, Faisal, I'm sorry.'

He shrugged. 'We have bigger things to worry about.'

'Your Excellency ...' Charles began.

'Call me Faisal.' The prince knelt next to Charles, who reached into his shoulder holster, drew his pistol and handed it to Faisal.

'You're in a better position to use this than me.'

Bullets thudded into the wreckage near them and Joanne and Faisal dropped to their bellies, searching for targets.

Sonja leopard-crawled across the ground to them. 'This is where we circle the wagons,' she said.

They all looked up at the sound of a jet engine echoing through the night sky.

*

Hudson could see the RG-32 clearly now, the vehicle bathed in the glow of the burning helicopter. Suddenly, the flames went out.

'You still got it?' Hudson said.

'I can still see it thanks to the moonlight and the tracer. Hold on.'

Andrew pressed the cannon's firing button and a series of loud, lumbering bangs shook the entire airframe as the thirty-millimetre projectiles streaked out ahead of them. The metallic smell of cordite drifted up from the gun pod below them and filled the cockpit.

Hudson briefly registered the sight of mini explosions going off below and a spark that could have been a round ricocheting off the metal hull of the armoured vehicle, which had temporarily disappeared from sight as Andrew pulled up and to the left. Hudson felt the g-forces pushing him into his seat, and when the smartphone in its cradle started flashing and ringing, it took all his strength to lift his arm to press the answer button.

'You missed,' Sonja said.

'It's been forty years since I shot anything,' Miles said.

'The wind's picked up down here. Watch where the smoke from the burning lodge is drifting. You need to aim off more.'

'Sonja, I'm sure Andrew knows–' Hudson began.

'Sonja's right,' Thousand said. 'I should have allowed more for the breeze.'

'Get it right next time,' Sonja said. 'That armoured car is about to grease its wheels with us. I've got two paralysed WIAs down here as well.'

'Yes, ma'am,' Andrew said as he banked and climbed. When he had levelled out he ended the call and glanced at Hudson. 'I don't need more distractions and, besides, I've only got enough ammo for one more run.'

*

Rod, Thandi, Baye and Laurel used the noise of the low-level jet pass and the ensuing blasts of the high-explosive rounds and the .50-calibre returning fire at the Hunter to launch their assault.

With Stephen laying down covering fire they rose and charged forward. The men arrayed against them fired a few desultory shots, but it was their turn to retreat.

Perhaps, Rod thought, the enemy had been ordered back to the RG-32, but whatever the cause the good guys were moving forward again, regaining the initiative. Rod and Baye moved as a pair, one covering while the other darted forward to a new place of cover. Laurel and Thandi did the same, with Laurel swearing again. Their opposition melted away as they ran forward.

*

The RG-32 toppled another tree and the driver was finally able to accelerate. Sonja stood and took aim, trying to get a shot at the gunner, in case he raised his head a fraction above the shield. Mercifully, the man must have run out of ammunition. Sonnet, crouched behind the shield, fired an M4 at her. Sonja pressed herself against the still-hot metal fuselage of the downed Huey. Joanne had found Sandy's Mini-14 rifle and was also firing at the armoured car, as was Faisal, but their small-calibre rounds were pinging harmlessly off the vehicle.

Sonja knew that as soon as the gunner reloaded, they were finished.

Then came the scream of a Rolls Royce jet engine from above as Miles lined up for his second run. This time the high-explosive cannon shells were landing close enough for Sonja to have to dive for cover. She could see the first four hit too soon, in front of the vehicle, but the next two found their mark. One blew off the left front wheel of the armoured car and the second slammed straight into the machine gunner's shield, penetrating it and pulverising both the gun and Lindeque, the man behind it, in an instant.

Sonja saw Sonnet half fall, half jump off the top of the vehicle. She stood up and ran forward as the Hunter streaked overhead. She climbed up on top of the disabled beast and, ignoring the gory remains of the gunner, fired down through the hatch, killing the driver before he could pull his pistol on her. Faisal had charged forward as well and now joined her.

Sonja looked around and saw Sonnet running off into the bush, in the direction of the prince's lodge, which was now completely engulfed in fire. 'Look after Joanne and the others,' she called down to Faisal as she jumped down and headed in pursuit of Sonnet.

*

Sonnet called Rafik Keita on the radio as he ran: 'How many men have you got left?'

'Six,' Rafik said. 'We've taken plenty of casualties.'

'The jet took out the car and the last of two men loyal to me, but we can still win this—we have to kill them all so there are no witnesses.'

'Understood. My men will die trying.'

'I don't want them to be martyrs,' Sonnet said, 'I want the other people dead, especially Joanne Flack and the prince. They're by the RG-32. I'm heading to the lodge to get a vehicle. Get me some muscle.'

'Understood. I'll send three men to you and take three with me to finish off the rest of them.'

Chapter 33

Joanne, Faisal, Charles and Sandy lay close to each other by the wreckage of the Huey. Charles seemed stable, but they did not want to risk moving him because of his possible spinal injury. They knew they needed to win this fight before they could call in medical help.

Faisal had braved the carnage inside the disabled armoured car and returned with a pistol for Joanne and an M4 rifle for himself. They had very little ammunition, as did Sandy for her Mini-14, which Joanne had returned to her. They waited and watched the bush for signs of movement. All was quiet.

'I'm sorry to have dragged you into this mess,' Faisal said to Joanne.

She looked at him. 'It's not your fault. I know now it was Sonnet who was behind the theft of the two cycads and the attempt to hi-jack the ivory.'

He nodded. 'Yes, and it appears he was training his own private army here at the same time. I can't believe how naive I was. That's what comes from a life of isolated privilege, I suppose.'

'I'm so pleased you weren't involved,' Joanne said.

He sighed. 'You really thought I was some petty criminal?'

She shrugged. 'Or terrorist.'

He laughed. 'I like Celine Dion and table dancing clubs too much to ever become a committed fundamentalist.'

She chuckled. 'I don't know which of those two things turns me off more, Faisal.'

He grinned. 'I like you a good deal, Joanne. My offer of a job here still stands, if we survive tonight.'

'As your head gardener? Or something more?'

It was his turn to shrug. 'You would have a very comfortable life here.'

She sighed. 'I think I want more than "comfortable".'

'Money? We can negotiate a package I'm sure you will find favourable.'

'No. I want more than money.'

'I enjoy your company, Joanne. I'm sure we could come to some mutually beneficial arrangement.'

Faisal didn't get it, she thought. She wanted what she would have had with Peter – if they hadn't lost everything and he hadn't turned to crime – and what she should have had with Rod.

'Target, one hundred metres,' Sandy said, then fired.

Joanne ducked instinctively at the sound of the gunshot then raised her head. She saw a man running through the bush and took aim and squeezed the trigger. Faisal blazed away.

'Take your time,' she said to him. 'Conserve your ammunition.'

'This is madness, this is my own property.'

Joanne ignored his incredulity and searched for another target. A burst of automatic fire from an AK-47 passed low over their heads, making Joanne bury her face in the dirt.

'*Allah-u-Akbar!*' A young man, wild-eyed, broke from the cover of the trees and charged towards them, firing from the hip.

Sandy fired at the man and the bullet hit him in the forearm. He kept running towards them, but her second shot dropped him.

'I'm down to my last two rounds,' Sandy said.

Faisal fired two shots at a moving shadow, then his weapon clicked on an empty magazine. He took out his phone.

'Who are you calling?' Joanne asked.

'The leader of my anti-poaching unit. They're based on the far side of the reserve, near the main road, the most likely avenue of entry for criminals. I have to hope that they, at least, are loyal to me. Sonnet said they'd been called out to investigate a poaching incursion, but I'm sure now that was a ruse.'

'I'm not sure they'll get here in time, but go for it.' Joanne had allowed herself to get her hopes up and now she realised they were probably doomed. She and Faisal could run, but that would mean leaving Charles and Sandy behind, something she was not prepared to do.

Ammunition clearly wasn't a problem for their enemies, because the bush in front of them exploded with a fusillade of automatic fire that forced them all to burrow into the dry dirt. The final attack was coming.

*

Rod heard the renewed crescendo of gunfire and surged ahead of Thandi and Baye. Thandi was the best shot of all of them, but she was also the oldest and the most out of shape. He looked over his shoulder. 'Are you OK?'

'Don't let me hold you back, Rod,' she huffed. 'But just be careful.'

He knew Joanne was somewhere by the crashed helicopter. He couldn't bear the thought of losing her again so he surged forward, his cracked ribs and tired legs protesting.

Men were yelling in Arabic ahead of him as he fought through the thorny, cloying bushveld. Rod passed the body of a man in camouflage; he had been shot through the forehead.

Panting and sweating he pushed himself harder, his finger on the trigger, bloodlust carrying him onwards. The firing had stopped now and Rod made his way through some bushes to see two men standing over Joanne and the man he guessed was the owner of the game reserve. Sandy and Charles lay in each other's arms by the wreckage of the helicopter.

'Don't shoot, please,' the prince was saying.

'Kill them,' said one of the two men.

Rod raised his rifle and shot the man in the back.

The other, younger man spun around, bringing his AK up. Rod squeezed the trigger and the firing pin clicked on an empty chamber.

In that split second of distraction Joanne leapt up and onto the man's back, clawing at his face with one hand and his weapon with the other. The man fired wildly. Rod surged forward, but he had thirty metres to cover, more than enough time to die.

Faisal went for the man's legs in a rugby tackle that brought him down. The prince grabbed the man's rifle and tried to wrest it from him, but the man pulled the trigger and the prince was blown backwards.

Rod was almost with them when he saw the barrel of the AK-47 coming towards him. He charged on, hoping the man would shoot him in the chest, and that his bulletproof vest would take another round.

Joanne was reaching for the man's belt. She pulled out a knife from its sheath and stabbed the man up and under his ribcage. As Rod dropped to his knees, the man was in his death throes, and Joanne's hand and arm were drenched in blood.

Exhausted, she rolled off her prey.

Rod took her by the hands, heedless of the blood, and drew her up to her knees and into his arms.

'I thought you were dead,' they said, in perfect unison.

'Faisal,' she said.

They looked to the prince, who was getting unsteadily to his feet.

'Now that bloody hurt,' Faisal said. He reached into the right front pocket of his pants and, gingerly, pulled out a silver hip flask. He held it up and they could see how the bullet had scored the metal when it had ricocheted off. 'Saved by the Bell's whiskey.'

Rod brushed the hair from Joanne's eyes and kissed her. 'I'm never leaving you again.'

*

Hudson Brand felt useless as he and Miles circled the battlefield below.

He knew that Joanne was alive, but their side had taken casualties, one dead and at least two wounded. Sonja had last been seen running after another bad guy.

'Just like her to go off all lone wolf,' he said aloud.

'We can't stay around here, Hudson,' Andrew said. 'As it is I'm going to have to declare an emergency and land at Hoedspruit airbase. I'm going to have a lot of explaining to do to the air force and the civil aviation people, even though I have friends in high places.'

Hudson called Sonja again and this time she answered.

'What now, Brand?'

'Sonja, are you all right?'

'Relax. I'm by the main lodge building, or what's left of it after the fire. Frank Sonnet is lying on the ground in front of me. The idiot tripped over and I got the drop on him. Call the cops, Brand, and the ambulance service, ideally a chopper. We've got wounded people to take care of. This is the end of it.'

Hudson exhaled with relief.

'Can we go now?' Miles asked. He had heard the conversation in his headphones.

'You, flyboy, are excused,' Sonja said. 'Go back to base for your gin and tonic.'

Hudson grinned.

'Do one more pass over the lodge, Thousand,' Hudson said.

'OK. But that's it for us.'

Miles banked and lined up for a run over the lodge. Hudson saw they were at five hundred feet above ground level. He hoped he would get a glimpse of Sonja.

'I'll get back to the reserve as soon as I can after we land,' Brand said to her.

'Whatever,' Sonja said. 'I'll probably get hung up with the cops for hours when they arrive, and –'

Hudson waited. 'Sonja?'

She said nothing more, but a beep signalled an incoming message. Hudson reached forward and unclipped the phone from the instrument panel. Sonja had snapped a picture and sent it. It showed three men standing in semicircle, lit up by the burning lodge, pointing AK-47s at her.

'Shit.' Brand thumped the panel. '*They* got the drop on *her.*'

Miles glanced at the picture. 'I've got no ammo left, Hudson. Call Cavanagh and the others, maybe they can get to her.'

Hudson could see the fire at the lodge looming in front of them. They would pass over Sonja in a few seconds.

'See ya, Thousand. Thanks for the ride.'

Hudson reached up and behind his helmet with both hands, grasped the yellow and black rings of the face-blind handle, and pulled down.

If Miles had anything to say it was lost in the explosion of the Hunter's canopy being blown off and Hudson's ejector seat being fired into the sky. Hudson felt an immense kick in the butt and a gale-force rush of wind as he was tossed and buffeted in mid-air, until another bang signalled the drogue parachute being deployed.

This stabilised his wild ride, and when the main parachute was deployed and the seat fell away from under him, he had a few moments of total peace. The silence rang in his ears and he caught sight of the Hunter flying away from him. Poor Miles, he must also have been having a windy ride with no canopy.

But Hudson had other problems to deal with and, having ejected at such a low height, only seconds to regather his wits.

His timing, if not his plan, had been good, and he felt the hot thermals created by the burning roof of the lodge buffet him. He hoped he didn't land in the fire, and drew on his ingrained training at the US Army jump school at Fort Benning, Georgia, to steer his chute as best he could.

Something, maybe the noise of the ejector seat deploying or just the low-flying aircraft, had made at least a couple of the men covering Sonja look up, and one of them saw him descending and yelled a warning.

Bullets streaked past him, tearing holes in his parachute, and Hudson realised he was going to land right in the middle of the circle of death that Sonja had found herself in. His pistol was in the right-hand lower leg pocket of his flight suit. He would have no time to reach it before he landed.

*

Sonja made the most of the distraction and threw herself at Sonnet, knocking him to the ground. Her fists flailed into him and one of the other gunmen tried to get a bead on her, but didn't shoot, probably out of fear of hitting his boss. Sonja got hold of Sonnet's gun hand and, rolling with him on the ground, pointed Sonnet's pistol at the nearest foot-soldier and used her hand to force him to pull the trigger. The man fell.

Sonnet was strong, but Sonja was a wildcat. She punched him in the face and managed to wrest the pistol from him. He rolled and her shots at him missed as he crawled for his life. She pivoted and fired at the remaining two men, who had dropped back into the trees, looking for cover.

*

Hudson felt the never-forgotten, unnerving sense of ground rush, coupled with the fear that any second now one of those bullets would find its mark.

Sonnet stood and ran to the nearest fighter. Hudson watched as Sonja calmly took aim at Sonnet's back, but it was her turn to run out of ammunition. She swore and Sonnet snatched the AK-47 from his underling. He looked up to Hudson and seemed undecided for a moment as to who he should shoot first, him or Sonja. Never one to waste an opportunity, Sonja launched herself at Sonnet in a renewed assault, and he swung his weapon so that it was pointed right at her.

Hudson was about to land, right next to them. He remembered, only now, Andrew Miles's safety briefing about the ejector seat. Behind his legs, pressing against his calves, was the fibreglass container with a life raft inside. Hudson fiddled for the release catch and pulled on it.

The pack, which Andrew had warned was stout enough to break Hudson's legs if he forgot to release it, fell away beneath him, swinging from its fifteen-foot lanyard. The heavy container preceded Hudson's landing and smashed into Sonnet's head, knocking him to the ground.

Sonja headed for Sonnet while Hudson, who landed heavily, found himself being dragged across the ground as the stiffening wind caught his parachute. As he bounced along, he reached down for the Colt in his pocket. A man was shooting at him, but Hudson was a moving target and hard to hit as he skidded in and out of view. Hudson drew his pistol and fired three shots into the gunman.

The third and last jihadi exploded from the cover of some bushes, and aimed his rifle at Hudson as he continued to bounce along the ground. He fought to bring his pistol to bear again, but Sonja had seen the man. She put him down with two rounds into his back.

Hudson's parachute finally became snagged on a tree and the air spilled out of the canopy.

Sonja, filthy, scratched, bleeding and beautiful in a black dress, slung her AK-47 over her shoulder. As she came towards him she took her phone out of her bra and tapped at the keys.

Hudson wondered if she was messaging Emma. He unbuckled and shrugged his way out of the parachute harness, and stood, briefly surveying the body count around them. His phone beeped, but he ignored it for the moment, thinking it was probably a wind-blown and angry Andrew Miles. Sonnet looked to be unconscious, if not dead.

Sonja kissed him. 'You do know how to make an entrance, Brand.'

Hudson smiled. 'Andrew Miles won't be too thrilled about my exit, though.'

They both looked around, senses still on high alert, as the sound of movement came from the bush. It was Rod, along with Joanne, Thandi, Laurel and Faisal.

'Where's your fearless leader?' Sonja asked.

Joanne frowned. 'Jacqueline was the traitor in our ranks, Sonja. She tried to kill Laurel, but Laurel, well... found her phone, and there were plenty of messages on there, including one relating to Jacqueline being able to clear her gambling debts. None of us even knew she had a gambling problem; she kept that quiet.'

Laurel put her free hand to her eyes and began sobbing; she still carried Thandi's pistol. Joanne put an arm around her.

Hudson hoped Andrew had been able to call the police, ambulance and fire brigade, but in case losing his cockpit canopy had given him other things to think about, Hudson took out his phone and looked at the screen. The ping he had heard was a message from Sonja, which she had sent from just a few metres away from him.

He stared at the three words in the message bubble scarcely able to believe them. A grin spread across his face as he looked up. Sonja had her back to him, probably not wanting to discuss the subject of the message, which began with 'I' and ended with 'you'. He dared not mention the middle word in case she took it back.

Instead, Hudson, grinning, started making calls. He moved away from the group as they discussed what to do about the chaos around them.

A movement away from the circle of people caught his eye. 'Look out!' Hudson had put his Colt .45 back in his pocket and he was struggling to draw it as Sonnet, who had quietly come to and crawled to one of his dead henchmen, was aiming an AK-47 at the others.

Of all of them, Laurel was the only other one to notice Sonnet. She raised Thandi's Makarov pistol and shot him between the eyes.

Epilogue

Pretoria, South Africa, one week later

Joanne banged the gavel on the table. 'I call this meeting of the Pretoria Cycad and Firearms Appreciation Society to order. Are there any apologies?'

Sandy put her hand up. 'Charles is still in hospital. It's touch and go as to whether he'll walk again.'

'Shame,' Laurel said.

'But,' Sandy added, 'he's asked me to give you some other news. He proposed to me, in hospital, and I accepted. He's coming to live with me when he gets out.'

Thandi put down her knitting and leaned over to give Sandy a kiss. 'That is some good news, at least. I'm so happy for you.'

Baye stood and went to Sandy and hugged her, and Stephen Stoke, out of hospital but on crutches, blew her a kiss from the other side of the table.

'I'm so happy for both of you, Sandy,' Joanne said. 'Bubbly's on ice for after the meeting and it will be doubly deserved today. I'd now like to welcome our newest member, his excellency Prince –'

Faisal held up a hand. 'Faisal will be just fine. And thank you, madam interim president, for allowing me to attend.'

'Our pleasure. Perhaps before we get down to business you might like to update us on what's happened at the reserve?'

'Of course.' He looked, Joanne thought, as handsome and perfectly groomed as ever in his blue blazer, chinos and crisp blue Oxford shirt. He smiled at her. If she had known a hundred per cent for sure that he wasn't crooked a couple of months ago she might have let herself fall for him, properly, but she also knew she would never be completely happy being someone's bit on the side. Her infidelity had not sat comfortably with her when she had cheated on Peter – and he had been a bona fide criminal.

Rod, she thought, was also looking pretty good these days. She had taken him shopping for a new set of clothes and a trimmer for his ear and nose hair. She'd also taken him to the optometrist to get him some contact lenses. He hadn't protested the makeover. He would be waiting for her after the meeting at the Bond Cafe, along with Jed Banks, whom he was collecting from hospital in Johannesburg that morning. Jed would be flying back to the States that evening.

Sonja Kurtz and Hudson Brand would have joined them for the reunion as well, except they were on a beach somewhere in Mozambique.

Faisal cleared his throat. 'Thank you. The police and various intelligence agencies, including my country's, have been continuing their investigations. It seems, to my great shame and embarrassment, that a terrorist training camp was being run in secret on my reserve. However, I should add that the primary motivation for this operation was criminal. The impressionable young men recruited to this vile program believed they would be taking part in jihad, but in fact they were being trained to act as assassins for a Malian crime gang. It turns out my head of security, Frank Sonnet, had worked for a time as a mercenary in Mali, fighting the Islamic fundamentalists in that country, and at some point he fell in with one of the local gangs. Poaching and the trafficking of wildlife products, drugs, arms, cycads – as we now know – and even humans is used to finance terrorism in that part of Africa, but it also makes criminals rich. Sonnet and his partner in crime, Lindeque, saw this as a way to make their fortune.

'As to the female *woodii* cycad, it was only thanks to Joanne that it was correctly identified in the first place. I bought it in Nelspruit from the deceased estate of an elderly gentleman who never told his children exactly what was in his garden. The *woodii* female was so rare that I had no idea what it was. Although my lodge was destroyed, the cycad was found safe in the emergency room in the tunnel, where Joanne was held captive. Now that we *do* know what it is, I have been in touch with Kew Gardens in London and we are in negotiations over how we get the last male and female plants together again, as it were. What I have decided is that any money that comes from the venture will go towards conserving cycads in the wild, and other charitable causes. Given the stress and injuries you all suffered at my reserve I will also be paying everyone's medical and rehabilitation costs. Sandy?'

She blinked at him. 'Yes?'

'It's come to my attention that you are in need of specialist medical attention in the United States. It will be my pleasure to pay for that.'

She gasped. 'You can't, it costs—'

He held up a hand. 'Consider it my wedding present to you and Charles.'

Sandy dabbed her eyes as they rapidly filled with tears. 'Thank you.'

'Yes, thank you, Faisal,' Joanne said. She consulted a sheet of paper in front of her.

'Can we have the champagne now?' Laurel asked.

'Not quite yet,' Joanne said. 'Our next item is something tabled by Jacqueline at the last meeting.' Most of them looked down at the mention of Jacqueline's name, Joanne noticed. It was hard, almost impossible, for any of them to accept that their Queen had betrayed them. 'This item was to do with an investigation into me, that was put in place at the last meeting. Thandi, if you would care to take it from here?'

Thandi put her knitting in her basket and folded her hands on the table. She looked to each of them in turn. 'I was, as those of you who were here will recall, asked to investigate Joanne's apparent theft of the *Encephalartos woodii* female cycad which, against the odds, has been returned to its owner.'

'Another good excuse for a drink,' Laurel said, tapping her watch. 'Carry on, Thands.'

Thandi looked at Laurel and gave a small nod, then addressed the room again. 'From my investigations and those of the police and other agencies, it seems that Joanne made the right decision to, um ... borrow ... the *woodii* and replace it with a more common variety, wrapped to resemble the real thing. Joanne then went off on her trip to London knowing that either nothing would happen while she was away, or, if her theory that one of us was a criminal was correct, that the fake *woodii* would be stolen and the blame pinned on her. Joanne was suspicious because we, her closest friends, were the only people with whom she had indiscreetly shared the details of the prince's planned shipment of ivory and the existence of both the *woodii* and another rare cycad which was also stolen from Faisal's garden earlier. Joanne's fears were realised, and the Malian crime syndicate that eventually received the fake *woodii* cycad were none too happy to have been duped. Their inside man, or woman, as it were, mobilised the Malians to take down Joanne, first in London and later at Victoria Falls and then here, so they could find out where she had hidden the real *woodii* and if she knew the identity of the alleged mole.'

Thandi looked to Joanne and she nodded back at her to continue.

'I have been following some extra lines of enquiry this week,' Thandi went on, 'since the momentous events at the game reserve. I wanted to check out some things about Jacqueline, and the local police were kind enough to share some information with me in return for me supplying them with certain details they were lacking.'

She paused to take a sip of water from the glass in front of her. Everyone was silent, watching her.

'A couple of little things were nagging away at me,' Thandi said. 'Not big things, but enough for me to be curious. Firstly, we live in a country where gambling is rife and there are several major casinos in our province of Gauteng alone.'

A few of them nodded and tutted.

'Have any of you,' Thandi asked, 'ever seen Jacqueline go into a casino?'

They looked at each other and shook their heads.

'I interviewed several members of her family and none of them could ever recall Jacqueline gambling in her life. As for owing money, her daughter actually showed me her bank accounts. Jacqueline, as it turned out, for all her penny pinching actually had nearly two million rand in her bank account. Of all of us she was the least in need of money. Her daughter told me that in fact, Jacqueline abhorred gambling.'

'Some people are good at keeping secrets,' Stephen said, shrugging and looking away.

'Too true, SS,' Thandi said, 'but there was something else.'

'Do tell,' Baye said. 'Are you going to point out how desperate the rest of us are for money, and examine our various failed business ventures?'

Thandi noticed the way Joanne avoided looking at Baye. She continued. 'No, Baye, I don't think that is necessary. However, I wanted to talk to you about two things that are very common in all of our lives–cycads and telephones.'

'Telephones?' Sandy asked.

'Yes, Sandy. Do you remember what sort of phone Jacqueline had?'

Sandy rolled her eyes. 'Yes, that silly old Nokia 3810 that looked like it belonged in a tech museum.'

Thandi nodded. 'Exactly. And do you remember what she often said about smartphones?'

'She loathed them,' Baye said.

'She said,' Laurel added, 'that she would rather die than waste money on a smartphone. That's how stingy she was.'

Thandi rested her eyes on Laurel. 'And yet it was the latest model iPhone that you found her carrying.'

Laurel nodded. 'Exactly. I was distraught at the time, but later it struck me as odd. I can only guess her boyfriend Sonnet gave it to her.'

'Boyfriend?'

Laurel shrugged. 'Well, partner in crime. Whatever.'

'That's odd, Laurel, that you would think they were having a romantic as well as a business relationship.'

'Why? Jacqueline was quite attractive, for her age.'

Thandi paused and looked around the room at each of them. 'We ended up with a priceless plant, and the loss of many lives, including one of our own, because Laurel's son-in-law asked us to look after it, when he became aware of its value. Isn't that right, Laurel?'

She nodded. 'It is.'

Thandi got up and went to the meeting room door and opened it. James, Laurel's detective son-in-law, came in.

'Hello, darling,' Laurel said. 'We were just talking about you.'

He nodded. 'So I understand.'

'James,' Thandi said.

'Yes?'

'Did you ask your mother-in-law if our society could look after the cycad when you learned of its value?'

He shook his head. 'I did not. I told her the best place for it was in the police lock-up. She convinced me, as did his excellency Prince Faisal's head of security, Frank Sonnet, in a phone call, that it would be best for the cycad to be stored here at the society's committee room, until Sonnet could send an armed escort to take it back to the game reserve.'

Faisal looked to Thandi. 'I knew nothing of that!'

Thandi nodded. 'I thought as much.'

Laurel looked at the faces around her. 'What's going on here? What are you suggesting, Thands?'

'Finally,' Thandi said, 'does anyone else remember Laurel yelling the word "bastards" repeatedly while we were under fire? And how the enemy gunfire would inexplicably slacken off when she did?'

They each nodded.

'I believe that was a code word agreed between Laurel and Sonnet, to help prevent her being caught in the crossfire while she was doing her best to hamper the battle flow by forcing me to withdraw, by tipping Sonnet off as to where we would land – so he could cut us all to shreds with that heavy machine gun when we set down at our original landing zone.'

'Preposterous,' Laurel said.

Thandi shook her head. 'I've never heard you swear before, Laurel, in all the years I've known you.'

Laurel folded her arms, but said nothing more.

Thandi looked to James. 'You did a search of Frank Sonnet's belongings, his office, his computer, phones, etcetera, yes?'

James looked at Laurel, the mother of his wife, and then down at the ground.

Joanne knew what was coming next, because Thandi had come to her with her theory and the two of them had worked together on finalising the investigation into Joanne's guilt – or lack thereof.

'Perhaps I'll discuss that with Laurel when I take her to the station, now,' James said.

Joanne stood, put her fists on the table and glared at Laurel. 'I thought you were my *friend*, Laurel.'

Laurel looked up at her. 'I was ... I am.'

'What was on Sonnet's computer and second phone?' Joanne demanded.

Laurel shrugged. 'How should I know?'

Joanne stabbed a finger at her. 'You. Pictures. Of you, naked.'

Laurel put her head in her hands.

Thandi held a hand up and Joanne sat. It was better to let the wisest, oldest member of their group wrap it up. 'You were the one who needed money, Laurel. Your love of gambling is no secret. The only thing you hid from all of us, and your immediate family, was the scale of your debt. You had a fling with one of your son-in-law's former colleagues – James told us of how you met Sonnet at a *braai* at his place, and how well you two got on.'

'You set me up,' Joanne said, quietly.

Laurel looked to her. 'Please, Joanne, I didn't mean any harm.'

'Why me?'

Laurel looked around them, searching for sympathy or someone to come to her aid, but received only angry glares or averted eyes. At last, she seemed to realise the game was up.

Laurel took a deep breath. 'When I heard, from you, of all the riches at the prince's reserve – rhino horn, ivory, and then the cycads, something I actually knew the value of – well, it just seemed like there would be no real victim in all of this.' She looked up, at Faisal. 'You're rich, right?'

Faisal nodded. 'I am. But your friend Jacqueline?'

'She was going to kill me. She shot me, look.' Laurel pulled down the shoulder strap of her expensive frock to expose the sticky plaster that covered her flesh wound.

'Probably because she worked out what you'd done, Laurel, or overheard you talking to Sonnet. There's a record of him talking to you just before the estimated time you killed Jacqueline. We believe you put your smartphone, or, rather, a burner as I believe non-traceable phones are known in the criminal world, in Jacqueline's hand after she died, in order to place her fingerprints on it, and that you later shot Sonnet to cover your tracks. I can only imagine that you thought Sonnet would have deleted the unsavoury pictures of you.'

Emboldened, Laurel looked around the room. 'I'll get a lawyer, the best money can buy. I'll go to the press. You're all trying to frame me.'

Joanne looked to James and nodded.

'Laurel,' James said, walking across the room to her, 'come with me, please.'

She looked up at him. 'With the money I owe they'll kill me, even in prison. You know that, right?'

Laurel stood, walked to the door, and turned just before leaving to look at each of them in turn. Then she left.

A few moments later the silence was broken when Rod Cavanagh came into the room assisting Jed Banks, who walked with the aid of a stick.

'Surprise,' Rod said to Joanne. 'I couldn't wait.'

Rod did a quick round of introductions as Stephen opened the bottle of champagne. The popping of the cork made more than one of them flinch.

Baye helped SS fill and serve the glasses.

Thandi stood and held her glass aloft. 'I would like to propose a toast to Jacqueline Smit. Our beloved Queen gave her life protecting her friends and doing something to save an endangered species. The Queen is dead.'

'The Queen is dead,' they all said quietly, then took a sip.

Rod raised his glass, went to Joanne and kissed her. 'Long live the Queen.'

Acknowledgements

O ne of the most enjoyable – and difficult – things about writing novels is learning about things you previously knew nothing about. Like cycads.

I'm indebted to my dear friend Liz Lapham, from Zimbabwe, who first told me about the importance and value of cycads and their perilous plight in the wild. It was Liz who told me about a real-life international undercover operation, which brought down a ring of illegal cycad traders back in 2001.

That operation, referred to in this book as 'Operation Green Thumb', was, in fact, 'Operation Botany' and one of its key players was US Fish and Wildlife Service Special Investigator Ken Mc-Cloud. Thanks to the wonders of social media I was able to track down Ken who, while retired from the service, remains active in conservation circles as a lecturer and advocate for wildlife and wild places. Ken, who went undercover for two years in 'Operation Botany', posing as a wealthy plant collector, graciously agreed to share some of his experiences with me and check the manuscript of *Last Survivor*. I am extremely grateful for his help and interest in this project.

In South Africa my thanks go to Wynand van Heerden, who answered my many questions on cycads and the illegal trade in these amazing plants, and read and corrected the manuscript. I am also grateful to Professor John Donaldson, from the South African National Biodiversity Institute (SANBI), and his colleague

Phakamani Xaba, Senior Horticulturalist at Kirstenbosch Botanic Gardens in Cape Town, who also provided some fascinating insights. My friend and passionate botanist and conservationist Michele Hofmeyr was also, as she has been in the past, a great source of information and inspiration.

Thanks go to Nigel Kuhn for his recollections of Mali, and for his service there as a member of Chengeta Wildlife, which is a real organisation whose members have found themselves in harm's way in the course of their work training parks rangers in Africa in the dangerous business of fighting poaching. I'm also extremely grateful to former Royal Air Force fighter pilot and test pilot Craig Penrice, who provided the descriptions of flying a Hawker Hunter, firing the ADEN cannon (something which would definitely *not* be legal–even in South Africa), and ejecting from an aircraft–an experience Craig has been through, twice.

As is and should be the case, if I've got something wrong it's my fault.

A number of good-hearted people paid good money to worthy causes around the world in order to have their names assigned to characters in *Last Survivor*. Thank you to the following individuals and the charities they support: Joanne Flack (Dine for Rhino/ Wild Support/Saving the Survivors); Baye Pigors and 'Queen' Jacqueline Smit (Wildlife and Environment Zimbabwe); Nikki De Villiers and Laurel Covey (Chengeta Wildlife); Cassandra 'Sandy' Burrell and Rod Cavanagh via Michele Cavanagh (Painted Dog Conservation Inc); Charles Borg (Heart Foundation) and Stephen Stoke (Wildlife Preservation Society of Queensland) via Mena Stoke; Frank Sonnet (Belmont Rotary Club, in support of Headspace); and Patricia Littleford via Richard Barry (South African National Parks Honorary Rangers).

Thank you, once again, to my team of unpaid, dedicated proofreaders–Annelien Oberholzer (whose knowledge of firearms as well as Afrikaans helped this time); firearms expert Fritz Rabe; Wayne Hamilton from swagmantours.com.au; and my wife Nicola, mother Kathy and mother-in-law Sheila.

I'd like to thank my publishing consultant Joel Naoum from Critical Mass Consulting for getting this edition of Last Survivor to you and if you've made it this far then thank you. I couldn't continue to live my dream, travelling and writing books in Africa, without you, which makes you the most important person in this whole wonderful world in which I live and work.

www.tonypark.net

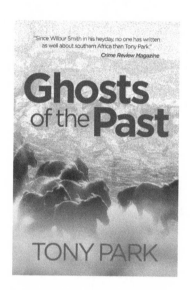

Ghosts
of the Past

TONY PARK

Africa, 1906: A young Australian adventurer is condemned to death.

Sydney, the present: journalist Nick Eatwell has just lost his job, but his day is brightened when a fellow reporter, South African Susan Vidler, comes into his life looking for his help with a story.

Susan is investigating Nick's great uncle, Cyril Blake, who fought in the Anglo-Boer War and later joined the struggle for independence across the border in the German colony of South West Africa, now Namibia.

A long-lost manuscript proves Nick's forebear was a somewhat reluctant hero. Soldier, deserter, cattle rustler and freedom fighter, Blake was helping the lost cause before the Kaiser's forces ordered his assassination.

In Germany, historian Anja Berghoff is researching the origins of the famed desert horses of Namibia. She's also interested in Blake and an Irish-German spy, Claire Martin, with whom Cyril had an affair.

Nick and Anja head to Africa on the trail of a legend, but someone else is delving into the past, looking for clues to the secret location of a missing horde of gold that's worth killing for.

Spanning two centuries, Ghosts of the Past is based on a true story.

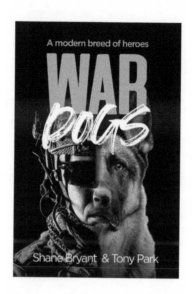

In Afghanistan, sometimes all that stands between coalition troops and death or serious injury is a dog.

Highly trained dogs and their handlers search for improvised explosive devices or hidden weapons out on patrol with combat troops.

It's a perilous job, often putting them right in the firing line, and making them high priority targets for the Taliban insurgents they're fighting.

Shane Bryant, a former Australian Army dog handler, spent 10 years in Afghanistan working with elite American special forces and training other handlers and dogs. War Dogs is his story – a riveting true account of the hidden war in the mountains and cities of the world's most dangerous conflict, and the comradeship between man and dog that has saved numerous lives.

This re-released and updated edition of War Dogs looks at the effects a decade of service as a contractor had on Shane, his personal life and his mental health as he faced new enemy, post-traumatic stress disorder.

Lightning Source UK Ltd.
Milton Keynes UK
UKHW010632011020
370850UK00001B/17